Praise for Rowan C...
Touching Bo...

The Accidental Family

"Winning . . . turns up the heat on Coleman's trademark romantic humor."

—*Booklist*

"Rowan Coleman weaves a tale of romance and love that is fast-paced and sure to keep you speculating until the end."
—Fresh Fiction

Mommy By Mistake

"An entertaining view of motherhood that will have readers laughing and crying along with the inimitable heroine and her band of appealing friends."

—*Booklist*

The Accidental Mother

"Fun, poignant."

—*OK* magazine

"A disarmingly sweet tale of motherhood and reluctant love."
—*Publishers Weekly*

"Coleman creates witty and endearing characters and delivers an exceptional and touching read about loss and love."
—*Booklist*

"Brilliant . . . moving and funny."
—*New Woman* magazine (U.K.)

"A charming tale . . . sophisticated."

—*Heat* magazine (U.K.)

The Home for Broken Hearts
is also available as an eBook

Also by Rowan Coleman

The Accidental Family

Mommy By Mistake

Another Mother's Life

The Accidental Mother

The Home for Broken Hearts

ROWAN COLEMAN

GALLERY BOOKS
New York London Toronto Sydney

Gallery Books
A Division of Simon & Schuster, Inc.
1230 Avenue of the Americas
New York, NY 10020

First published in Great Britain in 2010 by Arrow Books

First Gallery Books trade paperback edition September 2010

GALLERY BOOKS and colophon are trademarks of Simon & Schuster, Inc.

For information about special discounts for bulk purchases,
please contact Simon & Schuster Special Sales at 1-866-506-1949 or
business@simonandschuster.com.

The Simon & Schuster Speakers Bureau can bring authors to your live event.
For more information or to book an event contact the Simon & Schuster
Speakers Bureau at 1-866-248-3049 or visit our website at www.simonspeakers.com.

Designed by Kate Moll

Manufactured in the United States of America

10 9 8 7 6 5 4 3 2 1

Library of Congress Cataloging-in-Publication Data

Coleman, Rowan.
    The home for broken hearts / Rowan Coleman.—1st Gallery Books trade pbk. ed.
      p. cm.
    1. Widows—Fiction. 2. Boardinghouses—Fiction. 3. Mothers and sons—Fiction. I. Title.
PR6103.04426H66 2010
823'.92—dc22
            2010007878

ISBN 978-1-4391-5685-8
ISBN 978-1-4391-8250-5 (ebook)

Almost One Year Ago

Ellen braced herself against the unforgiving expanse of faultless blue sky that stretched endlessly above her head and wondered if such a perfect day was quite seemly on an occasion like this. Not a breath of wind stirred the leaves of the oak trees that surrounded them, and the warmth of the sun prickled through her cotton shirt and suit jacket, causing a trickle of sweat to drip between her shoulder blades. The sheer weight of the heat seemed to compress her, squeezing her ribs together, imprisoning her heart. Struggling to catch each breath, Ellen had to fight the urge simply to run away, to find some small, quiet, dark place where she could breathe again and close her eyes and pretend that none of this was happening. If her younger sister hadn't been there, gripping her arm so tightly that she would have bruises in the morning, then perhaps she would have. But Hannah was there, supporting her, restraining her, helping her—*forcing* her—to get through it, no matter how much Ellen wanted to turn away. It was Hannah who had told her to wear something lightweight and comfortable, a dress or a skirt, but Ellen had stuck to her guns and stuck to a suit. It was fitting, respectable, and suitable for such an important occasion.

Funny, Ellen thought without a trace of amusement, focusing with determination on a single blade of bright green grass that lay against the toe of her shoe, it had rained on her wedding day. A cold, drenching drizzle had sheeted from a steely spring sky in a relentless onslaught.

They had laughed, Ellen and her brand-new husband, when they had looked at their wedding photos, the pair of them standing outside the church, teeth gritted in rigor mortis grins against the cold. Ellen hadn't minded the weather that day, the chill that had raised goose bumps on her bare arms or the needles of fine rain that had consistently assaulted her face, teasing her heavily applied mascara loose from her lashes. On that day, all that she'd needed to fight off the elements was the knowledge that the man who was now her husband, the man she still could not believe had chosen her above anyone else, was standing by her side, his hand in hers, and that from that day on, he always would be. That sodden, foggy, miserable day had been her friend.

This day, this perfect July day that wheeled so recklessly around her, was her sworn enemy, a predator waiting for her to break cover and bolt for safety, waiting to pounce and rip her to shreds, because this was the day of her husband's funeral, and a world without her husband in it became her enemy, determined to assault her with every weapon in its armory. As the business of burying her husband went on around her, Ellen thought of home, of the cool, clean stone tiles of her kitchen floor, the shelter of her shadowy bedroom, curtains still drawn as they had been since the day Nick died. At home it was easier to believe that he had not gone; at home she still felt safe.

Finding every single further second that required her to stand at her husband's graveside intolerable, Ellen gasped for breath, drenched from the inside out by the suffocating heat, flinching as she felt her son pry open her clenched fist and slide his fingers in between hers. Ellen looked down at ten-year-old Charlie and mustered a smile for him; he squeezed her fingers in return. He was supporting her, Ellen realized, ashamed. He was coping when she was not, fearless, bearing the unbearable with the kind of valor that her husband would have had. Ellen took heart from Charlie, determined not to let

him see how frightened she was, how lost, panicked and confused, hurt and bereft she felt. She wouldn't let him see that at
that precise moment, standing under that blazing sun next to
Nick's grave, she had no idea how to live from one minute to
the next, let alone another day, another week, or another year
without her husband.

That all she knew was that she longed to be at home.

CHAPTER One

S *lowly the tip of his sword slid between the laces of her bod-*
ice, each breath from her heaving bosom forcing the open-
ing a little farther apart, revealing ever more of the milky white
flesh concealed beneath . . ."

"Mum."

"'Please, Captain, if you are any kind of gentleman don't—
oh, please . . .'. Eliza begged, her heart fluttering with both fear
and undiscovered longing as the captain's dark gaze roamed
over her tender form."

"Mum?"

"'You are mine now,' he rasped, his voice husky with desire.
'Just like this house is mine now, just as this sword always has
been!' Eliza gasped, her eyes widening as she laid eyes on the
captain's burgeoning weapon. 'Reconcile yourself to the knowl-
edge that you are mine and I will have you at my will, first
body, then soul . . .'"

"Mu-uuuuuum!"

Ellen's head snapped up as finally the voice of her son
dragged her out of the seventeenth-century darkened cham-
ber with a locked door, where a young puritan maid was about
to be ravished by her rakish royalist captor, and back to her
kitchen table in Hammersmith. Discovering Charlie at her
side, she slipped a folder on top of the latest Allegra Howard

manuscript that she had been sent to proofread by the publishing company she freelanced for and fixed her gaze on him.

"Yes, love?" she asked, mildly.

"What does 'burgeoning' mean?" Charlie asked with wide-eyed curiosity. Ellen squirmed. How long had her eleven-year-old been standing there reading over her shoulder?

"Burgeoning?" It means . . . um, to, um, grow rapidly or sprout—like . . . um, like buds in the springtime."

"How can a weapon, like a sword, burgeon, then?" Charlie asked, his level blues eyes searching out her gaze and holding it. "Because it's made of steel, isn't it? Hard steel. Steel doesn't burgeon."

"Obviously it doesn't!" Ellen agreed. "I'll be correcting that! I don't know—these writers, they haven't got a clue about metaphor. I swear I could do it better myself. Now, what would you like for tea?" Ellen asked, even though she knew the answer, because it was the same every day.

"It might be a metaphor," Charlie said, casually loosening his school tie. "Maybe the writer is using his burgeoning sword as a metaphor for the man's erection, for example."

"Charlie!" Ellen exclaimed, folding her arms across the offending manuscript as if she might somehow stop any further indiscretions from escaping it.

"What?" Charlie said. "I'm only discussing literature with you, Mum."

"Yes, but . . . Charlie, you're only eleven—you shouldn't be discussing . . ."

"Erections," Charlie repeated. "I shouldn't be discussing erections with my mother? Who should I discuss it with?"

Ellen's mouth opened and closed as she fought for an answer. For the millionth time, at least, in the last eleven months, the thought *If only Nick were here* flashed across her mind. But Nick wasn't here, and Ellen had to try to learn again how to manage without him—something else that she felt she had to learn and relearn many times.

"Well, because you're only eleven and I'm not sure it's appropriate for a boy of your age . . ."

"I'm nearly twelve," Charlie reminded her.

"Your birthday's not for two months. Don't wish your life away, Charlie. . . ."

The pair held each other's eyes for a second, an unspoken thought passing between them.

"James Ingram's mother talks to him about sex all the time," Charlie challenged her, papering over the gulf that stretched between them with practiced ease. "James Ingram's mother told him he could ask her anything he liked, and she's an *accountant*. She doesn't read porn for a living, like you."

"Por . . . Charlie, you know full well that I don't read anything of the sort. I copyedit romantic fiction for Cherished Desires, you know that. And if . . . if you have any questions about anything, you can always come to me, of course you can." Ellen felt heat color her cheeks. "Is . . . is there anything you'd like to talk to me about? Sex-wise."

Charlie stared at her for a long time, and finally Ellen detected the spark of mischief in his deadpan eyes; he was teasing her in that way he had. Deadly serious, edged in equal measure with humor and what Ellen often thought might be anger. Or perhaps frustration that he was changing so rapidly and she was failing to keep up with him.

"Er—no—that would be too weird!" Charlie grinned. "I think James Ingram is a freak anyway."

How Nick would laugh, Ellen thought. He'd come in from work sometime between nine and ten and they'd stand in the kitchen, he leaning against the counter while she cooked for him, she telling him every last thing that Charlie had said or done, and he would laugh and say something like, "That's my boy." With some effort, Ellen held back the threat of tears and smiled at Charlie.

"So how was school today?"

"Same as ever, only I have to get my permission slip in, you know, for the skiing trip—so can I go or not?" he asked, and Ellen realized that she would have preferred the most explicit question about sex that he could think of compared to that one.

"Well, Charlie—the thing is . . ."

Ellen sat back in her chair and wondered how to tell him what she herself didn't yet fully understand. She and Charlie were broke.

Nick's accountant, Hitesh, had visited her just before lunchtime. He'd been a regular visitor over the last months, taking on the financial mess that Nick had unwittingly left her with and battling on Ellen's behalf to try to get it sorted out, which Ellen was eternally grateful for, especially when neither of them knew how or if she would be able to pay him for all the time he'd given her. He'd told her on the phone that now that at least her affairs could be finalized, she should try to think through any investments or savings that she might have tucked away. Ellen had been unable to think of any. Nick had dealt with all the money stuff; Nick had dealt with everything.

When Hitesh had gone, she made herself a cheese sandwich and a cup of tea and sat at the table for a long time, staring unseeingly at the pile of washed saucepans gleaming like long-lost treasure on the draining board.

There had been two options open to her—to deal with the situation head-on, as Hitesh had advised her, to look at her incomings and outgoings to see exactly how bad her position was, or to finish reading the first segment of the latest Allegra Howard novel, *The Sword Erect*.

So, once Hitesh had left, the choice had been an easy one, and within a few seconds Ellen found herself lost once again in the heat of that locked room, struggling along with Eliza to fight her barely understood desire for a man she ought to hate but yearned to have.

Then Charlie had talked about erection metaphors and

asked her about the school skiing trip and Ellen was firmly back in the last place she wanted to be, the real world.

"There is no money," Hitesh had told her, sitting at her kitchen table. He spoke kindly, slowly, as if he wanted to be sure that she really understood him.

"None?" Ellen questioned. "But the insurance, the appeal—you said . . ."

"I said I'd try, and I have—you know that I've been on the case since they first refused to pay out, months ago—fighting with them for the best part of a year," Hitesh reminded her, sipping the glass of cold lemonade she had poured him, loosening the top button of his shirt. "Nick was insured up to the hilt; if he'd got cancer or been run over by a bus, you'd be fine, sorted for life. But he didn't. Death by dangerous driving, Ellen, *his* dangerous driving. Look, I know you don't need to hear all this again—but the skid marks on the tarmac, the distance from the road they found the car—the state of the wreck. The level of blood alcohol. It showed he took that bend at around a hundred and twenty miles an hour, and he was just above the legal limit for drinking. I've come to the end of the road: there is no other appeal process or arbitration board I can go to. The insurance company doesn't care about you, Ellen, or your mortgage, or the years of premiums Nick paid. It doesn't pay out on death caused by reckless behavior. You won't be getting any money from them. I'm sorry, but we need to face that and work out what to do next."

Ellen twisted her wedding ring around and around her finger. She heard Hitesh, but nothing he said seemed real. For the last year she had just carried on as normal, financially at least. She and Nick had had almost twenty thousand pounds in a savings account, which Hitesh had helped her transfer into her household account to tide her over until the insurance money came through. It was meant to be a temporary measure, but month after month had passed and still there was no payout. Everything, the mortgage, the electricity, gas, and whatever else there was had all been paid by direct debit from the household account. Ellen hadn't even thought to check the dwindling balance, confident that everything would be resolved. But now Hitesh was telling her that that money was running out. And then what?

"Hitesh, the money we had in our savings account—it's nearly all gone? Won't there be anything left from the business?" Nick had run a small but successful advertising agency, or at least he'd always told everyone, including Ellen, how well it was doing. When the recession hit he'd pointed to their five-bedroom Victorian villa and his Mercedes in the driveway and told Ellen not to worry.

"Advertising is recession proof," he'd assured her, planting a kiss on her forehead. It had fallen to Hitesh, not only Nick's accountant but the executor of his will, to spend the better part of the last year winding up his business affairs, a murky affair that Ellen did not want to even attempt to understand.

"Wages, rent, bills—Nick was behind on all of them and he was late paying his taxes. I'd got him some wriggling time with the revenue to sort out his cash flow, but he . . . didn't manage it. Most of what little capital there was, was in the business; the sale of the premises et cetera has gone to them, and you're lucky that you're not left *owing* anyone any money."

"It's just . . . I don't see how—is it really that bad?" Ellen was disbelieving. "Nick never mentioned anything to me, he never gave the impression that things were tough, that we should economize."

"You know Nick, he was a traditional man. He never wanted to worry you, and if he hadn't had the accident you probably would never have known. He'd have got all of this sorted out and everything back on track." Hitesh smiled fondly. "I don't know how, but he always did."

"Do you mean we've been in this sort of mess before?" Ellen asked edgily, uncertain if she wanted to know that the tranquillity and certainty of her married life had been compromised before.

"Now," Hitesh said, avoiding her question, "I've had a look at your expenses. The interest-only mortgage you took out on this place is sizable; if you tried to borrow that much these days, no bank would give you the time of day. And you're tied into a fixed rate for another three years, which is a shame because interest rates have plummeted—you'd be paying a fraction of what you are now if Nick had gone for a tracker mortgage. Should you try and sell and repay the loan, the redemption fee runs into the thousands, so . . ."

"*What?* What can I do?" Ellen asked. For the first time, the reality of her situation was nudging its way into her consciousness. All she had concentrated on in the months since Nick's death was living from minute to minute without him, and that had been more than enough for her to deal with; it still was. And now time had run out and she would have to do something for herself, would have to find a way to deal with this situation—and she had no idea how. Ellen twisted her fingers into a tight knot in her lap, feeling panic gripping her chest.

Hitesh paused, and Ellen wasn't sure if it was the warm day that made him so uncomfortable or what he knew he had to tell her.

"Right—well, let's look at the facts. This house is a good size, well located—you and Charlie could move out and rent it, enough to cover the mortgage until you can sell up and pay it back without charges. You'd still need to find a way to support yourself and Charlie, of course, but rent on a two-bedroom place will be a fraction of your current costs and . . ."

"Rent out our home to another family? Move out, you mean?" Ellen swallowed, her mouth suddenly parched.

"Well, no, you won't get the same revenue from renting it whole as you would renting it room by room to young professionals or perhaps students. What you're looking for is to maximize your assets. Now, it's a bit hooky, renting out without converting the mortgage to a buy-to-let, but I know a letting agent who deals with it on the QT. . . ."

"But this is *home*." Ellen barely heard her own voice as she whispered the words. "It's Charlie's home, his safe place. You know how he's been since the accident. But at least he has his home, his room, his things around him. I can't take that away from him, too. I can't."

Hitesh sighed, pinching the top of his nose between his thumb and forefinger, closing his eyes briefly. When he opened them, he held Ellen's gaze, making her look him in the eye.

"Ellen, you know Nick was a friend of mine. Shamilla and I consider you and Charlie like family. I don't want to see you in this position. If there was anything else I could do, I would do it, I promise you—but there isn't. Nick thought he was invincible, he never thought he was made of flesh and blood like the rest of us. He knew that everything was riding on him coming up with the goods, pulling off a miracle like he always did—it was that kind of risk he thrived on. But this time he couldn't make everything all right. And even though he didn't mean to, he's left you in a mess. Now, if you want to stay in this house without it being repossessed, then you either need to come up with two and a half thousand pounds a month pronto just to survive, or you need to think again. When I say pronto, I mean it—you don't have enough money in your account to pay next month's mortgage." Hitesh leaned forward, his voice softening. "I'm sorry to be harsh, but there it is. I have to make you see. Is there anyone else who could help you—I know Nick's parents are dead but perhaps yours . . . ?"

"They don't have any money," Ellen told him, thinking of her mum and dad in their chilly bungalow in Hove, surviving on a state pension and very little else.

"Then you need another plan," Hitesh explained. "Look,

take some time. Think about it. Talk it over with someone. If you find another way, then great. If not, come back to me and I'll put you in touch with that letting agent."

And Ellen had taken some time. But she had chosen not to think. How could she? How could she think about something that was as incomprehensible and irreversible as Nick's death?

If only Nick were here. The thought escaped her before she could stop it.

"Well?" Charlie asked. "Can I?"

"I don't know yet," Ellen hedged. "I need to think about it. It's a long way away, and you've never been skiing before. I'm not sure I want you so far away. It sounds dangerous to me."

"Climbing the stairs sounds dangerous to you," Charlie complained, frustrated. "Mum, if you don't let me go, everyone will think I'm a mummy's boy. They'll think I'm on free school dinners! You have to stop treating me like a kid. I'm not going to die, you know; I'm not Dad."

Ellen dipped her head, feeling the warmth of the manuscript beneath her fingers, as if the heat between Eliza and Captain Parker were escaping between the lines. Just a few flimsy pages away, another world—without debt, or dead husbands or angry boys who didn't know what they were saying or why—was waiting for her. A world where intensely passionate men stole you from your problems and ravished you into delirious submission, conquering you with their love. A world where you didn't have to do anything except be irresistible. How could she explain to Charlie that even though she knew he wasn't his dad, and even though she knew it was highly unlikely that she would lose him as suddenly and as violently as she had lost Nick, she couldn't persuade her heart to feel the same way.

"So, what would you like for tea tonight?" Ellen asked, weary from the constant onslaught of emotional battles that raged in her head.

Since Nick's death, Charlie had eaten only the same thing he had on the last day he saw his father alive: fish fingers, white bread, ketchup, and Frosties with low-fat milk. She'd seen in turn a doctor, a child psychologist, and a dietician, and all of them had said that the best thing was to let him get on with it as long as his health wasn't being compromised, but every time she fed him something from that all-too-short list, Ellen felt like a failure: a mother who couldn't even nourish her own son, either with the kind of food he should eat or the love and security he needed to feel in order to eat it. It was proof that no matter how much she tried to fight it, Charlie had been steadily drifting away from her since they had lost Nick, each day edging a little further out of her reach. It wasn't just the money that made it difficult for her to say yes to this skiing trip. It was the thought of him so far away, even farther away than he was standing right next to her now, that she couldn't stand. Ellen didn't think that Charlie blamed her for his father's death exactly. It was more that he seemed disappointed with his remaining parent. The quiet, loving little boy he'd been now strove more and more each day to be entirely independent from his mother, and Ellen was sure that the skiing trip was part of that, too, another thing he could do without her. The more he struggled to be free of her, the more she wanted to bind him to her, to keep him that same adoring little boy who had held her hand at Nick's funeral.

Charlie dipped his head, his shoulders heaving in a sigh, and then after a second or two he put his arms around Ellen's neck and hugged her, leaning his body into hers. She tensed, taken off guard by the gesture of affection that had become so unfamiliar to her, missing the opportunity to return the embrace before Charlie withdrew.

"I'm sorry, Mum," he told her, his lashes lowered. "I'm sorry I'm a pain sometimes. I don't know why I say the stuff I do. I'm an idiot."

"No, you are not." Tentatively, gently, Ellen put her hands

on Charlie's shoulders and looked into his eyes. "Charlie, this last year—we've had a lot to deal with, you and I. And you— you have been anything but an idiot. You've been an amazing, strong, brave little boy." Ellen winced inwardly at her choice of words. "Learning to get on without Dad. It's hard for us both, and sometimes we do and say things we don't mean to. None of it matters if we love each other and stick together."

Charlie held her gaze for a second, as if he wanted to say something more, something important. But instead he shrugged and stepped out of her embrace.

"Anyway, I don't care what the boys at school think," he told her bullishly, that relic of sweet boyishness passing as quickly as it had arrived. "It doesn't really matter if I don't go skiing, I suppose. Emily Greenhurst isn't going, and she plays the electric guitar."

"The electric guitar. Really?" Ellen nodded; this Emily Greenhurst name had started to crop up a lot recently. "Charlie, I'll be honest. I don't know about the holiday. It's a lot of money and we're still sorting out our finances," Ellen hedged. There was one person she could ask for help to pay for the holiday, even if the thought of letting Charlie go horrified her. These school holidays were always supersafe, Ellen told herself, de- spite her instinctive misgivings. The school had to make sure they were safe these days . . . although there had been that case on the news a few weeks back about a boy drowning in a canoeing accident. Ellen stifled her anxiety. She didn't want him to be the only one of his friends who missed out, even if this mysterious Emily Greenhurst wasn't going. Ellen knew that her younger sister, Hannah, would give her the money, if she was prepared to ask for it, but she just wasn't sure that she was, not even for Charlie. Hannah, the bright, beautiful, successful one, had made it her business to be around for Ellen a lot since Nick had died. Hannah had always glided through life so effortlessly, the world falling into place around her. For most of her life, Ellen had felt as if she were trailing along behind her little sister, plodding along through life while Hannah blazed a trail, like a bright shooting star. And then Ellen had met Nick, and for the first time in her life she'd had something that Hannah didn't. A loving relationship, a husband and a son, a proper family home. And as foolish and as shallow as it was, while she had these things Ellen had felt like her sister's equal, her superior, even. But now all but one of Ellen's treasures had either gone or were on the brink of being lost, and it would cost her a lot to have to turn to Hannah for help. Even for Charlie.

"I'll try my best, okay? And in the meantime, please don't call people trash. Or 'gay,' if you're using it as an insult."

"But it's okay if you're using it as a compliment?" Charlie quizzed her. "Like, oh, Simon Harper, you are so wonderfully gay!"

"Charlie." Ellen repressed a smile. "You are nearly twelve years old. You know what's wrong and what's right—try and stick to it, okay?"

"Okay." Charlie grinned. "I actually think Simon Harper is gay, though."

"So, fish fingers?" Ellen smiled, ever hopeful that one day he'd change his answer.

"Yes, please, Mummy."

Ellen didn't know what broke her heart more, the scars left by his father's death or the fact that sometimes, just for a fleeting moment, her little boy forgot to be all grown up.

CHAPTER TWO

W ell, I would have thought it was obvious," Hannah said, stirring her third spoonful of sugar into her black coffee. Ellen's sister, younger than she by some nine years, lived on coffee, cigarettes, and sugar, and looked annoyingly good on it; "slender as a willow tree and just as bendy" was how she'd been known to introduce herself to potential lovers, which was pretty much any male within a five-mile radius. "You have to do what that accountant says. You have to consolidate, let the place out, and get somewhere small for you and Charles. I mean, Ellie, it's only a pile of bricks. It's not even as if you and Nick lived here all your married life, as if he carried you over the threshold on your wedding day. You've only lived here a few years and I never did get why you bought such a huge place when there was only going to be the three of you. . . ." Hannah faltered, realizing that she had put her foot in her mouth yet again, and stirred her beverage furiously, unable to meet Ellen's eye for a moment. Both of them knew that when Ellen and Nick bought the house they had planned to fill it with children, a real family home for a real family. But circumstances had changed, and that had become an impossibility long before Nick died. Ellen smarted inwardly; it was just like her sister to pick up on the details that could wound her the most, calling her home a pile of bricks. It was so much more than that—it was symbolic of what her life used to be—of what it should have been.

"Anyway—it's just a place," Hannah stumbled on. "A reminder of everything that you've . . . lost. A fresh start—that's exactly what you need. If anything, this house is a burden, and it's one you don't need."

Ellen said nothing for a moment. It had taken her two days since Hitesh's visit to bring herself to call her sister, and of course she hadn't really invited Hannah over for coffee to listen to her opinion or advice. The two sisters were so different in every respect that before Nick's death they had barely seen or spoken to each other, apart from required occasions, birthdays, Christmas—that sort of thing. After his death, though, Hannah had been around much more, which Ellen supposed she ought to be touched by, her kid sister making an effort to be there for her when neither of them really liked or understood each other. But Ellen didn't get that feeling from Hannah; for some reason, it felt like Hannah wanted to be around her and Charlie for her own sake, as if it were she who needed distracting from Nick's death. Not long after the funeral, when Ellen had been at her lowest point, Hannah had found her lying in her room, her head buried beneath the pillow, and carefully sat on the edge of the bed.

"Mum's made egg and mayo sandwiches," she'd said. "Do you want one?"

Ellen had not replied.

"Look . . ." Hannah had reached out and laid a hand on her shoulder. "Look, I know how awful this is, how horrific—but you have to think that at least you had him for a while. At least he belonged to you and everyone knew it. And now he always will."

Unable to face her sister, Ellen had simply pulled another pillow over her head and cried herself to sleep. But later, when Hannah started making her regular visits, she thought about what she had said on that morning and wondered if her sister, who was so fond of personal dramas and life complications, was a little envious of her. If Hannah somehow found grief and the attention it garnered glamorous . . . or perhaps it was just the attention that Hannah was envious of. It made Ellen remember the day she graduated from university. It had been one of the rare days of her life when she was the center of everything. Mum and Dad, a miserable and sulky twelve-year-old Hannah in tow, had traveled all the way from home to see her receive her degree. Hannah had moaned and complained the whole day, but what Ellen would always remember was that at the very moment she stood up to collect her degree under a blazing August sky, Hannah fainted, slipping off her chair like a wisp of chiffon and collapsing on the grass. Ellen's parents had not been looking at her when she was awarded her first-class degree, and rightly or wrongly, Ellen blamed Hannah for that.

It should seem impossible that anyone would ever envy a widow, but much of Hannah's life and the way she lived it seemed impossible to Ellen.

She often wondered if it was because of the age difference. She had been born at the beginning of the seventies, when the world was still an optimistic and gentle place. Hannah, however, a surprise baby if ever there had been one, had entered this world on the cusp of the eighties, kicking and screaming for more, seeming to embody the decade she grew up in, a brash and confident high achiever always hungry for more success, more possessions.

Now almost thirty-eight, Ellen was dark, olive skinned, with green eyes that Nick had loved, and what Allegra Howard would describe as a comely figure, comfortably curvy, not that she gave much thought to her shape, which she covered with supermarket-bought jeans and an assortment of T-shirts, most of which had been Nick's. Ellen had never been one to care what she looked like, and Nick had often told her that was one reason he loved her so much. He'd called her his pocket

Venus in the bedroom, his goddess alone for him to adore, her hidden charms a veiled mystery to all but him.

Ellen inhabited the world that Nick had created for her and rarely strayed from it. She existed in her home, in her books, and for her husband and son. It had been a comfortable, comforting cocoon of a world, one that she struggled to find the energy to emerge from now, and one that she simply did not want to leave. Ellen did not want the world outside; she didn't need it. Her life was small, detailed and rich in the minutiae that only she cared about, and that was exactly how she wanted it, especially now.

Hannah, on the other hand, thrived on being noticed. Taller than anyone else in the family, including her father, and unfeasibly leggy, she had long ago perfected her glamorous look, boosting her naturally reddish hair with a monthly shot of chemical auburn so that it fell in luscious and glossy waves to the middle of her back. She was one of the those lucky few for whom slim hips and a flat stomach did not rule out enough natural cleavage to put on a reasonable display for her many admirers. At just thirty, she was one of the few female fund managers at T. Jenkins Waterford Asset Management, and she had ridden out the financial storm of the last few months with better success than many of her colleagues, whom she'd left by the roadside without so much as a backward glance. Ellen knew that Hannah earned well in excess of six figures and that she probably had enough money in various accounts to buy her house outright if she wanted to. But Ellen would no more have dreamed of asking Hannah to help her out financially than she would have hammered nails into her eyes. At least she wouldn't if it were not for Charlie's ski trip. The real reason that Ellen found it so hard to ask Hannah to help her out was that she knew her sister would want to help her and Charlie, knew that it would give Hannah pleasure, and Ellen balked at that. It wasn't an impulse that she was proud of, particularly when it meant that

Charlie missed out, especially when she didn't really understand her motivation herself. Maybe if Hannah was envious of her, she was envious of Hannah, too—life had always been so easy for her. Even when she frequently got things wrong or made mistakes, it always seemed that the universe rearranged itself around her to smooth things over and make everything better. Ellen had given herself a good talking to before Hannah arrived, telling herself that this request was not about her, it was about her son—but still she hesitated, unable to bring it up.

"This house is not just a pile of bricks—it's Charlie's home," she stated quietly instead, sipping the frothy cappuccino that she had made with the elaborate and expensive coffee machine that Nick had bought her for her last birthday even though she mostly drank tea. "And when Nick and I bought this house it meant something special to us, it was the house we always dreamed of. The place—the place we planned to get old in together. Nick was going to do up a vintage motorbike in the garage and I was going to take up writing stories, you know, just for fun, and read them to him in the evening. And when . . . when we realized there would be no more children, we decided that when Charlie was old enough we were going to convert the attic rooms into a little flat for him so he could have his privacy, and we were going to get a dog, two dogs—a Labrador and a red setter. Nick always wanted a red setter."

Ellen glanced up at Hannah, whose features had tightened as she listened, as if just the very idea of such a mundane and domestic existence offended her. Ellen knew that Hannah understood so little of what she was saying that she might as well have been talking in a foreign language.

"Yes, but, Ellie—none of that is going to happen now," Hannah said impatiently. "Don't you get it? Nick is dead." Hannah paused for a second, disbelieving, as if she, too, were hearing the news for the first time. She swallowed and took a breath. "Your life has changed, it's not going to be like you thought it was. You need to wake up and deal with it."

Ellen sucked in a sharp breath. "I think you should go," she said, pushing her chair back and handing Hannah her bag.

"Ellie—please—don't." Hannah leaned across the table and rested her hands on Ellen's forearm. "Don't throw me out, I'm only trying to help."

Ellen shook her head. "No, Hannah—you're not trying to help. You're trying to march in here and tell me how pointless and pathetic my life is and how I should just sweep it all away, sweep everything that I have left of Nick away and go and live in a poky little flat somewhere because that's the sensible thing to do, and because it's only me, it's only quite boring Ellen—what happens to me doesn't really matter, does it? Well, since when have you ever done the sensible thing? Just because none of what matters to me matters to you, it doesn't mean you have the right to trample all over it. I'm not going to let you."

Hannah stared at her for a second, taken aback by her sister's uncharacteristic outburst. "Is that really what you think?"

Ellen shrugged, surprised by the rapid acceleration of her heartbeat.

"Ellie, all the things that matter to you matter to me," Hannah insisted. "I want the best for you and Charles. Look, you know me, Ellen—tact isn't my strong point. Haven't you heard of tough love? Look, I know I sound like a heartless cow—but it's not just me that thinks this, there's your accountant, Mum and Dad—we're all worried about you, Ellen. You just can't go on sticking your head in book after book, thinking that everything will turn out all right in the end—there aren't those kind of happy endings in real life—there is no tall, dark, and handsome stranger waiting to rescue you. . . ." Hannah hesitated, and Ellen wondered if she heard a catch in her voice. "Or any of us. And I know it's hard. I know Nick did every single thing for you and Charles—you're not used to coping. But now you have to. You have to, otherwise the mess you're in is just going to get worse and worse until there's no way out, and what about Charles then, when your house is repossessed and you don't even have that?"

Ellen sank back down into her chair. Hitesh, Hannah, her dad on the phone last night—they were all right: she had to do something. But it wasn't just that Ellen had no idea what to do, she had no idea how to do anything. She closed her eyes briefly, fighting the urge to tell Hannah to get out. Hannah was right—she had to do something, and if anyone could think of something to do, it would be Hannah, clever, resourceful Hannah. Her personal life might lurch from one catastrophe to the next, but when it came to problem solving and lateral thinking, Hannah was the expert.

"Okay," Ellen said. "Okay, I know you're right. But it's Charlie that I'm thinking about. He's lost so much—I don't want him to lose his home, too. There has to be another way, doesn't there?"

"Well, you could earn more, for a start," Hannah said, chewing her bottom lip, the way she always had from girlhood. "I mean that job you do for that publisher, Naked Desires, or whatever it's called—how many books do you copyedit for them?"

"Well, it depends—Simon knows which writers I enjoy, so he waits until he's got a new work from one of them. Somewhere between one and two every couple of months."

"Well, that's crazy, for starters." Hannah spoke quickly, words tumbling out of her mouth at a million miles an hour, as if there were never going to be enough hours in the day for her to say everything she had to. "Especially when you only get—what—fifteen quid an hour? You need to stop treating the manuscripts like a hobby and start thinking of them as cash-making opportunities. They publish hundreds of those books, don't they? The horny old ladies can't get enough of them, right? If you stopped actually reading them and just concentrated on crossing the *t*s and dotting the *i*s, then you could probably do one or even two a week. As for that Simon—he is the one that's gay, right?"

"We don't know that he's gay, just that he's a bachelor," Ellen interjected, although she had to admit that the chances of a man as well dressed and attractive as Simon Merry still being single in his midforties were unlikely, unless his preferences did not include commitment-hungry females, and even then he seemed to have a distinct lack of men in his life, too. Ellen suspected that he simply liked to keep his private life private, and she respected him for that.

"Yeah, single, forty-something, never been married, and runs a raunchy pot-boiling publisher—um, hello? If he's not gay, then I'm not a ravishing redhead, and I obviously am. Anyway—talk to him. Maybe he could do more than just farm out bits and pieces to you. Maybe he could bring you in house—or maybe he knows someone who knows someone. You have skills, Ellen, not to mention a first-class history degree that you've never used since you met Nick. You need to maximize your earning potential. How much do you earn per month right now?"

Ellen pursed her lips; Hannah's conversational style could be somewhat relentless, but she sensed that her sister was working toward forming some idea, so she went with it. "Not enough to pay the mortgage, the bills, and keep Charlie in fish fingers. Not even if I read a book a day, which I don't want to do. I don't want to go through them like they're cannon fodder. They're *books*, Hannah. Wonderful books that someone has labored over for months and months and put all their care and attention into. I want to treat them with the respect that they deserve."

"We're talking about romances here, Ellie, not Booker Prize nominees. Everyone knows the writers churn them out to a formula. I read in *The Guardian* that if the heroine isn't being ravished every ten pages, then the so-called writer's not doing their job."

"Well—that's just ignorance and prejudice," Ellen said crossly.

"Okay—so if you worked a bit harder you could make up maybe half of what you need to pay the mortgage. Let's think laterally—how can you make money with you and Charles still living in the house . . . well, even with you two still in situ that leaves three good-size bedrooms . . . *that's it!*" Hannah clapped her hands together; she was clearly pleased with herself.

"That's what?" Ellen was alarmed.

"You become a landlady. You take in lodgers! You said it yourself—those attic rooms are practically a self-contained flat already, what with the loo and shower that's up there— that's worth seven hundred a month. Six hundred for the other double, with the en suite, and I know you won't move Charles out of his room, but even that third bedroom is worth about five hundred. That will more than cover the mortgage, and what you earn from copyediting you can use to live on. Ellen, I've solved all your problems, you may thank me now!"

Hannah beamed at her, her eyes burning brightly, and Ellen longed to get up and walk out, only this was her kitchen. Hannah had done exactly what Ellen knew she would— she'd come up with an idea that no one else had, that could work for Ellen if she had a few minutes to think about it—but her first instinct at being presented with the idea of filling her house with strangers was to run away. Ellen fidgeted in her seat as Hannah waited for her reaction, getting the feeling that Ellen had somewhere else that she really had to be. And then she realized that somewhere else was the book she was working on. A make-believe world that felt safer and more familiar than the one she actually existed in was her only escape route now. Ellen sighed. She was desperate to find out exactly how Eliza planned to escape the evil clutches of her nefarious uncle who had snatched her back from the captain after he'd been called away on secret business for Charles I. But her son, her bills, and her financial worries would not be solved in Civil War–torn England.

Ellen looked up at Hannah, who was studying her intently.

"But lodgers?" Ellen said. "Two, maybe three strangers in the house? I'm not sure that would be good for Charlie—and besides, I haven't the first idea how to be a landlady. I mean how would I split the bills? Would I have to make them breakfast? Where would they sit?"

"Where would they . . . ? Ellen, it would be like a house share. They'd cook for themselves, you could add on an amount to their rent to cover bills—you need to get a tenancy agreement drawn up, but I'm sure there's probably a boilerplate of one we could print off the internet. You'd get a deposit in advance, have a few house rules—like no nudity in the living room, for example. You'd probably hardly know they were there, I mean this is London. We're not exactly all for hanging around making friends with each other, are we? And just think, you get to stay in your precious house, forever and ever if you want to."

Ellen wasn't sure which of the words that Hannah had just sprayed her with hit home, but suddenly she knew that Hannah was right. She was the only one who'd come up with an idea that could enable her and Charlie to stay in their home and survive. Yes, it meant opening up her refuge, the haven where Nick had promised her she could always close the door on the world and feel safe, to complete strangers, but as far as Ellen could see, there was no alternative. Nick had done his best to look after her and protect her. He'd sheltered her from the world, made himself a cushion between her and its hard edges. But he was unable to continue to do that in death, no matter how carefully he'd planned to. Hannah had come up with a way out, as imperfect as it was, and despite herself Ellen was grateful that she had Hannah, a sister who could always see a way around things. There had never been any obstacle, not since Hannah was a very little girl, that she couldn't find a way to surmount to get what she wanted. It was something that Ellen simultaneously admired and disliked about her; the way she flashed her charm, beauty, and intellect with unwavering confidence was almost indecent. Still, she got things done.

"Okay," Ellen said carefully. "So, explain it to me from the beginning—what would I have to do?"

CHAPTER Three

A thin, piercing trill cut through the air. Ellen sighed, pushing the manuscript of *The Sword Erect* back across the table. For a few blissful moments she had been lost in the passion and drama of the seventeenth century, but then the doorbell sounded, ripping through the morning with its sharp, invasive ring. Phones could always be ignored. Doorbells could often be ignored, but not this time. This time Ellen had to answer it—her first lodger had arrived, exactly on time.

Hannah had procured Ellen her first lodger through work. Sabine Neumann was on a secondment from the Berlin office of T. Jenkins Waterford. She was to be posted in the London office for three months and needed a place to stay. As soon as Ellen had deferred to her sister's moneymaking idea, Hannah had pounced on her BlackBerry, remembering an email requesting temporary accommodation that had been sent out the preceding day.

"This is perfect," Hannah chirped, pleased with herself. "She wants a recommendation, and you don't want just any old weirdo turning up on you doorstep. I'll sort this out now—I'll tell her that it's the room with the en suite that's available. Let's hold back on the attic rooms, we want to get as much as possible for that, put in the room rate, and presto—it's sent."

"Whoa—wait a minute—how do we know that she's not a weirdo?" Ellen asked, her panic rising as her ever-decisive sister took action on her idea within seconds of having it.

"She works for my company." Hannah shrugged.

"Ted Bundy had a job, you know," Ellen told her.

"We do all that NLP business at the interview stage—so they'd definitely spot a psycho—then again, they gave me a job, so who knows!" Ellen did not laugh. "Anyway she's German, so she's bound to be tidy, efficient, quiet, and well mannered."

"If you choose to conform to a racial stereotype, that is," Ellen muttered.

Hannah's BlackBerry pinged. "See? What did I tell you, efficient. She's replied already and . . . she wants the room! She's arriving in a week. Right, now—what should I tell her about bedding, towels, et cetera—do you want her to bring her own or do you have enough? I'll tell her she has to supply her own, after all, you don't want to be lumbered with a load of laundry, do you?" Hannah beamed at Ellen, in her element, and briefly Ellen was reminded of her sister as a little girl, mastering riding a bike without stabilizers. It had taken Ellen a whole summer to teach Hannah how to ride a big-girl's bike, and the look on her face as she had sailed past Ellen, who'd been whooping and clapping, was exactly the same as the one she wore now. Ellen found herself smiling; there had been a time once when the two of them had been the center of each other's universe. What had happened to cause them to grow so far apart—when had Hannah stopped being the adoring little sister that Ellen doted on? If she stopped to think about it, Ellen knew that she would actually be able to pinpoint the exact moment, but she never stopped to think about it. She didn't want to remember that.

"One down, two to go," Hannah went on, oblivious. "You should ask around, too, Ellie, but in the meantime I could draft an ad for *Time Out.*"

"I don't know, I'm not sure—that really would be a stranger," Ellen said uncertainly, that fleeting memory of a summer morning fading rapidly.

"Just as a backup, I'll put my email and number on it—so you won't have to deal with it—and I promise I'll weed out all the weirdos, right after I've dated them. Let's see . . . 'Rooms to let. Well-located shared house. Must be a nonsmoker. No pets.' Perfect. I'll just log on to their website and . . . there—that's posted. I'll pay for it on my credit card—you can pay me back when the rent starts to roll in, along with the money for the skiing trip."

Ellen blinked.

"Hannah! But I haven't asked you to lend me any money for Charlie's trip—wait—how do you even know about it?"

"Charlie called me a couple of days ago and asked me if I'd spot him the cash. Of course I said yes, after I'd talked it over with you, obviously. So when do you need it? I could write you a check now if you like." Hannah smiled brightly, clearly feeling like she was on a roll in her new position as Lady Bountiful. "You don't mind, do you, Ellie? After the year he's had, a change of scenery, a chance to spread his wings a bit will do him the world of good, won't it? And it's not as if I'm giving you the money, just lending it—that's all."

Ellen felt outmaneuvered. Since Nick died, Hannah had gone out of her way to form a special relationship with her nephew. She had always been mildly fond of him, but now he had become the official apple of her eye, and Charlie loved it, loved the outings, shopping trips, and visits to the cinema. He loved his cool aunty Hannah and it rankled Ellen that he seemed more comfortable with his aunt than with his own mother. Even so, it had never occurred to Ellen that he might take it into his own hands and call Hannah and ask her for money himself. Ellen was so used to knowing every aspect of her little boy's life, it came as a shock to realize that he had a world outside of hers. More than that, she had unconsciously been glad to have a reason not to let him go so far away on the school trip, a reason other than the one that really unsettled her, the idea of him out there, vulnerable and unprotected.

"I'm not sure if he's ready to be so far from home . . ." Ellen began.

"It must be a worry for you, to let him go," Hannah said. "But you need to, Ellie; if anything, now is exactly the time when he should be finding his feet, finding out more about the world. We'd hate what happened to change him, wouldn't we? To take away his joy of life."

"Are you saying that's what I do? Take the joy away?" Ellen was offended.

"No, no! I'm saying that you're still grieving, it's not been a year yet. It wouldn't hurt to let Charlie have a break from that—it's not until September anyway, is it, this trip—so let's just agree that I'll lend you the money, you'll pay me back, and see how you feel about it nearer the time. How's that?"

Ellen nodded, mute.

"So anyway, you'd better get that room sorted out. Today's . . . Wednesday, and Sabine is arriving Friday—so that gives you two days to get ready."

"She's coming already? Hannah, that's too fast. I haven't had time to think about it, to even discuss with Charlie what he thinks about strangers living in the house. Not all of us live our lives at high speed you know."

"You can say that again." Hannah pursed her lips as she studied Ellen's face for a moment, her expression opaque. "Ellie—time has run out for you—there aren't any more opportunities for procrastination. If I know one thing, it's when to take action, and now is that time. Besides, what is there to discuss? You're out of options. Charles will understand that, he's a bright boy. I could talk to him if you like."

"No, no—I'll talk to him about it when he gets back from school later."

"Okay, well, you do that—and with a bit of luck we'll have all your spare rooms occupied before you know it."

"Good morning. I'm Sabine Neumann." Ellen looked somewhat taken aback by the perfectly manicured hand that was extended toward her. Sabine Neumann was not at all what she had pictured. To her shame, she had expected the German businesswoman to be rather mannish, with short hair and a very firm manner, somewhere in her fifties. Her first impression could not have been more different.

Sabine was about Ellen's age, with long, blond hair that spiraled over her shoulders in a natural corkscrew curl; she had a bright smile and blue eyes that seemed actually to sparkle. Instead of the dour business suit that Ellen had expected, she was wearing a white shirt over faded jeans, finished off with a pair of red Converse shoes. It was an outfit that Ellen could never picture herself in, not outlandish or over the top but confident, stylish.

"Welcome, Sabine," Ellen said, feeling suddenly dowdy and mannish herself. "Please come in. I hope that everything here is to your liking. I've never had lodgers before, I'm not at all used to it. I don't really know the etiquette, but I hope if there is something that I'm not getting right, you will tell me."

"Okay, I will," Sabine agreed, with barely a trace of an accent, looking around the sunlit hallway. "You house is lovely, it's very Victorian—just how I pictured it."

"Thank you," Ellen said, casting an eye over the restored oak boards that glowed a deep gold in the morning sun, and the pale green and cream paints that Nick had chosen for this space, which made it such a warm and inviting entrance. They had spent an age touring reclamation yards to find the perfect lighting, settling eventually on a modest little crystal chandelier that Ellen noticed needing dusting as she glanced up at it. Immediately she pictured Nick on his stepladder, swearing as he wrangled with it, the beams of sunlight captured by its glass drops dancing on the floor and walls.

"And this is your family?" Sabine had wandered over to a photograph of Ellen, Nick, and Charlie that hung on the wall. It had been taken a few months before Nick's accident, and it had been Nick's idea. He had come home one day and told Ellen that they should make a record of their family, something permanent they would be able to look back on so that whatever might change in the future, they'd always remember how things had been. Ellen remembered feeling rather puzzled, and she'd asked him if there was anything wrong, anything he was worried about. But he'd just laughed and ruffled her hair in that way that he'd taken to doing and told her not to be so foolish, that real life was nothing like those books she was so obsessed with, stuffed with tragedy and intrigue. He'd found a photographer he liked and she had come to the house, shrouding their seldom-used living room with white sheets and throw cushions. Ellen remembered how Nick and Charlie had had to make her laugh to get her to loosen up after the photographer had shown them the first digital images on her laptop. Nick had joked that it was like having his photo taken with a maiden aunt. They had told her stupid jokes until finally Ellen had forgotten that the camera was there at all, and now there they were, the three of them. That single moment captured them lounging together, arms around necks, legs intertwined, laughing.

"You are very lucky to have such a wonderful family," Sabine observed

"I, well—yes, I was—I am." Ellen fought that familiar prick of tears behind her eyes. "Nick, my husband, died last year in a traffic accident. It's just me and Charlie now—hence the lodgers."

Sabine nodded. "I'm sorry. My husband is not dead," she informed Ellen, her pretty mouth forming a thin line. "My husband is in Berlin; I've left him. I couldn't stand looking at him for another second more, the lying, whoring piece of shit. It's not fair, is it? If my husband was dead I wouldn't mind, but you—you loved yours and now you've lost him. Life isn't fair." Sabine shrugged as if she'd just missed a bus she wasn't especially bothered about catching and put one foot on the bottom stair. "So now, perhaps I might see the room?"

The phone was ringing as Ellen left Sabine unpacking her bag and she prayed that it was not Hannah with news of another enforced lodger.

Ellen was still trying to adjust to having one stranger move into her house and her life. Sabine was right, it wasn't fair. If Nick hadn't decided on a whim to borrow his friend's Lotus and take it for a spin down some quiet country roads after a late pub lunch, if he hadn't exceeded the speed limit by nearly double, if he'd *thought* just for one second about . . . Ellen halted that train of thought before it could develop any further, consumed with guilt that she could allow herself even to begin to feel angry with her husband. Nick would never have left her and Charlie in this kind of mess on purpose. He hadn't set out on that summer morning to kill himself, purely to inconvenience her. He had loved her like no other man ever had or ever would again. And Nick had been an adventurer, an explorer—the kind of man to seize the day and ring every ounce of life out of it, reluctant to waste any precious seconds on sleep. That was what Ellen had loved about him first, his drive, his passion. That and the fact that when she was around him, for the first time in her life she felt vibrant, a three-dimensional being of flesh and blood who was finally present in the world that Nick embraced so readily—she felt alive. It was a feeling that she hadn't been able to re-create since the moment she had discovered that Nick was dead.

Biting her lip, Ellen quieted the circle of thoughts that constantly ran around in her head and picked up the phone.

"Ellen, good, you're in." Simon's voice sounded deep and

melodious. Ellen breathed a sigh of relief. Her boss was one of the few people who would not demand that she take some kind of action, who would not persist in telling her where she was going wrong. If anything, with a little bit of luck he'd have something nice for her to work on—preferably the next installment of *The Sword Erect,* as she had almost finished the pages she already had.

"Hello, Simon." Ellen's voice was warm. "I'm in and I've just greeted my first lodger."

"Ah yes, you told me about your new career as a landlady in your last email. In fact, in a roundabout way it's sort of my reason for ringing today."

"Really?" Ellen was puzzled. "Why, do you need a room?"

"No, no, my dear—I'll get to that in a minute. First off, tell me all about your first lodger," Simon said, deciding to put whatever urgent request he had for her on hold for a second. That was the other thing Ellen liked about Simon. While Hannah seemed to feel that it was her duty to talk at her and boss her around, Simon, a man she rarely spoke to and saw even less, actually seemed interested in her and how she was coping. He was one of the few people who ever asked her how she was. Sometimes Ellen didn't want to answer. Sometimes she hated the fact that he asked, but at the same time she appreciated it, too.

"She's nice, I think." Ellen recalled the ten or so minutes that she had spent so far in Sabine's company. "She seems it, anyway, and she is happy with the room as far as I can tell. It's just strange, you know—different."

"I know, Ellen, it must be hard for you," Simon said, his voice softening. "I'd hate to share my flat with anyone but Tibalt." Simon referred to his ancient and grizzled cocker spaniel, who accompanied him every day to the Cherished Desires offices on Fulham Palace Road and lay all day under his desk, emitting foul smells and loud snores. Simon was more devoted to him than to any human, at least that Ellen knew of.

"Oh well, no—not that hard. And it's money, isn't it, money to keep this house going and disrupt Charlie as little as possible—talking of which, do you have any more of the new Allegra Howard for me? It's not like you to give me a book in dribs and drabs."

"Not quite; I have something a little better." Simon sounded hesitant. "Ellen, I have Allegra Howard herself for you, if you will have her, that is."

"I beg your pardon?" Ellen glanced up at the ceiling at the sound of furniture being dragged across the floor.

"Allegra—she's in a pickle, and she needs a fair maid to come to her rescue. I immediately thought of you, the fairest maid I know."

"Me—but how could *I* ever help Allegra Howard?"

"Well, you know those dreadful spring floods they had a while back in Gloucestershire?"

"Oh yes, they were awful," Ellen said, thinking of the TV pictures on the news of houses half filled with water, a teddy bear floating down what once had been a quiet avenue. The whole of Tewkesbury was practically under water.

"Well, Allegra's seventeenth-century manor house took the brunt of it. It's going to take months to restore it, and apparently her insurance company isn't keen to put her up in a five-star hotel for the duration. Allegra refuses to go anywhere near anything as unsavory as a trailer or a strange rental house, so I was thinking about what you said—how you mentioned that you were looking for tenants—and I wondered if you'd have Allegra as one."

"Have Allegra Howard staying here—Simon, I can't possibly." Ellen pressed the palm of her hand to her chest, feeling her heart rate accelerate; it was a curious sensation. She'd read so many of Allegra's books over the years that she felt as if she knew the woman, and oddly as if Allegra knew her, too, more intimately than perhaps anyone else.

"Please, Ellen, she really needs somewhere nice and homey

to stay while she tries to finish *The Sword Erect*. All of the drama has rather blocked her creative flow. She's lost her confidence a little and she needs someone to boost her up. I can't think of anyone better to take her in than you, the very person who loves and understands her books so much."

"Allegra Howard in my third bedroom, Simon! She needs to stay somewhere much better than a shabby old house in Hammersmith. Besides, you said she wouldn't touch a rental!"

"That's where you're wrong, my angel. And your house is anything but a strange and unwelcoming rental house. Your shabby, old, beautiful, much-loved home is *exactly* what she needs, the poor old duck. And you wouldn't just be her landlady. As you know, the latest book is set during the English civil wars, and Allegra needs a bit of extra help—a research assistant, if you like. To find contemporary street maps, brush up on the history—that sort of thing. Allegra's never been one to let facts get in the way of a good story, but the readers do like things to be at least a little accurate. Her last PA left because of . . . artistic differences, so the position is happily vacant. Besides, Allegra will only write in pen—lilac fountain pen to be precise. One of your jobs would be to type up her work into an electronic format. Just imagine—you'd be the first person in creation to read the new Allegra Howard. And she'd pay you—it wouldn't be much but it would double your rental income, and I could top it up by a few quid—it would be worth it, you'd be saving my life."

Ellen paused, feeling her heart pounding. In truth, there was nothing she could imagine enjoying more than helping the great Allegra Howard with her latest work of genius. But could she really do it?

She was certainly capable of helping research the background of the novel, after all, she had a degree in English history—even if the only thing she'd used it for in the last ten years was to subtly point out some of the more glaring

historical errors in Allegra's books. She was a competent typ-
ist and her job as a freelance copyeditor (might as well be a
"free" lance, Hannah persisted in teasing her) meant she was
well versed in punctuation and grammar—something else
that Allegra seemed to find rather tiresome. But this was *the*
Allegra Howard—the woman who had supplied Ellen with the
alternate universe that she had so happily inhabited for the last
few years, even before Nick had left her so suddenly. Allegra,
who created the heroines that Ellen loved to transform into
for the few precious hours she spent wrapped up among those
sheets of paper. Allegra, who fashioned the kinds of manly,
magnetic heroes Ellen was ashamed to admit she frequently
imagined making love to her with the same fiery passion that
they lavished upon the shapely young maidens who popu-
lated Allegra's books. Quite often, on a quiet afternoon when
Charlie was at school and Nick was safely at work, Ellen would
find herself quite caught up in the moment as one of Allegra's
rakes urgently pinned some feisty young woman to, perhaps, a
ship's mast, or a tree trunk, or, in one of Ellen's favorite books,
The Stallion Rampant, a horse's back. Unable to contain his
desire for the heroine's lovely body a second longer, he would
rip her clothes from her, whipped into a frenzy by the exquisite sight of her naked breasts, whereupon he would take her,
his manhood searching deep within her, finding that sweet,
sacred spot, so that at last she would come to know the true
delight of physical love and be prepared to fall in love with
him. After reading a scene like that, sometimes *while* reading a scene like that, Ellen would feel compelled to find her
own sweet, sacred spot and imagine that it was her full, pert
breasts that the hero's lips were so firmly latched on to, and
her slender yet shapely hips that he gripped with his powerful
hands as he entered her again. And again. And again.

The physical side of her life with Nick had been lovely; it
had been tender and sweet and more than satisfying—he'd always been so gentle with her, as if she were made of cut glass

and might shatter in his arms. Over the last year she had spent many a night muffling her tears in her pillow, grieving over the loss of the intimacy that they had shared. But the orgasms that Ellen had had with Allegra Howard's heroes were more passionate and intense than any she had known even with Nick. And Ellen was not at all sure she could look in the eyes of the woman who had fueled her fantasy sex life for so long. The thought of meeting the woman who had occupied her imagination so entirely for so long seemed impossible, almost like meeting God and letting him know what you thought of creation.

"Look, Ellen." Simon's voice startled her out of her reverie. "I know that the idea of a lot of people you don't know in your home tortures you. No one understands that better than me. God knows if I didn't have bills to pay I'd live as a recluse, doing up my wreck of a cottage in Suffolk, and never talk to anyone again, except you and Tibalt. You'd be doing me a huge favor if you took Allegra in. To be honest, her name is one of the few on the list that is guaranteed to turn a profit for the company. Allegra's sales carry a lot of our less-established authors, not to mention pay my mortgage and hers. In this climate, I need her to finish this latest book sooner rather than later. Her readers are used to three books a year and *The Sword Erect* is long overdue already. You love her work, you know exactly what her readers want from her books; I've long thought that you've got far more potential to develop your career than merely copyediting, and I know you'll look after her like a seventy-three-year-old woman needs to be looked after—"

"She's seventy-three!" Ellen interrupted. "She looks at least twenty years younger in her author photo."

"That's because she *is* twenty years younger in her author photo," Simon told her. "Anyway, I can't think of anyone better to help her through this dry patch."

"So you're saying you want me to get her back into a wet patch," Ellen joked, quite uncharacteristically.

Simon chuckled. "Ellen! Have you been drinking during the day!"

"I don't know, it must be Allegra's latest book—this one is especially racy, Simon. I'll just have to hope that working on it won't corrupt me totally."

"So are you saying you'll do it?" Simon pressed. Ellen heard the anxiety in his voice. Clearly, she was his plan A and he didn't have a plan B, and the idea of helping Simon out of a spot gave her unexpected pleasure.

"Okay, okay—I'll do it!" Ellen exclaimed, feeling giddy with the rush of the unknown; it was a sensation she hadn't experienced in the longest time. Meeting Allegra would be fine. As Simon had said, she was a homeless old lady, not some soothsayer with psychic powers to see inside a person's brain.

"Ellen Woods—you are a magnificent woman," Simon told her warmly.

"Oh well . . ." Ellen found herself flushing with pleasure as she stood alone in her hallway. It was rare for anyone to compliment her these days.

"There's just one more thing. Allegra will need a ground-floor room near a loo—is that a problem? She's not too great with stairs, not that she will tell you that and nor should you mention it."

"Well, there's the dining room, we don't really use it, and it's got French doors that open out onto the garden. I could get Charlie and some of his pals to put the table in the garage. But what about a bed?"

"Oh, I'll buy you a new one; Allegra is quite fussy about only sleeping on virgin mattresses, as she calls them," Simon said. "Also, if you painted the room lilac, preferably with odorless paint, and got in some lilac furnishings so that it's all ready for her grand entrance in around a week from now, then we're all set."

"Lilac?" Ellen questioned, pinning her whirl of confusion on that one word.

"Yes, and a chaise longue, she needs a chaise longue to recline on while she's thinking up ideas. There's this website that delivers them in any color you like. I'll order it and pick up the bill and get it delivered to you, shall I? Plus, I'll have to ship in her desk—it was one of the few things that survived the flood, she's very attached to it. Don't worry about the expense, just send all the receipts to me and I'll settle them straightaway. Anyway, my dearest love, I must dash. I've got Bernadette Darcy due in for an editorial meeting. Apparently she's having a problem with her country-house orgy—can't think of enough positions for each chapter."

Ellen set down the phone and looked at it for a moment, wondering if that conversation had really happened or if she had imagined it.

Allegra Howard in *her* house in a week's time. Ellen wondered where she could get lilac paint delivered from, pronto.

CHAPTER Four

Charlie eyed Sabine across the dining-room table, where she sat eating a bacon sandwich that she had made herself. Sabine had asked Ellen when she might be allowed access to the kitchen, and Ellen, realizing that she hadn't given catering or kitchen arrangements a moment's thought, had told her to use the kitchen whenever she liked. Sabine had gone out for an hour, returned with several Sainsbury's bags, and then had politely asked Ellen if she might have a shelf in the fridge, one near the top would be preferable.

"It will save on labeling," Sabine explained, although Ellen had no idea what she meant.

"Useful to have a big supermarket so close," Sabine remarked as she munched on her sandwich.

"I suppose it is." Ellen smiled. "Although I must admit I get all my groceries delivered, once a week. I read that it's greener, because the delivery van has less of a carbon footprint or something. Besides, I don't drive."

"You never learned to drive?" Sabine asked.

"Oh, I learned, it's just that living in London you don't really need to, and since Charlie was born I sort of lost my confidence. I prefer not to drive, I should have said."

"You still keep Dad's car insured, though," Charlie said, arriving home from school, his hair tousled, his uniform Friday dirty. Normally, all that would greet him would be his mum, sitting at the kitchen table, up to her elbows in some book or other, but now he was greeted by a German blonde sitting in his usual chair. He had known that the first lodger was coming today. Ellen had discussed or at least attempted to discuss with him at length what he thought about the idea on the same day Hannah had suggested it, but Charlie had simply shrugged. "Yeah, okay then," he'd said. Ellen had been nonplussed.

"Well, hang on a minute, Charlie—let's think about this. It would mean a really big change, a house full of people—not just us here anymore."

"I know." Charlie had nodded.

"And you don't mind that?" Ellen had asked, wondering if she should feel put out that he was quite so relaxed about the end of their quiet little family.

Charlie had tipped his head to one side. "Mum, you really don't want to leave this house, do you?"

"Well, no—but you don't either . . . do you?"

Charlie had looked thoughtful. "The point is, you don't want to leave, you can't leave. You need to be here, and I know you think I don't know anything that's going on, but I know that money is tight, I know we need to make some. So we get in lodgers, it's fine."

"But are you happy about it?" Ellen had pressed.

"I'm happy!" Charlie had exclaimed, grabbing a piece of bread and stuffing it into his mouth. "Besides, Aunt Hannah says it's a good idea."

"Oh, she did, did she? Well, that makes it okay then." Ellen had never voiced how irritating she found the private joke that Charlie and Hannah had shared, ever since he was three years old, of only ever addressing each other formally, or that it drove her mad that Charlie was so interested in every word Hannah said, that he respected her lifestyle and her career and the travel and material prizes that her work brought her, while he increasingly treated Ellen like she was the one who needed looking after. Before, Nick's word had been law; if he said something was good, bad, or indifferent, then Charlie agreed with him. Now it was Hannah's word he trusted, and Ellen wondered if he would ever really open up to her again.

"She said we needed the money," Charlie had told her. "Yeah, it will be a bit whack—but mainly I'm cool with it, seriously."

Ellen had decided that this was not the time to remind Charlie that he was an English middle-class schoolboy and not a New York gangster rapper.

"Well, just so long as you know you don't have to worry about anything, okay?"

"I'm not worried," Charlie had insisted, chewing the corner of his thumb as he spoke.

Ellen watched her son closely now for signs of distress as he studied Sabine, but all she could detect was naked curiosity.

There were only three mismatched chairs at the kitchen table. When they moved into the house, Nick had taken them to a local junk shop where he had spotted a large, ancient, battered pine table that he thought would be perfect for their new kitchen. Ellen had complained that it didn't have matching chairs, and Nick had laughed, waving his arm around at the collection of disowned chairs of all shapes and sizes.

"I know," he'd said, winking at an enchanted Charlie. "Let's choose a different chair each. One that will suit us and be our chair whenever we sit at the table."

Ellen had chosen a chair that she thought was most in keeping with the table, a humble pine affair with a simple back and straight legs. Nick had managed to find a dark wood carver that looked like it had once belonged to a much grander set and had ideas far above its station, with its turned arms and sturdy, squat bowed legs. Charlie, much younger, still a baby really, had found a brightly painted chair that must have once belonged to an amateur artist. Every leg was painted a different primary color and the back rest was an acidic green decorated with a painted eye. Ever since that day, the three of them had always sat in their special chairs, until Nick had died, and then his remained stubbornly vacant, and even Hannah knew better than to sit in it. Today, Sabine was sitting in Charlie's and he took up residence in his mother's. Ellen leaned against the kitchen counter and watched, fretting about how to break the news to her lodgers that one of her kitchen chairs was off-limits.

"This is a delicious sandwich," Sabine said after she had finished chewing. "Do you like bacon, Charlie? I love Danish bacon."

"I don't eat bacon," Charlie told her. "I eat fish fingers, white bread, ketchup, and Frosties." He issued the declaration like it was a challenge.

"Ah—you're a fussy eater." Sabine nodded, as if nothing Charlie had said was out of the ordinary. "When I was a girl I would only drink milk and I wouldn't touch any vegetables."

"Even when you were nearly twelve?" Charlie quizzed her, making Ellen tense—wondering if he was as worried about his eating habits as she was or if some of the kids at school had said something.

"Oh yes, until I was much older than twelve. I didn't like vegetables until I was in my twenties, after several years of smoking and drinking. Your taste buds are young and tender, unsullied by alcohol or nicotine—it's normal for a young boy to only like a few things."

"That's what I thought." Charlie grinned at her, his shoulders relaxing, happily forgetting the ravenous appetite he'd had for nearly anything edible before his father died.

"So, Charlie," Ellen said from her observation point. "We got our second guest today. She's a writer, Mummy's favorite writer actually, and she's arriving on Tuesday—so you and I have our work cut out, turning the dining room into a bedroom and painting it lilac this weekend."

"Lilac! Gross!" Charlie and Sabine looked at each other and wrinkled their noses, striking up an easy camaraderie that Ellen could not help but envy. It hadn't been that easy between her and Charlie for a long time; he always seemed so disappointed in her.

"I know, but the best bit is I'm going to be her research assistant, which means more money—which means I can pay Aunt Hannah back for your skiing trip!" Ellen told him proudly. Whether or not she actually wanted him to go was moot for now, it was the fact that she no longer needed Hannah's money that was paramount.

"But Aunt Hannah's already paid for it."

"I know, but it was just a loan—now I can pay it back."

"Yes, but Hannah's loaded and you're skint, so why don't you—"

"I'm paying for it, Charlie, end of discussion." Ellen felt hurt that Charlie had rejected her announcement so roundly.

"Yes, but it doesn't make sense. What about the bills, the mortgage . . . ?"

"Charlie . . ." Ellen heard her tone rising, against her will.

"May I help you paint this weekend?" Sabine asked, taking a packet of cigarettes out of her shirt pocket, looking at them rather wistfully, then putting them back again. "I don't have any friends here or a social life yet. I would welcome the chance to get to know you better, plus I am an excellent painter. I do very straight edges. It's because I'm German, you know—we're very precise."

Sabine winked at Charlie, who chuckled, and it took Ellen a second to realize that her guest was joking.

"Well, Sabine, if you're sure, that would be wonderful." Ellen smiled. It seemed that for now, anyway, having a lodger wasn't nearly as dreadful as Ellen had feared, unlike the unexpected ring of the doorbell.

"Well, I will just go outside for a cigarette." Sabine nodded at the kitchen door. "Out there, okay?"

"Oh yes, fine," Ellen said, bracing herself to answer the bell, even though she knew who it was.

"Charles." Hannah nodded at her nephew as she entered the kitchen.

"Aunt Hannah," Charlie replied with a small bow. "A delight to see you as ever."

"Charmed, I'm sure," Hannah replied regally.

"Hannah." Ellen watched as her sister sprawled in her now-vacant chair. "It's very nice of you to drop by, again, but you didn't say you were coming over tonight and it's just I've got a lot to do, a lot of sorting out for the next lodger."

Ellen wanted Charlie to see that she could manage some things for herself.

"Oh, God, please say it's not the second-floor suite you've let out?" Hannah exclaimed.

"If you mean the attic rooms, then no—I'm converting the dining room into a room for an elderly lady—actually she's—" Ellen was keen to share her bit of news but Hannah rushed on before she could.

"Oh good, that's a relief. I came for two reasons. Because I thought I'd say hi to Sabine, and offer to take her out for lunch on Monday and show her around." Hannah looked around. "Where is Sabine anyway? Have you confined her to her quarters? I'm dying to see what she looks like."

"She's really nice," Charlie assured Hannah, making his aunt and mother look at him. "She's outside, smoking, and she's a total fox."

"Oh, Charles, you are growing up!" Hannah burst out laughing; Ellen did not.

Ellen privately smarted. Here was Hannah, marching in, making everything about her as usual, even the possibility of any fledgling friendship that Ellen might have with Sabine. Since Hannah had hit her teens, it had been characteristic of Ellen's life that once anyone she knew met her sister, Hannah's burning sun eclipsed Ellen's quieter personality almost immediately; this had happened so much that Ellen had taken to avoiding bringing her friends to her parents' house, because once they met Hannah they couldn't stop talking about her, how pretty, how delightful, how funny, how different from Ellen. Hannah's determination to claim Sabine was just the same as when at age twenty-one Ellen had brought her first-ever proper boyfriend home from university to meet her parents. When she had left the previous autumn to return to college, Hannah had been a sulky and sullen teen, resentful and jealous of Ellen's escape to more exciting—or at least different—climes. But when she and Jack had returned that summer, Ellen feeling especially grown-up, hand in hand with her first-ever lover, Hannah had been waiting for them, sitting on the front step in a pair of white denim shorts and a halter top, her flame-colored hair swinging down her back, grazing her sun-drenched shoulders. Ellen knew, from the moment she set eyes on her sister, that Hannah wanted to see if she could make her boyfriend like her more than he liked Ellen, and what really hurt was that it took just a few seconds for her to claim him. Not in actuality—as far as Ellen knew, Jack had never touched Hannah—but for the duration of his visit he could not take his eyes off her, and she pranced and danced and laughed for him, testing her budding sexuality with capricious delight. She had made Ellen feel so dark and clumsy and invisible that eventually she had picked a fight with Jack, accusing him of chasing her little sister, and he had looked at her, both shamefaced and disgusted, accusing her of petty childishness. Their relationship fizzled out quite soon after they got back to college and Ellen put the blame firmly on Hannah's shoulders. How she had dreaded taking Nick to meet her family, but it was probably on that day that she had fallen in love with her husband once and for all, because Nick was the only person Ellen had ever known who seemed quite disinterested in Hannah, even mildly irritated by her. It was one of the reasons that Ellen had loved him so fiercely. From that moment on, Ellen had done her best to separate her life from her sister's, and yet here she was again, laying claim to the new people in Ellen's life before she had a chance to get to know them herself.

"Oh well, the other reason I came is because I had a response from the *Time Out* ad," Hannah went on seamlessly. "Clever and beautiful Aunt Hannah has found you another lodger!"

"Please say it's not a little old lady who only likes lilac," Charlie begged, hauling himself up to rest his chin on the tabletop as he watched his aunt, with bright eyes, as if she were a particularly entertaining TV show.

"No, much better than that—he's a man! His name is Matt Bolton, he's twenty-six, a nonsmoker, and he's just moving down from Manchester to take up a job as a staff writer for *Bang It!*"

"Wicked!" Charlie's eyes widened.

"What on earth is *Bang It!*?" Ellen questioned, her expression pre-set to disapprove.

"It's a lad's mag—you know the sort of thing, photos of busty babes, articles about computer games, how to get a six-pack in six weeks—that sort of nonsense. Anyway, Matt had a column about being a single man in the *Manchester Evening News*, and apparently it caused a bit of an uproar amongst Manchester's feminist community, and he was on the verge of losing his job when he got spotted by the editor of *Bang It!* and was offered a job continuing the column down here. The offices are in Hammersmith, so this place is perfect for him. He was especially stoked about the idea of having his own loo and shower."

"So you've already told him he's got the room?" Ellen asked hesitantly. "Without checking with me first, like you said you would, remember?"

"I said I'd screen the applicants and weed out any weirdos, and Matt's not a weirdo, he seems really nice on the phone. Besides, he's got the money and he works down the road. I expect he'll be out most of the time, a young single man in London—you'll hardly know he's here."

"No, sorry—I'm putting my foot down," Ellen said firmly, feeling dizzy from how quickly her life was spinning out of control. "You'll have to tell him he's not coming."

"Oh, Mum!" Charlie exclaimed, disappointed. "I'll be the coolest boy in the school if one of our lodgers worked on *Bang It!* It'd make up for the old lady!"

"Hang on a minute, Ellie," Hannah countered. "Let's think about this a bit more. Why do you object to Matt?"

"Because my other tenants are females, and one of them is an older lady, a writer with sensitive needs. The last thing Allegra Howard wants is some man crashing around the place, swearing and talking about . . . God knows what. This is a house of women, we don't want any men."

"Oh, thanks very much." Charlie scowled.

"Allegra Howard—isn't that the woman whose books you love so much?" Hannah asked, completely breaking Ellen's stride and making her firm stand seem rather less effective.

"Yes, it is—she needs a place to stay while her flood-damaged home is being restored *and* she needs a research assistant and PA—and that's me. I've got the job. I'm getting paid and everything." Ellen nodded emphatically on the final word.

"Really—Ellie, that's fab news—well done, you. See what you can do when you set your mind to it?"

Ellen nodded, caught off guard by Hannah's enthusiasm for her. After all, she hadn't really done anything yet—except answer the phone. Still, Hannah didn't know that.

"But honestly, I don't see why that means you can't have Matt as a tenant. Like I said, he'll be out most of the time, and when he is here he and Allegra will be separated by a whole floor! Besides, if the covers of her books are anything to go by, she likes a strapping young man with his top off, and it wouldn't do Charles any harm to have a man about the place . . ." Hannah stopped herself, probably from saying "since Nick died." Her face was still and dark for the briefest moment. "You know, to watch footy with and talk about girls to."

"Please, Mum," Charlie begged. "I would get total respect at school." Ellen looked at him, puzzled. Was he really keen to have another man in the house or did he just want to please Hannah?

"You're really begging me to let a male lodger stay?" Ellen asked.

"Like Aunt Hannah says, it will be cool to have a bloke around, otherwise it will just be me and a load of old women. And Sabine."

"Hey, you, Sabine's not much younger than me," Ellen protested, self-consciously tucking a strand of her dark hair behind her ear.

"Oh, go on, Ellie—at least give Matt a try—I'll tell him he's on a one-month trial and if you don't like him you can kick him out after that. Just think, if you take Matt on, you don't need to look for any more lodgers. You can get stuck in your new job, and Charles will be settled with the new arrangements before you know it."

"I will," Charlie agreed.

Ellen felt her shoulders slump. It seemed that she was the victim of a fait accompli.

"Okay, I'll give him a trial, but if he smells or swears or is in any way a bad influence, then he's out."

"Great! He's getting an early train down from Manchester Monday morning; he's going to move his stuff after his first day."

"Hello." Sabine appeared from the garden, where she had been smoking among the ragged rose bushes that Ellen hadn't touched since last summer.

"Oh, hello. You must be Sabine. I'm Hannah—we spoke on the phone?"

"Ah, Hannah, hello, it's nice to meet you in person."

"Well, I thought you might like to meet for lunch tomorrow and get some of the inside goss," Hannah said. "Seriously, if I don't know it, then it's not worth knowing."

"That would be very nice." Sabine smiled. "I find that no matter how old or how well traveled I am, beginning work in a new place is still just like starting school. A friendly face makes things so much easier."

"That's what I thought," Hannah said, making Ellen feel bad for resenting her sister's visit. Hannah was only trying to help her, she told herself. Hannah was being a good sister. Whatever it was, whatever dark little nagging resentment that kept on nibbling away at Ellen, whether it was left over from their childhood or was something new that had sprung up in the wake of everything else, she had to shake it off. She had to remember that she was lucky to have Hannah, and put all her irrational irritations aside.

"While I was smoking in your beautiful garden I was thinking that it is such a pleasant evening, and I noticed a rather nice-looking pub down the road on an earlier shopping trip. Ellen, I wondered if you might take me for my first British drink?"

"Oh, can we?" Charlie looked at Ellen hopefully, his eyes bright with expectation. This was the first time that any-thing—well, anything different or interesting—had happened at home for him in a long time, Ellen realized, glimpsing an insight into what his life had been like for the last year. This change, this shake-up that she dreaded, was exactly what he needed. Perhaps it's what she needed, too.

Ellen checked the wall clock; it was only just past seven, it was the weekend tomorrow, and she supposed an hour wouldn't hurt. It would be nice to be the one giving Charlie a treat for once. Besides, Sabine did seem to have the most won-derful knack of pouring oil over troubled waters at just the right moment, her newness diluting the tension that always built between Ellen and her sister.

Ellen thought of the pub at the end of the road. Right now it would be busy with commuters on their way home, enjoy-ing a cold drink, standing in the evening sunshine. There'd be laughter in the air, a cacophony of voices, the scent of smoke mingling with the summer foliage. It would be crammed to the brim with happy, relaxed people. But she had so much to do for Allegra Howard and so little time to do it. Really she had to start right away.

"You three go," Ellen decided. "I've got to get on the internet, see if I can find someone who'll deliver paint tomorrow and start sorting out the dining room. I want you back in an hour, though—okay?"

"Marvelous! What fun to take my nephew for his first illegal drink."

"Hannah!" Ellen reacted just as her sister knew she would.

"I'm only joking, Ellie." Hannah giggled, winking at Charlie, who grinned delightedly at her in return.

"Hannah," Ellen heard Charlie ask as they walked out the door, the June evening still gilding the street with its warmth. "Can I have a cider?"

"In your dreams, sweetie." Hannah laughed. "Don't want to give your mum any more reasons to be cross with me, do we?"

Once they had gone, Ellen listened to the silence left in their wake for a second and then walked into the now-seldom-used living room, hoping to catch a glimpse of them walking by the hedge that was so desperately in need of trimming.

Ellen took a moment to look at the border she had planted so lovingly in front of the window, packed full of tall blue and violet delphiniums; yellow, spiky stars like goldstrum; a multitude of multicolored pinks and mauve coneflowers. She hadn't weeded or tended to the plants since last summer. In fact, she had a feeling that her gardening gloves were probably still where she had left them, wrung together and cast down, moldering somewhere in the depths of the border that she had been working on when the news came. And yet, despite being half choked to death with weeds and rogue grass, the flowers had fought their way through to bloom again.

For a moment Ellen pressed her palm against the glass, remembering the smell, the feel of the soil between her fingers, the pleasure in seeing her planting design mature and take shape. And for a moment, she missed being out there, passing a polite word here and there with passersby, feeling the heat of the sun scorching the nape of her neck. Ellen watched as a fat bumble bee tracked its way first up and then down the pollen-heavy head of a delphinium, ensuring its bloom would soon be gone. She wasn't ready for that yet, she wasn't ready to see her plants blossom and die, another summer over. She wasn't ready for it to be almost a whole year since she had last worked on that border, since the two very kind police officers had walked up the garden path and asked her if she would come inside so they could talk.

Ellen turned her back on the golden evening outside, pulled by the drag of the empty room that used to be so full of her and Nick, sitting together on the sofa any evening he wasn't working late. Holding hands, drinking tea, and sharing choco-late, talking about Charlie and where they would go, or what they would do next. Without having to look, Ellen knew that over the hedge the street was drenched with sunshine, and she could imagine the day's heat, absorbed by the pavement, that would have radiated through the thin soles of her summer shoes. Perhaps she should have gone, Ellen thought, running her hand along the cool, painted windowsill, but somehow it didn't feel right. Even when Nick was alive they hadn't really gone out together, always content to stay at home, curled up on the sofa that Ellen was trying not to look at. Home had been Nick's refuge, his break from real life.

Things were difficult now, they were painful and harsh, Ellen thought, turning her face away from the glare of the outside to cool her cheeks in the shadowy room. But at least they *were* changing. At least there was some letup to the un-relenting grief that had characterized every single minute of her life since Nick had died. Was it wrong to feel optimistic and even excited about the recent turn of events? Perhaps it was too soon to attempt to get on with things; perhaps if she started to pull herself together now, that would mean that she hadn't loved Nick enough. Queen Victoria had mourned the untimely death of her husband for over fifty years. Never again had she worn anything but black. She had made the rest of her life a mausoleum to her husband. Should that be how any grieving widow carried on, an empty shell, existing only because she had to?

No, Nick would want her to get on with things, he'd want her to be okay. He'd be so surprised that she'd made it this far without him; he'd always joked that she wasn't safe to be let out on her own. Besides, being okay, having something to look forward to, something to do, didn't mean that she wasn't still carrying a burning hole in her chest where her heart used to beat.

Life could still be livable, Ellen slowly allowed herself to realize as her eyes roamed over the empty sofa. Even without her husband, her existence could still be bearable, even perhaps happy again, in a way. It was a previously unimaginable thought that, when it dawned, came as an enormous relief to her. The idea that the burden of grief she had become so used to carrying could, *would* one day be at least lightened made Ellen feel a little giddy, and she felt just the first stirrings of something that had lain dormant in her for more years than she could remember. The pleasure of finding her own independence.

The outside world blazing at her back, Ellen found that she was smiling to herself. If two new people in her life could improve things for her so much, then a third could, at the very least, do her no harm. Like Hannah had said, Ellen would probably have hardly anything to do with Matt Bolton.

It wasn't too late to catch up with them, she could still go to the pub if she wanted to.

Ellen thought for a moment, and then, drawing the curtains on the living room, she went to the dining room and started to clear out the sideboard instead.

CHAPTER Five

M att Bolton blinked and pinched himself. He actually couldn't believe his eyes. Here he was on his first day on the job at *Bang It!*, watching a photo shoot. A photo shoot with two glamorous models, who were getting much better acquainted with each other's assets than they had been when they'd turned up a few minutes ago.

"Life's good, right?" Pete Grossman asked Matt. He was the features editor on the magazine and would be Matt's immediate boss and mentor. Standing a good four inches shorter than Matt, Pete was nevertheless an attractive and well-built man in his midforties. Matt could see with his journalist's eye that Pete would have been considered handsome once, and had probably been something of a pinup in his youth. A life of drinking and smoking, however, and at least two expensive ex-wives had taken their toll on him, his skin thickened and ruddy and his possibly dyed black hair thinning around the temples. Once, he'd been a cutting-edge young investigative journalist who battled on gamely in the middle of whatever war zone was most readily available. When he had bagged the job of the youngest-ever editor in chief of Britain's bestselling tabloid in his thirties, his future had looked golden. Something had happened to change all of that, though. Matt had heard dark rumors that there had been some incident between Pete and a lesser member of the royal family that had compelled him to resign from his job and be grateful for whatever work he could find since. And that had been as a feature writer at *Bang It!* for the last two years.

Pete had invited Matt along to the photo shoot as soon as he walked in through the office door that morning. He'd barely had time to park his suitcase under his desk before Pete had whisked him out of the office.

"Mag rules," Pete had explained on their way to the shoot. "We always get the rookies along to one of these as quickly as possible; stops them wasting time they could spend wondering exactly what goes on here. Truth is, it gets a bit dull after a while; you've seen one pair, you've seen them all—know what I mean?" Pete tossed his head back as he laughed. "No, of course you don't, it's the best job in the world! Play your cards right and I'll get you in on the next casting. That's when the models come in and we get them to strip in the office for us. Sometimes, if it's a bloke's birthday or some poor sucker's stag night, we hold a casting for them when there isn't even going to be a photo shoot. Brilliant, all these girls taking their clothes off for free, doing whatever we tell them without a clue that we're just having a laugh and there is no job at the end of it. Brilliant. When's your birthday?"

"Tomorrow?" Matt joked. This was his dream job: London, women, national-magazine journalism. This was what he had been working for, a room full of topless girls and a minibar in the corner. Some people might think that Matt was a little shallow, but he didn't care. Maybe this wasn't the kind of reporting that he'd had in mind when he set out on his writing career, maybe he had envisioned himself writing hard news from the center of the Gaza Strip, but life, his life, had brought him to a photo shoot for *Bang It!* magazine, and as far as he could see, there was no way a red-blooded man would complain about that.

Matt *had* been a little worried, as he entered the closed set in a photography studio in Ladbroke Grove, that he would let himself down, that he'd drool, leer, lose the power of speech—or worse still, get an unwelcome hard-on, which would mean he'd have to cross his legs and stay seated until it abated.

As soon as he was on the set, though, Matt realized that if he had done any of those things, he would have been the only one to care. The girls walked about in nothing but G-strings, laughing and talking as if they were fully dressed. The photographer took an interest in them only when they were in front of the camera, and the makeup-and-hair girl, a pretty redhead called Carla, dusted their breasts with glitter with all the erotic tension of basting a turkey. Even Pete seemed more interested in checking his emails on his mobile than watching what was going on.

The real test came when, during a break, Lindsey, a twenty-one-year-old from Doncaster, came over to talk to him.

"You're from up north, too, right?" she asked with a pretty smile. Matt tried very hard not to look at her breasts, which was difficult, because they were big and naked. And breasts.

"Yeah, Manchester—just got off the train this morning actually. You been down here long?" He attempted nonchalance.

"A couple of months." Lindsey's voice was sweet and light, which didn't seem to fit with her impressive physique, which Matt knew had to be natural because *Bang It!* didn't do fake, it was magazine policy. "It's all right once you get used to it—a lot like home really, only everyone's got a funny accent." Lindsey laughed and her natural breasts jiggled in Matt's peripheral vision. He prayed to all the gods he could think of that he would not blush. Until quite recently, all the women he was really attracted to made him go red from the tips of his ears to the ends of his toes. He'd literally boil with embarrassment, finding it impossible to make conversation with a girl he liked, unable to believe that any woman would take him seriously, even as a candidate to buy her a drink, never mind as a prospective sexual partner. It had taken Matt well into his twenties before he realized that women actually liked him, and he didn't even have to try that hard to make them. They thought he was funny, his girlfriends told him, charming, and, best of all, good-looking. They went on about his thick, blond hair and his intense blue eyes. Apparently he also had the kind of backside that a lot of women liked, and one girl had told him he had the sexiest hands that she had ever seen, although Matt failed to see how hands could be sexy.

Gradually, Matt's confidence had grown, and with it, his success with the opposite sex. He liked testing his luck, seeing how far he could get with girls who should, by rights, be well out of his league. He discovered that most women were accessible. All you had to do was make them laugh, look them in the eye, and really listen to them. Or at least appear to be really listening to them. He'd started writing a column about his dating exploits for the paper on which he was a music writer. It had started as a filler on the music-review pages one week when they didn't have quite enough column inches and advertising was down. It was meant to be a one-off, but loads of people emailed in, said they'd liked it, that it had made them laugh. Before he knew it, it was a regular thing. Friday and Saturday he'd be out with his mates, looking to hook up. And on Monday he'd be writing it up for the paper. He never used girls' real names, of course—but some of the things that happened, it was enough to make a grown man blush—only not him. Not anymore—not since the day he realized that a woman hadn't made him blush in months and he believed that he was cured. But rarely were the girls he met already mostly naked, and he wasn't sure if gently jiggling all-natural 34 Gs might set him off again.

"I'm only doing this while I'm at university so I don't end up thousands in debt."

"Wha . . . what are you studying?" Matt asked her.

"Forensic science; I want to be like the one on *Bones,*" Lindsey told him. "So far I'm on track for a first, so not just a pretty pair, hey?"

Matt could not have been more relieved when they were interrupted.

"Back on set, please, girls, we need to get your school ties on," the photographer bellowed.

"God, I hate it when they make me wear a costume," Lindsey joked, rolling her eyes. "Nice to meet you, Matt, and just between you and me, you should ask Carla out for a drink—she's been eyeing you since you got here."

Matt watched as Lindsey strode back to the set, slipped a tie over her head, then handled her fellow model like she was assessing the ripeness of a pair of melons.

"So are you cured?" Pete asked.

"Cured of what?" Matt said.

"Glamourous models." Pete nodded at the girls, who frolicked with each other with a most professional élan. "Today was your treat—your story to tell your mates back home—but your job is to be an average bloke and write about things average blokes want to know about, cars, footy, bands, gadgets, and how to get girls, and on a weekly like *Bang It!* that means you've got to get cracking today. We've got to get to a features meeting now; don't go in without any idea or your new god and our editor Dan'll rip you to shreds. You'll need to have uploaded all your copy, which means your column and two features to the features folder by Wednesday. We put that magazine to bed on a Thursday, we get bladdered on a Thursday night, and on a Friday we start all over again. So remember, even though your job is to be the average bloke, you're not. Average blokes don't spend all day around naked women, they spend all day thinking about them—which is why our magazine is the field leader in the weeklies and the boss liked your column so much. So you know where you stand right until your probation is up? Work like a bastard or get dropped, there is no in between."

"Yeah—of course, I'm up to it," Matt said with a bravado that he didn't quite feel. "I'm stoked that I've got a chance to write for a national magazine. I'm going to give it my all, Pete—I swear."

"Good. Let's get back to the office then and get you doing some real work."

While he waited, Matt noticed Carla leaning against a windowsill, powder brush in hand, the midday light igniting a fiery halo around her hair. She was about his age, maybe a couple of years younger, slender, with a nice figure under her shirtdress. Okay, it was only his first day here and he had to move into his digs later, but apart from the other articles he had to write, he needed to have his first installment of his column ready in two days—he needed some material. He could recycle something old, or make something up, but Pete had just made it perfectly clear that he needed to impress from the start, and what could be more impressive than bagging his first London date on the day he arrived. Perhaps hitting on a girl through work was a bit of a cheat—a bit lazy—but Matt's motto was always to strike while the iron was hot. Never pass up an opportunity, he lectured his regular readers.

"Hiya." He approached her, his smile warm and friendly— open and casual.

"Oh, hi." Carla looked him briefly in the eye before studying her chipped fingernails.

"This is all a bit mad, isn't it?" Matt nodded at the models. "You'd think it'd be a turn-on, but to be honest, I'm more interested in a bit of mystery, someone who's a bit less obvious." Matt noticed a smattering of freckles scattered across the bridge of Carla's nose. She had painted her fair lashes black but he could just see their natural pale gold right at the very roots, just where they met the near-translucent skin of her eyelids. It was these small vulnerabilities that really drew him to a woman, not how she was built or how she looked. It wasn't the tricks a girl used to make herself look better that Matt went for, it was the frailties that she failed to hide that really touched him. They all had them, even Lindsey from Doncaster, for as much as she'd caught him off guard with her easy bravado, it had been the white patches behind her ears where she failed to fake-tan that Matt had especially liked about her.

"You don't really think that." Carla looked skeptical, her light gray eyes narrowing. Matt tried to imagine her in the morning, her face clean of makeup. It was surprising how different some women could look in natural sunlight and without any cosmetic aid. Despite her profession, Carla was wearing hardly any, and Matt liked that about her.

"Listen, it's my first night in town tonight. I'm moving into my new place later—but could I take you for a drink first? It'd be great to have someone show me around a bit."

"Really? I mean yeah, okay—why not—a drink, yeah, that would be good. Great—I mean fine, whatever." Carla's face flitted through a range of expressions from surprise to delight to studied nonchalance within a fraction of a second.

Seeing Carla's mobile peeping out of the top pocket of her dress, Matt fished it out, careful not to touch her. He punched his number into it and saved it under his name.

"Text me, yeah? Let me know where to meet you." He slipped the phone back into her pocket, feeling more heat between the two of them in that second than he had felt the whole time he'd been talking to Lindsey.

"Bye then." Carla swept the bristles of her brush over the tips of her fingers, leaving them dusted with glitter.

"See you later," Matt told her. "Look forward to it."

Matt followed Pete down the concrete stairs of the studio and out onto the bright street, crammed with office workers clamoring for lunch and a little midday sun before they chained themselves back to their desks.

"So you've got your eye on Carla, then?" Pete nodded in approval. "Nice little arse on that one and not a bad pair for someone so skinny."

"It's just a drink," Matt said, laughing, as he followed Pete into the back of a black cab.

"It better not be! You and I know the score, Matt, and let me tell you, you might not spend your afternoons rolling around with naked models, but you mention to any pretty little blonde you meet in the pub who you work for and chances are most of them will be all too happy to show you what they've got, in the hopes that you'll get 'em on the next cover."

"Pete—you don't decide that!" Matt chuckled.

"I know that, you know that—but they don't." Pete laughed. "Best job in the world, mate. Best bloody job in the world."

Matt glanced at his watch and sat up. It was almost 8:00 P.M. He'd told the woman on the phone that he'd be at his new lodgings by seven at the latest. It was time to go. Carefully he eased himself off the bed, hoping not to wake Carla.

"Where you going?" she murmured, rolling over, exposing one delicate, pink-tipped breast.

"I'm moving into my new place tonight, remember I told you?" Matt smiled, bending over and kissing her freckled shoulder. "We were going to have a couple of drinks and then they turned into doubles and we came back to your place for coffee to sober up and . . ."

"Well, we did sober up." Carla smiled, leaning up on her elbows, her tangle of auburn hair nestling on her shoulders, her black mascara spread under her eyes, intensifying their pale blue hue. She stretched out two slender arms to him, cocking her head to one side and curling her mouth into the sweetest smile in her armory.

"Do you really have to go?"

"I do," Matt said. "I need to move in and I'm already late."

"Well, I'll come with you then," Carla offered, already pushing back the bedclothes and reaching for her discarded bra. "Help you get moved."

"I've only got a couple of cases," Matt said, nodding at his luggage that he'd left in the hallway. There were two reasons he didn't want Carla to come with him: first, he didn't really want anyone to know that he was going to live with a widow and her kid and, from what he could make out, some old lady and a German woman. It wasn't exactly cool, it wasn't exactly the *Bang It!*–lad lifestyle that Pete had told him he had to embody. But it was the only place he could find close to work that he could afford and that wouldn't mean spending a fortune in travel costs. It would do for now, at least while he was still on three months' probation; once the job was permanent and he knew he wasn't going to have to go back up north with his tail between his legs, he would look for a bachelor pad.

The second reason was that he didn't want Carla to think that what had just happened meant anything. That the sex they'd had would lead to greater intimacy. Matt had broken his own rules. He hadn't told Carla up front that he wasn't looking for a relationship. He hadn't told her definitively that he wasn't looking for a girlfriend, his usual blunt disclaimer when he approached any woman. In theory, his blunt honesty should have put girls off, but so far that had rarely happened. Women heard what he said, they shrugged their shoulders as if they didn't care—but almost all of them seemed to secretly think that he would change. Each one thought she would be the girl who would change him; one night with her and he'd change his mind, be desperate to settle down, get a couple of kids and a dog. Almost without fail, they were upset and hurt when they realized that Matt never stuck around for more than a couple of weeks at the most. When he'd remind them about his disclaimer, they'd look bewildered and hurt, as if they really believed that a few nights of sex, a few days of laughing and kissing automatically meant the beginning of a grand romance. Sometimes Matt felt bad about letting them down, but at least he always had his declaration to hide behind—proof that he had not led them on. But in the heat of a moment saturated with vodka, Matt had forgotten to make his intentions clear to Carla.

"You should stay right there, relax," he instructed her.

Carla flopped back onto the bed, stretching her arms above her head and smiling.

"If you insist." She smiled happily. "Today certainly turned out a lot better than I expected. Not that I do this sort of thing all the time—never, actually. There was just something about you that seemed . . . right."

"For me, too." Matt pulled his jacket on and sat briefly on the edge of the bed. "You are a fantastic girl, Carla."

He meant it—Carla was funny, beautiful, and warm and engaging in bed. She deserved someone a lot better than him.

"And life's for living, isn't it? I mean, how boring would it be if no one ever took a chance . . ."

Matt didn't reply, even though he knew that Carla was looking for some sort of reassurance. Obviously, going to bed with a man she had met only a few hours earlier wasn't normally her style, and she wanted him to tell her that she hadn't made a terrible mistake.

"So when do you want to meet up again?" Carla went on after a moment's silence. "I'm supposed to be hanging out with my girlfriends tomorrow, but I could cancel if you want."

Don't do that, Matt thought. *Don't just decide to change all your plans for me.*

"I've got to work," Matt told her, glancing at his watch. "New boy—lot to prove. Need to deliver a kick-ass column."

"Oh, okay, no worries—well, just call me when you're free then," Carla said, a tiny frown line insinuating its way between her eyebrows.

"Sure. See you." Matt got up, picked up his cases, and closed Carla's front door behind him, knowing that she'd be flopping back on the bed, her fingers in her hair, wondering what she'd done.

"Hello." A boy opened the front door and greeted Matt without the faintest flicker of a smile. He was a good-looking boy, with intense eyes and an odd smudge of lilac paint across the bridge of his nose. "Are you Matt Bolton, because if you are, you're late."

"I know, I'm sorry," Matt said, taken aback by the boy, suddenly very glad that the last remnants of the vodka he'd indulged in with Carla had receded to no more than a slight fuzziness around his temples. Somehow, he got the feeling that he was going to need all his wits about him. "I got held up at work, you know."

"What were you doing?" The boy questioned him closely, with slightly narrowed eyes. "Were you interviewing Chloe Brand, Britain's sexiest babe 2009—was she wearing a bra?"

"Wha . . . what?" Matt spluttered, glancing around as if this were a trap set to catch him out. "How do you know about Chloe, kid?"

"This kid, Harvey, from school, nicks his dad's copies of *Bang It!* out of the recycling bin and brings them to school. He charges us a quid a look. It's worth it, though."

"Christ!" Matt laughed. "Does your mum know?"

"No, and she'd kill me if she did, she still thinks I'm a little boy . . . so anyway—were you?"

"No, I was not." Matt shook his head. "I don't do that sort of thing—no one really does that sort of thing. They take those photos somewhere else, far away from the office, and then a staff writer makes up the interview."

"Really?" The boy looked disappointed. "You mean Chole isn't really a huge Arsenal fan, and she doesn't really love to watch a match wearing only the team colors and a pair of stilletos?"

"How old are you?" Matt asked, peering through the crack in the door to take in what looked like an ordinary hallway in an ordinary home.

"Twelve, nearly," the kid told him. Matt could tell that the "nearly" part was very important to him.

"Makes sense. I guess I was interested in the same things at your age. Guess I have been ever since." Matt lowered his voice. "Look, if you want to pay a pound a pop to look at your mate's mags, that's your business, but all I do is write stuff, all the words that you and your friends probably never look twice at. My job's boring, mate, I promise you."

"Oh." Charlie looked disappointed, then perking up slightly he added, "Do you have PS3?"

"Not on me," Matt said. "I shared one with my old flat-mate but I had to leave it behind when I moved. I've got a PSP, though, and a DS—is that enough for you to let me in?" Matt nodded at the doorway.

"S'pose." The kid shrugged and stepped aside, yelling, "Mum, he's here!"

A woman hurried out of a back room, wearing an over-sized man's shirt and a pair of baggy jeans; her dark hair was tied in a knot on her head, and, like the boy, she was splattered with lilac paint. She had the most remarkable pair of green eyes, like a summer meadow.

"Oh, you must be Matt," she said, greeting him with an out-stretched paint-spattered hand. "We were worried that you'd been mugged or got lost; it's a jungle out there. I'm Ellen and this is Charlie." She placed a hand on Charlie's shoulder and he reflexively shrugged it off.

"No, no—nothing so interesting . . ." Matt thought briefly of Carla's closed eyes as he had kissed her, the setting sun turning her skin a shade of pale gold. "Just caught up with work, first day and all that. Sorry, your sister, Hannah, is it? She gave me your number, I should have called and let you know I'd be late."

"No, no—I don't want you to think you have to keep me apprised of all your movements. I'm not that kind of landlady. To tell you the truth, I have no idea what being a landlady is all about yet. I'm sort of making it up as I go along."

She began to walk up the stairs, talking as she went, and Matt assumed that he was to follow her. "Well, I'm not sure what Hannah told you. You know what the rent is and that it includes utilities. You'll get a key, of course, and a shelf in the fridge in the kitchen if you want one—it saves on labeling, apparently—but there is room for a fridge in your room and a microwave if you like. Otherwise, just come and go as you please."

Slightly breathless as they reached the top of the stairs,

Ellen pushed open the attic door and stood back, allowing Matt into the room first.

"There's a large bedroom, and a bathroom, my husband and I always thought that . . ." She trailed off for a second, to a moment in time that Matt couldn't fathom, before snapping back into the present. "Anyway, I hope you like it."

Matt walked into the room and looked around. It was large, almost the whole footprint of the sizable house, with dormer windows on one side that looked out over the street and VELUX windows on the other, letting in plenty of light. It was furnished with a slightly aged-looking double bed, a rather worn red sofa, a dark wood wardrobe, and a desk. Through a door to the right Matt could see the bathroom. It was basic; it was perfect.

"It's great," he said, turning to Ellen, smiling.

"Oh, well—good." Ellen dropped her eyes from his and tentatively touched her hair, as if she had only just remembered that she had screwed it up into a careless knot a few hours earlier. Matt noticed the holes in her pierced earlobes, redundant without earrings.

"Um, Matt . . ." Matt watched as Ellen's mouth undulated with uncertainty.

"Yep?" he said, offering an encouraging smile.

From the look of her, she was somewhere in her thirties, pleasant-looking—something like the women who after getting married and having kids sort of give up on trying to attract men because they just don't need to anymore. Matt had to admit that he was relieved; after talking to the openly flirtatious sister, he'd been a little concerned that his new landlady would be something of a temptation, the kind of temptation that it would be a very bad idea to give in to and the kind that he invariably did, hence his swift exit from the *Manchester Evening News*. But as sweet as she seemed, there was nothing about this woman to tempt him. She was a widow and a mum, and as far as Matt could see, those two things defined her. There was no danger of entanglement here.

"Ellen, I'm hard to offend—tell me what you're worried about."

"Well, it's just that you've met Charlie." Ellen finally found the courage to look up at him again. "He's at an impressionable age and, well, it's only been a year since his dad died. I don't think he's even begun to work that out yet."

"Must be tough." Matt nodded; his father had walked out on him and his mother when he had been a little younger than Charlie was now. The fact that his dad was still alive somewhere didn't ease the sense of bereavement that Matt had felt for a very long time.

"You won't . . . I mean you wouldn't . . ." Ellen struggled to form a sentence. "It's just Hannah told me a bit about your work and . . ."

"You want to know if I'll be parading topless models through the house and leading Charlie astray?" Matt asked, thinking of Charlie's opening interview a few minutes earlier.

"Well, yes, frankly." Ellen's smile was bashful, and Matt noticed the very fine crinkles that blossomed prettily around the corners of her eyes.

"No, I won't. I promise."

"Of course, you're a young man," Ellen said, as if the twelve years between them were really a hundred and twelve. "You'll want to bring friends back. A girl sometimes, maybe even girls." She stressed the last letter of the sentence with a raised brow.

Matt couldn't help but grin as the color rose in Ellen's cheeks.

"All I'm asking is that you be discreet—you know, in the shared parts of the house."

"Of course," Matt assured her. "Look, Ellen, this is your home. I know that. Your sister told me what happened and why you're taking in lodgers. I don't want to make things any more difficult for you. You'll hardly know I'm here, I swear."

"Thank you," Ellen said. "I'm sorry. I don't mean to be rude or put you off or anything like that."

"Don't be silly." Matt picked up one suitcase and dumped in onto the bed, where it bounced once. "You're a mum, looking out for your kid. I wouldn't expect differently."

"Right. Well, if you want to come down and make yourself something to eat or drink, then feel free. I've got to finish painting the dining room for my last lodger. I think Hannah told you about her. She's due in a few days."

"Old lady who writes sex books, right?" Matt asked as he unzipped his suitcase and opened the wardrobe to find a selection of mismatched hangers.

"Well, it's more like historical fiction, but anyway, Charlie and I—and Sabine, that's our German guest—will be in there if you need us."

Matt glanced at his watch. It had just struck nine.

"She's arriving in a few days, you say?"

"Yes, I know." Ellen looked stricken. "I'll be lucky if the paint's even dry. I had no idea it would take so long. Trouble was, the patterned wallpaper kept on showing through the paint. We're on our fourth coat now and it needs at least one more, and apparently the room absolutely mustn't smell of paint by the time she arrives. Come to think of it, Simon hasn't even told me when her chaise longue is to be delivered. . . ."

Ellen frowned, the tiny crease deepening between her brows.

Matt pulled his work shirt off over his head, discarding it in a tangled heap on the bed as he fished a faded T-shirt out of his case.

"Sounds to me like you need a hand." He grinned briefly at Ellen before pulling the top back over his naked torso. "It's the room at the back, right?"

"Only if you're sure." Ellen's smile was uncertain.

"Sure I'm sure." Matt trotted down the stairs and Ellen waited for a moment before following.

For some reason, she felt more out of breath on her descent that she had on the way up.

CHAPTER
Six

Ellen jumped when the alarm clock sounded so that the pages of *The Sword Erect* that she had been reading slipped to the floor, skimming one over the other as they fluttered gracefully downward. Her clock was set for 6:30 A.M., but sleeping much beyond 5:00 in the morning was something that Ellen had been a stranger to since she'd lost her husband. She'd stay up late, as late as she could, fighting the drag of her heavy lids to the very last second in the hope that she would eventually wear herself out enough to sleep through until morning. But no matter how hard she tried, Ellen's nights had evolved into an exhausting routine. She'd drift off over a book somewhere around 2:00, sleep for a few fitful, restless hours, and just before 5:00 her mind would jerk her awake with the panicked sensation that she had forgotten something. Ellen's heart would be pounding in her ears, her eyes wide open as they adjusted to the dark, her weary mind seeking, against her will, to remember the terrible truth. Then it would all come back to her, and in those first seconds it would tear through her just as vividly and as painfully as it had when the poor young policewoman first broke the news. Nick was gone. He was not asleep in bed beside her and he never would be again. She would never again hear his voice, never feel his touch, never listen to the sound of his breathing. And as that reality washed over her yet again with the cold indifference of a wave breaking over a rock, Ellen would have to spend several moments gasping for air, fighting both for and against life, until her heartbeat slowed and she thought of Charlie, asleep in his bed, waiting for her to make him breakfast. Then she would have a reason, her only reason, to get up.

It was then that Ellen would turn to her latest book, losing herself with relief among its pages until her alarm clock sounded the official break of day.

Bending over the edge of the bed, Ellen gathered up the pages of Allegra Howard's latest work and carefully reordered them. She remembered with a shock of nerves that it was Thursday morning; today Allegra was due to arrive at 11:00 A.M., which meant midday, Simon had promised. As Allegra made it her business always to be an hour late to everything, Ellen was relieved that the extra time would allow the paint smells to fade, and the chaise longue was just about in position. Against all odds, she had got everything ready for her VIP guest, and even though it had taken the help of virtual strangers to do it, she was still proud of herself.

The timing of Allegra's stay could not have been better, since Ellen had just finished the last of the pages of her latest that Nick had sent her. She smoothed the sheets of paper out against her thighs and wondered about the book. Ellen couldn't deny that she was enjoying it; every second that she had been immersed in Eliza's story—a young puritan maid caught up with the passions of the Royalist captain whom she barely understood—she had been there with her, enjoying the guilty pleasure of imagining herself as the fulsome young woman with an exquisite body and beauty to match. Yet, in *The Sword Erect* the heroine had endured more ravishing than Ellen could remember in any other Allegra Howard novel or indeed any other book on which she had worked on the Cherished Desires list. Ellen had read only up to page thirty-three, yet poor Eliza had already had her body manhandled by three different men in the space of barely a week!

Hannah had been only half wrong when she'd joked that these kinds of books had a strict average of sexual encounters per page that had to be met. Sexual passion and erotic fantasy were what the readers wanted, they were what Ellen wanted— but all the other things that she loved so much about Allegra Howard's books were missing so far. Ellen wanted the adventure, the danger, the sights, smells, and sounds of a world and time gone by that Allegra conjured up so brilliantly and that made her novels more than just run-of-the mill bodice rippers. Simon had said that Allegra was having trouble with this book, and he wanted Ellen to help her get it back on track. The problem was, how did you tell a person whom you admired so very much that you thought she was getting it wrong? Particularly when all that qualified you to comment was that you enjoyed reading the books.

Ellen sighed as she leaned back against her pillow and thought about Allegra's formula. Allegra put all her heroines in sexual danger but they actually had sex with only one man, and by the end of the books they were not only in love with him but married to him, too, so that the usually inappropriate way that they had first become physically acquainted would be happily resolved. Still, three men in one week driven to a frenzy of desire by your mere proximity—at least it meant that Eliza knew she was alive, that the world took notice of her when she passed. The world went on outside Ellen's window and she had very little to do with it at all; most of the time that was just the way she liked it, but every now and then she'd wonder what it would be like to be more like Eliza—or even Hannah. To live life as if the world revolved around you and you had every right to expect that it would dance to your tune. Now this house was her world, because it had been Nick's world, too—and in many comforting ways it still was.

Ellen looked around her bedroom. It was exactly the same as it had been a year earlier, stripped and varnished floorboards, covered here and there with faded rugs covered with roses, an ornate oval Victorian mirror that Nick had bought her hanging over the solid pine dressing table he'd spent an age stripping down just after they had moved in. The wardrobe was still full of his clothes, the drawers still crammed with his things. There was still a dirty shirt in the laundry basket that Ellen could not bring herself to wash. And it wasn't just this room that was still so full of Nick; every room in this house was stamped with a presence that was still so strong it was almost tangible. Nick had labored long and hard over this late-Victorian house, spending all his spare time stripping off layer after layer of inappropriate wallpaper, finding just the right light plaster work to replace what had been ripped out when period detail wasn't quite so fashionable. It was Nick who'd dragged home the three small cast-iron fireplaces that now sat comfortably over the fireplaces he'd found when ripping out plasterboard. He had lavished the same kind of attention on this house as he had on Ellen when they first met. She remembered, for a time, feeling a little jealous of the time he spent lovingly blacking his newly acquired grate, his fingers caressing their organic curves as they had once caressed hers, but now she was glad that he had spent so many months making this house his own—it was as if he still existed here in every nook and cranny.

Ellen thought of the world outside her window, Thornfield Avenue, a quiet enough tree-lined street of Victorian houses just a stone's throw from Shepherds Bush Market and now Europe's largest shopping center, Westfield—although Ellen had never felt the urge to venture there, despite Charlie's tales of the endless retail and junk-food opportunities that he and his friends had discovered. Nick had chosen this road as the location of their home not only because he'd fallen so in love with the dilapidated old house but because it had residents' parking only, and a bus that went straight to a good school passed regularly at the bottom of the road. When they had first moved there, Ellen had wheeled Charlie around the market in his buggy every day it was on, more just to see the colors, hear the noises, and smell the smells than anything else. It had been a long time since they had done that together. Now, Ellen was content to get everything she needed delivered to her door.

A sudden breeze wafted in through the crack in the sash window that Ellen had left open through the night in concession to the stifling heat, carrying with it the scent of privet hedge and hot tarmac that brought her mind instantly back to that last morning with Nick.

He'd been sitting on the edge of his bed, fussing about which underwear to put on.

"Does it matter?" Ellen remembered laughing, stroking his back. "Who's going to see it but me?"

Nick had twisted to smile at her over his shoulder. "I always promised my granny that if they ever had to scrape me up off a road, I wouldn't bring shame on the family. Seriously, I've got this big meeting today—I think a man should be dressed to impress from the inside out."

"Do you have to get up right now?" Ellen had asked tentatively. Seduction was not one of her natural talents, and she had been unthinkingly brushed off by Nick enough times in the past to feel all the more hesitant about suggesting they share some intimate time together.

"Yep," Nick had said, standing up, pulling the chosen pair of boxers over his buttocks. "Lots to do today, love." He'd bent and kissed her on the forehead before retreating to the bathroom to shave.

If only he'd taken the hint, Ellen thought wistfully. If only she'd been a little more brazen and bold, and if when he'd turned to smile at her he'd been able to discern the look in her eye. If only he'd kissed her on the lips instead of the forehead, if only she'd wound her arms around his neck and kissed him back. Then at least she would have had one more memory of him, one more memory of what it felt like to have his arms around her, his lips on her neck, the sound of his breath in her ear. But none of that had happened; he'd walked out the door a few minutes later and had never come back.

Ellen lifted the neck of her nightshirt and peered shyly down at her breasts. They were rather fulsome, if not quite the perfectly pert twin moons that Allegra seemed to give all her heroines. Ellen was secretly proud of them, although she did not feel the need to squeeze every inch of cleavage out of them and put it on display like her sister. Nick had loved her breasts, he had loved all of her body, and when they were first married, his adoration had made her glory in the swell of her bottom, the reach of her hips, and the girth of her thighs. Ellen closed her eyes as she remembered the touch of her husband's fingertips dragging ever so slowly over the rise and fall of her curves, his lips following in their wake. They had not made love nearly so frequently in what turned out to be the last few years of their marriage, but Ellen had accepted that, albeit regretfully, supposing that after ten years the passion and urgency that Nick had once felt for her was bound to wane a bit. In fact, if Ellen remembered correctly, which she knew that she did, on the day that Police Constable Henderson and her colleague had walked up her garden path to break the bad news, it had been almost six months since the last time. And now, now there would be no next time.

Slowly, Ellen let her fingertips travel upward, over the thin cotton of her nightshirt, and for a brief second, for the first time in a year, she allowed herself to imagine that it was Nick who was touching her, his fingers that gently massaged her body, his lips that teased her skin, his eyes that looked up at her. . . .

Ellen sat up abruptly and snatched her hands away from herself, leaping out of bed as if she'd just discovered that she'd been sharing it with something awful.

Flustered, she pulled one of Nick's shirts on over the pair of jeans that she had been wearing yesterday and, unable to locate her brush, ran her fingers roughly through her tangled hair. Coffee, she decided, what she needed was coffee, that would wake her up properly, because what had just happened had been a sort of waking dream, not the thoughts of her conscious mind at all—not anything that she could have controlled. Ellen scowled as she headed barefoot down the stairs, furious and embarrassed.

It hadn't been Nick's face she had seen looking up at her when she closed her eyes. It had been her latest lodger's—it had been Matt's.

Matt stared at his Mac screen and waited. This was only his third full day in the office, and there was no more time for special excursions today—it was press day. The deadline was fast approaching and Matt still hadn't filed anything in the features folder. Pete had come up with a new name for the column. Apparently, Dan, the editor in chief, said that the name he'd used for the *Manchester Evening News* was not catchy enough and it didn't capture the spirit of *Bang It!* Pete and Matt had kicked a few ideas around and then Pete had come up with an idea that he loved so much, no further discussion was needed. Matt's new column in *Bang It!* magazine would be called "Wham Bam! A Single Bloke's Guide to Sex in the City."

Matt told himself that it was ironic, but to be honest, there wasn't that much about *Bang It!* that was ironic, except for maybe the equal-opportunities policy. Still, as Pete had said, as long as there were girls who chose to take their clothes off for money, then he was all for equality.

The cursor hovered on Matt's empty Mac screen. He looked around the office and saw that they all had their heads down, struggling to make the deadline. Pete had said that the pattern was always the same. On Monday, everyone was casual and relaxed. They'd often have that week's features meeting in the pub, or at the very least get the beers delivered and sit around talking about ideas with their feet up; the magazine staff looking up stuff on the internet, inventing some new kind of office-based game—Matt himself had taken part in his first Olympic ten-meter chair dash. Tuesday, things started to get done. Wednesday, everybody remembered there was a ticking clock, and by Thursday there was no time for fooling around anymore, work got done in the run-up to deadline.

"Don't be late with any of your copy if you want to make it past your probation period," Pete had warned him. "Dan doesn't put up with that."

Problem was, that was exactly what Matt was worried about. He'd also been worried about running into Carla since their encounter on Monday—but then he'd realized that she was freelance. The chances of his bumping into her were slim. That left him with the dilemma about what to do. He should call her, he should at least explain to her that although he'd had a great time with her, and although she was a lovely girl, he wasn't ready for anything serious, especially not when he'd just arrived in London. The trouble was, if he rang her up and told her that, she'd probably say she was cool with it, she'd probably suggest that they get together, no strings attached, and then after a week or two she'd want more. She'd want to plan stuff, make dates more than twenty-fours hours in advance. She'd want to introduce him to her friends, expect him to be available every Saturday night and hang out with her every Sunday. And if he reminded her that that was not at all what they had agreed on, she'd cry and get upset and tell him that she thought things had changed, that she meant something to him. Inevitably he'd end up hurting her anyway. No, if he rang her, if he slipped into that mistake, he'd be breaking his first rule, which was never to date a girl more than three times. Any more than that and they thought you were in the dreaded R word, no matter how clear you were that you weren't up for it.

He could visualize exactly what his first column should

be—cocky jack-the-lad steps off the train and into a hot-girl's bed. He should write about his technique, how he'd made the moves on Carla, how he'd let her think it was her plan to get drunk in the June sunshine and her idea to drag him back to her place. He'd lie about how voracious she had been in bed, transforming their brief encounter from one that had been sweet and hesitant to one of a passion-fueled frenzy of lusty sex. He'd have to boost Carla's assets by a couple of cup sizes and make her a good deal more experienced in certain areas than she was, too.

Still, it did seem a little too caddish, even for him, to write about a girl quite so soon after the event. Especially a girl like Carla, who didn't really seem the type to be out looking for casual sex. From what he could tell, it was more likely that he'd caught her unawares amid what Matt thought was probably an uncharacteristic bout of spontaneity.

His mind made up, Matt took his laptop out of his bag and opened up the file in which he saved all his columns. He found one of his very first pieces and sent it to the desktop of his Mac. Rehashing an old piece was not how he wanted to begin his career at *Bang It!* And he was well aware that if Pete or Dan found out, he could well be ending it before it even began. He liked Carla enough not to turn her into trash. Not just yet.

"So you nailed the little makeup girl on your first day then?" Pete arrived at his desk in a fog of sweat and cigarette smoke. "Impressive."

"A gentleman never talks." Matt gave him a well-practiced "of course I did" smirk.

"No need to be coy about it, it's all over the place. She told Suze, Dan's PA, and Suze told everyone else."

"Really?" Matt shifted in his seat. Carla wasn't as comfortably distant as he had hoped after all.

"She raved about you, mate—you never put 'gentle and considerate lover' on your CV." Pete chuckled to himself, catching the eye of Raffa, a fellow features writer, who grinned in reply.

"Bollocks!" Matt's reaction was instinctive. "She was mad for it, mate, practically dragged me off the street—I didn't have a chance to be gentle or considerate. She had my pants off in less than a minute—and hers! That girl was ravenous!"

"Any good?" Pete asked him flatly. "You'll have to tell Keith in production, he's been trying and failing to get in her knickers for weeks, poor sod. Reckons he *really likes her.*"

"Mate, top marks for enthusiasm." Matt winked. "Besides, we all know there are some things that it's difficult to get wrong, know what I mean?"

Pete and Greg the layout guy laughed.

"So, you going to see her again?"

"No; it was just for fun, she knows that."

"You sure?" Pete asked. "Suze seems to think she thinks you're the next big thing in her life."

Matt shrugged. "I just got here. I'm not looking for anything serious, I told her that up front."

"Well, you got an office full of people waiting to read your write-up. You know what? You should award her marks out of ten—that would be a laugh."

"Great idea," Matt said. "Will do."

He watched Pete walk away and after a moment closed the column he'd been about to rewrite. He had no choice now. He'd have to start from scratch.

CHAPTER Seven

"She's a freak," Charlie hissed as he peered at Allegra Howard through the kitchen window. "And she smells funny."

"She is not a freak, and don't use that word!" Ellen chided. "She's an old lady and she smells of lavender. Admittedly rather a lot of lavender."

"A freakish amount of lavender, one might say, hey, Charles?" Hannah put in, digging Charlie in the ribs, the pair of them giggling like cohorts.

Ellen pursed her lips at her sister. Hannah had arrived just after five, at the same time as Sabine, and suggested that she treat everyone to takeaway, which had caused Charlie to question her on whom exactly she meant by everyone—was she including Matt or the old woman, for example? And would it be okay if he still had fish fingers?

Hannah had extended her largesse to whoever might care to join them, but Ellen knew that the only reason her sister would leave work any earlier than 9:00 P.M. was that Hannah hadn't met Matt yet, and it often seemed to Ellen that her sister was determined to meet and greet every member of the male species on the planet. Apart from everything else, she would be dying to see exactly how Ellen would cope with the elderly whirlwind that was Allegra Howard. Ellen guessed that because the lodgers had been Hannah's idea, she felt that she had some ownership of it, some responsibility to make sure that it went smoothly, so that Ellen wasn't suddenly overburdened, otherwise why else would she pop up here every five minutes? If she came around any more, Ellen was tempted to charge *her* rent.

"She's old and set in her ways," Ellen reiterated. "And a very keen gardener, by the looks of things. She's been out there ages now. Pruning."

Ellen had been fraught with nerves when Allegra had finally arrived with Simon at almost three in the afternoon.

"Ellen, darling." Simon had greeted her with a huge hug, lightly kissing both her cheeks. "Sorry we're late. Allegra had a little trouble deciding what to bring and what to leave in storage; we spent two hours deliberating over her Stafford china dogs." He winked at Ellen, stepping aside to reveal Ellen's new employer.

"May I introduce you to Miss Howard?"

Allegra Howard did not look at all how Ellen had expected. The publicity shot that graced all her book covers was dated and, besides, soft focused in the extreme. It showed a smooth-skinned blonde of indeterminate middle age, tenderly holding a single rose against her cheek while gazing into the distance with a faraway look in her eyes, as if at that very second she was dreaming up her next bestseller.

Simon had already warned her that photo had been taken a long time ago, but still Ellen had expected Allegra to be dressed from head to foot in some chiffon affair, her aged skin caked with too much makeup, her hair brittle with dye and hairspray. It was a cliché and an unfair one.

Allegra was a neat, stylish-looking woman, wearing a lilac suit and low beige heels, with her silver-blond hair tied into a frail chignon at her neck. Other than an ostentatious triple string of pearls around her neck, fastened with a ruby clasp, and three large diamond rings on her fingers, Ellen might never have guessed that she was a bestselling author of lusty romantic fiction with the kind of commercial success that any author would envy. At least not by her genteel appearance, which had a rather aristocratic air.

"M-Miss Howard," Ellen stammered. "I'm so thrilled to meet you, I'm such a huge fan."

"Nonsense, you are not a fan, writers do not have fans. You are a reader, a follower, or an admirer. I do not approve of fans, such a garish word. And I insist you call me Allegra. Just because one is great, one does not expect special treatment. May I see my room now? I do hope it's facing south, I did instruct Simon that it had to be facing south but he seemed to have forgotten."

"Um, I *think* it is," Ellen said nervously as she led Allegra into the former dining room. "It always seems to be sunny in here."

Ellen held her breath as Allegra looked around the freshly painted room, terrified that the shade of lilac would be wrong, the chaise longue would not come up to scratch, or that despite her leaving the french doors open since seven that morning, the faintest smell of paint would be detectable to that elegant, aquiline nose.

"I'd say southwesterly, wouldn't you, Simon?" Allegra arched a penciled brow, the corners of her mouth dropping minutely. "Still, it will do, it will do—which is more than I can say for those roses, what a disgrace!" Ellen had watched anxiously from the doorway, stricken, as Allegra stepped out onto the patio, its cracks filled with grass and weeds, tutted her head at the unkempt and overburdened rose bushes that had once surrounded the windows so decorously, but that now still endured the moldering dead heads of a summer long gone.

"I must have beauty and order to work—all this chaos simply will not do. Bring me your gardening shears, my dear, I must remedy this immediately. Fortunately I brought my own gardening gloves; you see, Simon dear, I was correct—one never knows when one might be required to handle foliage."

Ellen was frozen to the spot for a second, quite unable to remember if she even had gardening shears, or indeed what exactly they were. When her petrified brain did make the connection, she realized that they would be hanging on a rusty nail in the shed located at the bottom of the overgrown garden, its door probably jammed shut by inches of high grass and an invasion of convolvulus, its musty interior inhabited by various large and unchecked spiders. Ellen had not ventured down there in the longest time, the desire to prune her roses the very last thing on her mind. Feeling utterly inadequate, she remembered a pair of kitchen scissors that she thought might do the job and rushed to bring them to Allegra's newly gloved hands.

Allegra examined her offering with her neatly painted lips pressed into a thin line of disapproval and disappointment, but nevertheless she accepted them.

"If you'd bring me some tea, I'd be grateful," she instructed Ellen. "Oh, and before you go, you should know I'll take breakfast at seven thirty every morning in my room, a soft-boiled egg and wholemeal toast, no crusts, thinly spread unsalted butter. Before ten I only drink English breakfast tea and whole milk, after ten, Earl Grey. I begin work at ten, break for a light lunch at one, and then recommence until five. I take dinner between six and seven thirty and I retire by nine thirty every night. Simon will furnish you with a copy of my eating plan, but you should know that I do not eat red meat. We took the liberty of bringing the ingredients for tonight's meal with us, but from now on I will expect you to do all the grocery shopping." She looked at Ellen as if she expected a response.

Ellen stared at her, dumbfounded, as Allegra's instructions finally sank in.

"Oh, oh! You mean you want me to cook your meals, too?"

"You have accepted the position of my personal assistant, have you not?" Allegra questioned.

"Yes, but I thought . . ." Ellen floundered for a second, realizing that it was pointless to debate with Allegra. Either she was going to accept the old lady with all her needs and foibles or she was going to have to ask her to leave, and the latter was unthinkable.

Ellen glanced at Simon, who shot her a rueful look, mutely apologizing for not having told her quite all that he could have.

"Of course, whatever you say," Ellen demurred. "It's just—well, I'll need some time in the week to work on my other manuscripts that Simon gives me."

"I beg your pardon?" Allegra looked horrified. "You mean to work on other writers, 'material' while working on mine? Oh no, no, no. I can't have that—Simon, this will not do at all."

"Oh, no—Allegra, Ellen is mistaken and it's entirely my fault; I don't think I explained to her that from now on all the work she'd been doing for Cherished Desires would be exclusively Allegra Howard." He smiled at Ellen. "That's okay with you, isn't it, Ellen? You won't be losing out financially, and of course you'll need to concentrate your mind entirely on Allegra's work in progress."

"Yes, why deal with dross, my dear, when you can work with art," Allegra added.

"Not that Allegra is implying that my stable of writers isn't anything but wonderful," Simon countered.

"Aren't I?" Allegra winked at Ellen, who was so taken aback by the gesture that she was momentarily at a loss. It seemed that there was a sense of humor lurking somewhere underneath this grand facade.

"Well, of course, I'd be delighted to just work on your books. They are, after all, my favorites."

"Delightful." Allegra smiled approvingly. "Then in the meantime I shall endeavor to tame the wilderness you have allowed to rampage so willfully in the garden."

Allegra ventured into the garden.

Simon followed Ellen into the kitchen, where she was considering her supermarket teabags, wondering if they would do until she could stock up on Earl Grey.

"Don't look so alarmed," Simon told her, gently resting a hand on either shoulder and turning her to face him. "That woman, that's not the real Allegra. She's just old, and a bit lost and out of sorts. She's missing her home and her routine, poor old bird, she's just hiding all that behind that battleax out there. All of this is as frightening for her as it is for you. I'm sure that once she settles in, you and she will become great friends and she'll stop talking to you like you're the help."

Ellen relaxed as she looked into Simon's warm, amber eyes. He had a knack for settling her down, washing calm over her with a few simple words. It was one of the reasons she liked working for him so much—nothing in life seemed to faze him, and his confidence and optimism were somehow contagious, making others believe that the world was a much simpler place.

It was a shame that Simon had yet to find anyone special in his life, Ellen mused. A tall, good-looking man like him, well dressed, all his hair still intact, and financially secure even in these difficult times, deserved the right person to love him. Perhaps Hannah was right; perhaps Simon didn't want all that. Perhaps he chose a series of brief encounters rather than anything more, seeking out embraces in the dark, passionate kisses stolen under moonlight, names rarely exchanged, just a few moments of pleasure and then . . .

"Goodness me, Ellen Woods, what are you thinking?" Simon asked, cocking an amused brow.

"What, why?" Ellen pulled away from him, pressing the back of her hand to her cheeks.

Simon studied her face closely. "Just for a second there you looked like a smoldering, smoky-eyed siren planning your next seduction!"

"Me? Nonsense. I was thinking about cooking for Allegra,

you idiot!" Ellen laughed nervously. "Honestly, Simon, you and I spend too much time reading romantic fiction. We must remember that real life is much more mundane."

Ellen turned to pour boiling water into the teapot that she had found languishing at the back of the crockery cupboard, hoping that the rising steam would be reason enough to explain away the color in her cheeks. Whatever had come over her? First that incident this morning and now this . . . What was happening to her? Months, years, of being an essentially sexless being, at least outside the pages of a book, and now her rebellious brain was catching her unawares at every turn, mentally undressing more or less every man in sight, which amounted to only two, thankfully.

It was the upheaval, Ellen had told herself. All the change was upsetting her equilibrium—that and the particularly high ravish count in *The Sword Erect.* Once she had settled herself down to work, her brain would be properly occupied and thoroughly distracted from all the sorrow and anguish that had overshadowed it for so long. Her mind might even become a quiet and peaceful place once again, concerned only with the small things. The details that so many other people missed but Ellen loved to pore over.

"So do you think Allegra would like special fried rice or noodles?" Hannah broke Ellen's train of thought.

"Neither; she is having . . ." Ellen picked up one of the recipes that Allegra had furnished her with. "Grilled chicken with steamed broccoli and new potatoes—and so are we, Simon brought enough to feed a small army—so I thought I might as well cook it for Charlie and me, too."

"Not me," Charlie said. "I'm having fish fingers."

"Yes, but I thought that tonight you might like a change?" Ellen questioned. "You know, we're starting a new chapter in our lives and I thought you might feel like eating something new, too, you know—for a change."

"I thought you said what I eat isn't a problem?"

"I did, and it's not, it's just . . ."

"No, you know I don't like chicken or broccoli or any of that stuff. I'll have fish fingers. I can do it myself if you can't be bothered."

"Of course I can be bothered, it's just I thought you might . . ."

"It's not that big a deal, is it, sis?" Hannah asked, slinging an arm around Charlie's shoulder.

"I just said it wasn't, didn't I?" Ellen snapped. She took a breath and forced herself to lighten her tone. "I'll do you some fish fingers now. Sabine, would you like to join us for dinner? There's plenty to go around."

"Oh yes, please," Hannah replied before Sabine could answer. "I'll get a couple of spare chairs from the shed."

"Quick, she's coming in!" Charlie hissed, as if he expected them all to hide. He scrambled into his chair and did his best to look nonchalant.

Allegra opened the back door and peeled off her gloves, glancing around the room. Hannah grinned at her as she looked at the takeaway menu while she lounged against the kitchen counter, Sabine smiled politely from her seat at the table, and Ellen stood by the kitchen sink as if caught in the act of something dreadful, which in a way she had been. It was clear that Allegra did not find the willful neglect of one's garden at all acceptable.

"I've done my best, but someone will need to clear up the debris," she told Ellen. "I don't do bending."

"Thank you, Allegra, you didn't have to."

"Ah, but I did," Allegra said reproachfully.

"Let me introduce you to my son, Charlie." Ellen gestured first at her son and then at Sabine. "And this is Sabine, she has the room above yours, and this—this is my sister, Hannah."

Allegra nodded stiffly at each in turn. "I'll take dinner in my room. I like to listen to the radio in the evenings."

Just as she was about to exit, she collided with Matt, who all but took the poor woman off her feet, only saving her from falling by catching her in his arms.

"Oh, I am so sorry," Matt told her as he righted her. "I really didn't mean to."

Ellen watched in disbelief as Allegra beamed at Matt, her face lighting up with a smile that instantly took a good twenty years off her age.

"Please don't worry, it's not every day a woman of my age is swept off her feet," she told him sweetly.

"What, thirty-five?" Matt's compliment was quite without guile.

Allegra fluttered her lashes. "So you are the young man Simon warned me about? Matthew Bolton?"

"I suppose I must be, unless it's young Charlie here you need to watch out for."

"And you are a writer, too?" Allegra asked. "You are, I can see the creative fire in your eyes."

"That might be the two pints I had on the way home." Matt grinned at her.

"How charmingly male," Allegra said, placing the flat of her hand against his cheek. "One quite misses the scent of testosterone in one's life. Ellen, I think we might model our hero on this dashing young man; I think he might be quite an inspiration."

Ellen thought of Captain Parker, dark, moody, and dashing, and looked at Matt, blond, sexy, and full of light, and couldn't see the comparison.

Allegra patted his cheek and then, as coquettish as a girl, glanced over her shoulder and waved at him as she left the room.

"Top old lady." Matt grinned around at the others.

"She likes you, that's for sure." Hannah laughed, extending her hand. "You are quite the charmer. I'm Hannah, Ellen's sister, by the way; we spoke on the phone."

"And I am Sabine. Pleased to meet you, Matt."

Matt looked from Hannah to Sabine. A tall, leggy redhead, sexily dressed and with the kind of look in her eyes that if he'd met her in a pub or a bar, he would have taken as a challenge, and a shorter, curvier blonde, with what looked like a slamming body under her sensible work clothes. And both of them off-limits—that is, if he were to stick to his second rule, which he was determined to do this time. Never mess with girls you have to see on a regular basis. Not flatmates, not work colleagues (he didn't count Carla as one of those), and not friends' girlfriends. Especially not friends' girlfriends; he'd learned that from bitter experience—it was one of the reasons his PS3 was still in Manchester.

"You joining us for dinner, Matt?" Hannah asked. "There's plenty to go round."

"Really? If you're sure, that would be great. I haven't had a chance to get to the supermarket yet."

"That's okay, isn't it, Ellie?"

Ellen pursed her lips. "Well, not if you stay, Hannah—I might have exaggerated a bit about the small army. I've only got four portions."

"You could have a fish-finger sandwich with me," Charlie offered.

"Brilliant. If you're sure?" Matt looked at Ellen.

"Of course. I'll put the grill on."

"Tell you what, I'll do the fish fingers in payment for the sarnies." Matt grinned at her, taking the grill pan out of her hands and heading for the freezer.

Ellen watched him covertly as he rifled through the freezer drawers, and she tried to imagine him in tight breeches and a white shirt, open to the navel, with ruffled sleeves that fell over his knuckles. Turned out it wasn't quite as difficult as she had thought.

CHAPTER Eight

Ellen sat in her chair at the kitchen table, watching the clock ticking toward 3:00 A.M. on Saturday, sipping chamomile tea in the dark, wondering if she needed to do something practical in her new capacity as landlady, perhaps draw up a bathroom schedule or something that made her look as if she were capable and in charge of this house that was newly brimming with strangers, but she realized that such a schedule would be pointless. Matt had his own shower room, she had her own en suite, and Allegra preferred to attend to her toilette in the downstairs bathroom, which Nick had squeezed a shower into for when he came back from his runs and sometimes when he got in very late at night and didn't want to disturb Ellen. As for the main bathroom, Charlie so seldom went near it voluntarily that Sabine might as well have called it her own. Still, Ellen felt that there was something she should be doing, rather than merely sitting back and letting these people simply be here. It was just that she couldn't think of anything, and perhaps that was a blessing, because she had the distinct feeling that working for Allegra Howard was going to take up an awful lot of her time. The old lady was rather . . . demanding.

Cupping her mug of warm tea in her hands, Ellen relived her first day of working for Allegra Howard and what had followed. It hadn't gone *quite* as she had expected. In fact, it hadn't been like she had expected at all.

She had brought Allegra breakfast, right on schedule, and had found her reclining on her chaise longue already, neatly dressed in a pale lilac skirt and white blouse, open at the neck. Her fine hair had been expertly whipped into a chignon, her skin powdered, her lips coated with the kind of dry orange-red lipstick that looked like it had gone out of production in the 1950s. Ellen could not imagine how or when Allegra would have found the time to put together such a glamorous appearance, because she herself had been up since six thirty, getting Charlie off to school and choosing something to wear that seemed appropriate for Allegra Howard's research assistant, deciding that supermarket jeans and a secondhand man's shirt simply wouldn't do. Finally, Ellen had settled on a faded khaki linen skirt that she had found languishing at the back of the wardrobe and a once-white T-shirt that was now mainly gray, but had at least been designed for a woman to wear. She'd felt self-conscious as she showered, aware of the other people in her house. She heard the sound of Sabine's TV as the woman caught up with the markets around the world before she went in to work, and Charlie skulking about in his room, refusing to make an appearance until at least five minutes after he should have left, whereupon he would grab a piece of white toast from Ellen and munch it as he walked down the street. Most disconcerting, she had become aware, as she stood in the shower, letting the warm water run in rivulets over her shoulders and breasts, of the sound of Matt's shower draining away above her, and had realized that he was standing naked over her head at that very second.

Ellen had then switched the shower to cold for a moment, after which she'd briskly rubbed herself dry, hoping to chafe off all her foolishness along with her dead skin cells. It was just being near an actual man, she'd reasoned. Something about having Matt in the house, combined with reading Allegra's latest work, had combined to create these . . . very stupid, very foolish feelings. They weren't even feelings, they weren't even *ideas* of feelings. It was just that Matt was a young, attractive man, and she was a single woman who hadn't had any kind of meaningful male contact since long before Nick's death.

Her body had responded to Matt's proximity just as a flower opens its petals to the morning sun. These little flutters of desire that she felt when she looked at him, or thought about him, were physiological reactions, nothing more serious than sneezing when you get something up your nose. That was the reason behind all this foolishness. That, and that she had seen him with his top off.

In any case, soon, she'd told herself, she would build up an immunity to him, just as she had to her mother's cat whenever she went home to visit and sneezed her head off for the first hour at least. The rush of blood to her cheeks whenever he looked at her, or the hazy half-remembered dreams would fade away like a crop of hives.

Ellen had considered her flushed face in the mirror, her cheeks still ruddy from the cold water, her eyes bright with the prospect of something to do. In the meantime, she might as well enjoy it. A harmless secret crush on a man a million miles out of her league wasn't hurting anyone, and while a part of her felt a little as if she was being unfaithful to Nick for even thinking about another man, another very tiny, dark part of her that she was barely aware of was immensely relieved that she was still capable of feeling anything at all.

Allegra had examined her breakfast without comment and dismissed Ellen with a single wave of her hand.

"Return at ten and we will begin," she had instructed Ellen.

Ellen had returned to the kitchen, where she sat silently as Matt rushed around, pouring coffee down his throat in a single gulp and flapping about where he had left his mobile phone until she noticed it on the windowsill. And just as

Sabine popped her head around the door to say goodbye and before Charlie came crashing through to grab his daily bit of toast, Matt had bent his head and kissed her on the cheek, calling her a star.

Then all at once the kitchen had been empty again, and Ellen had been left alone with the sound of her heart pounding. She couldn't decide if it was the kiss on the cheek, the compliment, or the fact that in a few minutes she was due to start her new job. Or perhaps it was the shock of having her peaceful house filled with strangers and life again, talking, eating, laughing out loud. No, *shock* wasn't the right word; the *surprise,* the surprise of finding that she rather liked it.

"So." Allegra had repositioned herself on her chaise longue, her legs up, neatly crossed at the ankles. She motioned for Ellen to sit behind the burr-walnut desk that Simon had arranged to be brought in. "You've read the first few chapters of *The Sword Erect.* Your opinion?"

"Oh." Ellen sat rather nervously on the amber-colored leather of the heavily padded desk chair, thinking of the departure of the last PA over—what was it?—artistic differences? "You want *my* opinion? On . . . on *your* book?"

"Well, I certainly don't want it on the price of eggs." Allegra scowled at her. "Of course I want your opinion on my book. Simon told me you have read all of my books—how does *The Sword Erect* compare?"

"Well . . ." Ellen hesitated, aware that she was anxiously knotting her fingers together like a schoolgirl caught out on a difficult math question. She felt her mouth dry up, her tongue sticking to the roof of her mouth. No one had asked her opinion on anything in years, but for Allegra Howard to ask Ellen what she thought of her book was like Shakespeare dropping by and asking if she liked his rhyming couplets.

"Good God, woman, it's a simple enough question," Allegra snapped impatiently.

"I'm sorry . . . it's just, um, well—you know. I feel a bit . . . self-conscious, because after all what do I know, really?" Ellen chewed on her lip as the question hung awkwardly in the air.

"Let us hope you know something," Allegra exclaimed. "Simon told me you had an excellent eye and an instinct for fine-tuning a story. He promised me that if I came to stay here in this . . . *house* that you would be useful to me. So—be useful. Tell me what you think of the book so far."

Ellen took a deep breath, feeling a level of anxiety that she had experienced before only when telling Nick that she was pregnant with Charlie. It had been an accident, one of those things that happened despite the number of precautions used; Charlie had arrived at least two years ahead of schedule in Nick's life plan—before they had the house, the business, and their lives together well established. Ellen had worried that Nick would not be happy, that he would blame her somehow, but after he'd had a few minutes to let the news sink in, he couldn't have been more delighted. Her fears had been foolish fears then, and Ellen was sure they would be again. People were not nearly as frightening as she often believed them to be, even artistic geniuses like Allegra.

"It's a real page-turner, that's for sure," Ellen blurted. "I couldn't put it down and when I ran out of pages I was very disappointed. I'm desperate to know what happens to Eliza at the hands of that dreadful man who accosted her as she was trying to run away from the clutches of Captain Parker. . . ."

"But?" Allegra observed down the length of her aristocratic nose.

"But? There is no but, I think it's brilliant in every respect." Ellen smiled at Allegra, as if the intensity of her smile might somehow incite one in Allegra.

"Oh, Ellen, please don't insult my intelligence. Of course there is a 'but.' I know it, Simon knows it, and you know it. It's just that Simon and I can't decide exactly what the 'but' is.

That buck, I'm afraid, has been passed to you. You must see the flaws with that keen eye of yours. What are they?"

Ellen swallowed and took a moment to frame her sentence. "Well—I know it's only your first draft—and I probably usually read your second or even third draft for copyediting purposes—"

"You don't. I only ever write one draft," Allegra argued.

"Oh well, it's just that it seems that this book is a little lacking in . . ." Ellen lost her nerve.

"Lacking in . . . ? Spit it out, woman!"

"Substance."

Ellen spoke the word quietly, as if she were revealing an unpleasant secret.

"Substance?" Allegra's tone was neutral, her expression implacable. Miserably, Ellen realized that she was required to elaborate.

"Well, what lifts your books above the others," she battled on, "is the historical context, the attention to detail, the way that you bring alive the sights and sounds of another age. The characters . . . the plot is brilliant but—correct me if I'm wrong—but I think *The Sword Erect* is the first book you have set in the English Civil War. It's such a rich and interesting time, yet you skirt around it almost as if it were incidental, and . . ." Ellen faltered. For a moment her passion and interest had swept her along, but now she remembered that she was standing in her former dining room, telling one of the greatest historical-romance writers ever how to do her job. How could she, Ellen Woods, who had never done anything more than read books and correct grammatical errors, even presume to tell Allegra where she was going wrong?

"Of course that's just my opinion, and my opinion is hardly worth knowing; in fact, when I think about it I'm not altogether sure that it's right anyway."

"And?" Allegra questioned.

"And?" Ellen repeated the word as the faintest echo.

"You told me that I was treating the backdrop of the English Civil War as if it were incidental and *then* you were about to add something further. What?"

"It hardly matters." Ellen squirmed, wishing the voluminous folds of the overstuffed leather chair would swallow her up and spit her back out in *her* world, the world where she existed in simple suspended animation and read and daydreamed and waited for her husband to come home and her real life to begin at the touch of his lips on her cheek.

"Ellen." Allegra enunciated her name with such care that it sounded as if it should have a good many more syllables in it. "If you and I are to work together, then we must be straight with each other. I know that you are sitting there wondering how you could possibly have anything to say to me about writing, and I understand why you would feel that way. But let me assure you, one does not become as successful as I have without listening to criticism. I might hate it, but I can take it, and I am not in the habit of shooting the messenger, only torturing them a little. Yes, you are little more than a housewife with barely any experience of the creative arts but you are my reader, you are the person I write for, and now that I have an opportunity to meet you face-to-face, I want to know what you think. You need not be afraid." Allegra's mouth hinted at a smile. "Not very afraid, anyway."

Ellen braced herself.

"Your characters, especially your female characters, usually have something else about them. Wit, intelligence—bravery. Something else apart from their beauty and perfect bodies that makes the reader wish they were them. I know that in the end everything will come right for Eliza—knowing that is sort of half the fun of reading about the other things that happen to her—but at the moment I wonder if she is just a little bit too passive. Look at Helga in your Viking trilogy—despite being sold as a slave and ravished by her new master, she always maintained her dignity until he had no choice but to fall in love with her. And Caroline in *The Pirate Lover*. Beaumont snatches her from the docks when she is lost and locks her in his cabin to have his wicked way with her for weeks, but she challenges him, constantly. She doesn't let her circumstances change who she is. Although Eliza puts up a bit of a fight and runs away, she just seems to lurch from one ravishing to the next. I started to feel sorry for her, and I've never felt that for your heroines before."

Allegra nodded once and then was silent. Not for a few seconds or a few minutes but for almost half an hour. For almost half an hour Ellen sat in the chair and waited for Allegra to speak, unsure if she should stay or go—or even if she still had a job. Finally, her thighs cramping from being clenched for an extended period, she moved to stand up. But just as she moved, Allegra spoke, forcing her back into the chair.

"You're right," she said simply. "You are quite right. I've been relying on all the clichés, all the things that make a work of art no better than pulp fiction. Sex sells and I know that; I've become little better than a whoremonger."

"Oh, well, I wouldn't go that far . . . ," Ellen began.

Slowly and with some difficulty, Allegra stood up, straightening her vertebrae one by one.

"Ellen, can I confide in you?"

Ellen gripped the arms of the chair, not absolutely sure she wanted the responsibility of being Allegra Howard's confidante. Still, unable to refuse, she nodded.

"Of course."

"Ellen, I'm seventy-two. Last year my home was destroyed by a flood, nearly everything I've ever loved, all my memories, all my photos, my works of art—they were all swept away in a river of muck and sewage. I didn't think that it mattered. I always believed that mere objects weren't what made a person human—that it was her feelings, her experiences and memories that made a person exist. But when I was alone in my hotel room I realized that without my things, my photos to look at or my books to pick up, my memories were slipping away from me. And I'm slipping away with them, a little more each day. I'm vanishing."

"No, no—you couldn't be more alert and sprightly," Ellen assured her.

"Sprightly." Allegra pursed her lips. "It is always the curse of the elderly to be either 'frail' or 'sprightly.' I don't mean that I am suffering from dementia, I mean simply that I have reached a crossroads in my life. After seventy-two years of knowing who I am and what I want and what I *do,* suddenly I'm no longer sure, suddenly I'm afraid. With this last book I've been writing by numbers, papering over the cracks and hoping that no one will notice or care—but if you can see it, then so will everyone else, and I'll be vilified as a fraud. They'll see that I don't feel like a writer anymore. They'll see that I am not a writer anymore. My creative fire was quite drowned in that flood along with everything else. Ellen, I am finished."

Ellen sat across from Allegra Howard and looked into her pale blue eyes. "No," she said. "No, you're not finished. You've taken a knock, you've had a setback, and when you're . . . a more mature person, then, well, it's harder to move on from them. When my husband died, I couldn't imagine another day, another hour without him in the world. If it weren't for my son, I would have happily curled up and waited for my heart to stop beating. But I couldn't do that, I had to keep going, and somehow I've got through my first year, and then the lodgers happened and working for you and for the first time I feel as if . . . there is a future."

"There is a future for you." Allegra looked down at her. "You are young and beautiful. But for me? My future is behind me now and suddenly I find I don't have the energy to keep going. I don't have a husband or a son to keep going for. After all of these years writing grand romances, I forgot to find the time to have one myself. I just can't do it anymore. I just don't want to."

"But you do have someone to carry on for." Ellen stood up,

her legs on fire with pins and needles, and came around the desk, only just resisting the urge to touch the older woman. "You have me and all the tens of thousands of people who have read your books. We need you, Allegra. We need the next Allegra Howard book and the one after that. You give us . . . hope. And even if what I said about your book is true, that doesn't make it a bad book; I still couldn't put it down. I still couldn't wait to find out what happened to Eliza." Ellen smiled. "It still made me daydream about having my own Captain Parker crazy with lust for me. All it means is it isn't as good a book as it can be—yet."

Allegra twisted her mouth into a knot of a smile.

"Let me help you fix those things," Ellen went on. "I know a little about history, and what I don't know I can find out. I can find the facts and backdrop and you can weave them into the story and make Eliza a true Allegra Howard heroine. Fearless, defiant, and undefeated by whatever life throws at her—just like you."

Allegra looked into Ellen's eyes and slowly one featherlight hand floated upward to cup Ellen's cheek in its papery palm. "I believe that you might just be a very passionate person, Ellen Woods," she said solemnly.

"Who, me? No, I'm just . . . normal."

"A passionate person with a whole undiscovered universe locked away inside."

"Really?" Ellen was skeptical.

"Really, and I hope that you and I will work very well together. The question is, where do we start?"

"Here," Ellen said. "Well, not here in my dining room. Here as in London during the Civil War. You see, it was a Parliamentarian stronghold throughout the war. With Eliza intent on escaping from Captain Parker, it's natural that she would head here, to a place where she would feel safe. Imagine the historical figures she could encounter, perhaps even Cromwell himself. She could become a sort of seventeenth-century poster girl for the cause. And I thought if the captain followed her into the enemy's lair in order to win her back, then—" Ellen stopped herself. "I'm sorry, of course it's not up to me to think of the plot."

"Nonsense. Keep talking," Allegra said, easing herself back onto her seat. "Keep talking. I will see the pictures."

And as the morning rolled into the afternoon they had talked over ideas, Allegra painting plotlines in the air with a sweep of her hand and Ellen suggesting historical figures and events that they could weave into the plot.

Finally, Allegra held up her hand.

"You must forgive me, Ellen, I'm not as invincible as I used to be. We missed lunch and I fear I must eat something soon or perish."

"Oh no!" Ellen looked at her watch; it was just after three, and before she knew it Charlie would be ambling through the front door. "How awful!"

"Not at all, it was rather wonderful, actually." Allegra's smile was warm. "Let's finish now. Today we laid the foundation. Tomorrow we will write."

As Ellen had shut Allegra's door behind her and headed for the kitchen, she realized that she hadn't felt so excited, so optimistic, or such a part of something in a very long time. It was almost as if she had only just started to exist.

Charlie had bowled into the kitchen as Ellen had been making a smoked-salmon salad for Allegra, one of the components of her eating plan that had been delivered by the supermarket earlier that day along with Earl Grey tea.

"That stinks," he said, peering over Ellen's shoulder briefly.

"So what did you get up to at school today?" Ellen asked.

"You know, the usual," Charlie said, ripping open the packaging of a new loaf of bread even though there was still a third of a loaf left in the bread bin.

"No, I don't know, because you never tell me anymore."

Ellen turned to face her son as he slathered the slice of bread with butter. "When you were a little boy I couldn't shut you up, you'd tell me about what you'd learned, the games you played—you'd skip home holding my hand and talk and talk." She smiled at him, seeing that tousle-headed little boy who'd once been her best friend. "Now I can barely get two words out of you half the time. I know you're growing up, and changing, but—well, I'm still your mum. Come on, *something* must have happened today."

Charlie crammed a bite of bread into his mouth and observed Ellen while he chewed.

"Not really," he said on a swallow. "Oh, wait—James Ingram asked Emily Greenhurst out and she said no."

"James asked a girl out!" Ellen felt unsettled. "Really, you are all asking each other out now, are you, getting girlfriends and things?"

Charlie looked gratifyingly horrified at the idea. "No, not all of us—just James. Most of the girls at my school are right skanks. James likes Emily because she's in this band and she's cool and not like the other girls, you know—she doesn't just giggle and talk about crap. She has opinions and she's funny, and she's got long hair sort of like the color of honey right down to her waist and . . . well, anyway—James likes her but she knocked him back. It was funny."

"*James* likes her." Ellen smiled, reeling from the longest burst of conversation she'd had out of her son in a long time. It took her some effort to ask him exactly how he felt about this mysterious Emily Greenhurst.

"Yes," Charlie said. "He was gutted. It was really funny."

"So you gave him lots of friendly sympathy then?" Ellen asked.

"No! We told him he was gay for liking girls in the first place."

"I think that's probably a contradiction in terms." Ellen smiled.

"A what?" Charlie looked at her.

"Never mind—so you're not planning on asking any girls out just yet, then? Not this Emily, for example?"

"God, no, Mum—I'm not gay!" Charlie exclaimed in horror before scrambling up the stairs, no doubt to find his DS, leaving Ellen alone with her salad, wondering exactly when and how "gay" had started meaning the opposite of . . . well, "gay." And she wondered if she had been sticking her head in the sand a little, determined to still think of him as her little boy. Clearly he was becoming interested in girls, even if he wasn't ready to admit it. If Nick were alive, it would have been simple. Nick would have guided him along the rocky road of adolescence, helped him find his way from boyhood to manhood. But, as Ellen had to keep reminding herself daily, Nick was not here—she was all Charlie had in the way of guidance, and she was only too aware of her inadequacies. She barely knew anything about being a woman, let alone how to be a man.

Later, when he had reappeared for fish fingers, his eyes still glued to his video game, Ellen had tried to talk to him.

"Charlie, you and I have never really talked about . . . well, about the things that you are beginning to be interested in. . . ." She slid the plate of fish fingers garnished with ketchup toward him. "The thing is, you are learning to grow up and turn into a man, and I'm learning, too, learning how to be the mum of a young man. But you know, if you ever want to talk to me about those *things*, then of course you can, and I will try and help as best I can."

"Things?" Charlie looked up from his DS. "Are you talking about sex again?"

"Yes, I suppose I am. When you talked about it the other day, I don't suppose I took you seriously enough. But you are growing up, there are things that you will want to know, and, well—I'm just saying that you can ask me. I won't mind."

Charlie had picked up his fork and stabbed it into a fish

finger. He looked at Nick's empty chair and said, "I wish Dad was here."

Before Ellen could respond, Matt arrived with a packet of fish and chips, and, after ruffling Charlie's hair, he promptly plonked himself down in the one vacant chair. Nick's chair.

"Just gonna dash this down, then I'm off again, got a date," Matt told an immobile Ellen as he unwrapped his takeaway. "Girl from the chick magazine downstairs, she lives round here, so I'm meeting her down the road. . . . What?"

Finally, Matt realized that he was being stared at.

"It's just that—," Ellen started.

"You're sitting in my dad's chair!" Charlie bellowed.

"Am I?" Matt jumped up, spilling greasy chips into his lap, looking around as if he fully expected to find that he'd been sitting on a dead man's lap. "I'm really sorry, mate, I didn't know."

"You don't just come in here, move in, and sit in my dad's chair," Charlie shouted, sliding his plate off the table with a sweep of his hand, sending it crashing onto the tile floor.

"I hate you!" he shouted, and Ellen wasn't sure whether it was her or Matt or his absent father he was talking to. In a second he was gone, thundering up the stairs, slamming the door behind him.

Matt stood there for a second, trying to work out what had just happened.

"Oh, fuck, I put my foot in it, didn't I?" he said, squatting on the floor next to Ellen and beginning to pick up the spilled food.

"No, you weren't to know. I was going to mention it, but I didn't really know how . . . it's not something you just drop into conversation after all. You know, we've all got special chairs—and by the way, please don't sit in my late husband's. I suppose Charlie and I just fell into our little ways over the last year . . . we forget other people won't know what they are." Ellen took a breath, retrieved the dustpan and brush from under the sink, and knelt down beside Matt, sweeping up the pieces of the broken plate. "Besides, it was my fault, I put him on edge, trying to talk to him about 'becoming a man.' I didn't know he'd be so sensitive about it; it only seems like yesterday that he was obsessed with Power Rangers and took his teddy to bed." Ellen bent her head, letting her hair curtain her face as she struggled not to cry. "And it's not as if he's got a dad to talk to or learn from anymore."

"Eleven, nearly twelve, it's a weird time for a boy," Matt said, leaning back on his heels. "Everything's changing, you know—your body, the way you feel—the way you speak, even. It's all up and down, and no one understands. I remember when I discovered . . ." Matt paused, popping a chip he had just picked up off the tiles into his mouth.

"Discovered what? Girls?"

"In a manner of speaking." Matt's smile was rueful. "When I discovered—you know, the pleasure of my own body."

"Oh, I see." Ellen put the dustpan and brush down, feeling suddenly exhausted. "But you were much older than twelve, weren't you?"

"Not so much," Matt said, breaking the news gently. "Anyway, it's difficult for us men, you know. We've got to work out what it all means, how it all works, even how to walk down a road like we've got control of all our arms and legs, and we try our best to do it without anyone noticing, especially not our mums." As they both sat on the kitchen floor, he reached out and tucked the curtain of her hair behind an ear, chucking her under the chin like he might a chubby child. Even at that moment, sitting on the floor among debris, Matt felt comfortable with Ellen. There was something about her that was enticingly familiar, as if he'd met her before and couldn't remember where, only that he was glad to see her again. "It's nothing personal, Ellen," he assured her. "It's not anything you're doing wrong. It's something he has to get through on his own, and for what it's worth, by the time I was his age my dad was long gone and I turned out all right in the end."

Whether it was his touch or the softness in his voice, Ellen didn't know, but the tears that she had been battling broke free and rolled down her cheeks.

"He must miss his dad so much," she said, her voice barely more than a whisper. "And I'm not enough, I'm not nearly enough to make up for him."

"He does miss his dad," Matt said quietly, wiping away her tears with the ball of his thumb before stretching a hand out to Ellen as he rose, helping her to her feet. "And it hurts him like hell and he's angry and confused. And so are you. Look, I know I barely know you, but for what it's worth, it looks to me like you are doing an amazing job. You are a bona fide role model." Matt shrugged. "My dad left home and my mum spent the rest of her life in the bottom of a vodka bottle. You're keeping it together for Charlie, and once all this settles down, once he sees the light at the end of the tunnel, he'll realize that, I promise." Matt ran his fingers through his hair and winced. "What a fuckwit I am, crashing in here, treading all over your feet. I'm sorry I sat in your husband's chair. But look, don't cry, yeah? Give us a smile. If you don't smile for me now, it's going to be *nearly* impossible for me to enjoy my date with a leggy blond associate editor who works on the mag downstairs."

Despite herself, Ellen complied. "I'm quite sure that a weepy middle-aged woman is not going to enter your head once," she told him.

Matt shrugged. "First of all, you're not middle aged, and second, contrary to popular belief, I'm a sensitive guy. It'll ruin my night if you don't stop crying by the time I go out." Matt paused for a second, his eyes roaming over Ellen's face as he thought. "I know—there's this secondhand furniture shop down the road from work. How about if tomorrow I go there and get myself a chair, just for me? Save any further confusion."

"There is a distinct lack of chairs in here," Sabine said, joining the conversation with a smile as she entered, back from work a little earlier than usual and laden down with an armful of files.

"Exactly," Matt said, nodding at Nick's chair. "And for the record, that one's off bounds, too. I could pick three or four if you like, and then we will all know where we stand. Or rather sit. And Charlie will have one less thing to worry about."

"Really?" Ellen asked. "You'd do that?"

"A man's got to have a place to sit and eat chips." Matt nodded. "I'm sure I'll be able to pick up a cheap set."

Sabine crossed her arms and tipped her head to one side, appraising the vacant chairs that huddled around the table. "No, Matt, that will not do. These chairs have personalities, too. If you buy chairs, you must buy three different ones, one each to represent Ellen's three lodgers—isn't that right, Ellen?"

"Oh well—that's why we have these chairs, but you don't have to go to that trouble," Ellen said. A glow of warmth began to spread through her chest. It touched her enormously that people she barely knew were making such an effort to make her feel at home, when she was certain it should be the other way around.

"Cool," Matt said, chuckling. "So, some sleek European design for Sabine, something irresistibly attractive and comfortable for me, and . . . something velvet and sexy for Allegra?"

"Young man, you know me so well," Allegra said, appearing in the doorway. "Don't mind me, I have just come for a glass of water, this heat is unbearable." Allegra went to the sink and let the cold tap run for a few seconds. "New chairs, wonderful idea—what clever person thought of that?"

"Matt," Sabine said, taking a bottle of wine from the fridge and a glass from the cupboard. "He pretends to be a player, but you see, deep inside he is a sensitive soul," she teased Matt gently.

"Oh yes, it's written all over his beautiful face," Allegra agreed. Carefully carrying her glass, she walked across the kitchen, obviously at pains to hide any signs of frailty. "You can never hide a romantic disposition, no matter how much you might try."

"Hang on, ladies, don't let anyone else hear you talk like this, you'll damage my reputation!" Matt laughed.

"My husband also has a reputation," Sabine said, opening the door for Allegra, who went back to her room. "For being an arse. Now I am off to drink this wine and catch up on some work." Sabine regarded Ellen as she stood watching the cast of unfamiliar characters revolve around her. "Smile, Ellen," she said softly. "You are not so alone here anymore, you see? Now you have people to buy you chairs."

Alone with Ellen again Matt glanced at his watch; he was going to be very late for his date, and he was surprised that a considerable part of himself didn't want to go out at all. He found that he enjoyed bringing a smile to Ellen's face.

Ellen wiped her eyes with the heels of her hands and looked at him. "There, temporary relapse over with. Feel free not to give me a second thought. Honestly, I'm quite sure that you didn't imagine moving in here would include comforting your landlady in the rent."

"Well, it wasn't specified in the *Time Out* ad. . . ." Matt grinned. "Look, I like Charlie, he's a good kid. Maybe next time I'm in I'll get him to link our DSs and play Mario Kart or something." Ellen looked blank. "What I'm saying is, maybe, if he likes, him and me can be mates. And maybe if there's any guy stuff he's worried about, then maybe he'll talk to me. I am, after all, an expert on guy stuff. I've got a column to prove it and everything."

"Yes, your column—I'd like to read it sometime."

"Er . . . I don't think you would." Matt looked bashful. "I mean it's not exactly my finest work. And it's probably not exactly your cup of tea. But anyway, like I said, me and Charlie, we can hang sometime."

"You don't have to do that." Ellen shook her head.

"I know," Matt said simply. He looked down at his grease-stained trousers. "But Sabine is right, you and Charlie are not alone anymore—whether you like it or not. And as you are stuck with us, you might as well let us do something for you. I know I could have done with someone to talk to when I was his age. Anyhow, I'd better leap in the shower and get changed. Don't want the associate editor thinking I'm a takeaway-eating slob; I told her I'm into fine dining and that I love to cook."

Ellen had waited until Matt went out before checking on Charlie, who was watching TV in his room with his headphones on, at first resolutely refusing to acknowledge her.

Ellen hovered for a minute; she considered turning off the TV but then decided to sit beside him on his bed in silence. After a minute or two he sighed and ripped off the headphones, flinging them onto the bed.

"Matt didn't know," Ellen said. "I should have told him, but I didn't exactly know how to . . ."

"Well, put up a notice or something," Charlie said. "That's Dad's chair, Mum!"

"I know, I know . . . We've sorted it now—Matt felt terrible about it. He's going to buy some more chairs tomorrow. Special ones, for him, Allegra, and Sabine."

Charlie glanced at her. "Really? That is *quite* cool, I suppose." He turned back to the TV, and Ellen watched him for a few seconds, drinking in the outline of his profile, which was slowly evolving into a carbon copy of his father's.

"Look, Charlie, how are you?" Ellen reached out and smoothed her thumb over his scowl, as she used to when he was a little boy. To her relief, Charlie didn't flinch at her touch.

"I'm okay," Charlie said, looking up at her. "How are you, Mum?"

"I'm okay," Ellen said. "I even think that I might be . . . good."

"Do you think you're starting to feel better?" Charlie questioned, watching her closely. "Not so sad?"

Ellen hesitated, uncertain of how to answer.

"Because it's okay, I mean if you felt better, I'd like it," Charlie told her.

Ellen looked at him, pressing the tips of her fingers to her mouth. "Oh, you poor boy, have I been awful to live with these last months?" she asked.

"No, not awful, just not you. It's almost like you're not really here," Charlie struggled to explain. "Like you're fading away. You get up, you feed me, you wait for me to come home, you feed me, I go to bed, and the next day is the same. I like it that there are people here, that you have things to think about. I even like Matt. I want you to be more like you again, like you used to be before Dad died. We used to do stuff . . . go places."

"I know," Ellen said. "But I do think that I'm feeling a bit better, just a little bit. I think it will be good to have people in the house and a new job. It's not that I don't miss your dad terribly, but it is good to have something else to think about."

"Yeah, it is," Charlie said carefully. "So maybe soon we might do stuff again, go places?"

"You really want to go places with me?" Ellen asked, gently skeptical.

Charlie shrugged. "As long as no one I know sees me."

Ellen swiped him lightly, skimming the top of his head with the flat of her hand.

"Mum, do you remember when you, me, and Dad went sailing in that really flat place—what was it called?"

"The Norfolk Broads." Ellen smiled; Charlie was talking about a holiday that Nick had taken them on a little over two years earlier. He'd developed a brief but passionate interest in sailing and had even owned a share in a boat for a little while. That summer he'd taken them down to see it, full of enthusiasm for the outdoor life, the fresh air and the wind in his hair.

Charlie chuckled. "And Dad got really, really seasick and

in the end you and me did all the sailing. He went actually green—do you remember?"

Ellen nodded, thinking of that flat Norfolk horizon, the endless expanse of sky that made her feel breathless just to think of it, all that space.

"We had a laugh then, didn't we? You and me?" Charlie asked.

Ellen nodded. "We had the best time."

"And we will do stuff like that again, won't we? We won't always just be here in this house missing Dad, because sometimes when I think like that and feel like that—that's when I worry. I worry that I won't ever be able to live just like a normal person again. In case I shouldn't, in case it's wrong. Like it might not be allowed."

Ellen felt the muscles in her gut clench. Had she done this to him? Had her descent into grief dragged him down with her so deeply that he was afraid he might never resurface again?

"Of course it's allowed, sweetheart—more than that, that's the way it should be. Especially for you, you've got your whole life ahead of you."

"So do you, though," Charlie reminded her.

"Yes, I suppose I do," Ellen said thoughtfully. Until recently, the concept had been an unbearable prospect, but now—now it wasn't such a terrifying idea.

"So then you have to start feeling better and maybe you and me could do something like go sailing. I think we'd have fun," Charlie said, his tone hopeful.

"And if I start to feel better, do you think that you can, too?" she asked.

Charlie's smile faded, his shoulders hunching, his body almost halving in size as he absorbed the question. "Sometimes, like at school or when I'm playing the DS or watching telly, I feel all right, I feel normal, and then something will make me remember and . . ." He shook his head, unable to complete the sentence. "Sometimes I feel a bit better."

"I think that's what it's like," Ellen said. "I think sometimes you feel better and sometimes you don't, and that as the days pass, the times when you feel better get longer and the times when you don't get shorter. And I think that it is okay, it's okay to feel better. Dad would want you to be happy, Charlie. He'd want that more than anything in the world."

"He'd want you to be happy, too," Charlie told her.

"I know," Ellen said simply. "Well, let's give it a go for him then, yeah?"

"Yeah." Charlie nodded. "But you will tell everybody about the chair?"

"I will."

Charlie leaned into Ellen as she put her arms around him, resting his head on her shoulder for a second before pulling away and picking up his headphones.

"I know there's no school in the morning," Ellen told him. "But I still want this off by eleven."

But Charlie's eyes had already fixed on the screen.

Exhausted, Ellen lay on her bed, closing her eyes and finally letting the tensions of the day drain out of her. The events of the day—her conversation with Charlie, the mess on the kitchen floor—gradually faded and she found herself thinking of Matt and the sensation of his thumb tracing her cheek. Letting her weary mind drift anywhere it chose, Ellen imagined how it would have felt if that thumb had journeyed farther, running down her neck and brushing lazily over the tops of her breasts.

As Ellen drifted off into her fantasy she saw herself as Eliza Sinclair, her body transforming into the impossibly perfect ideal that was Eliza's, and Matt as the captain, unable to take his eyes off her, his desire for her tangible in the air that crackled between them as they stood alone in a . . . in a hay barn, Ellen decided.

"I love you," Captain Matt whispered, taking a step closer

to her so that she could feel his hot breath grazing her earlobe. *"Oh, Ellen, I love you."*

"And I you," Ellen whispered back, allowing one lily-white hand to flutter to rest on his manly chest and then boldly travel lower, where no maiden should ever venture.

"I long for you," Matt groaned, clasping her hand and clutching it to him.

"Then take me, for I am yours, my love," Ellen said breathlessly, finding herself an expert seductress.

In seconds Ellen found that her thin white cotton gown had been ripped from her body, and her perfect breasts were being crushed against Matt's firm body as his hands and kisses consumed her in a burning sea of fire that she delighted in drowning in.

Hours had passed when Ellen woke to find herself still fully dressed, tangled in her bedsheets, and suddenly wide awake. She looked at the bedside clock and sighed, pushing herself out of bed, peeling off her clothes and changing into a pair of Nick's pajamas, a bright red cotton with green trim that she'd bought him one Christmas as a joke and that he had never worn. Still, Ellen liked the feel of them, hugging the outsized shirt around her body. It was guilt that was keeping her awake, she realized. Fantasizing about another man—worse still, a real-life man—as if Nick had never existed, as if he hadn't been her lover, the love of her life. As if sordid fantasies could ever replace what they had once had.

Feeling the same sort of lurching horror as a drunk who has awakened to remember exactly what horrors happened the night before, Ellen took herself downstairs to drink tea and sort herself out. She paused at Charlie's room, pushing open the door to see the TV still flickering, despite her command, tuned to some music channel that he seemed permanently glued to, and her son sprawled facedown on the bed, his covers kicked to the floor. Treading carefully to avoid damaging any of the various possessions that he preferred to keep on the floor, Ellen swept up the duvet and laid it over Charlie's prone form.

"What the . . . ?" he questioned sulkily in his sleep.

"It's just me, darling," Ellen whispered, and within seconds Charlie was lost again in the deep sleep that seemed to overwhelm him these days. She stood for a few seconds outside Charlie's room and listened. Faint music and the sound of hushed female laughter drifted down the stairwell. Matt must have brought his blond associate editor home, she thought. While Ellen had been imagining them rolling about in a pile of hay, he'd been plying this girl with drinks and charming her with the sweet smile that he'd treated Ellen to earlier. And as this unknown woman had come back with him on their first date, he must have done a pretty good job.

Ellen shook her head, the tender soles of her feet jolted by the cool kitchen tiles. This day, a day of things happening, had gone to her head. For a moment she'd forgotten who she was and what she was here for. She was Nick's wife and Charlie's mother and she was here to do the best for her son that she could. While that included the guilty pleasure of working for Allegra Howard, it did not include wasting hours of her life dreaming about a man who'd never look at her in a million years. Her fantasies were far from harmless if they took her mind off the things that mattered.

She'd made herself a strong cup of tea and sat at the kitchen table staring at Nick's chair, wishing she could will him into existence just by thinking of him.

Ellen jumped when she heard footsteps on the stairs. Hoping it was Charlie coming down for a drink of water, she went to the kitchen door and opened it a crack. It was Matt and his associate editor. She had her coat on, and he had . . . well, nothing but a towel wrapped around his waist. Ellen stifled a gasp, clasping her hand over her mouth.

"I can't believe you're kicking me out!" the girl giggled,

swinging her arm around Matt's neck to steady herself as she stumbled, clearly the worse for wear. "Not after what we just did!"

"I know, and I don't want to," Matt purred. "It's just the landlady—she's old school, you know. A bit of a dragon. I'm risking getting evicted, bringing you back here at all, but you're so gorgeous that I was powerless to resist."

The girl giggled again and tightened her hold on him so that their lips met, and she kissed him, swaying gently from side to side like a willow bending in the wind as they embraced. As they kissed, Matt's hand departed from her waist and headed for the door latch; he opened it a crack and maneuvered the girl into the gap.

"Good night," he whispered.

"You'll call me?" the girl asked.

"But of course." Matt nodded.

"Promise?" There was a hint of desperation in her voice.

"For sure," Matt said as he shut the door on her. He stood there for a moment, his hand on the latch, as if he suspected that she might come back. And then, horrified, Ellen watched him rub his hands through his hair and over his face and head straight for the kitchen.

Panicking, she shut the kitchen door and ran to the back door, instinctively planning to escape into the garden, but then thinking better of it she ran first to the pantry and then to the fridge, as if she might climb into it. She was still flapping when Matt flicked on the unforgiving spotlight, illuminating the kitchen and catching Ellen red-handed and barefoot in Nick's pajamas.

"Oh shit!" Matt yelped. "You scared the shit out of me!"

"I'm sorry, I was just up when I heard your . . . friend leaving. I didn't want you to think I was eavesdropping."

"No worries," Matt said cheerfully, and then he frowned. "Were you eavesdropping?"

"No," Ellen said. "Well, a bit. Okay, I heard everything."

"Oh no," Matt groaned. "Listen, that bit I said about the landlady being a dragon, you know I was only saying that to get her to go, don't you? I don't think you're a dragon. All that stuff I said earlier—that's what I really think about you."

"Honestly, it's none of my business," Ellen said, pausing, confused and unsure of exactly what she wanted to say or how. She had known that Matt worked for what was called a lads' mag, and that he wrote about women all the time, but the man she'd met and just begun to get to know over the last few days hadn't seemed the sort who would meet a girl down at the pub and then bring her back to bed on the very same night. She had foolishly forgotten that he was virtually a stranger, had let her silly imagination run away with her and ended up feeling disappointed in him, even though she didn't have a right to be. Not in his choice of sexual partners, anyway. "Actually, Matt, it is my business a bit—we talked about Charlie, remember? About him being at an impressionable age—and I know I said it's fine for you to bring people back, and it is. But will it always be like that—some girl that you've just picked up? Because if it is, then you need to be a lot more discreet. What if Charlie had come down for a drink just then?"

"Shit, I'm an arsehole. I'm sorry," Matt said. "I just didn't think. I mean, I seriously didn't think." He shook his head, clutching his towel for dear life. "Next time I'll go to her place."

"So you liked her then?" Ellen asked.

Matt looked confused. "Oh no, not her place. I mean the next girl's place, whoever she might be. Next time I'll go there."

Not sure how to react, Ellen reached for her cup of tea. "Well, I'll leave you to it."

"I suppose you want to know why I got her to go," Matt said, stopping her with the question.

Ellen wavered. She'd never been around a man like Matt

before, a bona fide ladies' man, and she did sort of want to know. But she did also have to get up in a few hours and she had just recently, only minutes ago in fact, banned herself from having anything to do with Matt that wasn't essential. The last time she had "seen" him, he had been standing naked in front of her with an erection that would have rivaled that of any of Allegra's well-proportioned heroes, on the brink of flinging her into a pile of straw and penetrating her very soul with his thunderous passion. Under those circumstances, Ellen felt that standing in her kitchen alone with him while he wore nothing more than a towel at past three in the morning did not qualify as essential. Particularly as he was clearly the sort of man who would not shy away from a casual sexual encounter.

"Not especially, not unless you *want* to tell me?" Ellen waited, trying to picture how old and how prim she must look standing there in Nick's pajamas.

Matt took a pint of milk out of the fridge and drank directly from it, sitting down in her chair, the towel folding between his legs, barely maintaining his modesty.

"Too easy," Matt said.

"What, she was?" Ellen asked, leaning against the kitchen counter.

"All of it was. I met her in the elevator at the office. I'm on the fifth floor and she's on the fourth. I asked her if she fancied a drink on the third and she agreed and made plans with me by the time she got out. That should have been a sign, you know. Girls who are too eager, you've got to watch them. But she's got great legs and a really nice set of . . . eyes. And men are shallow. I am shallow. So I turn up at the pub, a bit late, and she's there, wearing this dress that's cut up to here and down to here." Matt chopped the flat of his hand first against the top of his thigh and then just below his nipples.

"I bet that really showed off her eyes," Ellen said, smiling at the surprise on Matt's face at her joke.

"It did." He nodded. "All the blokes were looking at her and I liked being the one she was with. And she was a laugh. Then two gin and tonics down and she's all over me, hands everywhere, wants to come back to my place."

"Sounds awful," Ellen said dryly. "How on earth did you cope?"

"It was a struggle." Matt's smile was rueful.

"Which is why you exercised your free will and said, 'No, thank you very much, young lady,'" Ellen observed, hating how much she sounded like his sensible maiden aunt.

"I know. I know that's what I should have done. But she's a woman, a hot woman, and she wanted to go to bed with me. Like I said, I'm shallow."

"Was it worth it, the sex?" Ellen found herself asking as she edged closer to the table and sat down.

"It was fine," Matt said. "It was nice, but the second it was over I didn't want to talk to her anymore. I wanted her to go. So I invented the whole dragon-landlady thing, sorry."

"I don't think it's me you should be apologizing to," Ellen said, sounding much primmer and older than she wanted to. "I mean you must have made the poor girl feel as if you were really interested in her, you must have made her feel that it was okay to come back to bed with you."

Matt scrutinized her long enough to make her break eye contact with him.

"Do you think I'm a shit?" Matt asked.

Ellen shrugged, suddenly feeling overwhelmed with fatigue. She wasn't sure if she was expected to work with Allegra on Saturdays, but she would definitely have to get up to make her breakfast.

"I expect that when the poor girl wakes up in the morning she'll feel foolish and vulnerable and she'll think that *you're* a shit." Ellen yawned. "But at least you're honest. You don't dress up how you feel or think about things, you more sort of sling on a towel and lounge around half naked."

"Oh shit." Matt looked down at himself as if he had just remembered what he was not wearing. "Shit. I've been here— what, five days? And I've pissed off your son, called you a dragon, and made an idiot of myself. Am I evicted?"

Ellen smiled at him, glad to see him like this, young, brash, half drunk, half naked, and awkward. The real Matt, as disarming and handsome as he might be, was nothing like the captain in her dreams. Perhaps avoiding him was the wrong thing to do after all; the better she got to know him, the less he would embody that perfect hero in her head.

"Good night, Matt," she said. "Get some sleep."

"Night, Ellen, and . . ." Matt paused, suddenly bashful. "I'm glad you were up. It's not often you meet a woman you can talk to."

"Unlike the ones you can have sex with," Ellen replied. "They're a dime a dozen."

CHAPTER
Nine

"Don't you reckon, heh?" Pete chuckled into his third lunchtime pint, which seemed to be reflected quite graphically by the rising tide of red that crept over his jowls and toward the tips of his ears with each swig of beer. "Heh? Matt?"

Matt looked up from his own untouched beer and realized that he hadn't been listening to a word that Pete had said since they'd sat down at the table. This was his third week at *Bang It!* and he was halfway through his probation. His first two columns had gone down well with Dan and, best of all, with the readers; he'd had quite a lot of actual letters, which was rare in the *Bang It!* office, which usually got Suze to make them up in her lunch hour. Dan was pleased with him, but the more he worked for Pete, the more he realized that half his job, at least, was comprised of babysitting his boss and keeping him at least vaguely on track. Nobody had said it out loud, of course, but the fact was that Pete was an alcoholic with a fondness for the odd line of midmorning coke. Matt had no idea how Pete kept his job, but he did, and he got the distinct feeling that as the rookie in the pack it was his duty to help him keep it. Still, the more he saw of Pete, who was permanently messed up— and even Dan, whose good looks and vigor were already being blurred by a lifestyle that would eventually kill off the best of them—the more Matt secretly wondered if this was his dream job after all. Was this really what he'd been hoping for all those years back, when he'd first tried his hand at journalism? A job that meant he woke up every morning with a hangover, that was giving him a worrying laissez-faire attitude toward naked breasts, and where the pinnacle of creative brilliance that was required of him was to think up ten different ways to write "blow job." He was sure he'd had other aspirations as a kid, when a report on the news at ten from a massacre in India had brought him to tears and inspired him to want to do what that reporter had done, bring the really important news home to people in a way that made it seem personal, that made it matter. Somehow, life had brought him here, an expert babe-hound, living the bachelor life surrounded by women. It had to be his dream job, how could it not be? Even if his drunken boss did somewhat take the edge off.

At just after twelve thirty, Pete had arrived at Matt's desk, looking hot and uncomfortable in a too tight shirt and food-stained tie, beads of sweat decorating his brow despite the air-conditioning in the office, and once again demanded that Matt join him for a liquid lunch.

"Got to get out of this shit hole for an hour," he'd said with a sigh, pulling at his shirt collar as he glared around at the rest of the room, studiously avoiding eye contact with his colleagues. Matt got the distinct impression that they were smirking at him behind his back.

"I'd love to, but the thing is, I still have to put this review to bed and I need to polish up my column a bit—," Matt began.

"What? No, you don't, that draft you gave me was fine. I sent it to the features folder last night."

"What? Pete!" Matt shook his head. "I thought I told you, that was a first draft, I hadn't . . . refined it yet."

"Refined it? This is *Bang It!*, mate, not *Woman and Home*. You're writing about shagging, not how to fluff up a muffin—although now I come to think of this, that makes a pretty good euphemism." Pete's chuckle was filthy. "Take it from an expert, that column was perfect. Now get your coat."

Reluctantly, Matt slid back his chair and followed Pete out into the midday glare of the street and to The Red Lion, the pub that was just around the corner from their office. That column *had* been perfect—perfect for Pete, that is. Matt had written it based on his evening with the associate editor, deciding to wait for a week or two before he used the material after what had happened with Carla. He had seen neither the associate editor nor Carla since, which was a blessing that he knew he didn't deserve. Last week he'd rehashed a column from his Manchester days but he didn't know London well enough to make it completely authentic. He had thought that one city would be very much like the next, but that wasn't true. While Manchester was big, vibrant, and packed full of all kinds of life, it seemed almost like a village compared to London. Of course, he felt more at home in Manchester, it *was* his home—he'd grown up there. But it was more than that. London was so huge, both dirty and beautiful, sprawling and crawling with humanity. It was built not just of mere bricks, concrete, and steel but of layer upon layer of life that he'd barely had a chance to scratch the surface of. Matt wasn't sure he could begin to get his head around what made the place tick, or even the little bit of it that he had seen so far. But he knew he had to work harder to capture the essence of his "hunting ground" in his column, so he'd written his column with Pete in mind, and as a consequence it was dirty and graphic and treated its female focus in turn as an object of lust and then of ridicule. Matt had knocked it out in minutes, returning to the office one evening after a stint in the pub, feeling gung ho and keen on impressing his new bosses. But since then he'd had second thoughts. Thoughts that involved the associate editor, who had been funny and generous, passionate and open. He had called her easy, but *easy* wasn't really the right word. It was more that she was willing—willing to take a chance on him, willing to live life to the fullest—and after all, that was pretty much his motto. The poor girl hadn't really done anything wrong other than trust him, and it seemed unfair that she should be pilloried for it; even though he had invented a name for her and changed her job title to that of editorial assistant, she would know it was about her. And now the piece was out there and there was nothing that Matt could do about it unless he wanted to make himself look like an idiot. He'd probably hurt a perfectly nice girl, for no good reason.

Matt struggled with this latest bout of guilt. For some reason, everything he did now, everything he wrote, seemed more real than it ever had before. Back home, he'd written piece after piece about girls he'd met in passing and it had never seemed to matter then. But recently, maybe after everything that had happened just before he'd left, he had started to see, to feel, the consequences of his actions. It was a new awareness that was not a particularly useful skill for a features writer on a lads' mag, and it was one he'd have to stamp out if he wanted to really fit in at *Bang It!* Matt couldn't put his finger on when exactly a little inkling of conscience had started to insinuate its way into his makeup, but he was fairly sure it had begun before he got on the train to London and he was certain that his landlady had an awful lot to do with the way it had gone, at precisely the wrong moment in his life.

His small-hours chats with Ellen in the kitchen had become almost a regular feature over the last couple of weeks, and Matt began to realize that he looked forward to finding Ellen sitting in the kitchen, cupping a steaming mug of tea between her palms despite the summer's unremitting heat. Take last night.

He'd walked into the kitchen hoping to find her there, but had been careful to look surprised when he did, as if sharing a cup of tea with her was the last thing on his mind. She had apologized, like she always did for nothing in particular, and he had claimed that he was just getting a drink of water, while she told him she was taking her cup of tea to bed. Yet, they had sat and talked for almost two hours.

"How's life as the sorceress's apprentice?" Matt asked Ellen as she hesitated by the kettle—she always seemed as if she took the greatest thought over every tiny decision, even choosing a mug for her tea, as if making the wrong choice might have terrible consequences. Matt nodded at the chair he had found to represent Allegra, a reproduction of a fancy French affair, with a violet velvet seat pad and arms that had been spray-painted gold. "It must be a bit like working for the queen."

Upon seeing her chair for the first time, Allegra had sniffed, and had haughtily declared that she had no idea what Matt thought that she and that clapped-out, overdressed old fake had in common, but she had winked at him when she said it, and taken the opportunity to pat him on the chest and kiss him on his lips, commenting, "Still, I suppose I must be grateful that you didn't return home with a commode."

"Yes, I do have to fight the urge to curtsy whenever I see her." Ellen smiled. "But on the whole it's good . . . frightening, a bit like you've been thrown into the deep end of a swimming pool without knowing how to swim. Actually I think that might be what I like about it. I can't remember the last time I did something so . . . challenging or satisfying." Her bright look faded briefly. "Not that being a mother and a wife haven't been both of those things, *that's* not what I mean. . . ."

"You mean it's good to do something that is just for you?" Matt asked, dropping all pretense that he was leaving and sitting down in his new red-plastic office chair that had casters and swiveled 360 degrees. In the short time he had owned it, he and Charlie had frequently created chair Olympics all around the kitchen and hallway—at least when Ellen wasn't looking.

Matt felt a surge of pleasure when, after making both of them a cup of tea without asking him if he wanted one, Ellen joined him at the table.

"Yes, do you know what I mean?" Ellen asked, with a compelling intensity in her green eyes that Matt only ever saw in her at this time of day, when she was relaxed and, he guessed, more like herself than she was during all the other tense, wakeful, expectant hours. She had the kind of eyes that Matt wasn't used to seeing in women, although he routinely told many of them that they had the most beautiful eyes he had ever come across. Ellen's gaze hinted at hidden depths that he could only guess at. What really made Ellen tick? Matt had begun to wonder more and more often. It seemed to him that since losing her husband she must have developed a habit of shuffling through each day, growing into her role as a staid widowed housewife and a stalwart grieving mother—and when Matt had first met her, that was all that he had seen. But when they had started talking late at night, letting the conversation slip and slide between them with careless ease, he had begun to realize that she was nothing of the sort.

"Not really," he admitted. "There hasn't really ever been anybody else to please, apart from myself, in a long time. I'm not in touch with my dad . . . Mum's got her own problems. I think I've been more or less doing as I pleased since I was sixteen—which has its own kind of pressure, because if I stuff it up, it's nobody's fault but my own."

"But you haven't stuffed it up, have you?" Ellen raised one quizzical eyebrow as she watched him across the table. "You have your dream job, any man's dream job apparently. And if you've achieved all of that on your own, then that makes you all the more impressive."

"Impressive," Matt repeated with a wry smile. "Honestly, Ellen, do you think I'm impressive?"

Ellen paused, and Matt heard the blood beating in his ears as he waited for her to respond.

"I think the fact that you've gone after what you want and you've got it is impressive," she hedged, dealing a crushing blow to Matt's ego with the lightest of touches.

"And what do you think about me?" Matt asked. He'd couched the question carefully, keeping his tone light, a smile playing around his lips. "Do you disapprove of me terribly?"

"As if you care what I think of you!" Ellen chuckled into her tea, and the steam that rose from the mug glistened on her flushed cheeks.

"But pretend I do." Matt encouraged her. "Pretend you are writing my school report—what would you say if you had to sum me up?" Matt pressed her, despite suffering from a sudden bout of nerves. He had no idea why he needed to know exactly how Ellen saw him, but at that moment it seemed very important indeed.

Ellen sucked in her bottom lip and regarded him with a long, cool stare that he found hard to meet.

"I would say . . . shows real promise but could do better."

"Ouch!" Matt winced. " 'Could do better,' that hurts!"

"I only mean . . . well, is writing about sex with girls you barely know really your dream job? I mean, you have this real gift for communicating with the written word; what I've read of your stuff really delivers its message, quickly and clearly, and you have a distinct style of your own—but, well—does it have to be so trashy?"

"You don't think it's funny?" Matt asked.

"Well, that piece you gave me to read the other night . . ."

Matt nodded. It had been a recycled piece about a beautician he'd met back home, who'd made the mistake of hurriedly waxing her bikini line into a Brazilian while Matt waited for her in the living room. It had turned out that it was a job best not rushed and the poor girl had emerged in pain and bleeding quite profusely from some rather delicate areas. She'd tried to cover it up but had eventually confessed, and Matt, ever the faux gentleman, had soothed the affected area with an icepack. There were jokes about plucked chickens and stubble rash. Pete had loved it.

"It was funny, I suppose," Ellen said uncertainly. "But it's also kind of . . . mean. Does your column always have to be mean?" Matt thought about it for a moment and concluded that for *Bang It!* it probably did. When he thought about it, though, when he thought about what he *had* wanted and envisaged for his career when he set out to become a journalist, he had to conclude that writing a sex column in a men's magazine probably wasn't going to lead to the awards and accolades he'd hoped for.

"Oh, God, I'm a total failure," Matt half joked.

"Don't be silly! You are still young, this might be where you are starting out, but it doesn't have to be where you end up."

"And what about you," Matt asked. "What new heights will you achieve now?"

"Oh, I don't know," Ellen answered absently, curling a tress of hair around her finger. "I'd like to get the oven cleaned by Friday, though."

When Matt laughed, Ellen couldn't see what was so funny, which made him like her all the more.

He couldn't exactly claim that he had made any friends since he'd arrived in London—mates, yes, through work; lads to have a laugh and a drink with. He had underestimated exactly how much it mattered to have someone you could really talk to without needing to put on a front or an attitude. Matt had left his lifelong best friend behind in Manchester along with his PlayStation, and it was his fault that they didn't talk anymore. Unwittingly, Ellen had become the nearest thing to a friend that he had in the huge, sprawling, unforgiving city, and theirs was small-hours friendship characterized by crumpled cotton pajamas, tangled scooped-up hair, and steaming cups of tea on sweltering summer nights.

As Matt had traveled to work that morning he kept picturing her as they had both knelt on the kitchen floor that day when Charlie had flipped out about his dad's chair, the tears welling in her eyes, displaying her raw vulnerability in front of a virtual stranger. And then he could not shake the image of her when they had first met in the kitchen later that day. She had been wearing those stupid red pajamas that hid whatever curves she might have, her face worn with worry. He sat in the kitchen, the body heat of the associate editor still cooling on his skin, and yet he realized that he would rather have spent time talking to Ellen than be in bed with any willing blonde. And she had told him off, only a little and so mildly that he might not have noticed, but when he finally tumbled into the already rumpled sheets of his bed alone, he realized that he felt regret about what had happened between him and the associate editor. It was not a sensation that he was familiar with. He decided that he would call her, not to ask her out again or to try to take the relationship further, but just because calling her seemed like the decent thing to do, and after fifteen minutes in the company of Ellen, Matt found that he wanted to be decent. It was a complaint that intensified the more he got to know her. Nevertheless, it was two weeks since his night with the associate editor and he hadn't called her yet. It seemed that the desire to be decent and the actuality of it weren't quite on a par yet.

What had begun to trouble Matt was just how often he thought about his landlady, and whether or not the kinds of things he was thinking or feeling were the kinds of things that invariably ended up trashing a friendship. Even now, as Pete went on about some women at the bar, Matt kept thinking about Ellen standing barefoot in those pajamas. There could not have been a less sexually stimulating image of a woman, and when he thought about her, it wasn't sex that was at the forefront of his mind at all; but for some reason he was unable to shake that image that seemed so firmly lodged in his brain, and it would pop up at any given moment, quite taking him off guard.

"Bloody hell, mate—that brunette—look at her, you can tell she likes sex. Look at them hips, they are the hips of a girl who doesn't mind getting flipped over, grabbed by the arse, and properly shagged from behind."

Dragging his thoughts back to the present, in the pub, Matt looked up. Sitting at the bar were two women enjoying a lunchtime drink, both dressed in what seemed like the unofficial uniform of office workers around here, pencil skirts and white shirts, although the blonde's had a faint pink candy stripe. They both had long, glossy, straightened hair. The blonde was slightly skinnier, with what looked like small, high breasts that offered no challenge to the buttons of her shirt, and the brunette was curvy, rounded in all the right places. They were both pretty, Matt thought, but he especially liked the way the zipper at the back of the brunette's skirt strained against the girth of her hips. She was by no means fat, but like so many women, she'd chosen to squeeze into a skirt one size too small for her, which, personally, Matt didn't mind at all. He imagined the red welts that her discarded garments would leave bitten into her skin when she removed her clothes that night and absently thought about how he'd like to trace a finger along those phantom seams and find out where they led.

"You take the blonde, I'm going for that hippy little minx." Pete surged up out of his chair and, finding his feet entirely out of touch with his legs, immediately blundered back down into it again. He scowled at his empty glass.

"Fuck, they've made the beer stronger in here."

"Or you had a couple of vodkas on the quiet before we even came to lunch?" Matt asked mildly. How on earth was he supposed to police a man who kept bottles of spirits concealed all around his office?

"I'll be all right in a second, I just need a few of these peanuts to line my gut," Pete slurred. "Here's the plan. You go over there, sweeten them up; keep your hands off the one with the big tits, she's mine. Tell 'em we work at the magazine, offer 'em a photo shoot, tell 'em you can make them rich and famous, and then arrange to meet them in here later. I'll be your wingman."

Matt looked up at the girls, who by now had noticed the attention they were getting. They looked neither impressed nor flattered, and the blonde waved her credit card at the barman, clearly keen to settle up and get back to work.

"I don't think they're interested, mate," Matt said. "Tell you what, how about we get you back to the office and get a few coffees down you before the features meeting this afternoon. Maybe you could have a little kip in your office."

"No, no, no—they're interested," Pete insisted, slamming the palm of his hand firmly on the tabletop, talking loudly enough for the whole bar to hear. "That blonde's giving you the eye—go on, mate, you go over, give 'em some of that charm you're so famous for, go on. Warm the frigid bitches up."

The two women stood up, collected their bags, and, shooting Matt a contemptuous look, mouthing something under their breath that Matt strongly suspected was the word *arseholes*, left with their noses in the air.

Relieved, Matt glanced at his watch. "Time we should be gone, too."

"Fucking hell!" Pete shouted, angrily gesturing with his hand so that Matt's nearly full pint shot across the table and rolled onto the floor, spreading a sea of lager across the polished boards. "You fucking let them get away! I haven't had a decent shag in fucking weeks. Fucking hell, Matt, you . . ."

"Get him out of here now." The barman had leaped across the bar and now stood with his hands on his hips, glaring at the sodden man. "I can't have him in here, intimidating the customers, swearing his head off. It's my job on the line if my boss hears of it. One more stunt like that and he's barred and so are the rest of you cocky bastards."

He glared at Matt.

"God, I'm sorry—we're going, I won't let it happen again. . . ." Matt tried to imagine the aftermath of Dan and the lads finding out that they'd been banned from their favorite pub because the rookie had let Pete get out of hand.

It shouldn't be a reason for him to fail his probation, but he wouldn't be surprised if it was.

It took Matt some minutes to drag the angry and resentful Pete to his feet and then a good deal more to stagger with him, reeking with stale alcohol and something more, which Matt didn't want to think about, to the door and out into the hot, exhaust-filled, oppressive afternoon on Fulham Palace Road. The hundred yards to their office entrance and the air-conditioned shelter it offered seemed very far away.

"Let's not go back," Pete coaxed blearily in Matt's ear. "Let's go over the road to that Irish pub. They'll serve any fucker. . . ."

"Pete, we've got an editorial meeting in under an hour and you're totally fucked. You need to get back and sober up quick." Matt was resolute.

"I'll be fine," Pete said, lurching into Matt so that he in turn staggered into a passing woman, nearly knocking her off her feet and unleashing a tirade of curses from her in a language that he was very grateful not to understand.

"No, you will not. We're going back." Matt put one arm around Pete's back, supporting him under his hot and fetid armpit, and with gritted determination propelled him down the road and into the office building. With relief he saw the lift doors slide open, and he bowled his charge into the cubicle before it could move.

It was only when he had Pete propped in a corner, pinned in place by Matt's steadying hand on his chest, and the doors had closed that Matt realized he was not alone. The associate editor stood in the corner, staring resolutely at the panel of illuminated numbers. His gut sinking, Matt really wished that he had found the time to make that call after all.

"Hello . . ." Matt had called her associate editor so repeatedly that her actual name had escaped him.

"You got home okay then?" he inquired belatedly, talking to her back. "The other night?" Matt watched her shoulders rise and fall in an almost imperceptible sigh before she turned to face him, her pretty features set and tense.

"Yes, thanks, luckily I found a taxi driver at the end of the road who didn't turn out to be a mugger or a rapist." Unsurprisingly, she was angry with him, but not as angry as she would be if she ever got sight of that column, he thought. He remembered Ellen in the kitchen, her quiet disapproval when he'd told her about his night with the associate editor, and he squirmed internally.

"Everything okay then . . . ?" Matt cursed himself inwardly, her name simply would not come to mind.

She barked a mirthless laugh. "Lucy," she said flatly. "My name is Lucy, and yes, everything is fine, except that I'm the kind of idiot who wakes up with a fuck of a hangover after letting someone who is obviously an utter, utter twat take me home, get me into bed, and then kick me out in the middle of the night without so much as even phoning me a taxi. And you don't even remember my name, you arsehole!" She rolled her eyes to the ceiling. "God, I hate myself. I make myself sick. I just did everything the magazine I work for is constantly telling its readers not to do—and for *you*, of all fuckwits—I mean sure, you're pretty, but that's about it. You've got the conversational skills of a mentally impaired rottweiler and your bedroom skills are frankly lacking in finesse." She sighed as the lift stopped at her floor. "When will women finally learn what cunts men are?"

"Hey, hang on, that's not fair—Lucy!" Feeling compelled to go after her and to have his moment of decency, albeit a couple of weeks late, Matt momentarily stepped away from Pete, who immediately threatened to topple like a felled tree, forcing Matt to stay where he was to shore him up again. He called out of the lift just as the doors began to slide shut, "I didn't turn you out, it was like I told you, my landlady . . . and anyway, I was going to call you . . ." The lift doors closed before Matt could finish his explanation, which he realized belatedly wouldn't have exactly done him any favors with Ellen.

Still, Matt felt unjustly slighted. How did Lucy know that he hadn't been about to call her and ask her out again, how did she know that he hadn't been telling the truth about his landlady being a dragon and that of course he would have called her a cab only his mobile was dead and . . . and the land line had been cut off? Matt sighed as the elevator rose one more floor, groaning as if it, too, could smell Pete's rancid fragrance. Lucy was right, he'd behaved like an awful shit. She had him bang to rights, and, weirdly, he liked her more in that moment than he had in any other in their brief acquaintance. What he should do, what he wanted to do, was to find that column and pull it from the shared folder and replace it with something else. That would be the fair thing to do, but Pete and Dan had already seen it and liked it, so he would look like some kind of cowardly idiot if he tried to come up with a reason to change it now.

"You fucked her, too? You bastard," Pete slurred as Matt dragged him into the magazine office. After a moment's hesitation about what to do with his addled charge, Matt bundled him into the men's toilet and pushed him into a cubicle.

"Stay there, don't move, I'm going to get you coffee."

"Bastard," Pete murmured, resting his forehead against the cubicle wall, his eyes closing and his jaw slackening simultaneously.

Matt paused briefly to look at himself in the mirror, running his fingers under the cold tap and then through his hair, before patting his damp palms against his hot cheeks. Then he headed out to find coffee.

"That for Pete?" Suze asked him coolly as he filled first one and then a second plastic cup at the coffee machine. Matt considered lying, but as Dan's PA, Suze missed nothing; besides, it was fairly obvious that Suze did not like him, which was a bad thing. Suze seemed to wield a disproportionate amount of power in the office. She was the only woman whom none of the lads talked or joked or made smutty innuendos about, and she ran Dan like a military operation, making him look much more efficient and good at his job than he really was, and everybody knew that if you were on the wrong side of Suze, it was only a matter of time before you'd be on the wrong side of Dan. Matt had been trying to warm her up to him since he'd first arrived, but no amount of flattery or charm would coax that perfect pout into a smile. Maybe by showing that he was taking care of Pete, if accompanying a known alcoholic to the pub could strictly be called taking care of, he would somehow impress her, show her that he was more than just another jack-the-lad.

"Yep," Matt told her, grimly serious. "I'm trying to sober him up again. He does this a lot, doesn't he? This is the worst I've seen him, but I bet it's not the first time."

"Or the last," Suze said primly. "Dan puts up with it because Pete helped him a lot when he was a rookie, got him some breaks that got him where he is today. That's why he's practically the only person in the industry who'll give Pete a job—but he won't be able to turn a blind eye for much longer. The old fool's getting out of hand."

"What should I do?" Matt asked miserably, hoping that by appealing to her expertise, she'd be flattered and impressed by him.

"Get that down him, then get him into his office to sleep it off. Whatever you do, don't let him come to the meeting. If he turns up drunk, then Dan'll have no choice but to sack him, which would put him in a foul mood, which is bad news for the rest of us. The trick is to keep him on an even enough keel to make it okay to keep him on."

"Right," Matt said, staring at the two coffees and wondering if the watery gray concoctions would be nearly enough to perform the required miracle. "But how do I stop him leaving his office if I'm at the meeting?"

Suze looked him up and down with an ill-disguised sneer

that made Matt worry about what exactly he'd done to deserve it, and shrugged.

"You'll have to stay with him," she instructed. "Don't worry, Dan loves your columns, especially the one about Carla—he laughed out loud when he read it. Everyone thought it was the funniest thing they'd read in ages. You did a real hatchet job on her, didn't you? You don't need to be at the meeting to impress him."

"You do realize that it wasn't really about Carla, don't you?" Matt winced, beginning to understand the chill in the air that had persisted ever since his first column had been printed.

Suze pursed her glossy lips and tipped her chin back. "Let me see—how did it go? 'Redheads are supposed to be fiery in the bedroom (and every other room) and this makeup-girl minx was no exception,'" she quoted verbatim. "'It was obvious from the first minute that we met that it wouldn't take much to get her to take her clothes off, but what took me pleasantly by surprise was how quickly she ripped off mine! The second we got into her apartment, she had me pinned up against the wall, powerless to resist as she rubbed her gorgeous body up against me. . . .'" Suze broke off, shaking her head in disgust. "I get it, I get that I work for a magazine that treats women like lumps of meat to be pawed at. But at least those girls in the pictures choose to take their clothes off and want a load of men they don't know to whack off over them. It's their choice. Carla didn't choose that."

"She chose to come out with me, though," Matt defended himself. "And she chose to go to bed with me, even if it wasn't exactly like that. It's not as if I forced her. She chose to be with me."

"Yes—the poor bloody bitch," Suze said bitterly. "And it's all my fault. *I've* been encouraging her to get out there again and meet men. *I've* been telling her that not all men are bastards like her ex and that she should take a chance." Suze shook her head. "Did you think for a second to find out anything about her apart from her cup size? For the last year she's been trying to break free from some tosser of a photographer who cheated on her, stole from her, and beat her up. A few weeks ago she finally got the guts to get shut of him for good and the poor girl's been in pieces ever since. Then you turn up and act all sweet and charming, act like you're interested in her, and she makes the mistake of taking you at face value and going too far too fast. That makes her naïve—but it doesn't give you the right to treat her like a joke and it doesn't give you the right to spread her all over the pages of a national magazine like one of those cheap sluts on the cover. She was just about getting her act back together and you've destroyed her all over again. But don't worry about it, Matt—because Pete and Dan and all the arseholes out there on the floor think it's hilarious. So, good for you, Matt. Bravo. Enjoy babysitting Pete."

Suze thundered out of the office, jogging Matt's elbow as she went so that some of the coffee in the plastic cups slurped over the side and burned the back of his hand, causing him to drop both of them on the floor.

"Fuck," Matt muttered under his breath as he pulled out reams of hand towels from the dispenser, dropped them on the floor, and trod them into the slowly spreading lake of machine coffee. "Fuck, fuck, fuck."

What was it about the women around here that made them want to break his balls today? It must be something in the water, he thought; he'd never got this grief back in Manchester. But then again, he never messed about in his own backyard back home either, except on that one very, very ill-advised occasion. It probably wasn't that London women were more pissed off than northern ones, it was more that they knew where to find him.

And in his mind's eye there was still that image he couldn't get rid of that made him feel all the more uncomfortable about what he had done since he had arrived here.

Ellen in her red pajamas, standing in her bare feet on those cold kitchen tiles.

CHAPTER Ten

Ellen paused, her fingers hovering over the keyboard. Eliza, who was just on the point of being ravished by a Royalist rogue who had kidnapped her on the road, had broken free and killed her attacker in her first fiery display of determination not to be made a victim again. Ellen was breathless with excitement. She had fallen headfirst into the story as Allegra talked and she typed, the office, the computer fading out—her former dining room transforming into a stale-smelling bedroom in a seventeenth-century coaching inn. And then, just as Eliza put a permanent end to her attacker's assault, Allegra had stopped talking. Ellen raised her head to look at the older woman, who was reclining on her chaise longue, her eyes closed. They had decided that morning that considering how late Allegra was with the book, it would be quicker for her to dictate to Ellen, who would type it directly into an electronic format. Ellen waited and still her boss did not move a muscle.

"Allegra?" Ellen's voice was low. Perhaps the old lady had drifted off, although Ellen could not believe that was possible after the breathless excitement of the passage that she had just typed up. More likely she was in the throes of some creative moment of enlightenment—having never spent much time around truly creative people before, Ellen wasn't sure what the throes of creative enlightenment would look like. Simon had said that Allegra was suffering something of a writer's block, or at least a problem with establishing the flow of the story, but Ellen couldn't see what he meant. When she attempted to write her own stories, something she hadn't been able to bring herself to do in several months, she'd sit in her chair at the kitchen table and chew the end of a Biro until something came out, usually some stuff and nonsense about a woman and her house and her husband and her son. She'd um and er and huff and puff over a couple of paragraphs at the most, which had always made Nick chuckle—her attempts at authordom, as he referred to them; he'd come in, peer over her shoulder for a brief moment, then rub the back of her neck and say something along the lines of "still no inspiration strike then, I see?" And perhaps he had been right, perhaps her labored efforts and scribbling and scrawling had shown that she'd never had a real feel for writing. Look at Allegra, she had just mentally downloaded at least a couple of thousand words in one go. Perhaps for real writers, real *artists* like Allegra surely was, the process was much more spiritual, like an emotional release. Afraid of disturbing Allegra but uncertain of what to do now, Ellen whispered her name again.

"Allegra?"

"Ellen." Allegra spoke her name with some resignation, as if she had just been awakened from a rather wonderful dream.

"That was—that was utterly brilliant!" Ellen was unable to contain herself. "I was right in the moment, with Eliza. It's so exhilarating and liberating! What happens next? Will Captain Parker come and rescue her and take her back to the manor?"

Allegra's nearly translucent lids fluttered open as she observed Ellen from across the room.

"No, my dear, it's rather too soon in the story arc for a happy ending. We need to put Eliza in rather more peril first, I'd say."

"Yes, of course," Ellen agreed. "It's just that if it were up to me, there wouldn't be a story arc; all of the characters would start out happy, be happy, and then end up happy. But I suppose that would make for a rather dull read."

"Have you ever worked on any of Melanie Love's titles, Ellen?"

"Yes, once or twice." Ellen nodded, thinking of the sugary-sweet faux-regency romance novels where the nearest any of the characters got to peril was dropping a handkerchief.

"Well, then you'll know that dull is exactly what that kind of book is. Not to mention moronic, but still, if there are people to read that kind of rubbish, there will always be people to write it." Allegra's smile was razor sharp. "Now, it was you that got these rusty cogs working again, and the words flowing. What do you think Eliza would do next?"

Ellen thought for a moment, thinking of Eliza standing over the corpse of her attacker. How would she feel? Frightened, exhilarated, confused? Allegra had already decided to move the action to London, so now it was just a question of how to get a fugitive female murderer there.

"What if she dressed herself in his clothes, cut her hair, took his horse, and made her way to London dressed as a man? It was your idea that Eliza would fight off her latest attacker and escape to London dressed as a man," Ellen suggested tentatively.

"How very Shakespearean," Allegra mused. "It could work, though. How much of a fraud does it make me exactly? I wonder that my assistant is the one coming up with all the ideas."

Ellen got up from her chair and walked around the desk, resisting the urge to sit on its polished walnut surface, as she was certain that Allegra would not approve. Instead she leaned against it, enjoying the slight breeze that wafted in through the open french doors, carrying with it a scent of roses in full bloom, mingled with the perfume of next door's freshly cut lawn and beneath that the earthy stench of moldering plant life, last summer's dead splendor, never cleared away and still rotting slowly into the earth. Beyond the unruly and unpruned cherry tree at the bottom of the garden, its fruit rotting amid its roots, there would be the neatly trimmed and weeded borders of the garden that backed onto hers, and the garden that backed onto that one, going on and on forever in a suburban patchwork of love and attention, leading Ellen to imagine her own garden standing out, a single frayed, unruly square besmirching the whole design. Perhaps, she thought, perhaps it *might* be time to venture into the garden again. She watched a pair of cabbage white butterflies dance and flutter around the open door before lifting off in haphazard zigzags into the empty sky. Perhaps another day she'd go out there and assess the situation; she'd think about it, anyway. She turned back to her boss.

"I might have had the idea, Allegra—but you put it into words," Ellen said, her eyes shining from the thrill of being involved in the process. "You're the one who makes it so exciting and so real! I could never have done what you just did, I don't know how you do it—the words just streamed out of you, it's amazing—you're amazing, so just because you're a bit stuck on the plot, it doesn't mean you're not a writer anymore. You're more than that—you're a born storyteller. I feel so lucky that I get to see you in action."

Allegra's smile was wan, but she sat up a little and smoothed her hair back from her face, seeming a little bolstered by Ellen's enthusiasm.

"So," she said. "We have our heroine, in disguise, speeding toward London, where . . . she hopes to find sanctuary with her father's childhood friend."

"Yes, yes!" Ellen nodded.

"And for once he will be a kind and fatherly figure who will want to look after her and protect her and not rip her clothes off," Allegra added. "We always need at least one decent man per book, apart from our soon-to-be-reformed hero. It adds balance. Now, as you quite rightly mentioned, at the moment the book is lacking a little historical context—where should we send Eliza running to that will add that aspect to the book?"

"Well, I was thinking—and this is just an idea, so say if you think it's rubbish—that you might set it in the Tower of London—in the Civil War it was a Roundhead armory with a permanent garrison posted there; they also used it to imprison a couple of dangerous Royalist supporters. I thought we could make him protector of the garrison general."

"Perfect—he could be an honest and forthright man who believes in the true cause of the war and in a republic for the people."

"Exactly—the people of London were so sick and tired of Charles and his blinkered belief in divine rule, by that time," Ellen told her. "They really believed that England could be a republic, where all men and women were equal. It's quite revolutionary when you think about it, not that it would have ever worked, especially not with Cromwell in charge."

"And," Allegra said thoughtfully, "perhaps while she is there, Eliza can become involved in some secret mission, some way to help the puritan cause? Now is the point in the arc when we want to start to show that her experiences have changed her."

"That she isn't just a girl anymore—but that she's becoming a strong, independent woman," Ellen added, seeing herself for a moment as if through a window. A woman on her own, earning her own money, paying her own bills. It gave her an unexpected thrill of exhilaration.

Allegra nodded. "Yes, yes—it's perfect, and then our dear Royalist Captain Parker will have to stray right into the enemy's nest to track down the woman whom he does not yet know he loves. . . ." Allegra looked thoughtful. "Let's say he's followed her trail, gathered that it must have been she who murdered our villain—a villain that we can make into someone important to the Royalist cause—and perhaps it is Captain Parker who is charged with discovering his murderer and then must bring his own true love to the noose!" Allegra's eyes sparkled as she spoke.

"Brilliant!" Ellen clasped her hands together. "You see? Now you are the one who's coming up with all the ideas. Soon you won't need me to do anything but type."

"I'm not at all sure about that." Allegra smiled. "I've known you only a few weeks and yet I have a feeling that you are my amulet, my lucky charm. You get this old brain creaking again, Ellen." The two women smiled at each other, Ellen feeling a rare moment of pure pleasure.

"I have a splendid idea," Allegra went on. "We've worked so hard these last two weeks, we haven't been out of the house! How about you and I go on a research trip to the tower, you know, soak up the atmosphere, find out a little more about the history, and afterward we can make Simon take us to lunch at that Conran restaurant—the one at the foot of Tower Bridge—what's it called? He's been promising me a good lunch for weeks now."

"Pont de la Tour," Ellen said slowly. "And yes, that would be a good idea—but don't forget—it's peak tourist season. We wouldn't be able to move for the crowds, we'd get no sense of atmosphere at all. And in this heat, with all of those people, I'm not sure you'd enjoy it, Allegra."

Ellen thought of the throngs that were always pressing into every nook and cranny of London's tourist hotspot, and her heart raced at the thought of being caught up in that great, indifferent crowd of strangers. She swallowed and shook the image from her head, choosing instead to focus on a ladybird that was crawling up the glass of the open french door. Now that the inside had been freshly painted, Ellen noticed that the outside was peeling and cracked. Vaguely she wondered if all the external woodwork was in need of similar repair.

"You have a point." Allegra wrinkled her nose at the thought of the mass of the great unwashed. "Although it rather irks me that I am getting too old for crowds. During my life I've found that almost all of the best things happen in crowds, parties, orgies—that sort of thing. Still, how are we to know our locations if we do not visit them?"

"Easy!" Ellen smiled. "Google maps." She opened the Web browser on her laptop and brought up the right page. After a few minutes she found the location and brought it over to show Allegra. "See, you don't actually need to go anywhere anymore, you can walk down almost any street without ever leaving the house. It's brilliant!"

"Good Lord." Allegra peered uncertainly at the screen. "I wonder that anyone will ever leave their homes soon; we will all be living virtual lives in a virtual reality."

"Yes, but when you think about it, that's sort of what a novel is, isn't it?—a virtual reality," Ellen said. "I don't think it's all that bad, is it? There's nothing wrong with having a place to escape to. A place to feel safe in."

"Perhaps." Allegra watched her. "But I tend to think that life is made up of the muck and grit, the dirt and danger of the real world. The world we are born into, kicking and screaming and gasping for air. To try to escape the daily fight is to excuse yourself from living, isn't it? And you want to be a writer, Ellen, and to be a writer you need to live life. Not watch it go by out your window."

"I don't want to be a writer!" Ellen smiled. "I don't have the talent for it. I just love reading and sometimes I've had a go at writing for fun, but I could never do what you do, Allegra. It's just not in me."

"Well, that is arguable, but if it isn't in you, then perhaps that's only because you are not in it."

"I beg your pardon?" Ellen asked, but Allegra shrugged the comment away.

"Very well, agreed that we will not visit the tower in person, but I am still determined to have my good lunch and I am determined that you will come with me; after all, you are just as deserving as I am, if not more."

"Well, um, thank you," Ellen said, her smile wavering. "Thank you. I'm sure that would be really nice and I'd love to come—if I can."

"That's settled then, I shall telephone Simon about it this afternoon," Allegra said. "Now let's talk about Eliza and Captain Parker. She hates him, and with good reason; after all, he took from her what was hers only to bestow. But now she's had that terrible experience with her uncle and the man she's killed, she might perhaps see a subtle difference. The captain did not hurt her and he made her feel the awakening of desire that she is unable to forget, so although she hates him she yearns for him, too."

"Mmmm," Ellen said. "The thing is, I've read all of your books and I love them, but I've never quite been able to get my head around the fact that the man who forces himself on a woman at the beginning of a book can be the same man she falls in love with at the end. I mean, while I'm reading it, I'm swept along with it, it all makes sense, but afterward, I wonder—would that really happen?"

"Of course not, but this is fantasy, dear—and whether we admit it or not, many women fantasize about being overpowered by a man, to be absolved of any responsibility for whatever sexual pleasure might be about to befall them," Allegra said. "Don't forget, most of my readers are married or older women, they are not practiced seductresses—in real life they would never stray from the right path, so in their fantasies they often have no choice. Goodness knows, the debate about whether my fiction glamorizes rape has raged on for each of the thirty years I've been writing, but what I'm writing isn't real, it's a safe environment where a woman can indulge in certain thoughts—I haven't met a woman yet who would not secretly like to be tied to the bedpost with a silk scarf or two and toyed with a little by her lover."

"Haven't you?" Ellen exclaimed, genuinely shocked.

Allegra's smile was mischievous. "Well, didn't you?"

"Me? Tied up and . . . No, it was never like that with me and Nick." Ellen found herself blushing, flashes of the last time that she and Nick had made love materializing before her eyes for one painful moment, him moving above her, his eyes closed, her watching him, willing him to look at her, just for one moment—to see her the way that only he ever could. It had been a quiet, sacred, special thing, the last time that they had made love, and afterward she had rested her head on Nick's chest and listened to his heartbeat as he slept.

"What a shame. So what was sex like?" Allegra asked flatly. Ellen hesitated; one thing she had never done was discuss her sex life with anyone other than her husband. Not even with him, to be honest—it simply wasn't something they ever sat down and talked about.

When she first met Nick, she'd been working as a research assistant at the British Museum, cataloging and dating the reams of various artifacts that the museum owned but did not have the room to put on permanent display. And when she'd come into work glowing after a night out with him, her friends and colleagues would quiz her on every tiny detail of her date, even on his prowess in bed. Ellen had told them nothing, partly because she was far too shy to talk about anything like that and partly because there was hardly anything to tell. For the first few months of their relationship Nick had barely touched her, their physical contact hardly stretching beyond a good-night kiss, his hand resting chastely on her waist, which would invariably leave Ellen on the wrong side of her front door, wondering exactly what it was he saw in her when he seemed to desire her so little. Once, after months of dating him, over dinner after one glass of wine too many, she had asked him flat out if he fancied her. Nick had laughed, making Ellen feel, she remembered, rather foolish.

"Do I fancy you?" He'd repeated the question. "Have you seen yourself, Ellen, with your black hair and green eyes and those curves . . . my God, I don't think there is a man alive who would not want you."

"But then why haven't we . . . I mean it's been nearly six months and we haven't even, you know." Ellen had leaned across the table, feeling the excess of wine slosh around inside her skull. "You haven't even tried to put your hand up my top."

Nick had given her this look, as if he was very slightly disappointed in her for even asking. It was a look that had set her back in her chair.

"Don't you get it, Ellen?" he'd asked, looking a little offended. "You are the woman I'm going to marry. The woman who's going to have my children and who I'm going to spend the rest of my life with. What's six months in a lifetime? When we make love for the first time I want you to know that it's special, that it's forever. When I make you mine, I want to make sure that you *are* mine—we have all the time in the world, Ellen. We have forever, after all."

Ellen remembered how breathless she'd felt when his fingertips had reached across the table and touched the back of her hand, the electric shock that had shivered through her body at the merest suggestion of contact. She had been overwhelmed by the romance of the moment, consumed with happiness at her luck in finding a man who would cherish her so.

"Yes," she'd whispered happily. "Oh yes, Nick, I will marry you."

"Hang on, darling." Nick had chuckled. "I haven't asked you yet. All in good time. You'll find out when I'm ready—and in the meantime, let's just take our time, shall we?"

And after Nick had chosen his moment, proposing to her over a picnic held on the banks of the Seine, and they were married on the date that he chose, Ellen had decided to take Nick's advice and give up working for the museum. Her female friends had gradually dropped away, and little by little Nick, and then a little later, Charlie, had become her life, a life that she reveled in. It was funny, but in all those years, up until that very moment, Ellen had never once missed the tipsy nights out that she used to enjoy with the girls, but somehow talking to Allegra brought back to her what it used to be like, how she never laughed in quite the same way or as hard with her husband as she had with her female friends. And yet now she wasn't at all certain that any of the numbers she had for them in her battered address book would still be relevant. She'd lost all of those people who had once been so important to her without even noticing, she'd been so caught up in her new life with Nick.

Once, Hannah had asked her with a raised eyebrow what her sex life with Nick was like, and Ellen had told her to mind her own business. She never talked about that kind of thing with anyone, and especially not with Hannah. Nick would have been appalled. And yet somehow it sort of felt okay to talk about it with Allegra. Allegra was impartial, like some Greek goddess reigning over a chessboard of mortals. Her interest in Ellen's sex life wasn't salacious or intrusive, it was impartial.

Ellen slid her bottom up onto the surface of the desk, forgetting what Allegra might think as she pondered her question.

"It was quiet—you know. Nick was always so gentle with me, so tender. I mean, he made me feel unbelievably beautiful. He used to love that he was the only man in the world who got to . . . well, look at me, you know—that way."

"You are unbelievably beautiful, that's simply a fact," Allegra told her. "It's a rare beauty when even in those sacks you insist on wearing, with your hair all scraped up and having clearly been nowhere near makeup in several years, you still have that glow about you, that look of a woman, to paraphrase Margaret Mitchell, who needs to be kissed, and well, by someone who knows how."

"I'm not sure about that." Ellen's eyes widened as she was haunted momentarily by her fantasy vision of Matt gripping her firmly in a hay barn.

"So your husband was gentle with you; was he passionate, too?" Allegra persisted.

"Oh yes—well, I mean he didn't rip off my clothes or fling me about. That just wasn't Nick, but he was very passionate about our marriage, about the way it should be." Ellen smiled fondly as she remembered. "He was an old-fashioned boy with old-fashioned ideas. He was the man who went out in the world, the breadwinner—and I was his sanctuary, his wife waiting for him at home. I know it seems outdated and archaic now, but the truth is, Allegra, that Nick was exactly the kind of man I needed. I'm not a go-getting career girl like Hannah; I don't . . . didn't . . . function all that well on my own, I haven't got what it takes. Nick made me realize that I didn't want to be out in the world, fighting for my corner. I wanted to be there for him and he wanted to make a safe place for me. When we bought this house, he closed the front door behind us and told me that I was home now, and I never had to worry about the world outside the door again. I felt so . . . cherished."

"And your husband was your only lover?" Allegra asked. "You were a virgin when you married him?"

"No, of course not! I was twenty-four when I married him. I'd had two other 'proper' boyfriends but it was nothing special with them. With the first one, I remember I was scared because I hadn't told him I was a virgin, and I didn't want him to think I was inexperienced, so I just lay there totally rigid with fear, until eventually he stopped and asked me what was going on. I had to tell him then and he was really sweet about it, turned out he was a virgin, too; we muddled through somehow. That was Graham. We went out together for a year, and then after him there was this man at the museum, my boss, I'm ashamed to say."

"And did he throw you across his desk, rip a hole in your tights, and take you?" Allegra asked hopefully.

"Goodness no, he was a lot older than me and he had a reoccurring slipped disk. We never really clicked in *that* way.

Anyway, it only happened a couple of times before I met Nick, and then I realized for the first time in my life what it meant to really want someone."

"What did Nick think of your lovers? Was he jealous?" Allegra asked.

"No—Nick never asked me and I never told him. It was as if when we came together we started on a new page, as if nothing that had happened before mattered. It was us two against the world."

"I see," Allegra said thoughtfully, eyeing Ellen, whose tawny skin was a little flushed from the conversation, the slight breeze that found its way through the french doors lifting tendrils of her dark hair away from her skin. "And now?"

"Now?"

"Ellen, you are still a young woman, a young, attractive, and clearly passionate woman. Now surely is the right time for a new chapter in your life. So—who will make love to you now?"

"Oh, God—no one! No, no one. I was, I am, Nick's wife. I always will be. I could never . . . not with anyone else. It would be a betrayal. And besides, what about Charlie? I have to think of him; the last thing he needs is me, you know, doing it."

"Are you sure?" Allegra asked. "Perhaps a more fulfilled and satisfied mother is just what he needs—either way, it's clear to me, even if it isn't to you, that you are a very sexual person."

"Me? Allegra, have you noticed that you think about sex a lot? You are obsessed!" Ellen laughed, but she didn't deny Allegra's assessment. "The truth is, I just can't ever imagine meeting someone who could replace Nick. There isn't anyone, it's as simple as that."

"Well, perhaps not as a life partner or a husband, those kinds of men are very hard to come by, which is the reason that I have never married. But lovers? Lovers are ten a penny. For example, what about your handsome houseguest?" Allegra's smile was wicked, her eyes sparkling with mischief. "I'm seventy-three, I haven't enjoyed 'congress' for many months, but I can still imagine that young man in a number of compromising positions."

Ellen's mouth opened and closed as she tried to process all the information that Allegra had just given her, and then, deciding that it was none of her business, she decided to concentrate on the salient bits. "Matt? As if he would ever be interested in *me*!"

"He's a man, my dear, he's interested in anything with a pulse, more or less—but that wasn't the question I asked you. I asked you if you were interested in him."

Ellen blushed, thinking again of her hay-barn fantasy, her face betraying her without a thought of loyalty to its owner.

"Well, he is very handsome," Ellen confessed. "And quite, you know, masculine—he's got very nice arms. Oh, look—the fact that he's a man and that he wanders about the house in a towel sometimes—and he's quite tactile—not in a sexual way—but let's face it, any man touching you when it's been so long, it reminds your body what it's like and . . . I did enjoy that side of my marriage. It's hard to come to terms with the fact that all that is over for me. But Matt and I—I'm like his older sister, we're friends." Ellen dropped her gaze to the floor, not wanting to reveal quite how much she enjoyed her kitchen chats with her lodger. "I can't think about him in that way, it would just be wrong!"

"Rubbish," Allegra said stoutly. "Matthew isn't the kind of man to turn down any sexual experience. Here he is, a virile, experienced young man in your house. It's almost as if the gods have brought him to you for your personal delight. He might be the kind of man who'd open a world of possibilities up to you, and bearing that in mind, you might want to consider taking him as your lover."

"My *what*?" Ellen all but shrieked. "Allegra, don't be so ridiculous. As if I ever would, and even if I would, even if I could, as if Matt would ever look twice at me, as if *he* would ever want *me*! He just wouldn't . . . would he?"

"Certainly I don't believe he would fall in love with you, propose to you, or cherish you in quite the same way as your late husband seemed to," Allegra said thoughtfully. "And I'm sure that whatever interest he had in you would wane in good time. But I am also quite sure that, as long as you understood that and determined not to fall in love with him, that if you set your mind to it you could have him in your bed whenever you chose, at least for a while."

Words quite failing her, Ellen emitted a kind of strangulated squeak, and glancing at her watch was glad to see that it was past five in the afternoon; she had been so engrossed in her work with Allegra that she hadn't heard Charlie come in.

"Well, anyway—that's that for today," she said hurriedly, saving that day's work. "I'm going to see what Charlie wants for tea—would you like anything before dinner, Allegra?"

Allegra smiled, clearly satisfied with her meddling. "I am quite replete, thank you. I think I might take a nap now and indulge in some daydreams of my own. Thank you for today, Ellen. You don't know how much it means to me to have found you to work with."

Ellen was so touched that she forgot to be shocked, and she was glowing with the after effects of the praise when she called up the stairs to Charlie.

"Darling? Do you want tea yet, or do you want to wait?"

There was no reply. She thought he was probably plugged into some contraption or other, listening to music on the iPod that Hannah had got him or playing his treasured DS. Wearily Ellen mounted the stairs and obligingly knocked on the door before opening it, as Charlie had made her promise to do. But the room was empty. He wasn't back from school yet, Ellen realized, feeling a swell of panic balloon in her chest.

"Well, that's okay," she said out loud. "I mean it's only just five and he is nearly twelve. He'll be in the park or with a friend.

It's perfectly fine. Nothing to worry about." Yet she crossed to the landing window that looked out over street after street of houses and toward the park, which suddenly seemed so very far away. Ellen placed her palm against the glass and withdrew it quickly, as if she somehow might be sucked through it into free fall, like she had seen happen in a film once about a jet-liner that had lost cabin pressure.

"He's just off somewhere and he's forgotten that he's sup-posed to phone me if he's staying out with friends," Ellen reas-sured herself, the tremor in her voice belying her calm words. Quickly, she went back downstairs to the phone in the hall and dialed the number of the mobile phone that she had been furious with Hannah for getting Charlie soon after Nick had died, as if gifts could replace his father, but for which she was now grateful. Or at least she would have been grateful if it hadn't gone straight to voice mail, which meant that it was either turned off or didn't have a signal.

Ellen swallowed, staring at her telephone as if it were some kind of mysterious cipher that held more answers than it chose to reveal. Why would Charlie's phone be turned off, and where might he have gone where there wasn't a signal? There wasn't anywhere around here that didn't have a signal; Ellen knew that because there had been that campaign in the local paper about the phone masts that had been put on top of a block of council flats a few streets away. The residents had formed a protest group, anxious about brain cancer or some-thing. They had lost in the end, proclaiming that people in private housing would never be subjected to such risk, which Ellen had felt bad about—but still, the place virtually bristled with masts. Where around here could Charlie be that could be out of reach of a mast—unless he had gone somewhere very far away? Or what if the phone was turned off? Ellen felt freez-ing fear settle on her chest like a block of ice. Had someone turned off Charlie's phone to stop him from asking for help?

Her hands trembling, Ellen picked up the phone again and

pressed Redial and left a message: "Charlie, it's Mum. Look, darling, it's nearly six and you're not home. Be a love and give me a call when you get this. I know you think I'm a silly old thing, but I worry."

She had successfully managed to brighten her voice, but the artifice dissolved the moment she put the phone down, and she stood uncertainly in the hallway, looking at the front door, willing Charlie to come in through it.

Perhaps he was just down the road, she thought. Perhaps if she went to the garden gate and looked down the road, she'd see him coming, dragging his school bag along the pavement, his blazer tied around his waist by the arms, scuffing his shoes with every step.

Ellen went to the front door and put her hand on the latch. Her heart leaped as she heard a key turn in the lock, and happily she flung the door open.

Sabine stood there, her keys in her hand, surprised to find Ellen on the other side.

"What are you doing there?" she asked. "You nearly gave me a heart attack!"

"Oh, Sabine." Ellen did not mask her disappointment, her eyes traveling over Sabine's shoulder to the heat-hazed road beyond. "I was waiting for Charlie—he's late and I was worried—did you see him coming up the road?"

Sabine glanced at her watch. "Charlie is nearly twelve and it's a lovely summer's evening—he'll be playing football or something with his friends. There isn't anything to be worried about, I'm certain." She put her hand on Ellen's shoulder, frowning as she saw the concern etched on her face. "Ellen, you are shaking—please don't be so afraid. I'm sure that Charlie is fine. I know you must worry about him more after what happened to your husband, but I promise you, dreadful things like that hardly ever happen. Statistically the chances of a terrible accident befalling another member of your family are very slim. Come, let me make you a cup of tea."

Not exactly comforted, Ellen nodded and let Sabine lead her into the kitchen. She knew that Sabine was probably right, that Charlie was probably fine and that probably he hadn't phoned her because, as with everything he did right now, he was determined to prove to her that he wasn't a baby anymore, but still it was a struggle for her to master the cold sweep of panic at the thought of her son, out there in some unknown place in the world.

As the kettle boiled, Sabine smoothed four sheets of A4 paper out on the table in front of Ellen. Each side was filled with writing, divided into sections and color coded with a variety of highlighter pens.

"You are a professional with words, would you look at my list—tell me what you think?" Sabine asked, taking two mugs from the draining board. "I would ask Matt to—but I was reading his column the other day and I think perhaps he would be on my husband's side. Men! They are all the same."

"Oh, I wouldn't say that," Ellen said, briefly distracted as she gestured at the chair Matt had picked out for Sabine, a black leather affair supported over stainless tubular legs and arms. "He bought you a chair."

"This is true," Sabine said, a mischievous smile playing around her lips. "Perhaps he has hidden qualities waiting for you to discover, hey, Ellen. Perhaps on one of your midnight trysts you will find out what they are."

"Midnight trysts!" It had never occurred to Ellen that anyone else would notice or even care if she occasionally chatted with Matt over a cup of tea in the wee hours. Ellen felt a blush deepen across the bridge of her nose. "Sometimes we just happened to be having a drink in the kitchen at the same time—hardly a tryst—as if!"

"Of course." Sabine straightened her mouth with some effort.

"Right." Ellen turned her attention to the sheets of paper in front of her. "What's this, something to do with work?" Ellen scanned the list, temporarily distracted. "I'm not sure I'll know what to think. Hannah's the one you want to talk to."

Sabine snorted as if Ellen had just said something utterly ridiculous; then, seeing Ellen's raised eyebrows, she shook her head.

"No, this is not work. This is *my* list. My disgusting, treacherous husband and I talked and talked on the phone last night. He wants us to try again, he wants us to be together and have children and be a proper married couple like his awful parents. Well, I told him that I could not even consider it until he addressed all of the problems in our marriage. So he suggested we each write lists, lists of things that we don't like about each other—he believes it will start a discussion and perhaps enable us to reconcile, the vile, whoring adulterer. So I said, 'Yes, okay, I will do it.' After all, we have been married two years now and I am not the sort of person who does not try her best, even though that scum-sucking arsehole does not deserve my best. He emailed me his list after we talked but I am still working on mine. Please, take a look, see what you think."

As she spread the sheets out in front of her, Ellen glanced at the kitchen clock as it ticked toward six. With Sabine here she did feel a little calmer. It hardly seemed anything out of the ordinary that Charlie wasn't home yet, and Sabine was so sure he would be soon. If Sabine was unconcerned, then Ellen would do her best to be, too, at least for the next twenty minutes. After all, life would be impossible if every time things went a little unexpectedly she'd expect to see two police officers making their way up the front path. Ellen made a bargain with herself: if he had not appeared by six fifteen, then she would allow herself to be anxious and to panic again, but until then she would not worry. She tore her eyes from the clock and looked at the list as Sabine, sitting in Charlie's chair, put a cup of steaming tea down beside her.

"Pages one and two," Sabine explained, "are highlighted in green and come under the category of irritants. Little things that annoy me but don't especially mean the end of a marriage. There are thirty-seven items in this section. Please read it. I've written it in English so that I could ask your opinion."

"Why my opinion?" Ellen was puzzled.

"Because you had the perfect marriage, you know what it takes to make a relationship work."

"Do I?" Ellen wondered out loud as she traced her finger down the first side of the green list: item one—failure to pick up own dirty socks from floor; item fourteen—refusal to ever see a film at the cinema that does not involve violence and scenes of a sexual nature; item twenty-six—mean when it comes to spending own money; and so on and so on right down to item thirty-seven—leaving unpleasant stains on the bedsheets without any attempt to share the laundry chores. Ellen didn't care to know exactly what that meant.

"Well, that *is* quite a lot of irritants," she said.

"Exactly," Sabine replied. "Was your husband ever so annoying?"

Ellen thought for a long while. It used to annoy her that Nick never remembered to put the milk or the butter back in the fridge and that instead of loading the dishwasher he'd pile all the dirty plates in the sink, filling it with water that would soon grow clammy and cold—but then she'd remind herself that he was out at work all day and that it was her job to make sure the house ran smoothly, and she'd put the butter back in the fridge and pull the lumps of sodden food out of the blocked sink drain, and her irritation soon passed. And she would happily have tossed out a thousand more cartons of curdled milk and unblocked a thousand more stinking drains if it meant that he would be back in the house again.

"No, not really," Ellen told Sabine apologetically. "And although those things are annoying, well—we are all human, aren't we? We all have little foibles. If you love someone, you live with them."

"I thought as much." Sabine sounded resentful as she put the next sheet of paper in front of Ellen.

"Here is the amber list, the things that really upset me a great deal but which if he agreed to change sufficiently might not rule out us getting back together. There are twenty-one items in this section."

Item five—flirting with every single woman ever encountered, even my mother.

Item eleven—always mentally undressing other women, even unattractive ones, even my mother, and being really obvious about it.

Item sixteen—openly watching porn when my favorite TV shows are on.

Item twenty-one—spending more money on lap dances than on my birthday present.

"Oh my." Ellen looked from the list to Sabine. "He really does that?"

"Yes, he's a member of a gentlemen's club, the yearly subscription is hundreds of euros, never mind what he pays for lap dances while he is in there. And yet what did I get for my birthday? A juicer." Sabine pressed her lips into a tight knot and crossed her arms. "True, I asked for a juicer, but a little something more—something he chose himself would have meant a lot."

"So it's the fact that the strippers cost more than your birthday present that upsets you, not the actual strippers themselves?"

Sabine shrugged. "Men will be men. For my odious husband, going to a strip club at the end of a night out is like an Englishman going for a curry."

"Really?" Ellen wondered what heinous crime Sabine's husband could have committed for her to hate him quite so vocally, if it wasn't his going to strip clubs.

"So finally the red list." Sabine's expression dropped, pain etched across her face, and Ellen braced herself. "There is only one thing on this list." She pushed it over so that Ellen could read it.

Item one—writing love letters to another woman.

"Writing . . . you mean you found out he was having an affair?" Ellen gasped.

"Yes." Sabine nodded sadly. "Not a sexual one—a sexual one I could have understood, perhaps even forgiven. No, it was much worse than that. He has always stayed in touch with his childhood sweetheart, I knew that. But then a few months ago I found these letters from her, so passionate, so full of love and regret that they could never be together. So I looked on his laptop; he thought he'd hidden them, but he never was very good at keeping a secret. I found copies of all of his letters in his accounts folders. Telling her how he would always love her, how if things had been different, if they had taken a chance when they had the chance. He was so tender, so romantic—he is never like that with me." Sabine pressed her palm to her chest. "Honestly, Ellen, if I had come home to find him in bed with another woman, it would have hurt less. Now I know that I am second choice, that he settled for me because he can't have her. How do I get over that?"

Ellen looked at the words printed meekly on the page before her. A simple collection of letters that when organized in this one particular way became so brutal.

Ellen felt another tiny rent in her heart as she realized again just what she had lost. Nick had been her first choice and she had been his; their marriage had been rare and fortunate indeed.

"Sabine, I honestly don't know. All I can say is that he does seem to be trying; I mean if you meant so little to him, then why would he try to save your marriage at all?"

"She is a Catholic. She will not divorce her husband," Sabine said wanly. "If she were free, would he still be trying to save our marriage or would he be running into her arms?"

Ellen didn't have an answer for that. "What did he write on his list?" she asked instead.

Sabine's laugh was hollow. "There are three items on his list in total. One of them is that I do not laugh enough. Laugh enough! I would laugh if only he were ever funny. But there is nothing funny about this."

"No, there isn't," Ellen agreed. There was Allegra, encouraging her to go out in the world again, even to take a lover, as if such a thing might be possible—and yet here was Sabine, living proof that men like her late husband were very rare indeed. She was lucky to have had a man who respected and loved her as much as he did, perhaps luckier than she knew. No one would ever care about her like that again.

"That I should be more spontaneous, but I don't like to be spontaneous. Not without thinking about it first." Ellen thought that Sabine was joking, but she managed to stifle her laugh when she saw that the other woman was deadly serious.

"That I care too much for appearances. Would he want me if I were fat, or gray, or never took any care with my hair or clothes?" Sabine unconsciously gestured at Ellen, who determined not to be offended, because after all she never thought twice about the way she looked.

"So what do you think? Do you think that these lists will help us reconcile?"

Ellen glanced at the clock; it was twelve minutes past six.

"I have to be honest, Sabine. I'm not really an expert on relationships, I've only had one important one—but if the list of things you don't like about your husband is this long and if one of the things on it includes him being in love with another woman—I don't really see how you could ever get over that. I know that I couldn't."

Sabine's face crumpled and she buried her face in her hands, as if she had just heard the bad news for the first time.

"But what do I know?" Ellen added hastily, putting a hand

on Sabine's shoulder. "I am probably completely wrong—only you know what your marriage means to you and him."

"You are right, of course." Sabine sobbed. "Of course I can't take him back, what honor or pride would I have left if I did, knowing he was always thinking of another woman? It's just that I love him, Ellen. I love the evil, disgusting pig. I love him, I always have, and he's ripped that all to shreds."

Ellen wrapped her arms around Sabine and let her sob into her neck, keeping her eye on the clock. In twenty seconds she would officially start panicking again.

Just then the front door slammed shut and Ellen heard voices in the hall. Charlie's and someone else's . . . Hannah's. For a few seconds she was flooded with relief, an emotion that in turn drowned in her fear-fueled anger.

Ellen withdrew her arm from Sabine, who stood up and went to the sink to splash water on her face, piling her list back into her bag as she went, clearly keen not to be caught crying.

"Hi, Mum," Charlie said happily as he slammed open the door, adding to the dent in the plaster that he'd been working on for some months even though Ellen repeatedly begged him to be more careful. "You'll never guess what, it's really cool. Aunt Hannah's brought me a PlayStation 3 and a load of games!"

"Charlie—it's past six. Where have you been?" Ellen asked, her voice low and tight, the terror she had been fighting to repress suddenly galvanizing into a heavy lump in her chest.

"With me, Ellie," Hannah informed her brightly. "Thought to myself what a beautiful afternoon, too good to waste in an office, so I left work a bit early, picked up Charles from school, and we went to the West End for a bit of shopping. After all, what's the point of having money if you don't use it. Don't mind, do you?"

"Don't mind?" Ellen found that she was shaking again, shocked to her core by exactly how frightened she had been at not knowing exactly where Charlie was, thinking of him out there alone in the world. Her cheeks flushed and her voice trembled. "You take my son off for nearly three hours, buying him expensive presents without asking me, without even letting me know where he is! Hannah, I've been worried sick!"

Hannah blinked at her, rubbed the end of her nose, and laughed. "Ellie, don't be so ridiculous."

"I am not, I am not, I am *not* ridiculous!" Ellen shouted, advancing on her sister with each word, until they were just a few inches apart. Hannah stared at her, her confusion reading as if she were mildly amused by Ellen's outburst, which just served to aggravate Ellen even further. "Don't you get it, Hannah? You might be Charlie's aunt, but you don't get to just take him! You don't get to take him places, buy him things he doesn't need without asking me first. I am his mother, not you!"

"But—" Hannah looked perplexed.

"I told her you'd said it was okay, all right?" Charlie shouted, stepping between his aunt and his mother, shielding Hannah from her older sister. "I told her I'd phoned you and that you didn't mind because I *knew* that if she asked you, you'd say no because you just want me to be stuck here in the house all day like you are and to *never* go anywhere and to *never* have any fun at all. And I turned my phone off so that you couldn't spoil everything like you *always* do. And anyway *everyone* else has got a PlayStation except for me and if Aunt Hannah wants to buy me one then I don't see why she should have to ask *you* and at least she does take me out, at least she will go places with me, which is more than you ever do!"

"Charlie." It was Sabine who spoke, her voice calm and level. "You are unfair to speak to Ellen like that, she was only worried about you."

"And you can shut up—it's none of your fucking business!" Charlie yelled at Sabine.

"Charlie Woods, go to your room right now!" Ellen thundered, shocked by the volume of her own voice, which was seldom, if ever, raised. Needing no further prompting, Charlie picked up the bag his console was in and made to leave. "And you can leave that there, for a start," Ellen told him.

"What?" Charlie whirled around, his eyes burning. "It's mine. I'm setting it up upstairs."

"No, no you are not." For those few seconds, Ellen concentrated every ounce of her anger, panic, and anxiety on him and realized that she was glad when she saw him shrink a little under her glare. "You are leaving it in its bag with its receipt until I decide what to do with it."

"Or what?" Charlie challenged. "Going to take it back to the shop, are you?" Ellen felt her brief moment of power dwindle away. "No, didn't think so. Fine, do what you like with it. I don't give a toss." He kicked the bag halfway across the kitchen floor, its journey stopped with a thud by one of the kitchen cupboards, and slammed viciously up the stairs.

Ellen turned to Hannah, who stood fidgeting with the strap on her bag; her eyes were bright, and a nervous half smile was fixed on her lips, as if she didn't quite understand what was going on. "Don't you see at all what you've done?" Ellen asked.

"Honestly, Ellen, Charles shouldn't have lied to me about calling you, but really, what's the big deal if I buy him something every now and then. God knows his life is so depressing, he deserves a treat or two. And I thought what with . . . well, it being nearly a year since the accident, it would be good for him to have something to take his mind off of things. And you know how much he's wanted one of those. I really didn't think it would do any harm."

Ellen shook her head. It was as if her sister lived in her own impervious little bubble, immune to the effect she had on the lives of those around her.

"Hannah, perhaps you should go," Sabine said quietly, but if she was attempting to defuse the situation, it was too late.

"How dare you," Ellen growled at her sister. "Charlie and I have been through hell together over the last year and we're not back yet. Don't you think I know how hard it's been on him? It's been hard on me, too. But I'm his mother, and I'm the one doing my very best to keep things together for him. You know how hard it is for me to make ends meet and you swanning around playing the big 'I am' doesn't help! It's almost like you're trying to make him like you more than me!" Ellen's revelation escaped her lips before she could stop it. Was that why she was so angry? Was it pure jealousy, seeing Hannah spend the kind of time with Charlie that she didn't seem capable of doing herself?

"Well, that wouldn't be hard," Hannah mumbled under her breath, rolling her eyes like an insolent teen, which blotted out all of Ellen's other thoughts.

"I've had enough of this, Hannah. I don't want you round here or Charlie for a while. Yes—yes it is the anniversary of Nick's death soon, it's going to be hard enough for Charlie and me without you trying to stir things up. So can you please just leave us alone to get through it—after all, *we're* the ones who loved him, *we're* the ones who lost him. You—you have nothing at all to do with what we are going through."

"Oh, you selfish, self-centered bitch." Hannah's laugh was shallow, rubbing disjointedly against the insult. "You really do think the whole world revolves around you and this fucking house, don't you? You love to play the martyr, don't you? To have everyone beating a path to your door to tell you how marvelously you're managing, how terrible it is for *you*. Well, what about me, Ellen?"

"*You?*" Ellen exclaimed. "What about you, Hannah? I'm his widow, I was his wife. You . . . you were his sister-in-law, who, frankly, he could hardly stand to be around. What the hell are you talking about?"

"What am I talking about?" Hannah paused, running her tongue nervously over her lips. "I'm talking about you wanting to keep Charlie locked up here like some little doll that only you get to play with, about you not sharing him, not letting him have any kind of life because you don't want one. *That's* . . . that is what I'm talking about." As she spoke, Hannah's face had transformed into an ugly, vicious mask, her finger jabbing into Ellen's face.

"You have no idea what it's like to lose someone you love—you have no idea what it's like to love anyone apart from yourself," Ellen accused.

"I have no idea? I have no idea—well, that is a laugh. If you knew—"

"Hello, all!" Matt walked in through the kitchen door, very glad to be home, immediately realizing that he'd walked into the middle of something. He froze on the spot. "All right?" he questioned weakly.

"Hannah, come on." Sabine stepped in, putting a hand on Hannah's arm and taking the opportunity to lead her to the front door. "Let's go down the road and have a drink, you and I. I have some work questions for you."

"Yes, let's—let's go for a drink, let's have some fun like normal people," Hannah shot over her shoulder as Sabine led her away.

Slowly Matt put his bag down on the table.

"Fuck—what was that all about? You two looked like you were about to rip chunks out of each other," Matt said as Ellen sank into her chair and found that she was trembling.

"I don't really know," she said, touching the back of her hand to her flaming cheek.

"Well, look, don't tell me if you don't want to, but in my experience booze usually makes a bad situation a million times worse."

"Booze . . ."

"Yeah, Hannah—she was tipsy, wasn't she? I'm sure she didn't mean anything she said."

"My sister hadn't been drinking," Ellen told him. "She

wouldn't, not when she was looking after Charlie. She might be thoughtless, but she does love him."

Ellen felt a pang of remorse. She had allowed herself to become so afraid that when Hannah and Charlie had arrived, she'd simply attacked without thinking. None of it had really been Hannah's fault; she had believed that Charlie had told Ellen where he was going—and could she really blame Charlie for wanting an afternoon out of the house, having some fun for a change? He had made it abundantly clear that he didn't get that with her, and he was right. Ellen saw herself for a moment, trapped in her home like a fly in polished amber, but even if that was true, even if she was trapped, she still could find the will or desire to escape. What was it about Hannah that made her so instantly furious? Privately she could concede that she was jealous of how easily Charlie and Hannah got on, but it was something more than that. Something that had happened since Nick's death that she couldn't quite put her finger on, that meant that whenever Hannah was around, she felt disjointed and uncomfortable. Theirs had not been an easy relationship, not since they were children, but rarely had it been so strained at it was now. Perhaps it was because Hannah was trying, because she was making such an effort to be there for Ellen now. It made Ellen wonder why she had never tried that hard before.

"No? Well, I'm wrong then," Matt said, taking her denial lightly. "It's probably because I'm spending too much time around alcoholics. It was just her eyes—you know, a bit bleary and bloodshot. She looked like people do when they've had a lunchtime drink. But still, I'm wrong. It seems to be my specialty today."

Still lost in her thoughts, Ellen looked down at the tabletop and reran everything that Hannah had said. There had been something, something that she hadn't said but that had been there in the room between them as real and as solid as this table. Hannah wouldn't have gone anywhere with Charlie if she'd been drinking, would she? She was stupid and selfish and vain; if Ellen put all the things she found annoying about her down on paper, the list would far exceed Sabine's in length. Hannah was about as irritating as a person could get, but she loved Charlie—she wouldn't have done that?

Ellen looked at Matt, sitting opposite her, looking at a loss as to what to do. *Poor man,* Ellen thought. *This is the last thing that he needs after a hard day's work.*

"Tell you what, you tell me what the fight was all about and I'll tell you how I officially became the shittiest man on earth today."

Ellen explained everything that had happened, looking at Matt as she spoke. "I let it all get out of hand, didn't I? I overreacted."

"I dunno," Matt said. "I mean, I'm not a parent, but I imagine that in this day and age, not knowing where your kid is can be pretty scary."

"Nick often told me that I was prone to overreacting," Ellen told him. "He said that I questioned him too much and sometimes made him feel like he couldn't go anywhere or do anything without me knowing about it. He said that I was too emotional, my skin too thin—that I responded to every little thing with my heart instead of my head." Ellen raised her chin a little as she remembered. "He used to say, 'Christ, Ellen, home is supposed to be a place I want to come back to, not somewhere I have to avoid. Try thinking once or twice before you open that mouth of yours.'"

"Really," Matt said, taken aback. "Not sure I agree with him there. Whenever you open your mouth, you usually have something pretty interesting or clever to say."

Privately, he thought that Ellen's late husband sounded like a bit of a dick, but there was nothing at all in the way that Ellen talked about him to suggest that she thought anything of the sort.

"I should go and talk to Charlie, shouldn't I?" Ellen said.

"Perhaps I'll tell him he can keep the games console but that he can't have it 'til his birthday in September. What do you think? I mean, Hannah meant well, trying to distract him from the anniversary—but it's not gifts he needs, or even distractions."

"Sounds like a good idea." Matt nodded.

"I don't want to lose him, I don't want him to drift away from me. He's everything to me—I'm not trying to stifle him, or keep him prisoner. I just love him, I just really love him—he must see that."

"I bet he does," Matt said. "I bet he's in his room right now realizing he's been unfair to you. He's just kicking out, testing boundaries. He's trying to grow up and for him it's going to be harder than it is for a lot of kids. It'll be painful for you both."

"I'll go and talk to him," Ellen said, half rising from the chair.

"You know what?" Matt rested his hand on her forearm. "Let me go and check on him—neutral party, that sort of thing."

Matt took the stairs up to Charlie's room three at a time and knocked on his firmly shut door. "Mate, got a sec?"

Matt waited, and after a second Charlie pulled open the door an inch and peered out at him with one watery, vivid blue eye. Matt's heart went out to him, the poor kid. Charlie was doing his best to look like he didn't give a damn, but Matt guessed that very probably the thing he wanted most right now was a hug from his mum.

"Well?" Charlie asked.

Matt reached into his pocket and pulled out a DS games cartridge. "Borrowed this off a bloke at work. Splinter Cell, he says it's pretty good. I was going to play it later but you can try it first if you like."

Charlie thought for a moment and then opened the door a crack more and took the game out of Matt's hand. "I could have been playing on a PlayStation if Mum wasn't being so unfair," he grumbled.

"Really?" Matt crossed his arms and leaned against the door frame. "You really thought you'd get away with that?"

Charlie shrugged.

"Your mum's downstairs worried sick about you. Cut her some slack, all right? She does her best."

"Why do you care?" Charlie asked. "Why are you sticking up for Mum? You're only the lodger, you know." Matt couldn't argue, nor did he understand why it mattered to him so much that things were okay between Charlie and Ellen. When he'd first moved in he'd been a little embarrassed to be renting from a widow and her son and not taking up residence in some swish docklands crib, but now, after years of getting by more or less on his own, without a thought about whether or not he liked it, he'd begun to get used to the rhythm and flow of a family around him again. A fairly odd, disparate little family, but the five of them were becoming just that all the same, and Matt had discovered that he liked it.

"I like your mum and I like you—you're a pretty cool kid, you know."

"Right." Charlie was tight-lipped.

"Yeah, and if there's ever anything I can do to help . . ."

"Really?" Charlie looked skeptical.

"Yeah, as long as it's not asking for back issues of *Bang It!* Don't want your mum to murder me before I end my probation period." Charlie rewarded Matt with a ghost of a smile. "Right, well, I'll leave you to it."

Matt was on the top stair when he heard Charlie say, almost under his breath, "Cheers, Matt."

Ellen looked up when Matt returned to the kitchen, her olive skin blanched, her face pinched.

"Is he . . . ?"

"He's upset, and angry and embarrassed. But I reckon he'll be all right in a bit."

Ellen nodded. "Thank you, Matthew."

Matt smiled, taking pleasure in hearing her say his name.

"Anyway," Matt said, picking up a thin plastic bag that had been resting by his legs, "I stopped off and bought some lagers on the way home. Want one?"

He cracked open a Stella and drank straight from the can. After a moment's hesitation, Ellen followed suit.

"So tell me about how you became the shittiest man on earth," Ellen said.

"You know what," Matt said, stretching his legs out and smiling at her, feeling an unfamiliar sense of peace descend. "It doesn't really seem that important anymore."

CHAPTER Eleven

Matt watched Ellen watching Charlie across the kitchen table over breakfast. For once, he had arrived downstairs and was ready for school on time, which was interesting because as far as Matt could tell, Charlie still wasn't talking to Ellen.

"Good morning, darling," Ellen had said, unable to disguise her surprise and pleasure at the prospect of getting fifteen minutes to make amends with Charlie before he went to school. "Did you sleep okay? I came up to talk to you last night but you were flat out already." Tentatively she reached over and touched the top of his head as if she were about to ruffle his hair, but then she thought better of it a second too late to completely pull out of the maneuver. Charlie shrugged off her touch and picked up a piece of toast that she had put in front of him.

"Look." Ellen sat down opposite him. "I'm sorry I shouted and got so angry last night. It was because I was worried, Charlie—I got all worked up and, well, by the time you came home, all the worry had turned into anger and I took it out on you. That was wrong."

Charlie said nothing, keeping his eyes down as he munched.

Ellen sighed and sat back in her chair. "But it was wrong of you to go off without telling me where you were going or who with, too. And it was wrong of you to lie to Hannah about telling me." Still Charlie was unresponsive. "So I've decided that I'm not going to take the games console back. . . ."

Charlie's snort was sarcastic and derisory as he rolled his eyes to the ceiling and shook his head, Matt noticed with interest as he ate his cornflakes leaning up against the fridge.

"And," Ellen continued, "if you apologize to me and to Hannah for lying, then we can say that it's a birthday present and you can have it in September. What do you say?"

Charlie looked at her, his blue eyes vivid in the morning sunshine as he appraised his mother with near-naked contempt. If Matt had been able to place a bet on what the boy was about to say just then, he would have put all his money on something bitter, reproachful, and insightful, something cruel but true, because the cruelest things were often the most true. But Matt would have lost all his money, because Charlie uttered only one word.

"Whatever," he said.

Matt watched Ellen's shoulders tense, her whole body a battlefield where her anger and her desire to be friends with Charlie again fought on.

"So what do you have to say?" Ellen asked.

Charlie got up, scraping his chair across the kitchen tiles so that they screeched.

"Take it back to the shop," he told her levelly. "I'm not apologizing."

He picked up his school bag in one hand and his remaining piece of toast in the other and walked out, slamming the front door behind him with such force that the mugs rattled on the draining board.

"I didn't handle that too well, did I?" Ellen said, more to herself than to Matt. "You know, this is my job, being a mother—it's what I've made my whole life about and now I can't even do that anymore. . . ."

Matt put his cereal bowl down on the table and briefly

rested a consoling hand on her shoulder before picking up his keys and laptop bag. He'd stayed in last night, watching TV in his room, aware that Ellen had gone to bed early and exhausted. As a consequence they had missed their post-midnight meeting, and when he'd woken up that morning, well rested and without a hangover, Matt realized that he had missed it.

"If he didn't care about you or what you thought or what you said, then he'd have just gone straight to school," Matt told her, grabbing his jacket. "But he didn't. He got up and ready early so that he could come down here and ignore and insult you—see, it's not all that bad!"

Matt paused to look at Ellen. She was dressed in a man's shirt again, her long hair as yet unbrushed, tumbling over her shoulders in a rare moment of abandonment before being twisted into the knot at the nape of her neck that she favored. She looked like she'd just got out of bed with a lover, Matt realized with a tiny internal thrill, letting his mind wander just a little further for one illicit moment, picturing Ellen in the seconds before she had pulled that shirt on, imagining her lying semiclad on her bed, her black hair spread out on the pillow, trickling between her breasts, which were . . . It was hard to guess exactly what her body was like under the clothes she wore, which was partly the reason why wondering about her was so interesting. Unlike the women who made it their mission to obliterate mystery with low-cut tops and high-cut skirts—and in the case of the models who graced the pages of *Bang It!*, barely any clothes at all—Ellen kept everything hidden, covered. She locked her body away, which just at this second and to Matt's great surprise made it seem even more intriguing. And Matt knew that even if, when he unbuttoned that shirt, the body underneath it was far from the air-brushed perfection that he was bombarded with daily, he would still feel that rush of discovering a newfound land; that he would still desire her, for all the physical frailties and scars that made her the woman she was, as vulnerable as a piece of glass—a piece of glass that for that dangerous moment he wanted to hold in his hands.

There are places that you don't go, mate, Matt reminded himself sternly as Ellen, feeling his gaze on her, looked up and then down quickly, heat flaring across the bridge of her nose as if she had guessed exactly what he was thinking. *And your widowed landlady is one of them.*

Women were wrong about him. Carla, and Lucy, the associate editor, and all the angry, bitter girls he'd left in Manchester thought he was a moral void, an incarnation of women-hating evil, even though he had always, mostly always, been up front and honest with them about his intentions, if not about the column that they were quite likely to appear in. But he had some standards, and Ellen was the line he would not cross. As much as she had started to fascinate him, there was something else going on—he liked her. He liked her too much to try to sleep with her, and more than that he wanted to help her, he wanted to do something to smooth that frown that dissected her brow so neatly in half.

"Better run," Matt said. "End of the week—the whole place goes crazy! But look, try not to worry, all right—this is just boy stuff, it'll pass."

Ellen did not look up at Matt as he left, which meant that she was probably still trying to work out just exactly what he had been thinking when she'd caught him looking at her as if he could see right through her clothes.

"Oi! Charlie!" Sweat trickled down Matt's back as he jogged to catch up with the boy before he reached the end of the road. "Hold up, mate!"

Charlie stopped and frowned, puzzled, as Matt came to a halt by his side, bending over and resting his hands on his knees as he struggled to reclaim his breath.

"Bloody hell, I need to get back in the gym," he wheezed,

nodding at the blazing sky. "It's going to be another hot one, by the looks of things."

"What are you doing?" Charlie asked flatly.

"Well, we go the same way, more or less," Matt lied. "Thought I'd walk with you."

Charlie scrutinized him through his mother's black lashes and shrugged his assent.

"So," Matt said as they began to walk slowly in the direction opposite his bus stop. "That was all a bit of a palaver last night, wasn't it?"

"S'pose." Charlie sighed wearily.

"You do know your mum was worried sick about you, don't you, mate? You do realize that all that shouting last night at you and your aunty Hannah was all about how much she loves you, that's all. And you know you were out of order with all the lying and shit."

Charlie giggled at the swear word, like a little boy would.

"So why'd you do it? Not tell your mum where you were going."

"Because I knew she wouldn't let me go, she never does. She doesn't like me going places. It's like if I'm not at school or at home, she freaks out; even when I do phone her and say I'm going to the park or round a mate's house or whatever, she pretends she's cool about it, but I know she isn't. I know she's sitting at home worrying, waiting for me to come back, and that spoils everything. I can't have any fun when I know she's in the house, all anxious. So I thought I wouldn't tell her— I thought if I didn't tell her, she wouldn't worry. I told Aunt Hannah we had to be back by five but she's always late, that's just what she's like—she doesn't worry about anything, you see. She has a laugh." Charlie shifted his school bag from one shoulder to the other, slipping his blazer off his shoulders at the same time in one practiced movement.

"Okay, I sort of get why you didn't tell her," Matt said. "But you must have known she wouldn't be best pleased about you coming home with a great big expensive present."

"Dad would have let me have it," Charlie muttered, kicking an empty Coke can with the toe of his shoe.

"Would he?" Matt asked tentatively. He wanted to know about Charlie's dad, Ellen's late husband—but he didn't want to frighten the kid off by asking too many questions. "Big on presents, was he—your dad?"

"He liked to surprise me." Charlie's mouth evolved briefly into a smile. "He used to go away a lot, on business trips and stuff, and he'd always bring me something really cool back and not just something you'd get at an airport. Once he brought me back a BMX, and I had an iPod before any of my mates, and the last time, the last thing he brought me was my DS. It never used to matter if it was my birthday or not. Dad never needed a reason to give me a present."

"He sounds like a pretty generous guy," Matt observed, privately wondering if the gifts were to make up for a father's long absences.

"He was," Charlie affirmed with a nod. "*And* he was funny. He was the funniest man *ever,* he really used to make me and Mum laugh. She used to laugh so hard that tears would come out of her eyes, seriously!" Charlie looked at Matt, determined to make sure that he believed him about his father's peerless comedy talents.

"I bet," Matt said, wondering what it would take to make Ellen laugh like that again. "What else do you miss about him?"

"His smell," Charlie said, softly. "He had this smell that was just Dad. When he'd get in from work he'd always come and see me, even if it was really late. Give me a kiss, because you know, I was still a little kid then and I liked kisses. And he used to smell of aftershave and the cigarettes that Mummy used to pretend she didn't know he smoked and just . . . him. Even if I was properly asleep when he came to kiss me good night, I'd still know he was there. I'd smell him in my sleep. And I miss his hugs. And playing football with him in the garden on the Sundays when he was home, and taking our bikes down to the park, and last May he had a bit of time off of work so he took me, just me and him on our own, to Center Parc for a long weekend and we did all these things, biking and climbing and swimming, just us. And we had dinner together and we talked and talked and talked, just us two. And he said that he'd always love me, no matter what happened. I should always re-member that he loved me more than anything. . . ."

Charlie trailed off and Matt didn't attempt to prompt him further, taken back fifteen years by those words. He'd heard that phrase before: "No matter what happens, remember I love you, son." His dad had said that to him one Saturday over a McDonald's after he'd taken him to see his favorite soc-cer team, Manchester United. Matt remembered that he'd blushed and told his dad not to be so worried that someone might overhear. What he hadn't realized as he sat there on those hard plastic chairs under the strip lighting was that that was the last Saturday, the last day he would ever spend with his dad. By Sunday morning his dad had gone, God knows where, with this woman whom he'd told his mother in a note, written on the back of a takeaway menu for the local Indian, that he "could not live without." Matt had never seen him again, and from that day on he had always considered his father a liar, and worse, that a father's love was a pointless, meaningless thing if it meant that you could live without your children. Had Charlie's dad been preparing his son for some change or upheaval, too? The anniversary of the accident was coming up; Matt wasn't sure exactly when but he knew it was some-time in July, because Hannah had warned him that it might be a sensitive time. Was it possible that Nick Woods had known exactly what he was doing when he crashed that car? Maybe things had been so bad with his business that he had thought that cashing in his life insurance was the only way to look after

Ellen and Charlie, and he'd taken Charlie away for a final holiday, to give the boy some memories. Then again, he hadn't exactly thought that through, Matt reflected; causing your own death ruled out any insurance payout, which was why Ellen was in such a financial bind now, and by the sound of him, Nick had been quite a controlling guy—not the sort of person who'd make such a basic mistake.

Besides, suicide didn't ring true. From what little Matt knew about the man, he didn't seem the kind of guy to throw it all in, no matter how noble his motivations might have been. Nick had been a huge man, metaphorically if not literally. He'd loomed large in his family's life. That kind of man wouldn't ever have given up, he'd have battled on to make sure that his wife and son always saw him that way, as their hero. So, if Charlie's dad hadn't been preparing him for his death, what had he been preparing him for?

More likely, Matt thought, dropping a consoling hand on Charlie's shoulder, he was letting his own past color what Charlie had just told him. It was more likely that Charlie had had the kind of father who'd really loved him, who had searched out time to spend with him, who had simply wanted his son to know exactly how important he was in his father's life, and for Charlie's sake, and in some small way his own, Matt really wanted that to be true.

"Mate," Matt said, "this must be fucking awful for you."

"It is." Charlie stifled a sob, half turning away from Matt, coughing up words on each gulp of air. "It is fucking awful because he's *dead* and he isn't coming back. I'm not going to get to go biking or swimming or do anything with him or . . . or smell him or hug him ever again . . . am I?" The question was so plaintive and desolately hopeful that Matt felt tears sting his eyes. He guided Charlie to a bench in a bus shelter and sat him down, standing in front of him to shield him from the prying eyes of passersby.

"Listen, if you want to cry, mate—you cry. It's good for a

bloke to cry every now and again. I'll stand here and make sure no one sees."

Matt felt a curious feeling in his chest, like a slow tear that ran from his sternum to his gut, as he stood there looking down at Charlie, who buried his head in his hands, his shoulders shaking with silent sobs. Matt dug a hand into his pocket and pulled out, along with some change and half a packet of gum, a screwed-up tissue.

"Here." He tucked it into Charlie's hand. "You can mop up the snot with that." Matt wasn't sure how long he stood there over Charlie as he cried, directing his threatening gaze at anyone who tried to intrude on what little privacy the boy had, but he knew that it was long enough to make him late for work and Charlie late for school. He would be even later to turn up at the office than he'd planned, as he'd have to take Charlie into school now, he couldn't let him go the rest of the way alone.

After a load of people had congregated at the stop and then lurched away on the next bus, Charlie screwed the heels of his hands into his eye sockets and blew his nose on the sodden tissue. He looked up at Matt.

"Do I look like I've been crying?" he asked anxiously, the blue of his eyes made all the more intense by his red-rimmed lids.

"Yeah, a bit," Matt said. "But you can say it's hay fever. Hay fever makes you look all puffy and shit, too."

Charlie nodded and looked at his watch and leaped up. "I'd better get to school, else they'll be calling Mum and she'll freak out again."

"I'll come with you," Matt offered. "Tell them it was my fault you were late."

"You don't have to do that," Charlie said.

"I know, mate," Matt said. "But I want to, okay?"

They stood side by side, swaying in silence as they waited for the next bus. After a while, Charlie asked him a question.

"When was the last time you cried?"

Matt glanced down at the boy. The last time he had cried was when his best mate from childhood, Gaz, had found him having sex with his girlfriend in the back of a night club last year. His friend had punched him in the face and told his sobbing girlfriend—the girl Matt knew Gaz had been planning to propose to that night, because he'd shown Matt the ring and already recruited him as best man—that she was a whore and a slag and he never wanted to see her again. Matt remembered the way she'd looked at him, Angie, tears and snot streaming down her face, blaming him, begging him to sort it out, to tell Gaz that it was all his fault, that he'd started it. But he hadn't done that.

Gaz had not been able to forgive either him or Angie, and Matt realized that he'd lost one of the few constant things in his life because he had been unable to resist the temptation of having that which was taboo. It didn't matter that Angie had been flirting with him for months, that whenever Gaz wasn't around she'd find a reason to touch him, brush against him, make sure that he could see down her top or up her skirt at every available opportunity. It didn't matter that she'd been playing a game with him. He shouldn't have gone there. He shouldn't have crossed the line, and when he'd realized that he'd broken Gaz's heart and his own, too, he had cried. He'd curled up on the floor and cried his heart out.

"Last time I cried?" Matt glanced skyward. "When Arsenal beat the mighty Man United—but that was ages ago, so I'm over it now."

Charlie smiled. "You've just been lucky is all. You wait, once our defense matures, we'll be back on top again."

"Yeah, back on top of the championship," Matt teased. "That defense has been maturing for about five years now—they'll all need a bus pass soon if they mature for much longer."

"Ha, ha." Charlie punched him lightly on the arm. "At least we don't cheat."

"What? It's a miracle any one of your lot can walk down the street without trying for a penalty, you dirty southern bastards."

Matt was pleased to hear Charlie chuckle; a good swear word never failed to amuse boys of a certain age.

"Look, I like a kick-about—so you know, if you fancy it, you and me sometime. We can re-create some great matches where my lot's whooped your lot's arses from the past, there's about a million to choose from. That's if you fancy it."

"Cool," Charlie said, looking up at him. "Thanks, Matt, that'd be cool."

The bus slowed and they got off.

"And I'm here, you know, if you want to talk about bloke stuff. Ask me. I'm a professional."

Charlie smiled and nodded, slowing as they reached the school gates.

"Before you go in there, promise me something, yeah?" Matt asked. "Be nice to your mum when you get home. Remember that she loves you more than anyone in the world."

"I know . . . I will." Charlie looked concerned. "I get angry with her, I get angry because she's stuck. She's broken and stuck and she doesn't want to get out. I can't even remember the last time she went out of the house—not for months, though."

"Well, maybe it's a bit soon, mate," Matt said, assuming that Charlie was exaggerating. "Cut her some slack—it's still not a year since your dad died. Maybe she needs a bit more time."

"No, you don't understand." Charlie was insistent. "She's stuck and she wants me to be stuck with her and that makes me mad."

"Well then, it's up to us to think of some way to unstick her then, isn't it?" Matt said, although he wasn't exactly sure what it was that Charlie meant.

"Us? Really?" Charlie asked.

"Sure. It's official, you are my best mate in London. Besides,

I like a challenge. Although I think your mum is doing pretty well by herself right now, new job, new lodgers—that's not exactly stuck in the mud, is it? She's really trying."

"Maybe." Charlie looked uncertain.

"Right. So tell me—your teacher a bloke or a bird?"

"A bird." Charlie laughed.

"Then we're sorted." Matt winked at him. "Never been a woman yet I couldn't charm."

CHAPTER Twelve

Oh, that's awful," Ellen said, looking up at Allegra. Ellen had typed breathlessly as Allegra described to her how, disguised as a man, Eliza had left the body of her assailant lying on the floor of the coaching inn and made her dangerous way to the shelter of the Tower of London, where she was certain her father's childhood friend would offer her some much-needed protection. But Captain Parker had been charged with bringing her to justice for being a murderer and a spy—forced to hunt down the woman he loved and abduct her from the tower in the dead of night to escort her to her death.

"Yes, I know," Allegra said thoughtfully. "The description is far too sketchy and halfhearted, it won't do at all. We will have to go back and rewrite the section where Eliza discovers a Royalist traitor in their midst and saves her guardian's life, otherwise the readers will feel cheated."

"No, I didn't mean that—I meant Eliza being captured and dragged off by Captain Parker. Surely he won't see her hanged, not if he loves her. Surely he'd rather be hanged himself, wouldn't he?"

"Would he, though?" Allegra mused. "We already know that he's a scoundrel. Handsome he might be, and a sensational lover to boot—but he forced himself on Eliza and now is racked with guilt. Perhaps he'd rather see her dead, and not have to think about her at all."

"Really?" Ellen was dismayed. "But I mean, doesn't he love her, wouldn't he do anything to save her? He is going to rescue her in the end, isn't he?"

"Who knows?" Allegra smiled. "But I can tell you one thing, Ellen: it's best that we don't know, because if we don't know, then neither does our reader."

"Ohhhh." Ellen smiled with relief. "But in the end he'll save her."

"Perhaps not. In life there isn't always a hero to save a damsel in distress. Perhaps it would be better if we made Eliza clever enough and brave enough to save herself; women don't always need men to rescue them, you know."

Allegra raised her eyebrows and looked pointedly at Ellen, but it was a glance that went over the other woman's head as she turned in her chair to gaze out the window, to the bottom of her garden, where her thoughts so often seemed to be drawn these days. Ellen saw a splash of color in the untamed greenery—the vivid blue of the irises that she had planted when they first moved in sang out against the lush green on the unkempt grass, and the hot orange of her lilies burned brightly in the sun, brought on early by this unlikely June heat wave. Across the fence, which was starting to rot and which sagged at one end since the spring storms had battered it, Ellen saw the neighbor's wash drying on the line. The woman had a new dress, hanging limp and still in the dead heat of the morning; red cotton, buttoned down the front and belted at the waist, it was the sort of dress that made other women look smart and sexy. Ellen would see her neighbor sometimes, walking down the road in one of her outfits. She always walked purposefully, as if she had somewhere really important to go. Ellen tried to remember the last time she'd had somewhere important to go.

"Do you hope for a hero?" Allegra asked, quite out of the blue.

Ellen turned back to her. "Me? A hero? Whatever makes you say that?"

"Well, your husband took care of you and your son so well, and now you are all alone and putting up with strangers in your home in order to make ends meet. Don't you wish some handsome man would come and whisk you off, take you away from all this? To float through Venice in a gondola, perhaps, or take you by the hand and lead you along the Great Wall of China. Or even just to kick pebbles on the beach in Suffolk. Don't you wish for something to happen, something unexpected and wonderful to take you out of this house and away?"

A brief image of sea stretching into a boundless sky flashed into Ellen's mind's eye and she felt her heart contract.

"I don't suppose I've really thought about going anywhere," she said mildly. "I suppose that all I've thought about for the last year is how to stay here. So no, I don't long for a hero. . . ." Ellen paused, thinking again about the way Matt had looked at her that morning. He couldn't have been looking at her *that* way, she must have imagined it. Young, sexy men didn't look at older frumpy women like *that*. It was simply impossible. She looked terrible and old and unkempt, and he looked young and fresh and like he could have any woman he wanted, and yet, just for that split second, their eyes had met and she'd felt like her fantasy version of herself, standing in a white dress in a hay barn, on the brink of ravishment.

"Just a lover then, perhaps?" Allegra asked.

"Oh, Allegra—stop it!" Ellen exclaimed. "I'm not at all sure it is seemly for a woman of your age to be constantly talking about sex."

"A woman of my age! Pah! Let me tell you, my dear, the body might sag, decay, and crumble all around, but inside I still feel the same desires and impulses I felt when I was eighteen, which is why you should be making the most of what nature gave you while you still have it, instead of keeping it shrouded away like a museum piece. Besides, if anybody is allowed to be obsessed by sex, it's me—it is rather my stock-in-trade."

"I don't keep myself 'shrouded away'—I just like to be comfortable, and besides, what's the point of dressing up when you work from home?"

"When you have a very desirable and probably willing young man cavorting around half naked in front of you, then I would say there is every point." Allegra stroked the tips of her fine fingers from underneath her chin to the top of her décolletage, as if she were remembering a lover's caress. "I had a younger lover once. I was sixty-three, he was forty-two. I recommend it, it was most exhilarating. Be assured I'd be setting my cap at young Matthew if it weren't for the fact that he is so clearly intrigued by you."

"He is not interested in me," Ellen retorted, surprised to find herself giggling like a schoolgirl. She looked up at the older woman, who regarded her with a kind of knowing smile that Ellen found quite disconcerting. "He spends his whole day with a bunch of half-naked twenty-year-olds!"

"Tell me what the best part about Christmas is," Allegra said.

"Pardon?" Ellen frowned.

"The best part about Christmas is the anticipation. It's looking at your presents, all so beautifully and temptingly wrapped, and wondering what on earth might be concealed beneath. In most cases, unwrapping the gifts is as good as it gets; usually there is something unutterably dull lurking beneath that requires you to look pleased and say thank you. But I think . . ." Allegra appraised Ellen for an uncomfortably long time. "Young Matthew would find delights equal to if not more pleasing than anything he might see at work beneath your wrapping."

"Allegra." Ellen flushed, briefly picturing Matt's hands on the buttons of her shirt, slowly undoing . . . no—rapidly ripping them asunder before burying his face in her soft flesh. "It is hot in here, isn't it?" Ellen said, glancing at the open patio doors. "I think I probably need to buy a fan if the weather's going to carry on like this. I can probably get it delivered with the next supermarket shop. Or maybe we could get one of those air-conditioning units . . ."

"Ellen," Allegra said over her. "Ellen. I'm sorry if I've made you uncomfortable. I can't help it, it's the prerogative of an old woman like me to meddle. Besides, I find that I like you, which is most unusual for me. I hardly ever like anyone. So if you feel my meddling goes too far, I give you permission to tell me."

Ellen looked into Allegra's hooded eyes and tried to imagine ever talking to her mother the way she talked to Allegra, and realized that it would have been impossible. Whenever she spoke to her mother, they discussed the weather, Charlie, Hannah's latest achievements, the height of the neighbor's privet hedge, and her father's back issues. They rarely talked about anything . . . internal. In fact, now that she came to think of it, Ellen had never had that kind of friendship with anyone. At school she had been at the bottom of the social heap, the shy, lumpy, awkward girl; at university she'd spent more time in the library than at the bar, and when Nick had come along, the friendships she'd forged at the museum soon became redundant. This was what it was like to have a friend, Ellen realized, feeling a bubble of pleasure rising in her chest. This wasn't uncomfortable; it was good. It was good to be rebuilding her life in her own modest way, finding her way in the world from within these four walls, forming friendships with people she hadn't known at all a few weeks ago. Nick had been so convinced that she would never be able to manage if left by herself out in the big bad world that he had persuaded her not to try, and yet here she was—not out in the big bad world exactly. But coping—no, more than coping . . . *living*. Nick would be so surprised and, Ellen hoped, proud. She hoped he would be proud of her.

"Look, if I'm honest," she said slowly, "I do think Matt is, you know . . . attractive, and I do sometimes wonder what it would be like . . . but even if he does want to unwrap me . . ." Ellen stalled as Allegra snorted with laughter. "Even if he did look at me like that this morning in the kitchen . . ."

"I knew it!" Allegra looked triumphant.

"Even then," Ellen went on, "it's not a year since Nick died, Allegra. The anniversary is in ten days, and to me it still feels like yesterday that the police turned up at the door and asked me to sit down in the front room. I love him. I love my husband. Thoughts and feelings and fantasies—they are okay, fun, even—like reading your books because they are safe, like you said. But I couldn't ever do anything for real, not ever."

"Not ever?" Allegra asked. "Ever is a very long time, Ellen. People will queue up to tell you that life is short, and you of all people have good reason to believe that. But I promise you, when you are alone, life can seem very, very long."

"When you love someone as much as I loved Nick, and when you know that he loved you every bit as much, that doesn't just go away, it doesn't just evaporate. I felt that way about Nick since the first moment I saw him. I don't think it's possible that I will ever feel differently. After all, that's what love is, isn't it? It's eternal."

Allegra leaned her head back against her chaise longue.

"It would be nice if that were true," she said. "But love is like anything else, it's ephemeral, as fragile as a spider's web on a windy day."

"But in your books, love always conquers all," Ellen said. "You've written some of the most romantic works ever; your job title is 'romantic novelist'!"

"Yes, I have always felt a bit guilty about peddling that myth, but like you said, I write fantasies and women want to believe in romance." Allegra shrugged. "Like children want to believe in Father Christmas and Christians are desperate to believe in God."

"But—" Before Ellen could respond, the doorbell sounded, spreading a trickle of fear through her chest the way it always did since she had heard it chime on July twelfth nearly one year ago.

"Well, it can't be Hannah," she said, looking in the direction of the front door as if she might be able to discern who the visitor was through a brick wall and two solid oak doors. "I wonder who it is."

"You could try the radical approach of answering the door and finding out," Allegra said dryly. The bell sounded again.

"I'm not expecting anyone. I had the supermarket delivery already," Ellen said tentatively, remaining firmly seated.

"Oh, for God's sake, woman—answer the bloody door before you force an aged woman to get up and do it for you."

Utterly reluctant to open her house to whatever might be waiting outside, Ellen forced herself out of her seat and, her heart pounding, made herself place her hand on the latch. Taking a breath, she opened it, flinching against the invasive sunlight that flooded into the hallway.

"Ellen!" Simon beamed at her, his arms outstretched, ready for an embrace. "I was beginning to think you'd gone out." He pulled her over the threshold and into his arms briefly before releasing her back inside. "Look at you, you look radiant. I hope you don't mind me interrupting you, but I read the pages that you emailed me last night and they were so fantastic that I thought I'd come and take you and Allegra to lunch to celebrate. I've booked the River Café at one."

"You've booked . . . but, Simon, look at me!" Ellen retreated into the hallway, gesturing down at herself. "I can't go anywhere dressed like this."

"My love." Simon smiled. "A woman as beautiful as you could go anywhere in sackcloth and still outshine every other soul there, but it's fine. I've booked a cab and it's not coming for half an hour. Plenty of time for you to gild the lily while I tell Allegra what a literary genius she is."

"And yet still no Booker nomination—where's the justice?" Allegra emerged from her room to greet Simon, having discreetly reapplied a little lipstick first and with a fresh spray of her favorite perfume lingering in the air; she kissed him lightly on either cheek, one hand resting against his chest with the practiced grace of a woman who knew exactly how to behave around men. It was an impressive skill, Ellen thought, realizing that she had only ever learned to behave around one very particular man. "I wondered when I might get the kind of attention that I deserve from you as the writer who singlehandedly pays your bills. Did I hear you say the River Café? Of course it's not as good as it used to be and it's not the Ivy, but it will do, I suppose."

"That's settled then." Simon took Allegra's hand from his chest and kissed it before turning to Ellen. "Darling, before you go and improve on perfection, do you have anything cold to drink? It's hotter than hell out there."

Ellen looked from Allegra to Simon and back again, her feet firmly rooted to the floor.

"Simon, it's just—I don't have anything to wear. I really don't have any clothes, nothing nice at all. I haven't bought anything new since . . . well, since Nick's funeral, and I just . . . I'm all grungy and hot and I'd need a shower . . . look, you two go without me. Allegra always looks so lovely, I'd just embarrass you."

"Nonsense," Simon protested, "you could never do that—Ellen, I've already said you look perfect just as you are. I mean that."

"Besides, if Simon is pleased with the new pages of our book, then it's just as much down to you as it is to me; you are my muse, Ellen—and you have the best ideas. I insist that you come and take the credit that is due to you."

Ellen chewed the inside of her lip, knotting her fingers together as she led Simon and Allegra into the kitchen and poured him a glass of cold water from the fridge.

"It's just . . . if you'd called and I had realized that you were coming, I could have got ready, I'm just not good at being spontaneous, not without thinking about it first. You and Allegra go. Please. I'll stay here and . . . tidy up a bit." Ellen gestured around the immaculate kitchen, which sparkled like a new pin.

There were several seconds of discomfort while the three of them stood there, not quite certain how to proceed.

"Actually, Simon dear," Allegra said, tucking her arm through Ellen's, "do you know, I think she might have the right idea, it is terribly hot out there. Probably too hot for an old lady like me, we drop like flies in this weather, you know. Too hot or too cold and the grim reaper has a field day. So, as I'd rather finish this book before I shuffle off my mortal coil, perhaps it *would* be better if we had lunch here, if my gracious hostess wouldn't mind?"

Ellen felt Allegra's fingers tightening briefly around her arm and felt reassured.

"Oh, I've got loads—the supermarket delivered this morning." Ellen went back to the fridge, letting the chilled air calm her hectic cheeks. "There's smoked salmon, and Brie . . . grapes—oh, and cold chicken from yesterday, fresh French bread, loads of salad, and some wine—I'm sure I could rustle something up." She turned back to look at Simon. "If you don't mind, Simon. As Allegra would feel more comfortable here, that is."

"Of course I don't mind," Simon said, looking a little bewildered. "Like Allegra said, the River Café is long past its best anyway. I'll just cancel the car and come and help you chop something."

Simon took Matt's chair, and the three of them settled down for lunch, Ellen content to listen as Simon waxed lyrical about the latest chapters of *The Sword Erect*.

"Who would have thought a suburb of Shepherd's Bush would suit you quite so well, Allegra," Simon said, leaning back in Matt's chair, sipping a glass of wine. "I'm thinking of phoning the builders and telling them to delay the restoration of your house for as long as possible."

"I must admit, it is far more tolerable here than I expected." Allegra smiled briefly at Ellen. "I find Ellen rather refreshing, a vast improvement on that last dreadful stain of humanity that I was saddled with. Shame she wasn't washed away in the floodwaters, the ungrateful wretch."

"Lord, I'd hate to get on your bad side," Ellen said. "What did she do that was so terrible?"

"Breathed," Allegra said, with such finality that Ellen considered the subject closed.

"And Eliza is really starting to live and breathe—do you know, I think she is your best female character yet," Simon said, deftly changing the subject.

"That's because in my mind's eye Eliza is Ellen," Allegra told him. "Or rather what Ellen could be if she would allow it." Ellen expected Simon to laugh out loud, but instead he simply watched her over the rim of his wineglass, until she lowered her gaze.

"Yes," he said, with just a trace of humor. "Yes, I can see Ellen rampaging around the countryside, offing assailants and saving the day. Leaving a trail of lovelorn men in her wake."

"Did you know that Ellen has a suitor?" Allegra said, that mischievous meddling glint returning to her eyes.

"A suitor?" Simon sat up a little. "Whom, pray?"

"Her young lodger is quite taken with her. I am trying to persuade her to take him as a lover but she is most resistant. Don't you think she should grasp the nettle, so to speak?"

"God, I hardly know!" Simon said, tucking in his chin and blushing. "But I would think that it would be something for dear Ellen to decide—and neither you nor I. Really, Allegra, when will you consider it time to stop being such a bad influence? It's hardly seemly at . . ."

"If you say my age I will off you myself with this bread knife," Allegra told him with some menace.

"Simon is right, though," Ellen said. "Next you'll be suggesting we put on miniskirts and go clubbing!"

"I wouldn't rule it out." Allegra smiled.

Simon shook his head. "Don't take Allegra seriously, she's

like Titania in *A Midsummer Night's Dream,* she can't help but
stir things up."

"I always thought that whole debacle was more Oberon's
doing than his poor queen's," Allegra said mildly. "But there
you are, that was ever the way of the world. Women get the
blame for the actions of men." Allegra leveled her attention on
Ellen. "Except for women who take action, that is."

"Is that the time?" Simon looked at his watch and sighed.
"Ellen, thank you for a lovely lunch. It kills me to have to leave
you with this old harridan, but I must get back to the office.
We've got a launch meeting for our new series, we're trying
something modern day. Unbridled passion on the photo-
copier, that sort of thing."

"Sounds appalling," Allegra muttered.

"Just make sure she finishes the book," Simon told Ellen,
cupping her face in his hand and kissing her briefly before
looking at Allegra.

"And as for you, remember you're a pensioner."

Simon escaped before Allegra had time to brandish her
knife.

After he had gone, Allegra sat at the table while Ellen bus-
ied herself putting away the lunch things. It was almost three
and she was secretly hoping that Charlie would come straight
back from school today, that there wouldn't be any tense minutes wondering what was happening to him, and that maybe,
just maybe, when he came he'd be smiling, perhaps even want
to talk to her. She worried about the anniversary of Nick's
death, which had started to loom large on the horizon; she
worried about what her son was thinking and how she was
handling it or even if she was handling it at all.

"Did you know that with just a little effort you could be
quite the siren," Allegra said as Ellen stacked the dishwasher, a
loose lock of hair trailing down her back. Ellen did not reply,
caught up as she was in her own thoughts. "Didn't think so,"
Allegra said quietly to herself.

CHAPTER Thirteen

Occasionally, so occasionally that when it happens you find yourself pleasantly surprised, things work out the way you want them to, which was how Ellen felt when Charlie came home just before four, bounding up the stairs and even humming.

She had been in her bedroom, released early from work by Allegra, who had decided that she felt a little tired (which was code for "tipsy") and needed to rest her eyes (which was code for "nap"), and had decided on impulse to go through her wardrobe. Spread on her bed were a selection of dresses and skirts, vapid remnants of a past life when she used to think about what she looked like. Ellen picked up one of Nick's favorite dresses, a pale blue cotton affair printed with tiny chintz flowers, with a square-cut neck, little cap sleeves, and covered buttons down the front. Ellen held it against her body as she looked in the mirror, smoothing it over her breasts and forming it to her hips.

Odd, how it didn't look like her dress anymore, or even like anything she would choose to wear. The color clashed with her olive skin and green eyes and the length, which fell just below the knee, made her look a good deal shorter than she was. And if Ellen remembered rightly, the little covered buttons used to pull uncomfortably over her bust and made her feel that if she made any sudden movements with her arms, they would ping off one by one. She had hated wearing this dress, and yet she had worn it because Nick had chosen it.

Hearing the sound of laughter on the street drifting in through the crack in her bedroom window, Ellen went to investigate, pulling back the thick, cream lace curtain that she habitually kept drawn. Standing on the street beneath her was her neighbor, wearing the red dress that she had seen on the line, and she was talking to someone else, perhaps another neighbor. As she hovered behind the curtain, Ellen peered at the man, but she didn't recognize him. That didn't mean anything, though, she realized—the whole street could have changed ownership in the last year and she wouldn't have known a thing about it. She remembered that just after Nick's funeral many of her neighbors had visited, most dropping cards through the letter box, wanting to show support but not intrude, but some knocking on the door and asking if there was anything they could do as if there was anything they could do. Ellen's red-dressed neighbor, Laura something, if Ellen remembered correctly, had arrived with a casserole. It had been the first morning that Ellen was alone in the house and she wouldn't have opened the door if she had remembered that she didn't have to, but habit had moved her body before her brain could engage.

Laura had looked tired and drained as she held out the dish.

"It's just chicken," she had said by way of a greeting. "I remember that after my husband left me I didn't have the energy to eat anything. You've got a little boy, haven't you, so I thought you might want this. It's nothing much, forty-five minutes in the oven at one eighty should do it."

Uncertain of what to say, Ellen had taken the casserole, the faint earthy scent of chicken and vegetables wafting upward, incongruous on that summer morning.

"Thank you," Ellen had said, at a loss as to how to respond.

"You don't have to thank me," Laura had said. "Just drop the dish back when you've finished."

Now as she stood at the window, Ellen realized that she still had the earthenware dish sitting in the back of her pots cupboard. She hadn't spoken to Laura since.

Laura laughed again and then leaned in and kissed the man, not on the cheek or even the mouth but on his neck, just beneath his jawline. Shocked by the unexpected moment of intimacy, Ellen withdrew farther behind the curtain, but she did not stop looking. It seemed that much more had happened to Ellen's neighbor over the last year than losing a casserole dish and acquiring a dress. Ellen watched as the pair linked fingers in one last gesture of familiarity before parting ways, slowly, until their hands pulled apart, and one last over-the-shoulder smile was exchanged.

A lot had changed for Laura in the last year. As Ellen watched her walking purposefully down the street in her red dress, she wondered if her life would ever be something like that again, a world of possibilities, a view with a far horizon. Her heart quickened a little as she thought about feeling the sun in her hair, the touch of her man's pulse beneath her lips.

Flinging her blue dress onto the bed, Ellen looked over her meager collection of clothes, wondering just for fun if there was anything in there that she might wear if she was going to seduce Matt. The thought made her chuckle as she rifled through sensible garment after staid dress. Even before Nick, her dress sense hadn't been desperately daring. She wondered whether Matt had ever been seduced by a woman in a stitched-down pleat and turtleneck sweater. Hannah always knew how to dress, Ellen thought, eyeing a pastel-pink cardigan that she had no recollection of buying. If not for the invisible, unquantifiable obstruction between the two of them, she would have asked Hannah to give her some tips. Sometimes, Ellen thought as she sat on the bed and raked her fingers through the clothes, she wondered how she and Hannah could possibly be related.

"There must be something in here worth wearing," Ellen muttered to herself. She had yet to find anything when Charlie came thundering in to her.

He stopped in his tracks when he saw her, as if he'd only just remembered that they'd been fighting.

"Hello," he said.

"Hello," Ellen said warmly, biting off the word *darling* before it could escape her lips. "Good day?"

"Yeah, not bad, actually," Charlie said, sounding surprised by his revelation.

"That's good." Ellen gestured at the bed. "Thought I'd sort some stuff out for charity."

"Dad's stuff?" Charlie asked, glancing at the half of the oak Edwardian wardrobe that was still crammed with Nick's clothes.

"No, not Dad's things. Not yet. My old things."

"You should get some new clothes," Charlie said, fingering a folded piece of paper that he'd pulled from his trouser pocket. "If you like, I could come shopping with you on Saturday. We could go to Westfield, it's got millions of shops, there's bound to be something you like—you should see it, Mum, it's massive."

"I know, with shiny floors and a cinema! You told me. Sounds like it would be an easy place to get lost."

"I don't get lost when I go there with my mates, I know it like the back of my hand!" Charlie told her. "I'd look after you."

"Really?" Ellen smiled. "You'd really go clothes shopping with your old mum?"

"If you like," Charlie offered.

"Well . . . shall we see, nearer the time?"

Charlie's shoulders sank just a fraction of a millimeter and he handed her the piece of paper.

"What's this?" Ellen asked, unfolding it.

"It's parents' evening, again. End-of-year things, you

know—see how we've been doing," Charlie said as she read over the letter. "It's next week, you have to fill in the time you want to come and give me back the slip. Mrs. Jenkins wrote you a note on the back."

Ellen turned the letter over. Sure enough, Charlie's teacher had written a message there in green Biro, with the fat round handwriting that all teachers seemed intent on passing on to their pupils.

"Dear Mrs. Woods—sorry to have missed you last term—really hope to see you here this time, it would be great to discuss Charlie's progress with you. All the best, T. Jenkins," Ellen read.

"Parents' evening, that's come round again quickly," she said. "I didn't know they did another one at the end of the year."

"You missed the last one," Charlie reminded her. "And the opening-evening talk about options. You didn't go to that, either."

"I know, Charlie. I'm sorry." Ellen looked at the piece of paper. "It's been a bit of a year."

"But you can come to this one, can't you?"

"Of course."

"Really?"

"Yes, really, of course really. We'll go downstairs now and write it on the kitchen calendar."

"I'm not allowed to come with you," Charlie said as he followed her down the stairs. "You know, so they can talk about me behind my back—but I was thinking that if you didn't want to go on your own, you could ask Matt."

"Matt?" Ellen frowned. "Why would I ask Matt to go to your parents' evening?"

"Because he wouldn't mind, and if you didn't want to go, you know, on your own, Matt would go with you. Matt's cool."

"Is he? Is Matt cool?" Ellen asked, amused. "When did you decide that?"

"He came to see if I was okay last night and he walked a bit of the way to school with me this morning." Charlie shrugged. "We talked a bit about stuff. He's a mate."

"Really?" Ellen was touched. Whatever they had talked about, it had obviously helped Charlie in some way; he seemed much brighter. She just had to remember that all the effort that Matt was making for her and Charlie was because he was a decent young man, not because he had any ulterior motives with her.

"I'm glad, Charlie, but I don't really think I can ask him to come with me to parents' evening. I'm sure he's got better things to do."

"I'll ask him then." Charlie was insistent.

"But there's no need—"

"Mum, I really want you to go to parents' evening this time. I *really* want you to go," Charlie said slowly and carefully, as if he were talking in a language that Ellen didn't understand.

"I will go," she said, pulling open a drawer and taking out a pen. "Here, pass me the calendar." Charlie took the calendar, "Seasonal Scenes of Sussex," which her mother always gave her every Christmas when they visited, just like she always gave Ellen a tin of Cadbury Roses every Easter visit, and passed it over to her. It was still folded open on January, showing a steel-skied blustery beachscape, snow dusting the wet sand. Ellen shivered when she looked at it before riffling her way through an entirely empty half a year, each month's page almost indecently bare of notes, dates, or events. Finally she stopped on June, and then, realizing that this month, too, had almost expired, she exposed July, illustrated with a park of flowers in full bloom, children in sun hats paddling in a toddler pool.

"There." Ellen scrawled the words *parents' evening* on July 2. "Now I won't forget."

"And you have to fill in the form, say what time you want to go," Charlie reminded her, spreading out on the kitchen table the form that she had left on the bed. "Do it now and I'll put it in my bag."

"Fine," Ellen said, wondering why she had begun to feel a little pressured by her son. After all, this was what she wanted, time with him, talking to him. She filled in a time slot, folded the letter along the dotted line, and tore off the response slip. "I'll say eight o'clock."

"Cool, Matt will be home from work by then."

"Charlie, for the last time, I'm not asking Matt to come with me!" Ellen exclaimed.

"Aunt Hannah then?" Charlie pressed.

"No! Why do you think I need a chaperone?"

"Come on, Mum, you know why," Charlie retorted, heat rising in his cheeks.

"Well? Are you worried I'll embarrass you or something? Get drunk and try and hit on the headmaster?" She had hoped to make Charlie laugh, but his expression didn't change.

"No, I'm worried that you won't go," Charlie said.

"But I've told you I will, I've written it on the calendar!" Ellen waved the article in question at him as proof.

"You said you'd watch me try out for the school football team," Charlie reminded her.

"Is that what this is about? You know I had a migraine that day, and anyway I thought that you'd rather not have your mother standing on the touchline embarrassing you."

"And you promised we'd go down and visit Gran and Grandpa this half term—"

"Yes, but Grandpa's back went out and I thought it would be better not to trouble them, they are getting old, you know; besides, they came up in the end. . . ."

"We haven't had one day out this year. If Dad were here we'd have done something. Gone to Thorpe Park, maybe—something."

"I know, I know, Charlie. I know I've been an awful

mother this year. The truth is I just haven't been able to face things—"

"That's not the truth!" Charlie said furiously.

"What then? Tell me, Charlie, what is the truth? Why are you always so angry with me?"

"The truth is you *never* go out. You *never* go anywhere. You never leave this house, and you haven't since Dad's funeral! That's the truth, isn't it? Admit it, Mum, just admit it—you're too scared to go out anymore. You've got that thing."

"What thing?" Ellen asked, reeling as each word her son had spoken was like a physical slap.

"I looked it up on the internet, and it's you. It's exactly you."

"What is?" she asked, with an exasperated laugh.

"Agoraphobia. You're agoraphobic, Mum."

Before Ellen could react, Sabine walked into the kitchen, dumping her bag on the table, her face set in an uncompromising frown.

"Ellen, I'm sorry, but I think Hannah is in trouble."

It took Ellen a second to register what Sabine was saying, because she was still reeling from Charlie's bombshell. This was why he was so angry with her and so distant. He'd got it into his head that she had *agoraphobia*?

"What's wrong with Aunt Hannah?" Charlie asked Sabine before Ellen could.

"I went to see her today, to ask her to lunch—she hadn't answered her extension or email—and when I got to her floor she wasn't in her office, so I asked her assistant to leave her a message. He told me Hannah had left, that she had been summarily dismissed over a week ago. For that to happen, without a verbal or written warning, means that she must have done something . . . bad."

Ellen sat down with a bump, struggling to process all the words that had been hurled in her face. First Charlie and now this . . . She looked at Sabine.

"What—wait a minute. You're telling me that Hannah's lost her job, that when she took Charlie out yesterday she'd already lost it—but why? Why wouldn't she have told us, and what could she have done that was so bad that she didn't even get a warning?"

Sabine shrugged, holding her fingers under the cold tap and then patting her face and neck. "The assistant wouldn't say, but I asked around. There are rumors. They say she'd lost her focus, made some bad decisions that cost a lot of money and . . ." Sabine glanced at Charlie.

"What?" Ellen asked.

"They say she was . . . turning up at work under the influence."

Ellen stared at her hands, which were pressed flat against the tabletop so firmly that the tips of her fingernails blanched white.

"Under the influence of alcohol?" Charlie questioned.

Sabine looked uncomfortable but didn't reply.

"What *do* you mean?" Ellen asked.

"I heard . . . I heard she'd been caught drinking on the job, but like I say, they are only rumors. I don't know anything for sure."

Ellen and Charlie looked at each other, each equally disbelieving. Hannah liked to party, and she enjoyed a drink. And Ellen wasn't so naïve that she didn't imagine her sister had taken part in some of the other excesses that were prevalent in the city. But it was incomprehensible to her that Hannah would have let things get so bad that she was drinking during work. Her career, her professional reputation, the way she looked—all these things were paramount to her. Ellen could not imagine what could have happened to change that.

"That can't be right, that doesn't sound like Hannah at all. Her work has always meant everything to her. Something really bad, really big must have happened to make her throw that away." Ellen thought of her sister's ever-increasing visits over the last few months, her sudden, uncharacteristic desire to be around. Ellen had been so caught up in her own emotional maelstrom that she hadn't stopped to think that Hannah might have problems of her own. "No, she would have told me if something really bad had happened."

"No, she wouldn't," Charlie said. "She knows you hate her."

"Rubbish! We fight and fall out and she drives me mad, but we're sisters. Hannah knows that I'd always be there for her. I mean, she's the strong one, she's the tough and together one."

Sabine shook her head. "All I can tell you for sure are the facts. She doesn't work for the bank anymore, that's all I know. I'm sorry to be the bearer of bad news. I didn't know what to do about it."

"I'll call her," Ellen said, fetching the telephone from the hall.

But when Ellen called Hannah's flat there was no answer, and her mobile went straight to voice mail.

"Perhaps it's because she knows it's you. I'll try her," Charlie said, fishing his mobile out of his pocket and dialing his aunt. Again, Hannah didn't pick up.

"Maybe Gran and Grandpa have spoken to her?" Charlie looked disappointed that his aunt appeared not to want to speak to him, either. "Call them, Mum—see what they know."

Ellen shook her head. "No, I'd better not ring, not until I know something. I don't want to worry them, not with Mum's blood pressure, and Dad'll just worry. He'll just want to come up here and look for her like he did that summer she ran off with that busker. No, Hannah is still Hannah; she's still a grown-up. I mean we only saw her yesterday and she was a bit off—but she was okay. We'll wait, she'll turn up or call. If she doesn't, it'll be the first day in months that I haven't heard from her in one way or another."

"But what if she's in trouble, what if she can't call or come round? We could go round to her place." Charlie suggested. "It's only a couple of tube stops to Ladbroke Grove."

"She's not there, Charlie, she's not answering the phone," Ellen said edgily, irritated that her son was picking this moment to illustrate his preposterous point.

"That doesn't mean she's not there," he insisted. "She might be lying on the floor choking on her own vomit or something. She might be dying and really, really need rescuing." As he spoke, he eyes filled with unshed tears. Ellen pulled him to her and put an arm around him. "I don't want Aunt Hannah to die."

"Charlie, Hannah's better at looking after herself than anyone I know," Ellen told him.

"So was Dad," Charlie said quietly. "Can't we just go and check?"

"Charlie," Sabine said softly and calmly. "I'm afraid I've panicked you. I'm sure that your aunt is fine. After all, it's been a week since she lost her job; you saw her just yesterday and she seemed okay, didn't she? There is no reason why she wouldn't be just as okay today."

"Yes, I suppose . . ." Charlie sniffed, brushing the back of his hand across his eyes. "If anything, she seemed even happier than normal, really cheerful, full of energy. I didn't say anything because . . . well, because I know you were cross, but she was talking about taking me on holiday to New York or somewhere," Charlie said.

Sabine and Ellen exchanged a look.

"Then she is probably fine, maybe even happy about what's happened. I expect she wants time alone to work out whatever is going on. She will tell you and your mum everything when she is ready. Your mum is right to want to wait."

Charlie looked at his mother. "But if she rang you now and asked you to go round, you would?"

"Of course I would, Charlie," Ellen told him levelly. "Look, I'll try calling again in a little while. In the meantime, let's get dinner on and get your tea sorted and try not to worry, okay? You go and play with your DS for a bit and I'll call you when things are sorted." Charlie looked to Sabine, who nodded—he seemed to need her extra affirmation—and then he picked up his school bag and slouched out of the room.

"How serious were these rumors?" Ellen asked her as soon as she heard Charlie's footsteps on the stairs.

"There was talk of some CCTV footage showing her drinking from a bottle of whiskey at a reception after hours. But I don't know, Ellen, it could just be gossip. It's a big office, a lot of people are very jealous of Hannah, they'd like nothing more than for her to have left in disgrace. Keep trying to call her. That's all you can do."

"Perhaps Charlie is right, perhaps I should go round there." Ellen pictured the street outside her front door, the yawning expanse of road that stretched to the tube station, with another four roads and an underpass to negotiate on top of that. Ellen didn't want to go, that was true. She didn't want to tackle the heat and noise and the throng of people who would be crowding the hot and stinking tube trains. She did prefer to stay at home, she did enjoy the quiet tranquillity of her house, and yes, the world that revolved around her here was enough for her. It always had been. But that didn't mean she wouldn't go to Hannah if Hannah needed her. That didn't mean she couldn't go, if she had to.

God only knew where Charlie had got this idea that she was agoraphobic.

"Ellen, forgive me, I don't know you or Hannah very well. But I do know sisters, I have a big sister myself, and there is nothing I hate more than her seeking me out to tell me how wrong I am and how right she is—you should have seen her crowing over what happened between Eric and me." Sabine went to the fridge and took two bottles of beer from her shelf. "If you want to be friends with Hannah, then it is best to wait for her to come to you. After all, if she wanted your advice now, she would have told you everything already, and she hasn't. Beer?"

Ellen nodded, and Sabine slid a bottle over to her. She hoped that a drink would quell the niggling feeling of discomfort that wormed its way into her gut and the underlying sensation that something was very wrong with Hannah. *That's just the way I'm built now,* Ellen told herself, pressing her hand against the fold of her belly as if she could physically quiet her concern. Anything, anything at all, that nudged her out of her daily routine set her heart racing as if she were balancing on a high wire. Something worse, something like Charlie arriving home late or Simon threatening to take her to lunch, made it pound and twitch, missing beats with reckless abandon, and for a fraction of a fearful second she felt nothing but a hollow, lifeless sensation in her chest until it thundered on, leaving her breathless and afraid. But that was her weakness, her legacy of losing her husband, not some prescient supernatural power. It couldn't be, because she hadn't sensed a single dark thing about the day that Nick had been killed. She'd been in the front garden, picking the dead heads off the roses, when the police car pulled up. There hadn't been a moment of discomfort or distress even then, even when they had walked up the garden path, not quite able to look her in the eye. Not until she'd sat down on the sofa in the front room and looked in the policewoman's eyes had the truth hit her like a sledgehammer. She'd felt short of breath, winded ever since.

"May I ask why things are so difficult between you and Hannah?" Sabine asked carefully, peeling the label off the beer bottle with her thumbnail.

"Half the time I don't even know, Sabine. When she was little we were so close. I would have done anything for her, and then . . . the older we got, the more different we became. I always felt as if she didn't want me to be good at anything, to have anything that was mine. Everything I did, she was always there doing it better; everyone I liked, liked her more; everyone I loved, loved her more. Mum and Dad always saw her as their sunshine girl—'Sunshine' is their name for her.

They didn't mean to play favorites, or treat me differently, it was just that Hannah is like . . . she's like a single star in a dark night—you can't help but look at her. Since she was a teenager I've felt like I was living in her shadow. That was, until Nick. Nick loved me, he wanted me—he was the only person who wasn't seduced by Hannah, and I can't tell you how much that meant to me. When I had Nick I finally had *my* life. And then Nick died, and now after years of barely ever seeing each other Hannah is here all the time, interfering, trying to take over. And I know I should be grateful that she cares and that she is trying, but you know what? I feel like she's doing it again. She's hijacking my grief." Ellen paused, caught off guard by her outpouring; all the feelings that had been building in her over the last few weeks had flooded out of her.

"None of that makes me sound like a very good person, does it," Ellen said as Sabine watched her.

"It just makes you sound like a person." Sabine shrugged. "Do you wonder, though, if maybe the way you see things isn't the way they are?"

Ellen frowned. "What do you mean?"

"I mean look at it another way and everything you've just told me could describe a younger sister who is in awe of her big sister. Who looks up to her and wants to be like her, who tries to emulate her, who wants the people her sister loves to love her. Maybe a woman who sees what a wonderful mother you are and what an amazing family you have and who looks at her own life and finds it wanting. A sister who understands how hard it is to lose something that she herself has never known and is trying in her own way to help you. You said you and Hannah used to be close—I don't know what's going on with Hannah now, but I do know if you want it, you could be that close again."

Ellen pressed her hot cheek against the cool glass beer bottle. She felt as if she were almost, but not quite, on the verge of working out a riddle.

"I don't know, Sabine," Ellen said. "I don't—she just . . . she drives me crazy. There's something, something between us that she's thinking and not saying, and whatever it is, just having her standing in the same room makes me . . . well, quite frankly it makes me want to slap her, so there." Ellen sat up in her chair and lifted her chin with an air of defiance.

"Oh well, that's just sisters all over the world." Sabine appeared not to be shocked by Ellen's latent violent tendencies. "If we are not tearing each other's hair out or scratching out eyes, then there is something wrong."

Ellen smiled. It had been years since she'd had any women around to talk to, and now she had two, three of them if you counted Hannah. Allegra's fascination with her had forced her to really think about herself, not only her thoughts and feelings but her physicality, from the tips of her fingers to the ends of her hair. And Sabine—Sabine reminded her of that wonderful gift of female friendship that she had let slip away when she married Nick, believing that if she had him, she didn't need anything else. But the truth was you never laughed so much, cried so hard, or talked so deeply as you did with your girlfriends.

"So, my husband received my list," Sabine said, leaning back in her chair and running her fingers through her heavy blond curls.

"And?" Ellen asked, touched that Sabine chose to confide in her. "What did he make of it?"

"He thought it was a little long. He said if he'd known that we were going to nitpick over every little thing, then he could have made my list much longer. He could have included things like I let my bikini line grow out or that I stopped putting makeup on for him, which isn't true. I just don't like to slap it on like a prostitute, that's all."

"So, what did you decide?" Ellen asked, sipping her beer and wishing she'd added some for herself on her supermarket delivery.

"I told him to go to her," Sabine said.

"To the woman he's been writing to?" Ellen gasped.

"I have to, Ellen. I thought about it and I realize I have no choice. After all, as Sting says, if you love someone, let them go. I've told him to go and see her, to see if he can be with her. How can I be happy living with a man I know is always dreaming of someone else? I can't, so I told him to go to her."

"And what did he say? Is he going?"

"Yes." Sabine nodded bleakly. "He is going to take leave next week and go and see her in Austria. She is *Austrian,* Ellen," Sabine added, as if that added insult to injury.

"And that's it, your marriage is over?" Ellen asked.

"Not quite." Sabine glanced at her watch. "We have an appointment for a Skype chat in a little while. To talk about my decision."

"So he's not rushing off to be with this woman then, even though you told him to go?" Ellen asked, as curious as she was shocked. "He still wants to talk? That's a good sign."

"Is it?" Sabine sighed. "Or is he just absolving himself? After all, if I've told him to go, given him my blessing, then he has no reason to feel guilty, does he?"

"Goodness," Ellen said. "Are you sure you want to give him that freedom?"

"Not really." Sabine sighed again. "But what other choice is there? If I force him to stay, I will always be wondering if he would rather be somewhere else."

"And you wouldn't think of, oh, I don't know, finding someone here to have a revenge fling with, or something?"

Sabine looked appalled at the idea. "Englishmen leave me very cold," she said, adding as an afterthought, "Well, Matt is very sexy, and you can tell by looking at him that he knows his way around a woman's body."

"Do you think so?" Ellen leaned a little toward Sabine, realizing that the third of a bottle of wine she had drunk earlier at lunch combined with the strong German beer had made her a little tipsy, almost tipsy enough to numb her body's physical tic. "Do you think he'd be a passionate lover?"

"Do you?" Sabine asked, amused.

Ellen leaned her chin into the heel of her hand but missed her mark, so that her head slipped and her neck jarred. "Allegra thinks I should take him as my lover, as if I could just sort of lift him off the supermarket shelf and get him to satisfy my every whim. Stud on a stick sort of thing."

Sabine spluttered beer as she laughed. "Allegra is probably right—Matt would go to bed with you. I'm sure you wouldn't have to go to much effort if that was what you wanted. But don't think it would be love, Ellen, or anything like it. For him it would be a sexual experience and nothing more. Don't go down that road unless you are prepared to accept that."

"Oh, God, I'm not going to go down that road at all." Ellen laughed. "Going down roads is the last thing I want to do, at least according to my son! No, I'm a widow and a mother. I'm thirty-eight, boring, and old. Besides, I have a lot more things to worry about. A sister who's lost her job and a son who thinks I'm agoraphobic, can you imagine?"

"Agoraphobic?" Sabine repeated the word as a question. "Interesting."

"Yes—you know, someone who is afraid of going outside. He's got it into his head that that's me. That I'm scared to set foot outside my own front door. Just because I'm a homebody, and I don't like people or crowds or a lot of noise. But that's just me, I'm quiet, and shy. I am a very quiet and shy person, Sabine. I am not at all the sort of person to be having emotion-free sex with a much younger man."

"Really? Are you sure?" Sabine looked in turn amused and then thoughtful. "Actually, Ellen, I have lived here nearly a month now and I hope you don't mind me saying that I don't think I have seen you go out once, not even into the garden."

Ellen shrugged. "Well, I'm not sure I have been out in the last month. But that's not that unusual for me. I mean, I work from home, I have to be at home for Charlie when he gets in from school. My life is in this house—there isn't any need for me to go anywhere."

"No need, perhaps, but don't you even want to go for a walk to the park, sit on a bench and enjoy the sun on your face?"

"That would all be very well if I had time, but I don't have time. Time is not something I have," Ellen insisted. "I really don't think it's that big a deal."

Sabine glanced at her watch again. "I expect you are right. Now I must go and talk to my husband. I hope you manage to get in touch with Hannah. I'm sorry that I worried you and Charlie so much."

"Don't be; I'm glad I know that something's going on with her, it sort of explains why she's been the way she has recently. It will be some big Hannah drama, some man at the bottom of it no doubt. Sooner or later I'll find out what it is and it will all blow over. Good luck with Eric."

"Thank you," Sabine said very politely, leaving Ellen sitting alone in her kitchen once again.

After a second Ellen rose from her chair and preheated the grill for Charlie's fish fingers. Then she started to get out the ingredients she needed to make Allegra's risotto primavera.

As she stood at the kitchen sink filling a pan with water, she looked down the length of the back garden toward the back gate, which had long been obscured by undergrowth, at the line of rooftops that serrated the skyline beyond it, silhouetted against the stubbornly faultless blue sky.

When *was* the last time she had gone out? she wondered as the water began to run over the edges of the pan, numbing her reddening hands as she stood there motionless. Ellen thought of the empty calendar that lay open on the table behind her, void of dates and memories. Her mind tracked back over the preceding months, struggling to recall anything particularly memorable in any of them. There had been Charlie, her books, and the pain—the horrible gaping, seeping, open wound that losing Nick had dealt her—and that was all she could remember. Each day—which at the time had seemed like an uncrossable desert that she had to claw herself across from dawn 'til dusk—now seemed like one featureless globule of time, a mass of existence that had been occupied by very little besides her treacherous body's continued insistence on staying alive, no matter how she felt about it.

The truth was that Ellen couldn't remember the last time she had ventured farther than her front door. Dropping the pan in the sink, and slopping freezing water everywhere she turned, with numb fingers she picked up the pristine calendar of Sussex views, gazing at each empty month, stretching her mind as far back as it would go, to last Christmas.

It had been a dark, desolate affair made all the more despairing by the effort that had gone on around her and Charlie to make it at least bearable. Her parents, confused and embarrassed by her grief, were driven up from Hove by Hannah, bringing Christmas lunch with them packed neatly in her mother's twenty-year-old Tupperware. After giving and receiving unwanted gifts, the five of them had labored over lunch in what would have been silence if Ellen's mother hadn't insisted on filling them all in on the details of Mrs. Hopkins' hysterectomy. Hannah had drunk herself slowly into oblivion; Charlie had bolted to his room at the first available opportunity; and Ellen, paralyzed by the memory of how Christmas used to be, of what it should have been like then and how it would never, never be the same again, had sat through the queen's speech with her mother while her father snored in the corner.

With a shock Ellen realized that she had no memory of going out of the house even then. What little shopping she had done had been online. Her family and a succession of well-meaning but unwanted visitors had come to her. Was it truly possible that she hadn't left the house in six months?

Suddenly feeling sober and filled with the kind of dread that she got when she had forgotten something important but wasn't exactly sure what it was, Ellen forced herself to scratch around in her memory for anything, any detail or incident in her life since Nick had died that would allow her to get some foothold on some happening. As much as she racked her brain, she could find no landmark event in her life until just a few weeks ago, when Hannah had told her that she had to take in lodgers.

Ellen sat in her chair and looked around at her kitchen, frigid with horror as she realized the truth.

She had not left this house since her husband's funeral. She had not been out in almost a year, and worst of all—she had not noticed.

Fourteen

Your round, rookie," Pete told Matt, his sweaty, booze-saturated face looming far too close for comfort. "Get 'em in, son."

"Yeah, yeah, okay—when do I stop being a rookie?" Matt asked, gathering up a selection of half-empty glasses and taking orders for the assembled staff of *Bang It!* magazine. It was Thursday night and that week's issue had just been put to bed, after what Matt was beginning to realize was a routine that involved panic, shouting, and large amounts of swearing blind that the whole thing was going to shit, even though somehow it didn't. Naturally, after they had pulled off their weekly miracle of getting *Bang It!* to press, everyone went down to the pub to celebrate by getting as many beers as possible straight down their throats in the shortest period of time, or in Pete's case, the whiskey that seemed to seep out of his pores. It was an exhausting and strangely dissatisfying routine that Matt still struggled to really feel a part of. He'd expected to thrive on the adrenaline rush of putting a weekly magazine together in a matter of days, but when the first fresh copies rolled in, looking and reading almost exactly like the previous week's, he'd found himself wondering what the point was. Then he'd reminded himself that this was his dream job, and that soon enough he would have killed so many brain cells through alcohol abuse that he wouldn't worry about it anymore anyway.

"You stop being a rookie when I say so," Pete told him, accompanying him to the bar, where Matt waved a twenty at one of the bar staff, knowing full well that he'd need at least another one of those to pay for everyone's drinks. "You're still on probation, and so far you haven't exactly excelled."

"What?" Matt said. "Bollocks."

"I'm serious, mate, you're not stretching yourself—you look lazy."

"Lazy?" Matt protested. "I've worked my arse off since I got here. Literally."

"Look, the writing's good, funny and that—but so far you've pulled two girls who work in the same building as you and rehashed a load of old stuff. We need more from you, more derring-do and adventure. Birds from the same office building are okay, but they're easy pickings. Our readers want you to be what they're not—the hunter, the master, the maestro—the man that can have any woman anytime. The dark destroyer. You need some variety in your shagging, mate. A police-woman maybe, or a nurse."

"So you're saying I should base my column around your top ten all-time-favorite stripper costumes?" Matt shook his head.

"It's not my worst idea." Pete shrugged, taking as many of the assembled drinks as he could carry, including his own large single-malt whiskey, and teetered off to the tables where the waiting hordes greeted him with a cheer after he'd lost only one of the drinks. Downing his own shot in one gulp, Matt ordered a replacement and went back to join his colleagues. They'd been in there for an hour and already he could feel his head swimming with the heat and the alcohol, not that he'd want any of them to know that; being able to drink like a bas-tard and still turn up for work the next morning was one of the job requirements, but for some reason Matt just had not been in the mood for it recently. The pub made him feel restless and uneasy, and he realized with something of a shock that just at that moment he'd much rather be at Ellen's house, sitting at the kitchen table while she pottered around, drinking cups of tea and seeing whether or not he could make her laugh. Steeling himself, Matt ordered another shot and downed that, too. He was far too young to want to be in instead of out; he'd have to drown the impulse with booze before it took hold completely and he bought a pair of slippers and started planning his life around television.

"I was just saying..." Pete belched at Dan. "I reckon we need more of a challenge for young Matt here. Give the readers something to be impressed by. I mean that Carla, anyone could have had her if they could be bothered with the stringy little thing."

"Everyone has," Raffa joked with a wink directed at Matt.

"Ha, ha," Matt said dryly.

"And that little blond tart downstairs, from the tarts' magazine—she's always got her arse and tits hanging out, looks like a hooker. Pulling her took about as much effort as scoring a burger from a drive-through McDonald's."

Matt chuckled as he gazed into his beer, but privately he was thinking of Lucy marching out of the lift, her eyes glittering with rage. He had the distinct feeling he'd underestimated her. Almost as if he hadn't seen her, even when they'd been in bed together.

"Drive-through shags, there's an idea," Dan said, stroking his chin. "Look that up on the internet, Raffa—do it now, son. If there isn't a drive-through brothel somewhere in Nevada, the next round of drinks are on me. If there is, which there will be, then, Matt, I want a feature on that by Monday, cool? Interview some of the girls, the punters, get some pics—you should be able to do it all online and on the phone."

"Sure," Matt said, wondering how the hell he was going to pull that off, imagining himself making a call that went, *Oh hello, are you the madam? I'm a journalist from England you've never heard of, writing a piece for a magazine you've never heard of. Please can I interview your hookers on the joys*

*of working in a drive-through brothel, and would you mind
sending me some pictures? But only of the fit ones.*

The sad truth was, that was exactly how the conversation
would go.

"I've got it!" Pete bellowed, making Matt wince. "We pick
his next victim. All of us tonight. We pick a girl from this pub
and that's the bird he's got to bed for his next column, and his
challenge is to make it happen, no matter who we choose."

"Right, well, hang on a minute," Matt started to protest, but
he was shouted down.

"What, like pull-a-pig night?" Raffa chimed in. "Like we
pick a proper minger and he's got to do her no matter what?"
The assembled men guffawed at the idea.

"Er, I don't think so," Matt countered, feeling the alcohol
tingle in his fingertips, his head swimming as he was swept
along on a tide of testosterone. If he was going to survive this,
he'd have to man-up and go with it; they'd eat him alive if they
knew that the last thing he wanted to do tonight was chat up
some random girl and that really he'd like to go home and
drink tea with Ellen. "I'm the man, the master—the maestro.
Anyone can pick up an old dog grateful for a sniff of any bloke.
If you're going to challenge me, then find me something special, something that's going to take a bit more effort than batting my lashes and giving her a smile."

"He's right, the readers want fantasy, not fact," Dan said.
"We've got to pick a fittie. Tell you what, to make it more interesting, we get to decide what your opening line is."

"Yeah, and you have to secretly record it on your phone so
we know you've done it," Greg chimed in.

"And you have to get a picture of her tits on your phone,
too." Raffa nodded. "Close-up, no face or nothing, just tits—
then we can print them in the magazine and score them one
out of ten."

"Oh my fuck, that's a genius idea." Dan clapped Raffa on
the shoulder.

"Whoa, okay," Matt said, laughing to cover his discomfort. "And if I pull this off?"

"Or if she pulls you off." Raffa snickered.

"Your probation ends tomorrow," Dan told him. "You're on the team."

"And if I don't?" Matt countered.

"Same deal, only you're off the team." Dan raised an eyebrow. "Got the balls to take that bet?"

"Don't need balls to take that bet. Fucking piss easy," Matt assured him with a beer-based bravado that he didn't enjoy.

"Okay then." Dan twisted in his seat, scanning the bar for a likely target. Matt felt uneasy as he watched him. What Dan was doing was no different from what he might do on any night out, looking for a girl to chat up—but when he did, it was random, chance, there was always a possibility that it wouldn't work out. Having Dan pick a girl out for him that he was definitely supposed to have sex with really did make it seem like they were choosing a victim, and Matt never liked to think of any of the women he spent time with as that.

"Her." Dan nodded in the direction of a pillar where two women, dressed in short, flowery summer dresses, showing a good deal of bare, tanned legs tapering down to high heels, were talking, their heads close together as they sipped from straws in some vodka-based cocktail.

Matt was dimly aware of sniggering and elbow digging as Dan made his selection. It had to be said that he'd picked the fittest women in the bar and, more than that, proper women. Well dressed and confident-looking, as if getting chatted up by a man was the very last thing on their minds. This really would be a challenge.

"Blonde or brunette?" Pete asked, with a death's-head grin that Matt found unsettling.

"Brunette; brunettes always have the best nipples." Dan nodded, making Raffa's shoulders shake with uncharacteristically repressed laughter. "Are we all agreed?" The group cheered their rowdy assent in unison, causing the unsuspecting woman to glance up briefly in their direction. Matt caught her eye and held it for a second until she lowered her lashes, turning back to her friend and whispering something that made the other woman laugh. If it was about him, Matt was fairly sure it wasn't complimentary. She looked about thirty, the high-maintenance type who obviously took a lot of care with her skin and her hair, and clearly worked out, judging by her lightly muscled thighs and arms. There wasn't a crease on her forehead or a line around her full-lipped mouth, she was perfect, and yet, if Matt had been making his own decisions, she would have been the last woman whom he would choose. There were no secrets there for him to discover, he was certain. She would have any hint of imperfection covered up.

"Yeah, I like her," Dan said. "She looks hot, like a right goer—might teach you a thing or two, Matt my son. And she's got a great pair, so she couldn't be more perfect. Off you go, son."

"Wait a minute. I can't just pile in there," Matt said. "I need to do a bit of groundwork first—fleeting eye contact, shy smiles, that sort of bollocks."

"Er, no you don't, you big gay," Dan told him. "Get in there and set your phone to record. You opening line is . . . 'I've never seen skin as beautiful as yours, do you moisturize?'"

The table erupted in laughter.

"Are you trying to make me look like a fucking serial killer?" Matt shook his head.

"Yeah." Dan nodded, taking Matt's phone off him to check that he wasn't cheating. Satisfied, he handed it back and nodded toward the girl. "Go on."

"Well, don't all look, okay?" Matt asked in vain. He downed his drink and headed for his target.

The woman spluttered into her drink when Matt delivered his line, glancing briefly over his shoulder at his assembled colleagues, who were now all suspiciously silent.

"You on a dare or what?" she asked, looking him up and down with barely concealed contempt.

Matt pulled out his self-deprecating "I know I'm a bumbling fool but look how cute I am" grin.

"There, that was a shocking line, wasn't it," he said. "But it is true—you have beautiful skin. Seriously, you look about sixteen."

The woman smirked. "So do you," she told him. It wasn't a compliment.

"Yeah, I am youthful, but that's not a bad thing." Matt tried his "I know where your clitoris is" eyebrow raise. "It means I've got the stamina to give a woman what she wants."

"What, a pair of Gucci shoes?" the woman retorted, quick as lightning.

Matt took a second to regroup, all too conscious of the baying pack of hounds at his shoulder, ready to rip him to shreds at the first opportunity. He needed to try another tack.

"Did you know that you could be a model?" he asked, cringing inwardly.

"Yes," she said. "I do know. I am a model. Model-slash-presenter, actually."

"Oh well, there you go. I was right then." Struggling, Matt listened to line after line fall totally flat. He'd always thought he was a proper charmer and mad with the X factor—but maybe that was because the women he normally picked were a lot more drunk and a lot more susceptible than this one, keen to lap up every hackneyed compliment as if it were gospel. Maybe he always sounded so shallow, like he got his lines from a Christmas cracker; maybe he'd just never heard himself properly before. Matt wondered what his chances were of finding another job. Maybe Lucy would put a word in for him at her magazine. But then again, maybe she wouldn't.

"Come on then," the brunette pressed. "You're trying to pull me, aren't you? Don't give up now—God loves a trier and so do I."

"Okay. You are an intelligent, sophisticated woman, you don't want any of the bullshit." Matt took a breath, pinning his career on the next few words: "The truth is, I really want to make love to you. What do you say?"

The brunette exchanged a deadpan look with her friend.

"I say if that was your best shot, you've blown it. Seriously, mate, you didn't ask me my name, or anything about me. Are you on the clock or something? Seems to me like you're just trying to pull any bird so you can write some sleazy magazine article about it."

"I . . . but . . . okay, how do you know?" Matt said, his words almost lost in the cacophony of jeers behind him. "You've been in the magazine, haven't you? Look, I know that makes me look like a prick, and I have no idea how I haven't remembered a woman as beautiful as you, but I promise you, that is not what this is about."

The woman slowly looked him up and down as if she were appraising a stud horse.

"Okay then," she said with a nod.

"Okay then what?"

"Okay then, I'll shag you." She looked him directly in the eye.

Matt suddenly felt quite nervous, and quite certain that the parts of him that were basic requirements for such an endeavor had just shrunk away to nothing.

"Really?" he squeaked.

"Yeah, but on one condition." She raised a flirty eyebrow, which made Matt think a million scary and exciting things.

"Name it," he whispered.

"You'd better ask my husband first. After all, he is your boss."

"He's . . . what?" He looked around to find the whole staff of *Bang It!* gasping with laughter and banging on the tables while Dan held up his glass and winked at him.

"I said you should have asked me my name. It's Aimee—

Mrs. Aimee Sutherland. And that moisturizer line, that was Dan's first line with me. It worked out a lot better for him."

Leaving Matt speechless, Aimee sashayed past him in her Gucci heels. Bending over her husband, she grabbed him by the collar. "Right, now you really owe me dinner. Come on— we're going."

As Dan stood up and kissed his wife, he was literally crying with laughter. "That is the funniest thing I've heard in years," he said. "Seriously, we should put that on the website. Babe, you were brilliant."

"What do you mean, put it on the website?" Matt asked miserably.

"I mean that when I checked your phone, I called my phone and put you on speaker. That was brilliant!"

"You? You bastard!" Matt proclaimed, picking up Pete's drink and downing it in one shot. "That whole thing was a windup." He looked miserably at Aimee. "Oh, God, I'm so embarrassed."

"You should be, love." Aimee laughed. "Don't know how you got your reputation for being a ladies' man."

Matt grinned; he had no choice but to take it on the chin. It was pretty funny.

"So am I fired then?" he asked Dan.

"You should be, but I can't bring myself to do it, you're too entertaining." Dan glanced at wife. "I'm too drunk to eat—how about a line and a club, yeah?"

Matt shook his head while everybody else was nodding theirs.

"You know what, I'm going to go back."

"Back where, to where you left your self-respect?" Raffa laughed.

"No, I . . ." Matt stopped himself from saying that he wanted to get home, have a shower, and go to sleep in front of the telly. "I've got a bit of a project going on."

"A woman?" Pete asked.

"Yeah, a real challenge, a little older—but, you know, really sexy."

"You mean like a cougar?" Raffa added.

"Or a milf?" Greg put in.

"Yeah, no—she's a lady. You know, refined, quiet, and shy."

"And you reckon you can crack her?"

"I reckon under those frumpy clothes she's got a slamming body," Matt said. "It's only a matter of time."

"Wait—are you talking about your landlady?" Pete slurred. "The one who's taking in lodgers because her husband snuffed it?"

"Whoa, low blow—you're going for a woman on the rebound from death, mate; that tops trying to pick up your boss's wife any day of the week," Raffa said approvingly.

"First, I didn't know I was trying to pick up the boss's wife, and second, her husband's been dead nearly a year," Matt said uncomfortably.

"You are a dark, dark bastard," Dan said approvingly. "Matt, the dark destroyer. Go for it, mate. There's a features idea, what depths a bloke would go to to get his way, hey, Raffa?"

Matt picked up his stuff and headed out into the mercifully cool air of the night; the sky was only just losing the last remnants of light even though it was getting on eleven. As he headed back to his much-longed-for room, his stomach churned and his head spun. It wasn't just that mixture of beer and whiskey, either; he felt disjointed and out of place. Like when he'd woken up after a big night and knew that he'd done something to offend someone, only he couldn't work out what, only this time he knew exactly what he'd done, exactly what he'd said, and he hated himself for it. He didn't think about Ellen that way at all. He did think of her sexually—that was inevitable, she was a beautiful woman, with a body that hinted at much more, and he was a man. Of course he thought about her that way, but he didn't think of her as a project, an easy target. That was the very last thing he thought about her.

If anything, he had an unfamiliar urge to look after her, to protect her.

As Matt turned down his road, his head hanging low, he considered turning back, finding his friends, and going out after all, but then he heard a noise in the shadows that stopped him in his tracks. He listened, uncertain of what he had heard.

"Matt?" A figure lurched out of the shadows and stood under the streetlight. It took Matt a second to take in what he was seeing.

"Hannah?" He stepped forward and caught the woman just as her knees buckled. Looking down, he saw her makeup smeared down her face, her eyes bloodshot and swollen, but there was more than that—a dark bruise inflamed her left cheek just under her eye, and her clothes were dirty and torn. "Fuck, Hannah, what happened?"

"Will you take me to Ellen's?" she asked drowsily, clearly still under the influence of something. "I need to go to Ellen's, I need to tell her something. I'm trying to get there but it seems so far and I'm . . . I'm hurting."

Matt folded his arm around Hannah's waist and bore her weight against his shoulder.

"Hannah, what the hell happened?" Matt asked.

Hannah swung her head around to look at him, her bleary eyes unfocused, her brows drawn together in a frown.

"I don't know," she told him. "I don't know what's happened."

CHAPTER Fifteen

In her dream, Ellen was in a library—no, not a library, *the* library, the one at college—where the tall, dusty shelves that stretched from floor to ceiling were so closely crammed together that the carpeted corridors that ran between them were narrow and dark. It was hot in the library, and dark; she felt sweat gathering at the nape of her neck. She was looking for something, looking for the way out.

Searching for a clue, she ran her finger along the shelf of books, like none she had ever seen in the university library, each one a fat, well-fingered paperback; the purple, pink, and red spines were cracked along their length, as if each one had been avidly read. Ellen pulled out one book and saw an illustration of a woman on the cover, the tops of her arms gripped and pulled back forcefully by a muscular, topless man so that her breasts surged forward, straining against the laces of what appeared to be a white nightdress. Ellen frowned, trying to puzzle out what was so familiar about the image. She tried to make out the title, gold-embossed swirling letters, but they seemed not to make sense no matter how hard she looked at them. She stared and stared at the image of the woman on the cover, her expression caught somewhere between agony and ecstasy, the internal struggle between desire and propriety expertly caught by the brush of the artist. There was something familiar about the woman, her long, dark hair tumbling over one shoulder, her full lips bared in what might have been a growl or a groan of ecstasy. Then, with a heated flush of embarrassment, Ellen realized that she was looking at an illustration of herself in the throes of undeniable passion. And the man who was restraining her, his lips buried in her neck? She could not tell who he was; he was fair and well built, but she could not see his face. Perhaps it was Nick? She tried to remember if Nick had ever grabbed her so purposefully. Ellen moaned, remembering the gentle pressure of his palm on her inner thigh, the first indicator that he wanted to make love. His first move always, even before kissing her. Or perhaps it was Matt, perhaps it was Matt who was seducing her away from quiet respectability, his strong fingers gripping her so hard that they would surely leave their imprints on her flesh, branding her as his. At last she could make sense of the title: *Ellen's Escape.*

This was it, this would show her the way out of this maze she was trapped in where every corridor, every room, led her around and around in ever-decreasing circles, always back to where she began. The book had to have the answers.

Desperately Ellen opened the book, anxious to see what secrets the words would reveal, but she flipped from page to page and each one was blank. Yellowing cream, slightly rough in texture, and entirely empty.

"But what happens?" Ellen's voice echoed between the shelves. "What happens to me next?" Perhaps she had to fill in the answers, Ellen found herself thinking. Perhaps to escape her story she had to write it.

"Ellen?" She spun around. Matt was standing behind her, shirtless, just as the man on the cover of her book was, his muscled torso glistening with what might have been sweat but which smelled like rose oil, his well-developed pectoral muscles rising and falling as he took each heavy breath.

"You've come," she whispered. "I've thought about it and I'm ready for sex. Let's have lots of sex."

"Ellen?" he questioned, softly insistent. "Ellen?"

"Yes, the answer is yes, yes, I want you, I want you. As a strong, independent woman I will let you take me now!" She flung herself back, bracing her body along the bookshelf. "Rip off my clothes, only be careful with the buttons on this top, it's my favorite."

Matt took a step toward her and gently shook her shoulder.

"Ellen? Ellen, wake up. Wake up!"

Groggily, Ellen opened her eyes and focused on Matt. She smiled, one hand lazily fluttering up to caress the side of his face. And she realized that she wasn't dreaming anymore and that Matt was actually leaning over her bed.

"Bloody hell!" She tried to sit up, but found herself pinned down by a tangle of sheets. With some difficulty, she unraveled herself with one hand while trying to maintain her modesty with the other. It would be tonight of all nights that she had finally conceded to the sweltering heat and given up Nick's pajamas in favor of one of Nick's cotton shirts.

"What are you doing here?" Ellen asked breathlessly, dragging the sheet up over her chest. She could have been mistaken, but she thought that the look on his face didn't exactly point to a seduction attempt.

"I'm sorry," Matt whispered, careful not to look at her. He sat on the edge of the bed, his weight causing her leg to roll a little closer to his. "I didn't know what to do. I thought I'd better wake you. You were having a pretty radical dream."

"Have I slept in? Is it morning?" Ellen was confused and then a flash of her dream came back to her. "Oh, God, was I talking in my sleep?"

"Nothing I could make out." Whatever he had heard or seen, Matt seemed utterly disinterested, which Ellen found simultaneously disappointing and a relief.

"Look, it's not morning," Matt went on. "It's about midnight I think." He paused, as if uncertain of how to say the next few words. "Hannah's downstairs."

Ellen felt her shoulders relax and leaned back against the headboard.

"Typical." Ellen ran her fingers through her hair. "She worries us all to death and then turns up on the doorstep whenever she feels like it. Seriously, that woman thinks the world revolves around her. She has to learn, she can't just turn up here attention-seeking at any hour of the day or night." Ellen swung her bare legs out of bed and hastily put on Nick's dressing gown, which she kept hanging on the back of the bedroom door. "I'm going to tell her she can bloody well go home and come back in the morning."

Just as Ellen reached the door, Matt put a hand on her shoulder and stopped her. She turned to look at him.

"Ellen, you don't understand." In the half-light coming through the open door, Matt's expression was unreadable, but something about the shadows under his eyes and the incline of his head sent an ominous shiver through her. "Look, I don't know what's happened, but Hannah's pretty messed up."

"Drunk, you mean?"

"Probably. She might have taken or been given something, too." Ellen's sigh was one of exasperation. "But wait, it's not just that. Something's happened to her, she's hurt, and she can't remember how. You need to come and see her, Ellen."

Matt took a step closer and finally Ellen saw his expression. He was really worried.

"Oh, God, what's she done now?"

Ellen didn't know what she expected to see when she pushed the living-room door open, but it wasn't the sight that greeted her. Matt had left Hannah on the sofa, where she had curled herself up into a tight ball and appeared to be sleeping. Ellen flicked on a lamp to get a better look at her sister, who unconsciously screwed up her eyes against the invasion of light. The first thing Ellen noticed was blood in Hannah's hair, dried now, a thick black lump matting the auburn strand. There was a bruise forming on her temple, and her lip was swollen and cut. The neck of her shirt was torn and there were scuffs of mud streaked along her skirt, which had ripped up the seam, revealing the tops of her legs. But the sight that sent ice through Ellen's veins was the smear of blood, dried and flaking, on the inside of one of her thighs.

Ellen pressed her hand over her mouth as she stared at her fitfully slumbering sister, forcing herself to stay silent. After a few seconds she peeled her fingers away from her lips.

"Where did you say you found her?" she asked Matt, her voice strained.

"At the end of the road; she just appeared out of nowhere, looking like that. She seemed really out of it. I think she'd been in someone's garden. Maybe she passed out there, I don't know, or how long she'd been there—but I think she was trying to get to you. I didn't find her, she found me. If she hadn't seen me I'd have walked right past her."

Hesitantly, Ellen knelt on the carpet beside the sofa, her hands hovering over her sister, uncertain of what to do. Then, biting down on her bottom lip, she gently touched Hannah on the shoulder.

"Hannah, Hannah," Ellen said softly, almost unwilling to bring her sister around, but knowing that she must. "Hannah. Wake up. It's me, Hannah."

Hannah opened one rapidly swelling eye with some difficulty and looked at Ellen through the tender slit of her lid.

"Ellen." Her voice was cracked and dry. "I hurt."

"I know, I can see that," Ellen said gently. Instinctively she pressed the back of her hand against Hannah's forehead as her mother used to do to each of them when she suspected a fever. Hannah's skin was cool, so she must have been outside for some time, Ellen thought. Unsure, she glanced up at Matt, who shook his head. He had no idea what to do, either. Ellen had to try to find out more.

"Okay, Hannah, Hans?" Ellen waited for Hannah to open her eyes. "You need to sit up, okay? Let me get a good look at you." Ellen was suddenly reminded of the last time she had nursed her sister, when they were both children, when Hannah had been her tiny little sister, utterly in awe of her and dependent on her for almost everything. Back when her mother's friends used to look at the two of them together and say, "What a lovely little mother your Ellen makes."

Hannah moaned. "Don't want to, Ellie, want to stay here. I like it here. Want to sleep now, hold my hand . . ."

"I know, I know you want to sleep, and you can soon. But first I need to see all your hurts. Let me look . . ."

Hannah grimaced in pain as Ellen awkwardly wrapped her hands around her and heaved her bodily into a sitting position. Hannah's head lolled on her neck, but she smiled when she caught sight of Matt standing by the door.

"My hero." She grinned, reopening the cut in her lip. "Matt rescued me, Ellie, I was lost and he found me. He's so brave and handsome—like a hero in one of your books. . . ."

Ellen knelt in front of Hannah, placing her hands on the sides of her head so that she could look into her sister's eyes; one was now almost completely closed, the other heavy lidded and sleepy. Once, long ago, Ellen had been the designated first aider at the museum, and she tried desperately now to remember something about head injuries. Hannah could be drunk, or she could have taken a serious knock to the head. Gingerly, Ellen felt over her sister's head for more cuts or bumps, but the only one she found was what looked like a fairly superficial cut on her forehead. Heads bleed a lot, Ellen remembered, but even so it was clear that someone or something had hit Hannah very hard.

"Hannah?" Ellen struggled to hold her sister's attention as her chin dropped onto her chest. "Hannah! Were you in a fight? Who hurt you?" Ellen asked, her eyes tracking the rest of her sister's visible injuries. Her knees were cut and dirty, fingerprint-sized bruises were blossoming on her forearms, and there was dirt beneath her broken nails.

"Don't know," Hannah said blearily, listing toward Ellen, who had to grab her shoulders to keep her upright. "Want to sleep."

"No, no you can't sleep. She can't sleep, can she, Matt? What if she isn't drunk—what if this is a concussion? They always say on TV that you mustn't go to sleep if you have a head injury."

"Shall I make her a coffee?" Matt offered.

"Yes, good idea. Make her a strong coffee."

Matt looked relieved to have an excuse to leave the room, and Ellen didn't blame him.

"Look, Hannah, I know, okay? I know you've lost your job, that you've gotten into some kind of trouble at work. I know all of that, you've got nothing to hide, okay—so just tell me, what happened to you?"

Without warning, Hannah flung her arms around Ellen's neck and dropped her head onto Ellen's shoulder, almost sending the pair of them tumbling back onto the carpet. "I'm sorry, Ellie." She sobbed tearlessly. "I'm so, so sorry."

With some difficulty, Ellen eased her sister back against the sofa cushions.

"You don't have to be sorry," she said, fighting the confusion and fear that made her want to run from the room. "Whatever's happened, it's not your fault. Please, Hannah, I'm trying to work out what to do."

"Will you promise to still love me, Ellie, promise me," Hannah begged plaintively. "If you still love me, then I'll be okay, I know I'll be okay."

"Of course, silly," Ellen said, remembering with sudden clarity how Hannah used to climb into her bed when she was scared at night. She could have been no more than three, and Ellen about eleven. Ellen remembered how she had loved the feeling of Hannah's small, warm body curled up against her, and how protective she had felt of her little sister, wrapping her arms around her and promising that no harm would come to her. Promising her that she would always love her.

"Come on now, Hannah. Come on, try to remember."

Hannah pulled her head up, her expression exactly the same as that of the little girl she had once been, caught with her hand in the biscuit tin. "I was bored so I went out." She frowned, which caused her to wince. "For a lunchtime drink. It was nice, really nice and hot and I sat outside and drank cider. I like drinking, Ellie, when I drink the pain stops for a bit. . . ." Hannah drifted off again, her eyes fluttering shut.

Ellen wanted to ask her what pain—what pain could her bright, beautiful, successful sister possibly be trying so desperately to drown out? But she held her tongue. As difficult as it was, she needed to keep Hannah awake, and she needed to know what had happened to her.

"Hannah? Hannah, look at me." Ellen waited as Hannah reluctantly wrenched open her one good eye. "Have you been drinking all afternoon?" Ellen asked. "Did you fall over? Did you get hit by a car?"

Hannah frowned. "I don't think so. Have I?"

"Okay." Ellen didn't know what to say. "Okay, so you were in the pub, then you were sitting in the sun, and then what happened?"

"Oh! I met some people, really nice. Lots of fun." Hannah nodded, smiling as she remembered. "They bought me drinks . . . it must have been later on, because they'd finished work for the day. City guys, you know. City guys are always the most fun. They bought me champagne and we . . ."

"What? What did you do?"

"I don't want to talk about this now, want to sleep, Ellie. Don't be cross with me anymore."

"I'm not cross," Ellen said. "Please, Hannah, I know this is difficult, but I think it's important—did you take anything, or did anyone give you anything?"

"I danced." Hannah frowned again. "I danced on the tables for them and then . . ." Hannah closed her eyes for a second, her face briefly clearing as she fell into a few seconds' precious unconsciousness. Ellen felt guilty for shaking her out of it again.

"Hannah!" Ellen's voice was sharp, her chest heavy with dread. "Then what happened?" Hannah's head snapped up again.

"We got thrown out, for being rowdy. So me and the boys went somewhere else. . . . Where did we go?" She looked perplexed. "I don't remember."

"Boys? Those were men you were with. How many, Hannah? What were their names?"

Hannah brightened. "One was called Nick! Nick—Ellen, can you imagine? I mean I know it's a common name, but it was nice. It was nice to have a reason to say it out loud again. Nick. Nick. Nick."

Ellen shook her head, fighting her frustration and worry.

"What happened with Nick, Hannah?" Ellen asked.

Instantly Hannah's face transformed into a picture of unhappiness. "Oh, Ellen, I'm sorry. I'm so, so sorry."

"You don't have to be sorry, I've told you that. You don't have to be sorry about anything, okay? None of this is your fault. Did this Nick have sex with you?" Ellen dreaded the answer.

"Yes," Hannah said, eliciting a sob from Ellen. "Yes, and I'm sorry, Ellen. I'm so, so sorry. I didn't mean for it to happen, it just did. I didn't realize what I was doing, or how it would change everything."

"Hannah, was it against your will? Was it this Nick who did this to you? Were you . . . were you raped, Hannah?"

"Raped? Don't be so silly. Nick would never hurt me."

Ellen sank back on her heels, unable to put together any of the pieces. Hannah had got drunk, met some men, taken something, and had sex. But none of that explained the way she looked, her injuries. Had something happened to her later?

"Then what happened to you, Hannah—how did you get hurt? What about the others? What about the other men who were with this Nick?"

Just then Matt reappeared with a mug of steaming coffee.

"I thought I'd better make real coffee, thought it would be more effective than instant," he mumbled, unable to look either woman in the eye. "Look, I'll get out of your way, shall I?" he offered.

"Would you stay?" Ellen asked, her green eyes large. "Please."

Unwilling to leave her to deal with this alone, as much as he might want to, Matt nodded and sat down in the armchair opposite the sofa, folding his hands and dropping his head as if in prayer.

"Hannah, you need to try and remember what happened tonight. After you left the pub with Nick and the others, what happened to you?"

"We went for a walk!" Hannah seemed pleased with herself. "The boys said I could do with some fresh air and we went for a walk, in the park. I suppose that must have been how I got so muddy."

"And you had sex with this Nick?" Ellen asked again.

"Oh no, no." Hannah shook her head slowly, contradicting herself completely. "No, they wanted to, but I didn't. I said I was tired and I was going to get a cab and go home but then . . . I think I fell asleep, that's right, I was so, so tired. And when I woke up again I was alone." Hannah sighed. "I'm still so tired. Can I go to sleep now, Ellie, can I? Will you hug me while I'm asleep?"

"No, Hannah. Listen, I need you to look at me and listen to me for a minute, okay?"

Hannah focused her gaze on Ellen.

"Hannah, I think . . . I think you've been attacked, beaten

up and maybe even raped. I think we need to call the police and an ambulance, okay? I'm going to do that now."

"No, no." Hannah shook her head again. "No. I just need to sleep, Ellie. I'm very tired now."

"I know, but we need to get you looked at and we need to find out who hurt you like this."

"Why?" Hannah blinked.

"So the police can arrest them!"

"No. I'm okay, I'm fine. I don't mind the pain. I deserve the pain, the pain is nothing at all, because now you know. Now you understand and you've promised to still love me, so everything is fine. So that makes all of this okay. Sleep now. Do you know, I feel like I haven't slept in almost a year. Not since . . ." Hannah drifted off.

"No, Hannah, this isn't okay. Hannah?" Hannah crumpled sideways, her head thudding against the cushioned arm of the sofa. "Wake up. I'm going to call an ambulance and the police."

"No!" Hannah suddenly sprang awake at Ellen's words. "No, no, no, no. Ellie, please, please don't. *Please.* I don't want the hospital, I don't want the police. I just want to sleep. I just want to stay here with you. I'm fine, Ellie, I'm fine, I'm fine, I'm fine." For the first time that evening, Hannah looked anxious and scared. "Please, Ellie. Please let me stay here with you, don't make me go to the hospital. I'm fine, I'm really fine. It's just like that time I fell out of the tree and you thought I was dead—I was fine then, wasn't I? I was fine." A dry sob tore through Hannah's throat. "I don't want to talk about it anymore, Ellie. Don't make me."

Resolute, Hannah dragged a cushion across her belly, drew her legs up beneath her, and closed her eyes.

Ellen looked at Matt. "I don't know what to do," she said bleakly. "Look at her. Should we call an ambulance?"

Matt looked at the slumbering woman.

"Maybe we should wait, let her sleep. Wait for her to wake

up and see if she can remember anything else. She looks bad but she was talking okay, and she didn't seem in too much pain; she didn't seem to have any trouble breathing."

"But what if she's got internal bleeding, or a brain injury?" Ellen was worried. "We should call an ambulance; they'll take her to hospital, x-ray her and things." She realized that it would be a relief to pass her sister into someone else's capable hands.

Matt bit his lip, leaning forward, resting his wrists on his knees.

"If we take her to hospital now, they'll call in the police. When I was a cub reporter they sent me to cover this case once, of a young schoolgirl attacked by a load of teenagers. I talked to her parents. They said that what she went through after the attack was almost as bad as what those lads did to her. If we take her in now, they'll be wanting to test her for all sorts of things, gather evidence. She'll have to talk to the police, give statements, hand in her clothes. They won't let her wash or sleep. Sure, she's messed up, but we don't know yet that anything bad happened. Do you really want to put her through all of that if all that happened is she's had too much to drink and a bit of a wild night out with some guy she picked up? And she really doesn't want to go, you saw that."

Ellen gestured at Hannah. "This is not a bit of a wild night out, Matt. Look at her."

Matt looked at Hannah, her head buried in her folded arms, her bruised and bloody legs drawn up and tucked under her.

"I don't know what to say, Ellen," he said, looking at her face, which was etched with worry and indecision. He had a sudden urge to go to her and put his arms around her, to tell her not to worry, to lean on him because he would look after her. "Call your doctor, there'll be an on-call GP who will come to the house. At least then, when they've had a look at her, we'll have a better idea of what to do."

A cold wash of relief swept over Ellen as she looked back

at her slumbering sister. Of course, if she called an ambulance now, she would be expected to go with Hannah. She tried to imagine accompanying her sister into the clammy night, sitting beside her as the ambulance sped to the hospital, listing from one side to the other, the siren ringing in her ears. Ellen felt every muscle in her body contract in panic. She'd been in the back of an ambulance before, and that time it had been she strapped to the gurney, frightened and alone as the paramedics talked over her head, and she had known that whatever happened, she had lost her baby at just twelve weeks. *But that was years ago,* Ellen told herself now. Nearly seven years since the ectopic pregnancy had ruptured her fallopian tube, since she had nearly bled to death and her chances of conceiving again had been slashed to nil when they discovered that her other tube was blocked. Seven years since she'd woken up alone in the hospital, waiting, terrified, for Nick to arrive back from a business trip to France, frightened of telling him that their dream of a big family had been ended, frightened about disappointing him again.

Ellen had been out of the house plenty of times since then, and she hadn't been scared of unfamiliar people or places then, even if her excursions had gradually dwindled. And even now, even though Charlie was right and she had spent the best part of a year indoors, that didn't mean she couldn't go out if she wanted to. She could if she wanted to, if she *had* to. But when Ellen looked at her bruised and battered sister, she realized how glad she was that she didn't have to test that theory. Not yet, anyway.

"I would feel happier if she would go to hospital," the doctor told Ellen gravely as they stood in the hallway. It had taken over an hour for the emergency GP to arrive, and that was only after Ellen had begged the dispatch handler, who told her after she'd described Hannah's injuries that she had to take Hannah to hospital. Eventually, Ellen had got the help she wanted but only after she had threatened legal action if anything happened to Hannah due to lack of medical attention.

"But I can't make her." The doctor sighed. "If she is competent and conscious, it's up to her. She's groggy, yes, but there is no sign of concussion or internal bleeding as far as I can tell. That doesn't mean it's not there, though." She handed Ellen a prescription. "There are no broken bones, and these anti-inflammatories will help with the bruising and pain, but I don't want you to give her anything for at least another six hours, just in case there is anything I haven't spotted. If she becomes unconscious, or anything changes for the worse, you will have no choice but to call the ambulance. Even if she doesn't get worse, try to persuade her to go to hospital for more extensive checks once she's sobered up. That's my recommendation; there's nothing I can do about it if she won't follow it."

Ellen nodded, acknowledging the disclaimer. She took the prescription and folded it first in half and then in quarters. She was aware that the exhausted and disheveled young woman was desperate to leave, but she had one more question she had to ask her.

"Doctor, do you think that . . . do you think she's been raped?"

The doctor lowered her head. "I'm only able to make a judgment on where your sister allowed me to examine her, so I can't comment. I would say that these injuries were inflicted on her by another person. These aren't the kind of injuries sustained in a car crash or from falling over."

"She wants to have a bath," Ellen said. "But if she does, then there'll be no evidence, will there?"

The doctor regarded Ellen with bloodshot brown eyes. "Look, my day job is police GP down at the local police station. I deal with this sort of thing all the time, and to be honest, less than fifty percent of rape victims report what's happened to the police, and of those who do, less than ten percent result in a conviction. If there was any forensic evidence, it would only prove that your sister had sex. *If* the police felt they had enough for a case, and *if* they tracked down who might be responsible, which is a big if, she'd be asked about her drinking, her drug consumption. About spending all day in the pub with the people who might have attacked her, or might not have. Even now it's still her word against his, if that's what happened, and we don't know that it did. I'm not even sure she knows."

"So you're saying I should let her have a bath and do nothing?" Ellen asked, incredulous. "That whoever did this to her just gets to carry on with life like nothing's happened?"

"I'm saying that one way or another, your sister has had a hell of day, and she still might be seriously injured. Let her do whatever makes her feel better, and keep an eye on her for any signs of deterioration. If she starts vomiting or blacking out, has difficulty breathing or any belly pain—especially look out for signs her stomach is becoming rigid or swollen."

"Thank you for coming," Ellen said politely. Then she watched the GP hurry down the path, on her way to the next emergency. Bleakly, she shut the door on the outside world and leaned her back against it.

"Here." Matt emerged from the living room and nodded at the piece of paper in Ellen's hand. "There's that pharmacy at the twenty-four-hour Sainsbury's, isn't there? I'll go and get it."

"Did you hear what she said? Do you think I shouldn't report it?" Ellen asked, handing over the piece of paper.

"I don't think it's up to you, I think it's up to Hannah—and for now all she wants is a bath," Matt said. He picked up his jacket off the end of the banister. "I'll be ten minutes."

"Matt?" He paused, his hand on the latch. "Thank you, thank you for being here."

"Not a problem," Matt told her.

After he'd shut the door behind him, Ellen stood looking for several seconds at the spot where he had been standing, and then after a moment she went upstairs and ran Hannah a bath.

"Hannah, what has happened to you?" Ellen asked, suddenly upset, pressing the back of her hand to her mouth. "This is . . . this is just so . . . typical." She was aware of the rising sun lightening the sky behind the kitchen blinds, casting a grayish, dreamlike light over everything, and she wished that she could wake up from this nightmare and wake Hannah up to a simple sun-filled morning where nothing bad had happened.

It was now almost five. A little more alert since the doctor had looked at her, Hannah had insisted on bathing alone, while Ellen had sat outside the door, asking whispered questions every few minutes, afraid that her sister would pass out again and slip beneath the water. Ellen was thankful that Charlie had gotten into the habit of sleeping with his iPod plugged into his ears. If she was lucky, he wouldn't wake up. She didn't want to have to try to explain any of this to him.

Hannah had stayed in the bath for an hour, not wanting to come out even when Ellen had come in with fresh towels and a clean pair of Nick's old cotton pajamas. At her sister's demand, she had turned her back while Hannah dried herself, gasping periodically in pain. The mirror clogged with steam, Ellen had found herself looking into the dirty bathwater, now pinkish in hue. When Hannah was dried and dressed, Ellen had taken her hand and led her into her bedroom, pulling back the covers so her sister might lie down, and tucked her in.

"How are you feeling?" Ellen asked Hannah, who rolled onto her side with her back to her sister.

"I'm starting to sober up, worse luck," Hannah said, as if she had nothing more than a hangover after a big night out. "And everything hurts."

"Not much longer and you can take something for that,"

Ellen said. "Hannah, do you think that after you've rested a bit more you should go to the hospital?"

"No," Hannah said. "No. I'll be okay. I just want to stay here. I want to stay here and I never want to leave."

Ellen nodded. That, at least, she could understand.

"What? What's typical?" Matt jerked awake. For the last few hours, since Hannah had drifted off to sleep again, he and Ellen had sat in the kitchen in silence, Matt's head nodding occasionally onto his chest. Ellen had not slept, but instead climbed the stairs periodically to check on Hannah, watching the rise and fall of her chest, the expression on her battered face, watching for any signs that her condition might be worse than it looked, just like a new mother keeping vigil over her new baby. Just like a big sister, just like Ellen watching out for Hannah when she was very little.

Ellen had not been pleased when her mother arrived home from the hospital with Hannah in her arms. She had not been pleased at all with her new little sister, a peaches-and-cream golden little thing, perfect from the moment she arrived in the world, charming everyone she met even before she could talk, even before she could smile. At eight years old, Ellen had felt like a gigantic and hulking changeling, the cuckoo in the nest, sticking out like a sore thumb in her newly re-modeled family, with her dark skin and dark hair that she apparently had got from some great-aunt she had never met. She was nothing like this stellar little creature who brought so much light into the house, who made everybody coo and smile. But still, despite herself, Ellen had loved Hannah; she'd had no choice but to love her and had been completely devoted to her from the moment that she first picked her up. They had shared a room from the beginning, Hannah's crib jammed alongside Ellen's bed in their narrow bedroom. Terrified that something might happen to her little sister when she wasn't looking, Ellen would force herself to lie awake, gazing through the bars of Hannah's crib, watching the rise and fall of her chest, checking the expression on her faultless face for any signs of dark dreams or distress.

When Hannah had been a little older, old enough to be afraid of the dark, she would hold Ellen's hand through the bars of the crib, her tiny, chubby fingers curled around Ellen's longer ones until she slept, and Ellen would never remove her hand from Hannah's. Even when her arm raged with pins and needles or she longed to be able to roll over, she would leave her hand in Hannah's for as long as her sister needed it there.

The last time she had gone upstairs to check on Hannah, who seemed immobile in what she hoped was oblivious sleep, Ellen had wondered when that had stopped, that love and devotion between them. Hannah had never done anything really terrible to her, except be more beautiful, more clever, and more successful, and Ellen had long ago accepted that it was her fate to be outshone by her sister whenever they were together. It wasn't envy exactly that she had felt at the realization—especially not after she'd met Nick and had Charlie. It was just that sometimes she wished that Hannah would leave her alone like she always used to; she felt like more of her own person when Hannah wasn't there. As if Hannah's mere presence highlighted the shortcomings in her life that Ellen preferred not to think about.

"What's typical?" Matt asked again, as he sat up straight, rubbing his palms over his face and blinking himself awake.

"When things went wrong, when she'd made a mistake, instead of admitting it or facing it or doing something to try to make it better, she'd always get herself into even more trouble, as if that would somehow blot out whatever the real problem was. Even when she was very little she'd take risks. When she was six she broke this china figurine that our mother loved—it was a dancing lady or something and Hannah had been playing with it and dropped it. Instead of telling Mum, she climbed the tallest tree in the garden. She got up it okay, but on the way down she panicked and slipped, knocked herself out on one of the roots. I thought she was dead, I really did, she was so still and pale—I had to run and tell Mum and it was a huge drama and of course no one minded about the figurine as long as Hannah was okay."

"Don't really think this compares to climbing a tree," Matt said, puzzled.

"Then, when she was eight, she wanted this doll from the toy shop. Well, it wasn't a birthday or anything, so one day when we were in town, looking round the shop with our pocket money while Mum was in the supermarket, she decided to just take it, and slipped it under her skirt. And she got away with it, only she realized that she couldn't go home with it. So while I was at the till, buying some sweets or something, she got on the bus that stopped just outside, no money for a ticket or anything. Just got on the bus and sat at the back and didn't get off.

"Mum and Dad were frantic. I was supposed to be watching her. A policeman brought her home when she got off at the last stop in Brighton. They were all so relieved to see her, no one but me noticed the doll at the bottom of her toy box. It's been the same ever since. Whenever she's done something stupid or wrong, she pulls a stunt like this, gets herself into trouble, gets herself hurt so that everyone will forget what she's done and feel sorry for her."

Ellen got up abruptly and put the kettle on again.

"You don't really think that's what she was doing this time, do you?" Matt asked. "Hannah wouldn't deliberately put herself in that kind of danger just so no one would be cross with her."

"No, no—I suppose not, I know this isn't the same—it's just . . . I feel guilty, I suppose. Something's been going on with her, something big and dark, and she's been spending all this time around me and Charlie, and I've minded. I haven't wanted her here. All she's been doing is trying to be a good sister, and all I've been doing is pushing her away, which is why I haven't noticed that she's been struggling with her own problems. I haven't seen anything outside those windows in a year." Ellen nodded toward the outside world as she poured boiling water onto two fresh teabags. "And now this—this awful, brutal thing. If I'd been paying attention, really looking at her . . . I always thought that we should be like two peas in a pod, me and Hannah. That sisters would have this . . . bond. But right now I feel like I know her less than ever."

"Maybe it's a kind of guilt," Matt suggested. "Maybe she's punishing herself."

"What on earth could she possibly have done that made her think she deserved that?" Ellen asked, glancing at the ceiling. "She drank too much, tried to drown out whatever it is that's been hurting her—but being attacked like that? That's not Hannah's doing. Someone . . . some people saw how vulnerable she was and they deliberately hurt her when she wasn't strong enough to stop them—and it's killing me that I don't know exactly what happened. The worst of it is, I don't even think she knows."

"Maybe, for now, that is for the best. Maybe she just needs some time to figure it out." Matt stood up and stretched. "Look, I need to get ready for work, take a shower—I'd stay home if I could, but I really can't."

Without thinking, Ellen went to him and put her arms around him, hugging him to her. It was only after he returned the gesture that she remembered she was wearing only a shirt under her dressing gown. She let a beat pass in his arms before she stepped back.

"Sorry," she said awkwardly. "I'm a bit overtired, it's making me inappropriate. What I meant to say was 'thank you.' You didn't need to be any part of this, but you were. I really needed a friend last night and I'm grateful. So, thank you."

Matt didn't speak for a second, caught up as he was in the briefest sensation of her soft body molded to his and every feeling that awoke in his exhausted brain. He hadn't wanted her to break the embrace. He'd wanted her to stay exactly where she was. He'd wanted to hold her.

"It's not a problem," he mumbled, glancing out the window rather than at her face.

"Here, take this with you, I've put extra sugar in it." Ellen handed him a cup of tea.

"You know what," Matt said, pausing at the door. "One thing is obvious about your sister."

"Oh, and what's that?"

"She cares more about what you think of her than anything else," Matt said.

CHAPTER Sixteen

The last person Matt expected to see sitting—no, lounging—at his desk when he finally made it into work was Lucy, the associate editor from downstairs. He'd thought it was oddly quiet when he'd walked into the office, none of the usual banter or jokes going on. Raffa, Steve, and even Pete were sitting at their desks, apparently concentrating on work, which was unheard of, particularly when there was a leggy blonde in the vicinity, in this case leaning back in Matt's desk chair with her ankles crossed on his desktop.

"Er, hello?" Matt slowed down as he approached her. If he wasn't very much mistaken, the last time he'd seen her she'd called him the baddest swear word he could think of, one that even he balked at using. What did she want with him now?

"You always this late?" Lucy asked archly.

"Had a bit of a heavy night," Matt said warily.

"Lured some other poor victim into your lair?"

Matt thought of Hannah's bruised and battered body curled up on Ellen's sofa and cringed inwardly. How much difference was there really between him, cruising bars, looking for tipsy women to talk into bed, and the men whom Hannah had encountered? The thought hadn't escaped him and it had been haunting him ever since.

"Look, Lucy, it's been a tricky night—"

"Ah, *now* he can remember my name!" she exclaimed. "I

thought you might think it was . . ." she picked up a copy of *Bang It!*, folded open to reveal Matt's column, " 'leggy blond bombshell' or maybe 'insatiable, curvy babe'?"

"So you've seen the column then," Matt said wearily, wondering why on earth he had thought it was a good idea to date a woman who worked one floor down—and what's more, why on earth he had decided to write about her. What had he been thinking? The truth was that he hadn't been thinking since he'd got here, at least not with his head. The truth was that he hadn't been thinking with his head especially since 1998 when his hormones kicked in.

"Yes," Lucy said. "And I've come to thank you."

"Thank me?" Matt shifted from one foot to the other. Suddenly he felt confused and afraid, very afraid.

"Er . . ."

"You see," Lucy said, snapping her legs down from his desk in one smooth maneuver and twisting his chair around to face him. "If you hadn't written your column about me, if you hadn't written, for example"—she scanned the page—" 'This little vixen was all over me from the moment we sat down, wearing a dress that left nothing to the imagination, and let me know just exactly what sort of a good time I was in for. I offered her another drink but she was already good to go and practically dragged me back to my place. . . .' If you hadn't written that, for example, then I would never have had the idea for my own piece. And I never would have been pissed off and ballsy enough to take it to my editor and ask her for a chance to write for the magazine. But you did and so did I, *et voilà!*"

Lucy handed him a copy of her own magazine. "You've given me my very first byline." She beamed at him, her bright eyes sparkling.

Dragging his eyes off her, Matt looked down at the glossy page. The headline shouted HOW TO AVOID TERRIBLE SEX! He read the first line: "We've all done it, we've all felt a little low, got a little drunk, and found ourselves in a compromising situation with a man we barely know. We think this liberates us, sets us free, but invariably the next morning we feel foolish and used and worst of all have usually experienced a night of terrible sex. The last time this happened to me was only a few weeks ago. . . ."

Matt looked up. "You've written about me and you?" he asked, incredulous.

"Yep." Lucy nodded, a wicked grin lighting up her face. "What? Not thrilled for me? Don't want to read on? Don't worry, I've memorized it. Let me recite for you: 'This guy, let's call him Matt . . .'"

"Hey—that's my real name!" he protested.

"Yes, but the readers don't know that." Lucy continued reading aloud: "'This guy obviously thought he was the cat's pajamas in bed. But the truth is, from the moment we got into his bedroom I was looking for a reason to leave. Was it his cheesy predictable lines that put me off? After all, how many times have you heard them tell you they've never seen a woman with eyes as beautiful as yours, yeah, right, like they care about your eyes! Or was it his fumbling, amateurish kisses that felt a bit like I was being slobbered all over by a Labrador? Why don't men ever learn that less is so much more when it comes to tongue? No, it was none of that, it was simply that the moment I let him get into my bed, I realized I was going to be bored—bored, bored, bored—and that for the next five minutes I was going to have to try my best to look like I wasn't.'" Lucy stood up and strutted to Matt, so that she was standing very close to him, her eyes sparkling with fury and laughter, the heady scent of her perfume in his nostrils. "'And that's what I'm talking about, ladies,'" she went on, quoting her piece. "'That's why we are all doomed to a terrible sex life unless we take action now. No more pretending that his fumbling at your privates is a turn-on, no more moaning and groaning out loud when really you're wondering if you remembered to record *Grey's Anatomy*. And most of all, no more pretending that you've had an orgasm after a couple of minutes of squelching about, when we all know that it takes a lot longer and a lot more effort to get one of those. Take a stand now! Say "no more" to terrible sex just to make some guy feel good about himself. If they're awful at it, tell them so. And if you're reading this, Matt—just so you know—you are shocking in bed.'"

As she finished her manifesto, she dropped her magazine at his feet, turned on her high heels, and strutted out of the office, to rapturous applause.

"Hey, mate?" Raffa clapped him on the shoulder. "Have you lost a bit of weight?"

"What?" Matt looked at him.

"It's just I think that bird just left with your balls!"

Matt blinked as the office doors swung shut behind Lucy. He'd had no idea that she was so . . . well, so cool.

"Wow, that's never happened before," Matt said, sinking into his chair. He felt embarrassed, exposed, and vulnerable—as if she'd told the world his secret . . . which was exactly what he'd been doing to various women for the last year. Matt closed his eyes. What a prick he was! What a prick he had been— he'd been doing to women what Lucy had just done to him for over a year. And as clever and as funny as Lucy's piece was, as much as it would make her readers laugh, it hurt him; it stung like a very hard slap. How many people had he hurt that way without a second thought?

"Never been bitch slapped in public before?" Pete sneered.

"Never been stung by a revenge column. You got to hand it to her, the girl's got balls."

"Yeah, yours," Raffa repeated his joke, clearly annoyed that it hadn't got a big enough laugh the first time.

"You need to pull it together, son," Pete told him. "Where's the dark destroyer, hey? And more important, where's your piece on that drive-through brothel?"

"Hang on—I only got the brief yesterday," Matt said, although last night in the pub did seem like an eon ago. "I wasn't entirely sure that Dan was even serious."

"Dan is always serious. Come on, mate, you've got a week to go until the end of your probation, and I've got to say it, you look knackered. Please tell me the reason you let that little tramp walk all over you is because you were up all night seeing to your landlady?"

"Lucy isn't a tramp," Matt said, defending his nemesis, and then, seeing the look on Pete's face, he added, "And yeah, I was up with Ellen all night. It's true what they say about older women being at their sexual peak!" Matt's grin was perfectly synchronized with his sense of inner self-loathing. Lucy, Hannah, the idea of writing a piece on a drive-through brothel—after what he'd seen last night and this morning, he felt sick to his stomach. Half-naked girls who were no more than breasts and bums, writing about sex week in and week out—that wasn't his dream job. It had never been his dream job, and Matt couldn't remember anymore why he had ever thought it was. Lucy, Hannah—especially Ellen. They reminded him that he liked women, he loved them. He found them interesting and funny and beautiful in ways that were somehow more subtle and complex than their cup size or how much they'd had to drink. How on earth had that joy and fascination with the opposite sex turned itself into this? Matt sighed. Now, on the cusp of completing his probation, was not the time to be developing a conscience or a desire for something better. But nevertheless, both of those impulses were there and he couldn't shake them off. What was happening to him? he wondered miserably. And then a memory of the scent of her hair as she had embraced him that morning came back to him, and he realized. Ellen, Ellen was happening to him. He had a crush on his landlady.

"Then there's your next column," Pete said. "Get your research on the brothel done and a first draft for your column today, and as for that piece of work that just came in here and stomped all over us?"

"Who, Lucy?" Matt said anxiously.

"That's war, mate," Pete declared. "That's magazine war. Come up with a plan of attack by the end of the day."

As Pete lurched away, Matt sank farther into his chair and considered what would happen if he just got up and walked out of the office and never came back again, because right now, after everything that had happened recently, after everything that had happened last night, the *Bang It!* offices were the very last place he wanted to be.

Ellen rubbed her eyes and looked at the monitor. Allegra had dictated to her, and her typing was riddled with red and green squiggly lines. For the first time since she had begun working for Allegra, Ellen hadn't really been involved in what Allegra was saying.

"So what do you think should happen next?" Allegra asked.

Ellen looked at the older woman. She was immaculately dressed, as ever, but there were violet shadows under her eyes, and there was something else about her that was different, too, that Ellen couldn't quite put her finger on. In the current scene the captain had visited Eliza in her cell to tell her that she was to hang at dawn. Ellen's tired eyes had welled with tears as Allegra described the emotion in the captain's voice as he struggled between his sense of duty and his love for Eliza. And then, just when Ellen could not see how Eliza could possibly escape, the captain had left a key and a dagger for her, hidden in a blanket. Allegra had stopped just at the point where Eliza was about to escape.

"I don't know," Ellen said wearily. "Is the captain waiting for her outside the gates with a horse? Is he going to rescue her after all?" She glanced at the ceiling, thinking of Hannah, who was still asleep. After Matt had gone to work, Ellen had gone back upstairs and, dragging the piles of clothes off the velvet armchair by the window, had sat and looked at Hannah, watching her closely. She had been sleeping peacefully, especially after she'd taken the pain medication, and as relieved as Ellen was to see her sister sleeping peacefully, she was fearful of how she would be when she woke, sober and with a clear head. Ellen was afraid of what Hannah would remember.

"That would be what my readers would expect," Allegra confirmed, as if the idea disappointed her.

"Maybe he could be waiting and then Eliza could murder him with her own knife, steal his horse, and run away to America? Maybe we could make this the first ever postmodern feminist bodice ripper," Ellen suggested testily, wondering what state the man who had hurt Hannah was in as he woke up this morning, if he even had any idea what he had done.

Allegra pressed her lips into a thin smile, and as Ellen focused on her she realized what was out of place. For the first time ever in her presence, Allegra wasn't wearing her vintage red lipstick.

"Feeling a little tense today?" Allegra asked.

Ellen shook her head, unable to talk for the threat of tears.

"I haven't asked because I don't like to pry," Allegra began deliberately. "I don't always like to pry, but, Ellen, I am an old woman. On a good night I barely sleep more than three or four hours, and what with all the comings and goings last night I didn't sleep a wink. I wasn't going to pry, but I can see that you've been up all night and that you are very upset. And if you are upset, we cannot work efficiently. And besides, I worry about you—I like you. Do you want to tell me what happened?"

Ellen looked out the open french doors, down the length of the garden. Of course Allegra had been disturbed last night, the poor woman must have heard almost everything. It hadn't even occurred to Ellen that her lodgers would be affected. She hadn't seen Sabine at all, not all of last night or this morning, so she had no idea if Sabine had been awakened by all the to-ing and fro-ing, or if Sabine had chosen to stay out of the way. But of course Allegra had been disturbed. Ellen felt she owed her an explanation, so, slowly, deliberately careful because of her own muddled brain and the strange dreamlike quality of the preceding night, Ellen began to talk.

"And so I don't know, I don't know what happened to her, I don't know why she lost the job that she loves, why she's gone so utterly off the rails or what really happened to her last night, and worst of all, neither does she."

Allegra nodded. "And what about Charlie? Does he know?"

Ellen shook her head. "I don't think so. He was plugged into his iPod all night and he didn't even mention Hannah when he came down this morning."

If anything, Charlie had seemed happier than he had been in a long time when he arrived in the kitchen in time for breakfast, probably because he'd been worrying for so long about her, feeling that he couldn't talk to her, shut out by her grief. The idea of him shut out, unhappy and alone with his problems, tormented her, because it was only now that she realized exactly how much he had been bottling up, and how much she had missed, shuttered up like a closed house as she had been.

When Charlie came down, Ellen had just collected Hannah's torn and stained clothes from the bathroom floor and had been holding them in her hands, dithering between putting them in the washing machine and saving them as . . . what? Evidence? Then she'd heard Charlie thundering down the stairs and hastily shoved them into the washing machine. She could always turn it on later.

"Matt gone?" he'd asked her.

Ellen had nodded, slotting two pieces of bread into the toaster. "You sleep okay?"

"I think so," Charlie said. "So have you had a chance to

think a bit more about, you know, what we talked about yesterday?" His voice was light and high, and Ellen felt her heart contract—he was trying his best to appear unconcerned.

"About my agoraphobia?" Ellen smiled, sitting down at the table with him. "You did make me think, Charlie. I checked the calendar and I realized something pretty shocking. You are right about one thing. I haven't been out since Dad's funeral. I haven't been out in nearly a year, and the frightening thing is, I didn't even realize it." Ellen had shrugged, conscious that Charlie was watching her closely. "But I'm not agoraphobic, Charlie."

"But, Mum—"

"No, wait. I haven't been outside for a year and that is strange and wrong and I have been hiding in here, but it's not because I just woke up one morning and decided that I didn't want to go out anymore, that I was afraid of the outside. To me it seems like yesterday that we found out Dad was gone. Somehow, the last year has both dragged by and gone in the blink of an eye. I've been caught up in all this grief and I haven't noticed or cared about the outside world. I haven't needed to. I didn't realize I'd been stuck in this house all those months—but I'm not afraid of going out, Charlie. I'm just out of practice."

Ellen covered his hand with hers and squeezed it. "I've been lost in sadness, but I think I'm coming out of it a little bit now, and I'm looking around and I'm seeing how things are and how things should be. So don't worry about me, okay? It's not as bad as you think, I promise."

"You mean you could just grab your bag and walk to school with me now?" Charlie asked.

"I think so, if you really want your mum walking you to school." Ellen smiled.

Charlie thought for a moment and then reached into his school bag, dumping a selection of printed leaflets and pages upon pages of information that he had clearly printed off the internet onto the tabletop, spreading them out with his hand.

"I still think you could have a form of agoraphobia, Mum. It's very common after some traumatic event; I've read about it and it's not unusual for the sufferer to be in denial about what's really going on. But it's totally treatable, you don't even need drugs, just something called cognitive therapy and a support group."

"So where do you go to find an agoraphobic support group—surely they don't get out much?" Ellen attempted to joke, but Charlie was not amused.

"Mum, all I'm trying to say is that this year it's been weird and difficult, it's been like you've been on another planet half the time, the house is full of weirdos, and now even Aunt Hannah's gone mental. I miss Dad—I miss him, too—but I'm ready now for life to be a bit normal again. I'm ready for you to be you again. I'd like for it to be okay to feel happy and have a laugh and moan when you drag me round the supermarket and make me push the trolley. I want to bring my friends home for tea so that you can be all embarrassing and offer them jammy dodgers like we're all still nine. So please, don't talk to me like I'm a baby or like I'm a stupid kid who doesn't know anything. I've thought about this a lot. I even went to the doctors and got those leaflets on my own, and I think I'm right. So I want you to take me seriously. I want you to find out about getting help. After all . . ." Charlie picked up a leaflet and read from it, " 'There is no shame in admitting that life has dealt you a blow you are finding it hard to recover from. Help is just a phone call or a mouse click away.' "

And at that moment Ellen had wished with all her heart that she wasn't so tired and confused by everything else that was going on so that she could enjoy this moment, she could enjoy her son really talking to her for the first time in a long time. Not to have listened to him would have been a crime. Ellen put her hand down on one of the papers and nodded once.

"Okay, okay—I'll take you seriously, I'll read all of this,

and if I think I need it I'll speak to someone about more help. Okay?"

Charlie's smile would have been reward enough, but his arm around her shoulder and the kiss he had planted on her cheek was a bonus that she had not expected. After he left for school, she had been smiling, until she remembered her sister lying beaten and battered upstairs, and the fact that Charlie had left his school bag sitting on the kitchen floor, something that Ellen knew she would pretend she hadn't noticed because the idea of picking it up and running down the road after him filled her with the dreaded certainty that if she stepped out the front door, something really, really terrible would happen to her or the people she loved.

"I think Charlie is fine, actually," Ellen told Allegra. "I actually think he is better than he's been in a long time. I think he feels like he's taking a bit of control about what's going on in his life. Which is exactly why I don't want him to see Hannah. Not like this." Ellen hesitated for a moment before adding, "Funny thing, he seems to have cheered up since he diagnosed me with agoraphobia."

She waited for Allegra to snort with derision or laugh at her son's eccentricity, but the older woman merely nodded, her expression passive.

"You don't seem that shocked!" Ellen laughed nervously.

"You forget, I saw how frightened you were about the idea of going out for lunch," Allegra said. "And I've noticed that you still dry all of your laundry in the dryer even though you have a perfectly good washing line at the bottom of your garden and this has been the hottest June on record. I don't know what you did before I arrived, but I know that in the last month you haven't gone anywhere, and as a consequence neither have I. So, if anything, I think your son might have a point. He's a very astute young man."

"Well, perhaps, and he's right about some things, but ... I'm not ill. I'm just grieving. I'm grieving, that's all."

"I wonder . . . ," Allegra said thoughtfully.

"What do you wonder?" Ellen asked impatiently.

"Ellen, describe your marriage to Nick for me," Allegra said.

Ellen sighed. "Why?"

"Please indulge me."

Ellen thought for a moment. "Nick was very caring, protective. He made me feel safe, and he was careful that I never had to worry about anything. He let me take care of our home and Charlie while he dealt with all the difficult stuff. I never had to think about anything, Nick took care of it all. He really loved me, he cherished me. I'll never have that again."

Allegra was silent for a moment. "Ellen, I'm only saying this because I care about you and because I want better for you than this closed-down half life you're existing in at the moment. When you describe your relationship with Nick, I don't get the same picture of it as you do at all. The picture I get whenever you talk about Nick," Allegra went on carefully, "is of a man who controlled and imprisoned his wife, who kept her like a bird in a gilded cage. Who told her what to think and what to wear, who slowly, systematically stripped her of her personality until she wasn't sure of any of her own thoughts or feelings. And I see you as the wife who became so reliant on him that when he was suddenly taken from her, she had no idea how to function in the real world anymore, so she simply stopped trying. I think Charlie might be right—I think perhaps you are agoraphobic—and I don't think it started on the day of Nick's funeral, I think it started a long time before that, because that's the way your husband wanted you. Whether it was conscious or not, whether he meant it or not. He wanted you pinned down. He wanted you trapped."

Ellen stood up. "How dare you, how dare you talk about Nick that way!" Ellen was surprised by the force of her fury.

"How dare you, Allegra. Nick loved me, he would have done anything for me, he was the kindest, sweetest, loveliest man and the best father, and you . . . you didn't even know him!"

"All I'm saying is that you're looking at this from one very narrow point of view, and that, as with all things, there are other interpretations—"

"Oh, this is ridiculous," Ellen said. "I don't know what I'm doing even trying to work this morning anyway with my sister lying upstairs beaten to a pulp after God only knows what's happened. I know you like to think you're some wise old woman, Allegra, who knows everything and sees everything, but you can't be that astute, otherwise you wouldn't have ended up old and alone."

Ellen finished her rant, her eyes blazing, the meaning of the words she had spit out catching up with her after a second's delay.

"I expect you are right," Allegra said stiffly, every one of her seventy or so years suddenly apparent on her face. "After all, here I am living in the former dining room of a woman I barely know. No husband, no children, not a single relative to turn to when I'm made homeless. The only friend I have ever kept is Simon, and the only other person I have met in decades who I am remotely interested in knowing is you. So I expect you are right, I expect I have got it all wrong. Now if you'll excuse me I think we should leave it for today. I think I might take myself for a little walk. It's been a long time since I felt the sun on my face."

"Allegra, I'm so sorry . . . ," Ellen began, but before she could say any more, the dining-room door opened and Hannah appeared. From that moment, for Ellen, everything in the room was eclipsed by the sight of her sister, her face swollen and bruised.

"Sorry, am I interrupting anything? Only I can't find the bread knife." Hannah's voice was thick and her words were still a little slurred.

"God, Hannah, look at you," Ellen whispered. "Go and sit down, I'll get you something to eat."

"Goodness," Allegra said, what little color there was in her cheeks draining rapidly.

Gingerly, Hannah touched her face. "Yeah, that was some drinking binge."

"Drinking binge—Hannah, you were attacked," Ellen said, wishing she could retract the brutal words as soon as she had uttered them, but realizing that she needed to hear them out loud just as much as Hannah did.

Hannah's face was so immobilized by swelling that it was hard to tell how she reacted, except that she turned her head away, unable to look Ellen in the eye.

"Anyway, I'm ashamed to say that last night is all a bit hazy. What exactly did I say when I got in? Didn't make a fool of myself, did I, Ellie?"

"That's it? That's all you're worried about? What you said? Hannah, stop it! Stop trying to pretend this didn't happen!" Ellen took her sister's wrist and led her into the kitchen, where she pulled dirty clothes out of the washer, holding up Hannah's skirt.

"Look at this. It's ripped, there's blood, and . . . and semen. Hannah, whatever happened, you don't have to put a brave face on it. You don't have to shrug this off like you've grazed your knee!" Ellen ignored her sister's wince as she took her by the shoulders and propelled her to the hall mirror. "Look at your face! Someone did that to you, Hannah. Why are you acting like it doesn't matter?"

Ellen stood behind Hannah as she forced her to confront her reflection, watching her. Hannah's one good eye stared back at itself for a long time and then slowly a tear tracked its way from her blackened and swollen eye, making its way down her vivid cheek.

"It doesn't matter," Hannah said, her voice tight. "I got drunk and took something, and got given something and had sex with some man, maybe men, that I didn't know who roughed me up a bit. It's my own fault, Ellen, I deserve it. I went out on my own, wearing next to nothing, got drunk and got fucked. I'm an adult, I knew what I was doing, I deserved it. So anyway, I was pretty far gone by the time I got here. What did I say again?"

Ellen stared at her sister's reflection. "Hannah, no matter what you were wearing, no matter how drunk you were, you didn't deserve that, no woman deserves that—you, you're so bright and beautiful and in charge of your life. You should know better than anyone else that whatever happened last night was wrong." Ellen released her grip on Hannah's shoulders, slipping her arms around them and hugging her from behind. "Please let me help you. I know I've been . . . stuck, stuck inside my own head and my own life, not just since Nick but for years, possibly. And I know I let you go, pushed you away. But I do love you, Hannah, and I can't bear this. I can't bear to see you of all people like this, as if . . . as if it doesn't matter what happens to you anymore."

"But don't you see, Ellie, I don't care. I don't care what happens to me anymore . . . ," Hannah said bleakly as Allegra emerged from the dining room and stood uncertainly in the hallway, just as shocked by Hannah's appearance as Ellen was.

"Look. I think you may be in shock or something, but even though you've had a bath it's not too late. We've still got evidence, I haven't washed your clothes. I can still call the police."

"Ellen, please, please—tell me, what did I say last night?" Painfully Hannah slipped out of Ellen's embrace and turned to face her. "Did I . . . ? Did I talk about Nick?"

"What?" Ellen struggled to understand. "Nick? Yes, yes—that's right. You said that one of the men you were with was called Nick, too, so that's something to go on, right? That's something we can tell the police. Please let me call them."

Hannah shook her head. "And that's it, that's all? I didn't saying anything else about Nick, about your Nick?"

"Hannah, why is this important? What if you did? What's important now is that you face this and do something about it. What if they attack another woman tonight? You have to . . ."

Hannah shook her head and with some difficulty made her way back into the kitchen, where she stood at the sink, filling the kettle. Ellen looked at Allegra, shaking her head.

"Give her some time," Allegra said. The two women followed Hannah into the kitchen, where Ellen stood for some moments, struggling to know what to say. If her sister wanted to know what had happened after she got here last night, then Ellen would tell her.

"Matt found you," she began. "You'd made your way to the bottom of the street and he found you. He thinks you'd passed out in some neighbor's garden. It was lucky you came round when he was passing. He brought you home and woke me up, and when I saw you I was horrified, I was trying to get you to tell me what had happened, but you were out of it. You told me that you had sex with Nick and you kept asking me to forgive you. You kept making me promise that I would always love you. Nothing you said made any sense, really. . . ."

Ellen stopped in her tracks as she ran the sentence over again, hearing the words as if for the first time. "You kept asking me to forgive you. . . ."

Slowly, Hannah set the kettle down and turned around. When Ellen looked into her eyes, she knew the truth.

"You had sex with Nick," she said slowly. "You had sex with my husband."

"Oh, God." Hannah buried her bruised face in her hands. "Oh, God, I was afraid I'd let it slip, after all this time. . . ."

Ellen battled against the words that demanded repetition and lost. "You had sex with my husband. My sister had sex with my husband. Oh my God . . ." She lurched forward, then steadied herself heavily on the tabletop. "Oh my God, I'm going to be sick. You threw yourself at him, you threw yourself at the one thing I had that was mine!"

"No." Hannah took a tentative step toward Ellen. "No, it wasn't like that. You have to listen. It wasn't just sex . . . and it wasn't because either of us didn't love you—it was . . . it wasn't just sex, Ellen, we . . . Nick and I loved each other, too."

Ellen stared at Hannah, every sinew in her body caught in the moment, every fiber straining against what she was hearing.

"Get out," Ellen said. "Get out of my home now."

"Ellen, please, I've tried. I've tried not to tell you, but I had to. I don't know what would have happened if I kept it to myself any longer. At least now you know, we can talk, we can work things through, we can support each other. . . . Please, all I want is for you and me to be okay."

In that second, Ellen snapped. She grabbed her sister by the arm, oblivious to the pain that shot across Hannah's face, and dragged and pushed her in turn into the hallway and out the front door, giving her one violent shove after the other up the garden path and onto the street.

"Get out, get out, get out," Ellen repeated, deaf to Hannah's protests.

Finally, with the midday sun blazing down on their heads, the two of them stood in the road. "You're right," Ellen told her sister. "I hope they hurt you, I hope they used you and hurt you, because you were right, you deserved everything that happened to you. You're nothing more than a common whore."

Turning her back on her sister, Ellen felt the world tip and tilt, felt herself no longer bound by the rules of gravity, about to slip off the face of the earth. She felt the oxygen rush from her collapsing lungs, her heart pounding, about to explode in her chest as sank onto her knees, the hot paving stones burning her bare skin. Suddenly the front door seemed a thousand miles away and still the world slipped on its axis, revolving ever upward as if she were a parasite it was keen to be rid of. Breaking her nails against the stones, Ellen began to claw her way to the shadow and shelter of the house, fighting for each breath as she went. After what seemed an eternity, she was aware of someone at her side, thin fingers supporting her under her armpits, dragging her, guiding her toward the distant country of her home, of what once had been her home, and at last the sun was eclipsed by shadow and Ellen felt the cool ceramic tiles pressed against her cheek.

As Allegra shut the door firmly on Hannah, Ellen lay there, waiting for the world to right itself again, and then she realized that was impossible now. Nothing would ever be right again.

CHAPTER
Seventeen

Since he had arrived at work that morning to find Lucy locked and loaded and waiting for him, Matt's head had been swimming with a thousand images, of Hannah beaten and bruised, of the photos of half-naked women tacked, taped, and spread out all around him, like an obscene collection of butterflies pinned up for his delectation, and most of all of Ellen in the moments before he had awakened her and dragged her into a world of confusion and chaos.

She had looked beautiful, not in an interesting or flawed way. Not because of the usual frailties that so often fascinated him about women, but because to him, she simply was beautiful. Her hair had been spread across the pillow, entwined between her fingers, her lips had been slightly parted as if in preparation for a kiss, and her bare throat had shone in the half-light, a glowing pathway that promised to lead to an undiscovered country. For reasons that Matt could not fathom, the sight of her then had taken him back ten years to an English class in which he thought he had not been paying attention, to a poem by some dead bloke whose name he would never remember in a million years. And yet, just then, one single line that must have slotted its way into his brain on that wet and wintry morning all those years ago presented itself to him as if it had been waiting all these years to make itself known: "Oh my America, my newfound land."

If in fact Matt remembered rightly, that poem was the reason he had become interested in writing in the first place. He'd forgotten that entirely until that moment, and he wondered how he could have forgotten something as pivotal as that. And what was it about Ellen that made him remember that moment all those years ago in a cold, dingy classroom where he'd been unexpectedly inspired to write a love poem, to simply write?

As Matt found himself in the middle of all the images of Hannah and the parade of topless models that assaulted him from all angles, he wondered, too, what would have happened if he had walked into Ellen's bedroom to wake her for another reason entirely.

He worked through his exhaustion, laboring away for the column over a fictionalized account of what had not happened between him and Ellen, but every time he tried to make it seem like a funny or racy anecdote, he'd realize that it had become romantic and fantastical. As if he was trying to remember that poem and rewrite it in prose for a men's magazine. Still, Pete didn't have to know that, so Matt went with it, allowing himself free rein to think about her, to describe her in every detail, and to imagine coaxing her to reveal herself to him, layer by layer, a lazy unveiling that when he pictured it got him much hotter under the collar than any of the photos that surrounded him. Which was odd, because Matt always maintained that men were simple creatures with simple desires, yet nothing that he had started to feel for Ellen was simple. "On His Mistress Going to Bed," that's what that poem was called; the title had suddenly popped into his brain. How odd that he'd remember that now, all these years later. Matt allowed himself to idle away a few more minutes, reimagining Ellen in that poem, and then caught Pete's eye across the office. He had to resign himself to the fact that there was no place for poetry at *Bang It!* Unless you counted the limerick someone had scrawled on the wall in the gents.'

As soon as the sun was up in Nevada, Matt put in a call to Fifi's Cathouse, which had a drive-through brothel where the self-employed girls chose between renting a room in the house or entertaining their clients in the comfort of their cars in a series of dingy garages. Of course, the sun coming up seemed to mean that the workforce went to bed, but eventually Matt got through to someone and he was not surprised to discover that his was not nearly the first request for information. A very pleasant-sounding woman called Angel Delight said she would email him a press pack and line up some Skype interviews with a selection of the professionals, but he would have to wait until eight o'clock that evening for them to begin, which gave him some time to kill. Matt wondered about phoning Ellen to find out how she and Hannah were. Then he wondered if it was appropriate—he thought it should be, after all, he was the one who had discovered Hannah, who'd brought her back and stayed up all night with Ellen. He was the one whom Ellen had embraced, but somehow Matt wasn't sure that gave him any special privileges. He remembered telling a girl he'd dated for a week or two back in Manchester that one of the reasons he wanted to break up with her was that she was too clingy.

"Too clingy? You call my calling you after nearly a week too clingy?" she had exclaimed. "You don't mind sleeping with me, seeing me a couple of times a week for sex, but only as long as I know my place and I don't expect that you sharing my bed gives me the right to actually talk to you every once in a while? I don't play those games, Matt. Either we're together or we're not. Which is it?"

Matt had responded with a resounding "not" and gone on his way without giving the girl a second thought. Except for today—today he understood how intimacy, even simple emotional intimacy, could lead a person to think it was okay to phone another person to see if she was okay. Only what if the other person thought he was being invasive, nosy, or even clingy? Matt realized that Ellen made him feel like a girl, which he wasn't entirely thrilled about. This was how he'd been making girls feel for years.

As the clock ticked on toward eight, Pete invited him to sit in on a casting; a couple of girls were in Dan's office, stripping down to their underwear in the hope of making a spread. But as several staff members, including the postroom boy, found spurious reasons why they absolutely had to be there, Matt realized that he didn't want to look at them. Instead, he had to resist the urge to walk in there and tell them to cover themselves up and have a little self-respect. That of course would have been career suicide, and even though he was beginning to wonder if this was the right career for him, he couldn't afford just to walk away from it. How would he pay Ellen rent then?

Matt decided to kill time in the pub. With a bit of luck, the rest of the lads who hadn't found a way into Dan's office would be caught up watching the secret filming of the casting in the conference room for at least an hour, and he'd get a chance to think.

Of course, Lucy was in the lift when Matt stepped in. She looked him up and down and then studied the wall with interest.

"I thought that was pretty cool today," Matt said.

"What's this, a line?" she asked, without taking her eyes off the wall. "Trying to trick me into thinking you're not so bad after all, to prove to all those gormless goons up there that you can get me back into bed?"

Matt smiled. "That would have been a plan of pure evil genius, but no—actually that thought hadn't occurred to me. Seriously, I . . . I treated you like shit and I used you and I deserved all of that. I really did." Matt seemed even more surprised by his confession than Lucy, who peered at him suspiciously.

"Have you found God or something, because even if you have, I'm still not going to have sex with you ever again."

"Well, I'd hate for you to be bored," Matt said as the lift

reached the ground floor and they stepped out into the foyer, pleased to see a tiny smile tugging at the corners of her glossed lips. "Or have to fake anything."

Lucy grinned at him as they walked out into the blaze of the evening.

"Isn't it funny that two people can do something so intimate and so . . . close and not really know each other at all?"

"I suppose it is," Matt said.

"I mean, here I am looking at you and you're cute and everything, but it seems like another person who went to bed with you, another person who I went to bed with. I never ever would have gone to bed with *you* if I'd gotten to know you."

"Bloody hell, Lucy." Matt winced. "You've had your revenge in a national magazine. Can't you lay off now?"

"No, that's not what I mean. What I mean is that you are far too nice to have sex with."

"Oh, God," Matt groaned.

"You're more like a brother, really," Lucy went on.

"Shut up!" Matt cried.

"Yes, that's it—a little gay brother."

"Right, fine, fine—I'm your nice little gay brother. Sex is totally off the table. Now we've established the facts, what are the chances you'll come and have a drink with me? We can talk about fashion, and shoes and . . ."

"What?" Lucy grinned at him. "Interior design?"

"Remember that dragon of a landlady I was telling you about?" Matt said, sensing that even after everything that had happened, he could trust Lucy. "Well, she's got me feeling a bit confused."

"Oh, so you are gay after all. Tell all to Agony Aunt Lucy, I'll set you straight."

Matt remembered that Lucy liked white wine spritzers and set one down in front of her as she openly flirted with a man in a tight T-shirt who was standing at the bar.

"Don't sleep with him," Matt advised, pushing the drink across the surface of the table. "He's even more of a prick than I am."

"How do you know?" Lucy asked. Matt nodded at the man's left hand, where a faint white mark was visible on his ring finger.

"Oh my God," Lucy moaned, covering her face with her hands. "Why am I such a terrible judge of character?"

"Start from the assumption that every man you meet is out to get you. Keep them far, far away until you know different, and then eventually you'll meet one who will see all the brilliant things about you, apart from your face and your body. They'll go dippy over the way you tell a joke, and how your eyes flash when you're mad, and that sweet weird little dimple on your right shoulder. And they won't be able to stop thinking about you, and wondering about you, and you'll have them wrapped around your little finger, I promise."

Lucy looked at Matt for a long minute. "You're sure you're not in love with me, aren't you, because you're nice and everything, but really . . ."

"No, it's not you. It's my dragon landlady. I've become a bit obsessed with her."

"In a stalky, weird, want-her-because-you-can't-have-her sort of way?" Lucy asked. "Because let me tell you, there is nothing that pisses me off more than a man who's all about the thrill of the chase and then as soon as he's got you, he goes off you."

"No, no—not in that sort of way. In a wanting-to-write-her-a-love-poem sort of way. In a caring-about-what-she's-thinking-and-feeling-and-worrying-about-her sort of way. In a wanting-to-lie-down-beside-her-and-hold-her-and-stroke-her-hair sort of way." Matt's confession poured out of him, because once he'd started to talk about the way he felt about Ellen, he discovered that he didn't want to stop. "She's got this inner quiet about her, you know. A sort of stillness and silence. I look at her and I get the feeling she'd bring me . . . peace."

"Fuck me, you are gay!" Lucy said, grinning as Matt blushed. "Sorry, I didn't mean that. What I meant was, it sounds like you have sort of written her poem already. And it sounds like you really do like her."

"I really, really do," Matt said. "And I have no idea what to do about it."

"Tell her?" Lucy suggested.

"I can't do that—it's the anniversary of her husband's death soon, and she's got a kid, and besides, she's in the middle of a great big awful mess with her sister. I can't just tip up and tell her how I feel."

"Maybe your doing that is exactly what she needs," Lucy mused.

"Plus, I'd actually die before I'd have the guts to," Matt added.

"You know what I don't get?" Lucy scrutinized him. "Is that you, Matt Bolton, trashy-column writer, coming up with all this poetic shit? Either it doesn't seem like you or you don't seem like someone who should be writing for *Bang It!*"

Lucy had repeated almost exactly what Ellen had said to him.

"Which is funny, because it's my dream job," Matt told her grimly.

"What, you set out wanting to fill in the gaps between photos of women's tits, did you? I do admire a man with ambition."

Matt laughed. "I thought I did—I thought there couldn't be a better job for me. But no, the first thing I ever tried to write was a poem, and then when I was a bit older I wanted to be a journalist, like a war correspondent. Then girls happened, my column happened. I fucked up my life in Manchester by having sex with my best friend's girlfriend and ended up here. I thought I was following a career path, but really I've just been letting stuff happen to me. And now I don't know what to do."

"Apologize to your best friend," Lucy said.

"That will solve all my problems?" Matt asked. "Anyway, I can't, he's not talking to me. He kicked me out and took custody of the PlayStation."

"Then try again and keep trying until you get through to him. Show him you care enough to persist. Best friends are hard to find, and if you're about to fall in love with someone, then you're going to need him for when it all goes horribly wrong and you're an emotional wreck. Besides, it's karma. You need to clear up your negative karma, and as tracking down all of the women you've upset or offended recently would take about a million years, your only hope is to sort things out with your friend, take stock of your work, and then tell your landlady how you feel about her."

"What if she runs a mile?"

"Life's not all about dead certs, sunshine," Lucy said. "It's not all about lining up some tipsy bit of totty in a bar for ten minutes of fun—"

"Hang on—it was more like twenty—"

"It's about taking risks, it's about putting yourself out there, really *living* your life. And I don't get the feeling that's what you're doing now. You're treading water, and you are too nice and sweet and clever to let that happen to you."

"Can you strike the 'nice and sweet' bit from that list?" Matt said. "I'm actually the dark destroyer."

"No, you are not!" Lucy snorted into her drink. "You're one of the nice guys. Which means two things: first, that it's time you admit it, and second, that I can never, ever fancy you again. There's always a bright side."

It was gone ten by the time Matt finished chatting to the ladies of Fifi's Cathouse, and all very nice they were, too. There were two single mothers who had discovered that this was one of the very few jobs that they could fit in around their children and earn enough to pay the bills. There were a couple of young girls, barely twenty, who just did it for fun, one of whom was putting herself through college while she studied for a degree in medicine, and there was one woman who just plain liked the work. It was only when Matt logged off that he realized he hadn't got any of the sort of stuff that Dan would be looking for; all the notes he'd made about the women he'd talked to were about them, their backgrounds, their motivations, even the names of their pets, in one case. He hadn't asked a single one of them what their favorite position was. Maybe Lucy was right, either he was going gay or . . . Lucy had used the term *falling in love.* Matt preferred to think of it as "having feelings." Having feelings seemed a lot less frightening than either of the alternatives.

When he finished work at last, he realized that everyone else was in the pub. He could have gone home to find out how Hannah was, and to see Ellen again. And yet as much as he wanted to, which was very much indeed, Matt decided to go to the pub again. Because as much as he wanted to see Ellen, he also didn't want to see her. He wasn't at all sure he was ready to be "having feelings."

Ellen stared at herself in the wardrobe mirror. She had been staring at herself for some time now, she wasn't sure how long except the afternoon had become evening. It was like reading a familiar word over and over again—the more she looked at it, the less it made sense. Sabine had come home to find her sprawled on the hall floor, an anxious Allegra trying to talk her to her feet.

"What's this?" Sabine had asked, with some consternation. "Why is Ellen on the floor?"

"She has just discovered that her sister, Hannah, who last night appeared to have been rather savagely attacked, was having some kind of sexual dalliance with her late husband," Ellen heard Allegra tell Sabine as if from a very great distance.

Sabine must have checked the time, because the next thing

Ellen heard her say was, "This is no good. Charlie will be home soon, Ellen. Do you want him to see you like this? You must get up at once and wash your face."

Ellen had rolled onto her back and begun to laugh but Sabine was clearly in no mood for joking. She had grabbed Ellen's hand and pulled her arm until Ellen realized that she either had to get up or have it torn out of the socket.

"Ellen, come now—you are not a lunatic, so stop acting like one."

"Actually I am." Ellen giggled. "I am officially mad. It looks like I am agoraphobic after all. I tried to kick my sister out onto the street and ended up nearly giving myself a coronary instead. Charlie was right, I'm afraid of the outside, I'm afraid of grass and flowers and bumblebees and . . . and noise and people and crowds and buses. No wonder Nick . . . no wonder he . . . You know, it all makes sense now. At least now it all makes sense."

"I've tried talking to her but she's in shock, I think," Allegra said anxiously. "I called Simon but he's not in the office. I really didn't know what to do."

"I'll tell you what we will do," Sabine said firmly to Ellen. "We will go to your room and wash your face and you will rest. When Charlie comes in, I will take him to the pub for tea, tell him you have a headache or something. Allegra will stay with you and you will talk about everything that's happened and you will see that it is not so very bad."

"Not so very bad?" Ellen laughed. "My deadbeat sister is in love with my dead husband. How can that not be bad?"

Sabine thought for a second before answering, "Well, at least he is already dead. That saves you from having to kill him."

True to her word, Sabine had bodily escorted Ellen up the stairs and into her bedroom, propelling her into the bathroom, where she scrubbed Ellen's face all over with a sponge, like a mother cat cleansing a kitten.

"You are very hurt," she informed Ellen as she guided her back in the shadowy room, curtains still drawn from the night before. "And you are very shocked. And you are very tired. You should sleep and get drunk and then talk to Hannah—find out exactly what this means."

"Do you think he had a list of things he couldn't stand about me?" Ellen asked. "You know, frumpy, sexless, boring, meek, never goes out. Do you think he had a list like that? Of course he preferred Hannah to me. I really thought that he was the first, the only person in the world who didn't prefer Hannah to me, but of course he did. I mean, look at her and look at me. Of course he did."

"Ellen," Sabine said, sitting Ellen down on the edge of her bed and crouching in front of her. "I know what it feels like to find out that the man you love is or was in love with another woman. I know it rips you in half. But think about it, you only have Hannah's word. Nick isn't here to defend himself. You only have her version of events, and who knows, perhaps over the last year she has made something that maybe was nothing into some grand affair—something that never was. And as for everyone preferring Hannah to you, I think that's in your head only. If you don't expect very much for yourself, you won't get it."

Ellen looked at Sabine. "Do you think so? Do you think that whatever it was that happened wasn't that serious?"

"Its possible." Sabine shrugged. "I'm just saying don't fall apart. Not yet. Not until you know something that you have found out for yourself."

"But if it wasn't true, if it was all in her head, then she wouldn't have been drinking, messing up at work—putting herself at risk. She wouldn't have let what happened to her last night happen if all this was in her head. You should have seen her, Sabine, she looked like a broken doll. She kept telling me that whatever had happened to her didn't matter, that it was just what she deserved. And I kept saying that she was wrong, but you know, what I kept thinking, even before this, even before she told me about Nick, I kept thinking she was right. I kept thinking she *did* deserve it, that she careens through life expecting everything to fall into place around her, and that maybe this time she'd learn that this is not how it works. What sort of person does that make me, to think that when she's been so badly hurt?"

"Ellen, sleep. Rest. I'll take Charlie out for tea, and later, when you have a clear head, we will talk. We can make a list, look for evidence. We can find out the truth ourselves. But for now, rest. I promise you, sleep is a welcome refuge from even the worst the waking world can offer."

Sabine had all but pressed Ellen back onto the bed and left her lying there staring at the ceiling, her head swimming in confusion. Ellen thought she must have slept for a little while at least, her body giving in willingly to the physical exhaustion that her mind fought, and she was dimly aware of the sound of Charlie's feet on the stairs and someone opening the door to look at her. When she woke again, the house was silent, and she sat up abruptly, coming face-to-face with her own reflection in the wardrobe mirror.

Her hair, which she hadn't brushed since yesterday, nested around her shoulders in a mass of dark tangles. Her face was creased with sleep, the seam of a pillowcase indented across one cheek; her eyelids were swollen and red. She looked like a grieving widow, and she felt like one. She felt that she had lost Nick all over again, and worse than that, she'd lost every memory, every moment they had shared together, which she had treasured so dearly. If what Hannah had told her was true, she would never be able to think about them again.

As Ellen stared at herself, she thought of the woman she had believed herself to be, the woman who was a little shy and reserved, who avoided crowds and noise and enjoyed nothing better than getting lost in a good book. A woman who was adored by the husband she had happily devoted herself to, a mother who always put the needs of her son first. A widow who, having faced adversity, had found the strength to carry on.

But Ellen realized as she looked into her own green eyes that she was none of those things. She was a woman betrayed by her own sister, deceived and mocked by a husband who, if Allegra was to be believed, thought of her as nothing more than a possession that he could control. A husband who had not loved her, at least not for the last year of his life, and very possibly even longer than that. She was a woman who had virtually ignored her son, so caught up was she in her sorrow, a woman who hid from the world, who shut it out along with life so that she could live a virtual existence between the pages of a book. She was a coward, and a fool. A misguided, smug, and selfish fool who had allowed herself to be led into a prison cell by the hand and who, now that the door was wide open, still didn't want to leave.

Ellen stood and pressed the tips of her fingers against those of her reflection. This could not be the story of her life, it couldn't end like this. A thought occurred to her and she flung open the wardrobe and rooted around in the back. Somewhere, somewhere . . . Ellen pulled out the dress she had worn on her first date with Nick. It was a dark bottle-green, figure-hugging cotton jersey with as low a neck as she would ever dare to wear and a hem that fell just above the knee. Ellen laid the dress on her bed and smoothed it out. She had felt so wonderful wearing it, so powerful and sexy. She remembered walking through the restaurant, returning to her and Nick's table after a trip to the ladies' and feeling heads turn in her wake. For the first time in her life, she had felt that she was on the brink of discovering who she really was, the woman who she could be, the woman who didn't merely watch the world go by but who took part in all life had to offer.

That night, Nick had told her that she was the most beautiful thing he had ever seen, which was why she had been surprised when a few weeks later, she put the dress on to go to some work function of Nick's and he asked her to change into something else.

"I thought you liked me in this," Ellen remembered saying, smoothing her palms over her hips.

"I do, I do like you in it," Nick had told her, glancing up briefly from the newspaper he was reading. "That doesn't mean I want the rest of the male population of the world to like you, too. You're mine now, Ellen; save that for the next time we're alone."

Although she had always kept it as a token of that first night with Nick, Ellen had never worn her green dress again. She racked her brain and thought and thought and realized that if she wasn't very much mistaken, that might have been the last piece of clothing that she had ever chosen on her own. Uncertain of exactly what she was doing, Ellen rummaged through her drawers. Pair after pair of sensible knickers floated onto the floor, along with firm-control bras in shades of white and beige, until she found what she was looking for. A set of underwear that she had bought to surprise Nick with the first Valentine's Day after Charlie was born.

Things had gone off the boil after Charlie came along; in fact, Ellen recalled getting the feeling that in those early days, Nick was more resentful of Charlie's demands on her time and her body than he was proud of his newborn son. What she was certain of was that Nick had thought of her differently after her pregnancy. He stopped looking at her in the way he used to or even touching her in the same way, his fingers never tracing the stretch marks that ran across her belly and hips, his mouth hardly ever seeking out her larger and newly shaped breasts. Ellen had been at a loss as to how to get him to come back to her as the lover she had come to depend on until she read an article in a women's magazine, something about how to keep the lust alive on Valentine's Day. There were several hints and tips, some involving ice cream and melted chocolate or some kind of dressing-up outfit; the only thing that Ellen had liked was underwear. She went out and bought some sexy lingerie. It had taken her hours to find exactly the right thing, steering clear of all the bright red nylon and feather-trimmed bras that seemed to line the shops that February. Eventually, after enduring the humiliation of a fitting by a very young, very pert girl, Ellen had chosen a black lacy underwire bra and matching panties. By most women's standards it was very tame, but for Ellen it was quite risqué. That night, as she waited for Nick to come home, she made preparations that would give them at least an hour to themselves, feeding Charlie and putting him down in his crib at just the right moment. She had timed it to perfection; the house was silent, Charlie was asleep, and as she heard Nick coming up the stairs she slipped off her dressing gown and lay on the bed in her new underwear.

Nick walked in and chuckled. This wasn't exactly the response that Ellen had expected, but still she tried her best seductress smile on him.

"Dinner's in the oven, Charlie's fast asleep, I thought perhaps . . . ?"

Nick had sat on the bed and kissed her on the cheek. "Bless you," he had said. "But, Ellen, you don't need to do all this for me. To be honest, I'm exhausted and I want a shower before I eat. Why don't you get dressed and talk to me while I clean up, okay?"

He hadn't been cruel or unkind, he hadn't mocked or insulted her, but as Ellen dragged on her clothes she had been awash with the humiliation and rejection.

Ellen felt the humiliation again as she relived the memory now. This was not going to be it, she decided. The way she had folded in on herself over the last ten years, losing herself to her house and her husband, was not going to be the sum total of what her life amounted to. She refused to let it be. True, she didn't know exactly what had happened between Hannah and Nick, but she knew that something had, because whatever Hannah was, she was not a liar. But even if she hadn't found that out, Ellen had been changing these last few weeks. She had been evolving and now she was determined that a wife, a mother, a flawed sister, a lost widow . . . an agoraphobic would not be the sum total of her existence. She would not let one more minute of her life slip away unlived to its fullest potential.

Spontaneously, she slipped off the clothes she had been wearing since last night and stepped into the underwear that she had bought all those years ago. After hooking the bra, she returned to look at herself in the mirror, shying away from making full eye contact with her reflection for some moments. The bra was now a little too small, so her breasts gently swelled over the lace trim, but Ellen was surprised to see that the effect wasn't too disgusting. She ran her fingers down her torso and into her waist before meeting the curve of her hips. Her gently curving stomach still bore the silvered stretch marks that her pregnancy had left her with, and her bottom was dimpled and a little more generously proportioned than it used to be, but as Ellen turned first to one side and then the other, she found that her body wasn't nearly as old or as repulsive as she had imagined. After a moment she slipped the dress on. It didn't fit her the same way it had all those years ago, it strained across her breasts and clung more to her bottom, but unless Ellen was very much mistaken, it didn't look that bad.

Impulsively she sat down at her dressing table and rummaged through her drawer. Thoughts and feelings about Hannah, Nick, and everything else clamored for her attention, but Ellen ignored them. She was certain that somewhere in here there was some mascara and lipstick.

After several minutes of looking, Ellen finally found a long-neglected tube of lipstick. Very slowly and carefully, her hand trembling, she applied the dark red gloss to her mouth. Nick had never liked her in lipstick, he'd always said it made her mouth look too big. But when Ellen checked her reflection in the mirror, she was fairly certain that the result gave her already-generous mouth a little more definition and color.

"Fuck you, Nick," she said out loud, utterly unaware that she had spoken at all. Then she unscrewed a mostly dry and caked tube of mascara and batted her lashes at the wand. The effect here was less pleasing: there were black clumps that she had to tease out of her lashes with her fingernails and a fine powdery dust that collected on her cheeks, which when she tried to wipe it away left a smudge—but after several minutes with a damp cotton-wool pad, Ellen thought she'd done the best job possible, and what remained of the black mascara did seem to intensify the green of her eyes.

After dragging a brush through her hair, Ellen knelt down and slipped a shoe box out from underneath her bed. Unwrapping the tissue paper they nestled in, Ellen took out her one pair of smart shoes, black and plain with a low heel. They were her funeral shoes.

Ellen looked at them for a long time, so sedate and sensible, the dull, smooth leather emitting a faint shine. She realized for the first time that she hated these shoes, they were ugly and frumpy—the kind of shoes that Nick would have picked for her, but that she had picked for herself, choosing only that which he would approve of, unaware that she despised them. Without a second thought, she took them to the window and threw them out, hearing them clatter on the path below. Then, just as purposefully, she marched to Sabine's room and knocked on the door, even though she knew that Sabine was still out with Charlie. Sabine had very many pairs of shoes and Ellen borrowed the highest, shiniest pair she could find, a pair of silver stiletto peep-toe sling-back sandals. Sitting on the edge of Sabine's bed, she fiddled with the minute jeweled buckles for several minutes before she finally managed to secure the shoes to her feet. They were a little small and the straps pinched her toes but Ellen didn't care. They were her finishing touch, the

final element to a plan that she barely knew she had been for-
mulating until she took her first teetering steps in those shoes.
Just as she was about to leave, Ellen spotted a bottle of wine on
Sabine's dressing table, a Rioja with a screw-cap top. Next to it
was an unwashed glass, and from what Ellen could tell, about
one glass's worth of wine was missing from the bottle. Pursing
her lips and shrugging, Ellen picked up both the bottle and
glass and took them with her.

Returning to her room, Ellen heard Charlie and Sabine
coming in from the pub, which meant it must be about eight.
Hastily she climbed into bed, pulling the covers over her head
as her son's feet thundered up the stairs, hoping that if he did
come in he wouldn't notice her makeup.

"Charlie," she heard Sabine whisper, "let Mum sleep, okay?
It takes a long time to get over a migraine. We could hook up
our DSs if you like and play Mario Kart."

"You've got a DS?" Ellen heard Charlie outside the door,
sounding clearly impressed.

"Of course, and I'm pretty good, too. Come on, let's go
downstairs and see if we can't teach Allegra how to race, too."

"Okay," Charlie said after a moment's hesitation. "Yeah, all
right then, probably best to let her sleep it off."

And then it was just a matter of waiting, taking one more
sip of the warming, numbing wine and waiting for Charlie,
who came in to see her around ten o clock.

"Mum? You okay?"

Ellen regarded him from over the edge of her quilt and
nodded. "Yes, Charlie, I'm fine. I think I just overheated a bit,
that's all."

"Your headache—it's not because of me, is it? Because of
what I said and made you look at the leaflets?"

Ellen held one bare arm out to him, careful not to let him see
any of the ensemble that she still wore beneath the covers, complete with the silver sandals; most of her lipstick had worn off
now anyway and she suspected she'd have to reapply the mas-

cara, too, which had flaked all over the pillow while she'd been waiting, dozing, thinking. "No, no—not at all. And you know what, Charlie? You were right. You were utterly and totally right. I have got a problem and I do need some help, I finally realized that today. I don't know if I ever would have if you hadn't been brave enough to tell me. I've a few other things to sort out, but I promise you, I will get better. I will be a good mum again."

"You are a good mum," Charlie insisted, taking her hand. "Anyway, guess what? I had scampi and chips in the pub. It was nice."

"Charlie, that's great!" Ellen said, sitting up to hug him, forgetting her secret ensemble for a moment. Fortunately, to an eleven-year-old boy, a green dress and an old shirt were virtually the same.

"Calm down, Mum. It's no big deal. It's just today I fancied a change, that's all."

"I know," Ellen said, "I know what you mean. Good night, love."

She kissed Charlie on the forehead and waited for what would be Sabine's inevitable follow-up visit. It came less than two minutes later.

"You borrowed my wine, I see," Sabine said, sitting down in the place Charlie had just vacated.

"Yes, do you mind?" Ellen asked.

"Of course not. I think under these circumstances alcohol is really the best remedy. Also it will help you sleep."

"And Charlie, he doesn't know about anything that's happened?"

"No; he was in good form actually. A little worried about you but not unduly. He seems . . . lighter."

"I think he is," Ellen said. "I think he's been carrying around this worry for months all on his own, and now he's found the courage to talk to me about it, he feels better. Which is exactly why he mustn't know about anything that has happened with Hannah."

Sabine nodded in agreement. "Allegra has retired. I think Charlie and I wore her out. Would you like me to make you some food before I go to my room? I'm having another Skype conference with Eric, but not for twenty minutes."

"No." Ellen mustered a smile. "I couldn't eat anyway. . . . It all seems so surreal. So artificial. Like I've just read it in a chapter of a book."

"I know," Sabine said. "Well, tomorrow when the sun is up and you have rested, we will think what to do next. For now, drink the wine and sleep and let it all seem unreal."

"Thank you, Sabine," Ellen said. "When I took in lodgers I never expected that I'd be taking in friends, too, but you and Allegra and Matt, that's exactly what you are."

"Well," Sabine said, "most people are good. Most people apart from my stinking, evil, good-for-nothing husband, that is."

When Sabine had gone, Ellen looked at the clock; it was almost eleven. Not much longer to wait and the house would be quiet and asleep. She would be able to go downstairs, find another bottle of wine, and implement her plan.

Because tonight, giddy with a kind of reckless abandon that she had never thought herself capable of, Ellen had decided not to let another minute of her life slip by unlived. Tonight she was going to take charge of what happened to her next. Tonight she was planning her second-ever seduction attempt.

Tonight, Ellen was going to have sex with Matt Bolton.

CHAPTER
Eighteen

It took Matt several seconds to locate the keyhole with his key. He hadn't considered himself very drunk at all, at least not by *Bang It!* standards. When he'd left the pub, the others had gone off to find a legendary and possibly mythical drinking club that was supposed to be open all night under an adult-entertainment shop called Venus Videos in Soho. Matt had questioned the point of an illegal drinking den when there were plenty of legitimate places that stayed open all hours these days, but he had been shouted down and pelted with a good many offensive insults regarding his sexuality and gender assignment. His sleepless night catching up with him at last, he'd bowed out and saved his reputation by telling them that he was off home to sort out his landlady.

Despite the weariness that crowded his head with ill-advised thoughts of Ellen's hair spread out across her pillow, Matt had elected to take the half-hour walk home, preferring the enduring heat of the evening to the crowded and noisy night buses that careened along the streets with the kind of reckless capriciousness that seemed to say "get out of my way, I'm out on the town."

Living a little dangerously, he'd tipped his head back as he walked, hoping to find some stars in the sky, but the city lights obliterated any chance he had of communing with the cosmos. Matt didn't know why he had the urge to chat to the heavens anyway, it wasn't as if he'd spent his childhood in some rural idyll, at one with nature. He'd spent it growing up on a Manchester council estate where nature was comprised of grass verges and the occasional privet hedge. But something had happened to him, something that made him remember snippets of love poetry from some sixteenth-century poet, that made him dream about curling a tress of glossy dark hair around his fingers, that made him want to look at the stars and try to find some meaning to his life in the random patterns of the universe.

"Fuck," Matt mumbled to himself as he tried to find the keyhole again. "I'll be reading my star signs next."

He took great care to close the door behind him and stood for a second in the quiet, cool hallway, appraising the situation. There was no light in the living room or under Allegra's bedroom door. But there was a low, greenish light coming from the kitchen, which meant that Ellen was in there having a cup of tea, because she always switched on the under-the-counter lights when she was in there alone, thinking. Matt considered his weary and confused mind, his exhausted body numbed by alcohol, and thought he probably had better not go into the kitchen to talk to Ellen now, not in his current state. Before he knew it, he'd be quoting her poetry and telling her that he loved her or something equally insane, taking risks, putting himself out there or whatever it was Lucy had said. Yet, even as the last tiny rational part of his brain was making these decisions, the rest of his body was propelled to exactly the last place he knew he ought to be.

He pushed open the kitchen door, but Ellen was not there.

Well, not there in any sense that Matt understood, at least not at first. She was not sitting at the table in some oversized shirt, with her hair tied up, embracing a mug of tea. She was leaning against the countertop directly opposite the door—more like lounging, actually—and she was wearing a dress. And not just a dress, but a *dress,* dark green and so figure-hugging that in one single second all the mysteries that had been Ellen's body were laid almost bare to him, and he was unable to tear his eyes from the curve of her breasts, the deep cleavage that ran between them, or the delicious flare of her hips, undulating from her waist with what seemed like a glorious decadence. Matt had heard the phrase *all woman* many times but had never really had cause to use it before, at least not so accurately.

Ellen smiled at him and tilted her head so that her long, glossy hair strayed over one shoulder. She had lipstick on, Matt noticed, confused. Why was she wearing lipstick and a dress?

"Glass of wine?" Ellen asked, pouring from a bottle that was on the counter into an empty glass that had been standing by.

She'd been expecting someone, Matt realized, wondering who it might be. And then with a sudden cold thrill he realized that she'd been expecting him. Fuck. *Fuck!* What was he going to do? He felt like he was fifteen again and Charlotte Mackenzie had told him that they could have sex if he liked as long as he was careful. Except he'd fancied Charlotte Mackenzie from the age of eleven, and just the thought of doing anything so intimate with her had meant that it was all over for him before he'd even laid a finger on her. Charlotte Mackenzie hadn't spoken to him again and he had hoped never to be so humiliated again in his life. But now, suddenly, it seemed like a very real possibility. This couldn't be happening, not here, not now. Not like this. He wasn't ready, he didn't know how he felt about her, and besides, he was really, really drunk. He was never any good at sex when he was really, really drunk, and . . .

"I wanted to thank you, for staying up all night with me last night," Ellen said. Slowly she walked across the kitchen toward Matt, which was when he noticed her silver high heels, an observation that was inevitably followed by an image of Ellen wearing nothing but a pair of silver high heels. Matt swallowed and backed away, praying that she wouldn't touch him. What had happened in the fifteen or so hours that he had been out of the house? Had some kinky alien life force with a thing for push-up bras come and taken over Ellen's body? Where was the offer of tea and biscuits? Where was the debriefing of the day, when he'd tell her what he'd done at work and she'd tell him about something Charlie had said or done?

It was going to be much harder to admire her from afar if she actually started throwing herself at him.

Please don't touch me, please don't touch me, please don't touch me, Matt pleaded silently as Ellen approached him. She handed him the glass of wine, which he took as a defensive tactic, assuming that a receptacle full of liquid would act as some barrier between them. He was wrong.

Ellen took one more step on her silver high heels into his personal body space and rested her palm on his shoulder. She looked into his eyes.

"I wondered if there was anything I could do to thank you?" she asked, batting her smoky lashes.

"Um . . . well, a coffee would be great," Matt squeaked as Ellen's hand traced its way down his torso, over his waistband, and . . . Matt grabbed her wrist before it got any farther.

"Ellen," he said, studying her face at close quarters, noticing the slightly swollen lids and the reddened eyes that hid behind the newly applied and flaking mascara. "Ellen, what's all this about?"

"Oh, God, you don't fancy me, do you," Ellen said, stepping away and stumbling a little. Matt realized that she was probably as drunk as he was, if not a little more so. "I knew it, I knew there was no way I could carry this off. Here I am being reckless and spontaneous, and it never occurred to me that you just didn't fancy me. I'm delusional, that's what I am."

"What, are you joking? Of course I fancy you, I don't think I've ever fancied anyone more," Matt told her. "You look stunning; that dress . . . your body looks slamming, Ellen. It's kind of hard for a man to ignore, which is why I'm wondering what all this is about."

"Really?" Ellen perked up, smiling a bit like the old Ellen—

the one who wasn't a sex-crazed, alien-possessed siren. Matt was more than a little bit pleased to see her. "Because you know, you spend so long not noticing yourself, or looking at yourself, that you sort of have no idea what you look like anymore. I used to be beautiful once, and I mean once. It was a Thursday evening in 1998. I was wearing this dress. That was the last time I was beautiful."

"That's not true, Ellen," Matt said. "You . . . you are one of the most beautiful women I have ever seen. And I know that sounds like a line but it's true. I've never, not since Charlotte Mackenzie, ever wanted so badly just to . . . touch your hair." Matt winced. "Which makes me sound a bit weird, doesn't it?"

"You can touch my hair," Ellen said in a low, husky voice, taking a step toward him again. "You can touch me anywhere."

She pressed herself against him so that they stood breast to breast, hip to hip.

"The thing is," Matt said, finding it quite difficult to keep his hands anywhere other than Ellen's beautifully rounded bottom, "is that I can't. I can't just come in from work and find you—you, Ellen Woods—dressed up and a bit drunk and up for it and take advantage of that. I can't."

"You mean you don't want to?" Ellen asked him, her hot breath tickling his neck.

"Oh, God," Matt groaned, knowing by the tone of her voice that she realized exactly how much he wanted to. "I want to, Ellen, I want to—but not like this. Not with you. I mean, when I left the house this morning you were in a full-blown crisis. How is Hannah, and what about Charlie, how's he coping?"

"I don't want to talk about any of that," Ellen said, her hand traveling along his inner thigh. "I'm a bit out of practice—in fact, totally out of practice when it comes to taking charge—so you must tell me if I get it wrong." She cupped her hand over Matt's erection and pressed it gently. "How's that working for you?"

"Oh, God." Unable to resist anymore, Matt put down his glass of wine and pulled Ellen to him, one hand cupping her bottom, the other finding its way immediately to one breast, which he squeezed hard as he kissed her deeply. He moaned low in his throat as he turned her around, thrusting her back against the kitchen counter that she had pinned him against only seconds earlier, tearing one hand away from her backside and entangling it in her hair, pulling her head back to expose her neck, which he covered with kisses and bites, pulling at the neckline of her dress, tucking it under the rise of her breasts, which he exposed to his lips with a tear of nearly new lace. Suddenly resolute and focused, Matt lifted Ellen by the hips onto the counter, pushing up her skirt to expose her panties, and with one fluid movement ripped them off and dropped them on the floor.

It was when her hand was on his belt buckle that he noticed the expression on her face. There was desire there, yes, a flush of heat traveling across the bridge of her nose and down her throat. But there was something else, too. Fear? Uncertainty? Even sadness? Matt let his hand drift to his side as he looked at her there, the woman who made him think about poetry and look at the stars, with her clothes asunder, her underwear ripped. At that moment she looked sexier and more desirable than any woman Matt had ever known. But this sordid centerfold affair wasn't how it was meant to be, not between him and Ellen.

They looked at each other for one breathless, silent moment and then Matt scooped Ellen up in his arms and held her. She wound herself around his body and buried her face in his neck. Matt increased the pressure of his embrace as he felt her frame begin to shake with sobs.

"Ellen," he whispered, retreating onto one of the kitchen chairs and pulling her onto his lap, cradling her in his arms. "Ellen, tell me. Please, tell me what's happened."

Ellen pushed her hair back from her face, which was streaked with tears, and looked into his eyes.

"You must think I'm such a fool," she said. "What would someone like you want with a past-it old woman like me?"

"I think you can see that someone like me would want someone exactly like you very, very much," Matt said, smoothing her tangle of hair off her face. "But when you're ready and when you're sure that it's what you want. And you're not sure, are you?"

Ellen looked into his eyes for a second and then shook her head, a response that surprised Matt by how much it stung and disappointed him. For the first time in his life, he wanted a woman who didn't want him back.

Ellen climbed off his lap and half turned her back on him while she rearranged her clothes to restore her modesty. Sheepishly, she quickly scooped her knickers off the kitchen floor and, uncertain as to what to do with them, hastily put them in the plastic-bag drawer.

"I mean I do, I do want you, but I'm not sure if it's for very sensible reasons." She sniffed, glancing nervously at Matt, who look uncomfortable as he sat, the heat of his desire taking some time to subside.

"What should we do now?" Matt asked. "I'm not sure what to do after some amazing making out and then a break to re-assess the situation. Apart from explode, maybe, or bash my head against the tabletop until I've got enough brain damage to stop me from coming over there and getting you."

They looked at each other for a moment longer, Ellen wondering exactly what was happening between them.

"I'll make us a cup of tea?" she offered.

"I'll make it," he said. "You sit down. And talk—start talking and explain to me what happened today to make you decide to give me the most difficult night of my life."

"I'm not really that difficult to resist, am I?" Ellen smiled shyly.

"Woman," Matt said, turning his back on her and closing his eyes. "You have no idea."

When Ellen stopped talking and looked up at Matt, she wondered just exactly how much he must pity her. He had not looked at her at all while she had told him about Hannah, and her claimed love affair with Nick, and how even venturing just to the bottom of her garden path had made her feel like she was going to slip off the face of the planet and die. While she had been wondering how to explain to Charlie why he was never going to see his aunt again, or if she should feel guilty that she'd thrown Hannah out when she was so badly hurt, he had not redirected his gaze from the tabletop. For a few seconds back there, Matt had looked at her and he hadn't seen Ellen Woods. He had seen a woman whom he wanted to rip the clothes off of and have unbridled sex with, whether she wanted it or not, just like Captain Parker, just like whoever it was who had hurt Hannah. But Matt wasn't like either of those men, imagined or real. He'd seen the expression on her face, he had spotted the uncertainty, and he had stopped. It was something that Ellen was deeply grateful for, and yet she mourned the passing of only her second beautiful moment. She wasn't sure that another one would ever come again, at least not with Matt. Not now that he knew everything about her.

Matt said nothing for a while, the muscles in his jaw tightening reflexively, as if he were actively trying not to say something. And then he shrugged.

"Well, this is a bit of a mess, isn't it?" he said finally.

"Yes." Ellen nodded. "The thing is, I've got a horrible feeling that I've seen the last ten years of my life slip by believing they were one thing when they were something else entirely. I thought I was one-half of a loving, committed marriage. That's what Nick made me think, but I wasn't—if anything I was his trophy for a while, his pet, and then . . . then I was this burden that he had to care for when all the time he longed to be with someone else."

"That's not true," Matt said.

"Isn't it? He was planning to leave me for my sister. Why did she have to tell me, Matt? Why couldn't she have just let me go on believing in my sad little delusion? At least then I had some . . ." Ellen wanted to say "pride" or "dignity" but neither one of those words seemed to fit. "At least then I had *something*. I was his widow. It was my reason for never looking in the mirror, never going out, never trying to live life. Now? Now I have no excuse. Now I am just a pathetic, drunk old landlady who throws herself at her lodgers. Now I am a character from a seventies sitcom."

"Listen." Matt seemed to be struggling with some emotion that Ellen couldn't pin down. "If anyone ever had an excuse to be fucked up, it's you, okay? You could dress in rags and never leave the house again and no one would blame you. But you can't let that happen, Ellen—I won't let that happen. Not to you. Some bloody, arrogant, selfish fuckwit didn't have the brains to see what an amazing, wonderful wife he had, and I can promise you, if he were alive now I would kill him. And I am not letting him or Hannah or the road outside stop you from being who you are for one more minute. You're great, Ellen, you're funny and strong and a brilliant mum and probably a great copy editor. There is so much more waiting for you out there. Starting tomorrow, we're going to get you back on track again."

"Really?" Ellen looked at him, trying to see if he was still drunk. "Only won't you be a bit busy, with work and bedding girls and all that?"

"I can handle work," Matt said, grinning a little sheepishly. "And as for girls, well—you're the only girl I can think about, and even if you need me to be there as a friend for you for now, that won't change in a hurry." Ellen dropped her gaze, not quite able to understand what she was hearing. "What I'm trying to say is, don't worry, Ellen, you're not alone. You've got me, Sabine, and Allegra—and that gay bloke who you work for, Simon Merry. And you've got Charlie. We all . . . care about you. Yes, someone's gone and ripped a fucking huge hole in your chest and filled it with despair, but it will get better."

"I don't know what I did to deserve such nice lodgers," Ellen said sleepily as Matt pulled her to her feet.

"Well," Matt said as he escorted her up the stairs. "You make a lovely cup of tea."

For the first few seconds after Matt woke up, he was confused, wondering where he was. It was a familiar feeling, opening his eyes to an unfamiliar room, searching around for some kind of marker or clue as to where he had ended up after a drunken night out. The pressure behind his eyes, the ache in his limbs, and his bone-dry mouth told him that he had a hangover, and normally that feeling, coupled with a foreign pair of curtains, meant that he had gone home with a woman. With the familiar mix of excitement and dread that always accompanied that sober first look at a woman he'd just spent the night with, he turned his head toward the sound of steady breathing. And that's when it all came back to him.

Matt felt something like a silent rent in his chest when he looked at Ellen sleeping next to him. When he had taken her up to her room sometime early that morning, she had asked him to sit and talk to her for a while, explaining that she didn't want to be alone because when she was alone she started thinking, and look what had happened the last time she'd done that—she'd decided to get drunk and throw herself at her lodger.

Matt didn't tell her that he didn't want to be alone, either, for almost exactly the same reason, except that he would be thinking about what would have happened if he hadn't stopped things when he had, so he sat on a chair by the bed, trying not to look at the strangely erotic array of sensible underwear that was scattered all over the floor and told her all about his drive-through-brothel assignment as she took a shower, struggling all the time with the image of the water running in rivulets down that body that he had experienced all too briefly. When Ellen emerged wrapped in a large towel, her hair dripping wet, Matt had been compelled to cross his legs and remove an embroidered cushion from behind his back and position it on his lap.

Ellen had peered into her already open wardrobe. "I don't know what to wear. For the last twelve months I've been wearing Nick's clothes, so that I could feel close to him, and now I don't want to. I don't want to wear anything that I had from then." She turned to Matt as if she'd just had a very controversial idea. "Maybe I'll sleep naked, why not?"

"I'll be off then," Matt said, feeling the heat sweep across his face. Ellen saw his expression of horror and her face fell.

"Oh, God, Matt, I'm sorry—that sounded like I was trying to seduce you again, didn't it? I promise I'm not. Here, this will do. Mum bought it for me at Christmas. I've never worn it." Ellen stepped back into the bathroom, emerging a few minutes later in a full-length white cotton nightgown with white lace trim. "I have no idea what she was thinking—I look like a heroine from a Victorian novel; any minute now I'll catch a chill and die!"

"It suits you, actually," Matt told her, trying not to notice how her damp hair that trailed down her back had made the material of the nightgown slightly translucent.

Ellen climbed into bed and pulled the sheet over herself. She looked around her, as if taking in every tiny detail of the room.

"This was our place, mine and Nick's. This was where we were alone. Do you know, I never guessed, I had no idea at all that he was seeing another woman, maybe even in *love* with another woman, let alone my own sister. There wasn't anything, not any of the signs that you read about. He didn't start changing his underwear more often or going to the gym. He didn't treat me any differently at all. Do you suppose that means that the whole thing was incidental to his life here, irrelevant to it?"

"Maybe it was," Matt said, thinking of that conversation that Nick had had with Charlie about loving him no matter what. "But if you weren't expecting anything, then perhaps you didn't notice."

Ellen lay back, her head on the pillow.

"Will you be very afraid of me if I ask you to talk to me until

I go to sleep?" she asked. "You don't have to, but if you will, I promise not to touch you."

"Of course I will," Matt answered painfully. Ellen patted the side of the bed, and with some trepidation Matt had gotten up and gone and sat on the very edge, leaning back awkwardly against the headboard, keeping one foot on the floor like he'd read the censors made them do in old films with any scene with a bed in it, so as to indicate that no sex was going to take place.

"Tell me about the Nevada hookers again," Ellen said. "Tell me about the one who's studying to become a doctor, what's her name?"

"Lola Lagoona, that's her professional name, but her real name is Paige Anthony. She's really clever, aced it all through high school even though her mum was an alcoholic and her dad was never around. . . ."

At some point they had slept. Matt had no idea who had drifted off first or when, but here he was stretched out on Ellen's bed with her sleeping next to him. The sight of her made him catch his breath.

> *License my roving hands and let them go*
> *Before, behind, between, above, below.*

As he propped himself on one elbow to get a better look at her, another line from that poem, which Matt had had no idea he remembered, popped into his head. Quite suddenly he remembered something else that he'd forgotten. In class, along with all his mates, he'd studiously ignored the teacher, talking over her, passing notes, throwing chewed-up bits of paper at the backs of girls he fancied. At the end of class he'd stuffed the photocopied handout into his bag and later that day when he'd been looking for something else he'd pulled it out and read it, and read it again. And then slowly, very slowly, he'd realized what he was reading. It was a man describing taking off his girlfriend's clothes, and then talking about having sex with her. Matt had been unable to believe that olden-day people even knew about sex, let alone wrote about it so explicitly. And for that one evening, he'd read it over and over again, trying to picture in his head exactly what the poet was describing, and though he would never have admitted it to any of his friends, it had been one of the most erotic experiences of his life. The next day, he'd screwed it up and thrown it in the bin and never given the poem a second thought. Not until he had met Ellen, for whom, it seemed to him, the poem had been written four centuries ago.

His head pounding, his mouth dry, Matt found that he was desperate to read it again, to know every line again, and, most uncharacteristically of all, to read it to Ellen. To experience it with Ellen. He turned onto his back and looked at the ceiling. What was happening to him?

Then two things happened at exactly the same time.

Ellen moaned a little in her sleep and, turning onto her side, flung her arm across Matt's chest. At that precise moment, Ellen's bedroom door opened and Charlie walked in.

"Mum, I've made you break—" Charlie halted in his tracks, a tray with some toast, tea, and a near-dead rose in a beaker in his hands.

"What?" Ellen sat up, confused.

"Charlie, mate," Matt said. "This isn't what you think."

Ellen bolted upright, catching up with the situation vital seconds later than Matt and Charlie. Rapidly she clambered out of bed.

"Charlie, Matt and I were just talking, that's all, and we fell asleep."

Suddenly galvanized into action by the sound of his mother's voice, Charlie flung the tray at the bed and ran out of the room. Ellen raced after him, and Matt ran after her, but as he reached the top of the stairs he could see that she was too late. Charlie had slammed the front door behind him, certain that his mother would not follow.

CHAPTER Nineteen

By the time Matt reached the bottom of the stairs, Ellen was beating her fists against the front door in frustration, tears streaming down her face.

"What the hell is wrong with me?" she said. "I can't go after him. I want to, I really need to, but I can't. I'm stuck . . . I'm stuck behind this bloody door. I'm too scared to go after my own son when he's upset!"

She turned to face Matt, and he was shocked by the genuine fear he saw on her face; she really was terrified of going out—he thought that he hadn't fully understood it until that moment.

"I'll go," Matt offered. "Look, he won't have gone far. He'll be at the end of the road or down at the shops or something. Give me ten minutes."

Matt opened the door and jogged up the garden path and onto the street in his bare feet. It was quiet for a Saturday morning, a toddler and her mother ambling down the opposite side of the road, a couple of kids kicking a ball around on the corner. Matt jogged on to where the boys were, hopeful that he'd find Charlie among them. But the kid was nowhere to be seen. Where would a boy who thought he'd just caught his mum in bed with her lodger go? Matt wondered.

Well, wherever it was, it was farther away than he could travel without shoes on. His hands on his hips as he caught his breath in the glare of the morning sun, Matt went back to the house.

"Where is he?" Ellen asked desperately the second he came in. "What did he say?"

"I didn't catch him," Matt said. "Maybe he got on a bus or something. What does he normally do on a Saturday?"

"He normally stays here with me," Ellen said miserably.

"What's happened?" Sabine asked, coming down the stairs, winding her long hair around and around one hand before tucking it into a knot at the back of her neck.

"Matt and I stayed up talking last night," Ellen explained, feeling heat flair across her cheeks as she thought of Matt pushing her skirt up and gripping her thighs. "We both fell asleep in my room and Charlie saw us, put two and two together and made five."

Sabine looked concerned. "He got the wrong idea and ran out?"

"Yes, and now we don't know where he's gone," Ellen said in dismay. "I should have gone after him, but I can't. . . . I hate this, I hate myself, I hate my shitty life!"

Ellen slammed her fist against the door again and again, making it rattle in its frame, her heart accelerating at the thought of being on the other side of it. "I can't have him out there thinking I've betrayed his father that way. I can't."

"Have you tried ringing him?" Sabine suggested.

Frantically, Ellen called Charlie's mobile, and she wasn't surprised that it went straight to voice mail. "Charlie, it's Mum. I swear to you, that wasn't what you thought it was, okay? Matt and I were just talking and we fell asleep, that was all, I promise. Please come home, darling."

"What did Charlie see?" Allegra emerged from her room. "Honestly, if I had known that there would be more comings and goings in this house than Piccadilly Circus, I might have taken the insurance company's trailer after all."

"He found Ellen and Matt in bed together, and ran off," Sabine explained, eliciting an expression of pure delight from Allegra. "But apparently no intercourse took place."

Sabine and Allegra looked the other two up and down as if they were searching for visible traces of indiscretion, which Ellen was sure must be written all over her face.

"How wonderful," Allegra said. "Well, let's go and have tea and you can tell me all about it. I want all the details, Ellen; it's been far too long since I was in the grasp of a virile young man. It seems to me that Charlie is a very sensible young man, I'm sure he'll be fine. . . ."

"Oh no," Ellen said, a thought suddenly occurring to her. "I know where he will have gone."

"Where?" Matt asked.

"To the same person he always goes to when he's angry with me," Ellen said anxiously. "To Hannah. Oh my God, what if she tells him about his dad. . . . I can't let him find out, especially not from her."

"Right, well, let's go then," Matt said, then remembered his bare feet and Ellen's nightdress. "Let's get dressed and go." He saw the look on her face and revised his offer: "I'll get dressed, you tell me where Hannah lives, and I'll go. Maybe Sabine could come with me? She knows Hannah better than I do."

Sabine nodded. "Of course."

"No, no," Ellen said, her body suddenly pumped full of adrenaline, her need to find her son eclipsing everything else. "No. I am not this person. I won't be. I can't be this person and be *me*. I can't be a person who abandons their son because they are afraid of . . . of what, buses and noise and people and certain death? That's not what a mother does. A mother does not abandon her child because she is afraid of anything. I'm going to Hannah's." Ellen's look of determination wavered a little as she looked at Matt. "But you will come with me, won't you?"

"Of course," Matt said. "Give me five minutes."

Sabine put her hand on Ellen's forearm. "Ellen, are you sure? Agoraphobia is not something you can just get over because you feel like it. You'll need a lot of help, therapy—medication perhaps. If you force yourself to go out now, you might make things worse."

"I have to go now, I haven't got time for therapy or drugs. I need to get to Charlie before Hannah says anything. I have to go now, before I lose my nerve, and that's that."

As Ellen and Matt rushed to get dressed, Allegra followed Sabine into the kitchen, where Sabine offered to make her breakfast.

"I hope she knows what she's doing," Sabine said anxiously.

"I think she does," Allegra said. "I think she has finally decided to become the heroine in her own story, and she is strong, much stronger than she realizes."

"She will have to be, that's for sure," Sabine said as she tugged a full bag out of the kitchen bin and dropped it outside the back door.

"So do you think anything else, apart from chatting and falling asleep, happened last night?" Allegra asked as Sabine looked for a replacement bin liner.

Sabine paused for a moment as she opened the plastic-bag drawer and then gingerly picked up a pair of black lace panties. She turned to Allegra and said, "I would say something else definitely happened."

Ellen stood on the threshold of her house. She knew perfectly well that what was actually outside the front door was a street of redbrick Victorian gardens with modest and mostly well-kept front gardens nestled behind neatly trimmed privet hedges. She knew that the pavement would be a patchwork of different shades of tarmac, depending on which utility company had dug it up most recently, and that the road would be relatively quiet except for the thunder of buses full of Saturday shoppers, rattling past the end of the road. She knew that the air would be warm, scented with summer flowers and traffic fumes, and that the most threatening thing out there that she was likely to encounter was an angry wasp. She knew this with her rational mind, but no matter what she might see with her eyes when she opened that door, she felt as if she would be confronted with a cliff edge, a precipice so high that she could not see its foot and over which she would be compelled to throw herself.

Matt opened the door and held his hand out to her. Ellen took it and stepped onto the path with him. Immediately the air rushed from her lungs and her head spun.

"I can't," she said, closing her eyes and clutching Matt's arm.

"You can," Matt said. "Come on, we'll just get to the gate, let's get to the gate and see how you feel." Screwing her eyes tight, as if she were on a roller-coaster ride that would soon be over, Ellen let him lead her to her garden gate. He put his hands on the rough wood. "This needs replacing, really," he said in a matter-of-fact voice. "The paint's peeling off and the wood's rotting around the hinges. A few more slams from Charlie and it'll be done for, don't you reckon? Ellen, don't you think?"

Slowly Ellen opened her eyes and looked down at her garden gate, a waist-high picket affair that she and Charlie had painted green several years earlier. It had suffered from lack of attention since Nick's death. Ellen ran her fingers over the rough and cracked surface, then glanced up at her house. It was the first time she had seen it from the outside in months. The wisteria had grown heavy for lack of pruning, its weight pulling away from the house in some parts, while in others it had begun to stray across the windows, including those in Ellen's bedroom. At some point the old cast-iron guttering must have become blocked with autumn leaves, because a tidemark of where it had overflowed could still be traced running down the brickwork. The front lawn, now standing a good ten inches high, had gone to seed and yellowed in the unremitting sunshine and looked in a sorry state, except for where it had migrated into the cracks in the garden path, where it seemed to be sprouting quite happily.

As Ellen looked at the neglected house that she loved so fiercely, she realized that one of the reasons she felt so safe inside it was that it had felt as if time stood still there. As if she were marking time, waiting for clocks to start ticking, hearts to start beating, and the world to start turning again. Waiting for order to be restored, for Nick to walk in through the door after work and her life to begin again. Ellen looked at Matt and her heartbeat slowed, the panic and fear subsiding a little.

"We'll go to the end of the road and get a cab," Matt told her. "There'll be loads, this time of the morning."

Casually, Matt opened the gate and, taking Ellen's hand off the wood, tucked it through his arm and began walking them up the street.

"I'm sorry," he said. "All of this is my fault. I didn't mean to crash out in your room."

"It's not your fault," Ellen said, fighting the rise of vomit in her throat as her stomach lurched and contracted painfully. She stopped walking, tried to turn back to the house, but Matt kept a firm grasp on her hand beneath his arm and walked her on.

"And I'm sorry about the other thing, the, you know . . . taking-a-lot-of-your-clothes-off thing," Matt said. Normally he never would have brought it up, but he decided that he needed to take Ellen's mind off exactly what they were doing and he didn't think small talk would do it.

"Oh, God." Ellen stopped for a moment, bending double and retching. "Oh, God, Matt . . . I have to go back. I can't breathe. . . . Matt, let me go back, this is too much. This is too far. I can't do it, I'm not strong enough." An overwound clock began unraveling in her chest, time spinning out of control as she fought for breath. Matt would not let her go.

"It's just as far to the end of the road as it is to get back now," Matt said calmly, rubbing between her shoulder blades. "Just take deep breaths in and out, in and out."

He paused while he waited for her breathing to even out a little, her eyes darting fearfully left and right.

"You know, I didn't stop what was happening in the kitchen because I didn't want to. I really wanted to, Ellen, a lot. But it didn't seem like the right time, I mean you were drunk and kind of throwing yourself at me. . . ."

Ellen straightened up, dragged the back of her hand across her mouth, and looked at him with watery eyes.

"I'm dying of a heart attack here and you're reminding me of the worst and most humiliating moment of my life," she gasped on a ragged breath. Matt smiled. His plan of extreme distraction seemed to be working.

He put his arm around her waist and propelled her forward as he talked. "You feel like you are dying, but you aren't. You're having a panic attack, which is pretty scary and very real, but it won't kill you. The trick is to try not to think about it. Which brings me to the next thing I want to say."

"You don't need to tell me, I know," Ellen said, looking around anxiously as Matt moved her forward. "I behaved ridiculously last night. I'm not exactly sure that's going to help when it comes to having a panic attack."

"No. Look, I've been thinking about you for a couple of weeks now. By which I mean I've become very attracted to you. You looked amazing last night, but you didn't need that dress or that underwear to turn me on. I've been thinking about what it would be like to make love to you since long before that."

"You . . . what? Are you trying to pull me now, when I'm on the verge of vomiting and there's an aneurysm that I'm fairly sure is about to pop in my head?" Ellen asked, aghast.

"I'm just telling you the truth," Matt said, aware that this was not exactly accurate. He was telling the truth about all his physical thoughts and feelings for her, but the emotional stuff, which seemed for the first time in his life to be tied up together with how much he wanted her, he kept to himself. If he thought too much about the emotional stuff he'd give himself a panic attack and then where would they be, two mental wrecks stranded in Shepherd's Bush. "You are a very attractive woman, Ellen. And if . . . when the dust has settled a bit and you're not quite so . . ."

"Insane?" Ellen asked, her eyes wide and wild as they approached the busy main road. She clung to him, winding her arms around his chest and pressing her cheek against his shoulder. "Oh, God, Matt, I need to go back. I need to go back. I can't do it, I can't do it, I can't. I'm going to die."

"You're not going to die," Matt told her as he hailed a black cab. "Anyway, what I was trying to say was that if you want to have sex with me, then I'm up for it. Whenever you're ready."

As Matt had predicted, Ellen was so shocked that she allowed him to bundle her into the cab and close the door behind them. "Ladbroke Grove, please, mate," he said to the cabbie.

Ellen sat wide-eyed in the backseat, looking like a wild cat that has been cornered, her chest rising and falling rapidly. Matt folded down the seat opposite and, reaching over, pulled her seat belt over her shoulder and clipped it into its catch, and for a second their faces were only millimeters apart. Matt sat back. He had no idea what or how she felt about him, if last night was just some crazy aberration brought about by everything that had gone on, or if it was based in something more, something that could be real. And he couldn't exactly press her on it now, but he found that he wanted to know. He hated not knowing what she was thinking or feeling, especially about him.

"A London black cab is one of the safest places you can be in the world," Matt told her as he looked at her wide, scared eyes. "No one knows the roads better than one of these guys, and these old things"—he patted the side of the cab—"are built for safety. You've done the hardest bit, Ellen. We'll get dropped right outside Hannah's front door, and after we've dealt with . . . whatever we've got to deal with, we'll get a cab all the way back to your house. You know you can go to the end of your road without anything terrible happening, so now you've really got nothing to worry about."

"I'm not sure about that," Ellen said, tucking her hands between her legs. "You just told me you'd have sex with me whenever I felt like it. Don't you know that I'm an agoraphobic widow who's just found out that her marriage was a lie? I'm the actual definition of a . . . of a fuck-up." For a second, she focused her gaze on him.

"Oh, you'd be surprised," Matt said, ignoring her last comment. "We like the mad ones, the complicated ones. The ones who are going to give us loads of grief and might very well turn up standing over us while we sleep, with a carving knife in their hands. Sex tends to be better with the mad ones. Well, you were on the verge of proving that last night; what happened in the kitchen—that was the best it's been for me in a long time."

"Ha!" Ellen gasped, but this time with incredulity rather than for air. As she watched West London slip past, transforming gradually from grubby redbrick Victorian shop fronts to the graceful, shabby chic of Georgian villas, punctuated every now and then with an exclamation mark of 1960s modernist architecture, she realized that her heartbeat had slowed and she was breathing easily. She felt almost normal, and much, much less afraid of dropping dead at any second. She did feel safe in the cab, sitting opposite Matt. And there was something else—she felt exhilarated. God only knew what mess awaited her at Hannah's place, but she had made it this far. With Matt's help she had made it this far . . . and then it dawned on her.

"You've been distracting me," she said. "All this talk of wanting sex with me, it's been to distract me, take my mind off of what I'm doing."

Matt hesitated, unsure of what to let her believe. But he saw the relief in her eyes and realized that his wanting her so much that every square inch of skin ached for her was the very last thing that she needed. So instead he grinned like a kid caught out planning a practical joke.

"It worked, though, didn't it?" he said, flinching as Ellen punched him in the thigh.

"You bastard!" she exclaimed, but she was laughing, high on adrenaline.

"Whereabouts, mate?" the cabbie asked them as they

turned onto the top of Ladbroke Grove. Matt looked at Ellen and raised his eyebrows.

"About halfway down, just past the tube station on the left," Ellen told him. As the cab pulled up to the curb, she looked into Matt's eyes and smiled, resting her hand on his knee.

"You are not the man you pretend to be," she told him.

"What are you saying? I'm a rubbish kisser?" Matt made himself joke, although her touch made him want to grab her and kiss her right there.

"No. In my admittedly limited experience, you are an excellent kisser. But you are not this man who doesn't care, who goes from girl to girl without a second thought. You are a very kind and generous and clever man and I'm very lucky that it was you who answered that ad, because I don't know how I would have managed if it had been anyone else."

"That's fifteen eighty then," the cabbie said, a touch impatiently.

"Ready?" Matt asked her as he stuffed a twenty under the Plexiglas screen that separated them from the driver.

"As I'll ever be."

Matt got out first and held out his hand to her. Inhaling deeply, Ellen took it, and the pair of them ran to Hannah's red-painted front door like children running through a rainstorm. When they reached the door, Ellen threw herself against it, pressing her palms against its hot, glossy surface; and as she stood there with her shoulders heaving, fighting to catch her breath, she remembered why she had come, and the light in her eyes faded as rapidly as the color in her cheeks.

"I've gotten this far," she said, more to herself than to Matt. "I can do this."

She pushed Hannah's doorbell and waited.

It was Charlie who opened the door.

"Oh, thank God you're okay," Ellen said, flinging her arms around him and hugging his rigid body. "How long have you been here? What's Hannah said? Did you get my message?"

Ellen released Charlie but he was immobile.

"Charlie, Charlie—look at me! I came to find you. I came all the way here to find you and tell you that there is nothing going on between me and Matt. Nothing at all! Aren't you pleased?"

Charlie looked at her and shook his head.

"Mum, it's Aunt Hannah—I can't wake her." His voice was tearful and tight. "I'm so glad you're here. I don't know what to do."

Ellen swallowed, finding her throat painfully tight, fear flooding through her veins.

"Where is she, Charlie?"

"In there." Charlie nodded toward Hannah's bedroom door. "When I got here there wasn't any answer, and I didn't want to go home, so I took the key out of the window box and let myself in. I thought she was out, so I had a look around and she's . . . she's in there. In bed. She's not moving. I can't get her to wake up. Mum, I think she might be dead."

When Ellen was confronted with her sister lying prone in her bed, two emotions tore through her in quick succession. The first was relief. Hannah was not dead; she stirred as Ellen came into the room, turning over onto her back. By her bed, though, was a packet of sleeping pills with two empty blisters and a bottle of vodka that was a quarter empty. Hannah might have been seeking oblivion but she had not been trying to kill herself. The second emotion was shame. Since the moment when Hannah had made her confession, everything else had seemed insignificant to Ellen; nothing else mattered anymore except that Hannah had betrayed her and her life had fallen to pieces. She'd forgotten that Hannah had been attacked and hurt. As she looked at her sister, lying on her back, her face swollen and misshapen, a livid rainbow of bruises tracking their way down her face and throat, ranging in color from shocking pink to sickly yellow, Ellen felt her stomach heave. She had abandoned Hannah at the worst moment in her life, and nothing, not anything that had happened between them, could justify that.

Yesterday she'd been furious with Hannah for putting herself in this situation, for getting herself attacked; she had blamed her for searching out the ultimate distraction technique to avoid getting into trouble for having slept with Ellen's husband. Ellen had been determined not to let her sister off the hook so easily. So *easily?* No one would choose to put herself through this to get off the hook, Ellen thought. She wasn't sure that it would ever be possible for Hannah to get over it.

Belatedly, she realized that Charlie was standing in the doorway, twisting his fingers in the hem of his T-shirt.

"She's not dead, Charlie. She's just very deeply asleep." Ellen pondered her sister for a second and then, turning, ushered Charlie out into the hall.

"You must have been very frightened," Ellen said, putting her hands on his shoulders and looking into his eyes. It was something of a shock to realize that Charlie was now almost as tall as she was and that it would not be long before he towered above her, like his father had done.

"I thought she was dead, her face is so . . . hurt," Charlie whispered. "And I didn't know what I should do. I was going to phone you—but then you came. *You* came here for me. That's brilliant, Mum."

"I didn't want you to get the wrong impression about me and Matt," Ellen said, dropping her gaze. "You're right about me, Charlie, I have got a problem. I wouldn't have been able to come after you if it hadn't been for Matt. He got me here, he more or less dragged me here, and I'm just as terrified of leaving here and going home as I was of coming. The world scares me to death, I think it always has, in a way—but when your dad died, when one of the things that I always told myself wouldn't happen happened, that's when it started. I lied to myself, and I lied to everyone else. You were the only one who was brave enough to face up to what was happening."

As Ellen talked, she glanced back up at Charlie and saw his eyes fill with unshed tears, and she realized how much pressure her son had been under, how much pressure she had unwittingly placed on him.

"I'm ill and I need to get some help to put me back on my feet, but the good news is, I can get the help and it will work and I will get better and I'll be dragging you round the shops in no time. So we don't have to worry about me anymore." Ellen glanced back at Hannah's bedroom door. "For now we have to look after Hannah."

Matt appeared from the living room where Ellen knew he had been listening to her conversation with Charlie.

"Tell you what, why don't you and Matt make a pot of coffee and I'll see if I can wake up Hannah and see how she's feeling."

Charlie scowled at Matt. "Can't I stay here with you and see how she is?"

"I think she'll want a bit of time to get herself together, Charlie. Give her a bit of space, okay?" Ellen watched her son eye Matt. "I did tell you, nothing happened between me and Matt. We're just friends."

"Okay, I s'pose," Charlie said. "Mum . . . she will be all right, won't she, Aunt Hannah?"

Ellen stopped herself from responding reflexively. How could she reassure him that everything was going to be okay anymore? If there had ever been any boy who knew that things weren't always all right in the end, it was Charlie.

"I hope so," Ellen said. "The main thing is to be here and to look after her and help her as much as we can. Go and put some coffee on and make some toast, too; if I know Hannah, she won't have eaten."

Matt put his hand on Charlie's shoulder and guided him down the hallway toward the kitchen. Taking a deep breath, Ellen went back into Hannah's room.

"So how the bloody hell does this work?" Matt said, staring at an orange Gaggia espresso machine. It looked like it had never been used and had been bought more to go with the other orange accent features in the smart kitchen than to provide a daily shot of caffeine.

"I don't know why you're here," Charlie said, reaching up and taking an orange cafetière out of a cupboard. "You've got nothing to do with this. And Aunt Hannah never uses that—she uses this. I can do it."

"Good one," Matt said, wondering why, as he went to the fridge to look for milk, he felt as if he were being interviewed by a stern father, which was ironic because he'd spent most of his adult life avoiding fathers of any description. The fridge was empty except for three bottles of wine, half a bottle of gin, two bottles of tonic water, and half a lime. Matt slammed the door shut and turned around to find Charlie carefully pouring boiling water into the cafetière.

"I'm here to help your mum, Charlie. She needed a hand to get over here, but I swear, nothing would have stopped her from coming after you. She didn't want you to get the wrong idea."

"And what about you?" Charlie asked. "Did you want me to get the wrong idea?"

"Not sure I follow," Matt said, perplexed.

"Well, first of all you're all matey with me, following me around, being a laugh, and then you make moves on my mum. On my mum! Why?" Charlie's blue eyes narrowed dangerously. "I thought . . . well, I thought you were my friend. I thought you liked me."

"I would never . . . That's not what it's about. I am your friend, Charlie, I made friends with you because you're a laugh and I like you, even if you are a gooner. And as for your mum, well . . . I like her a lot, too." Matt gestured at the empty fridge. "Look, fancy walking down to the shop with me to get some milk while that's brewing?"

"I can go on my own," Charlie said bullishly, and then after a moment's hesitation he held out his hand. "Give us a couple of quid."

"Look, mate—I get why you're pissed off," Matt said. "You think I've been trying it on your mum. You're bound to be riled about that. Any bloke would be, it's natural—you want to protect your mum."

"Well, yeah, I do—but that's not the only reason I'm pissed off." Charlie retracted his hand and crossed his arms over his chest.

"What then? 'Cause you and me are mates, and you know what—you're right—the first rule of mates is that you never go after a mate's woman, especially not if that woman is also his mother."

Charlie shook his head. "Arsehole," he said, deliberately failing to keep the utterance under his breath.

"Arsehole?" Matt laughed, noticing a twitch of a smile around Charlie's mouth in response. "Fuck, say it like it is."

"Well, you are," Charlie told him. "You are a proper arsehole. Look, my mum likes you a lot. I'm not a kid, I know she goes all stupid around you, and I don't think I mind if she wants a boyfriend. I want her to be happy and laugh and go out places and dress up again. I think Dad would want her to be happy, too. But not with you, because you won't even love her, because you are an arsehole."

"Wouldn't I?" Matt asked, even though he sensed that was the wrong question. "Why not?"

Charlie went over to his rucksack, which he had thrown in the corner, unzipped it, and brought out last week's issue of *Bang It!*

"I read your column," he said. "You have sex with girls and then write about it. If you do that to my mum, I'll kill you, I swear it." Matt fully believed the glare that Charlie shot at him with deadly accuracy. He watched as the boy flipped through to the center pages, where Kelly from Doncaster lolled, legs akimbo, squeezing bits of her anatomy together that were designed to make a grown man do a little more than blush. "*And you spend all your time around young, naked girls. My mum is pretty but she doesn't look like that.*" He nodded at Kelly, who pouted sulkily from the pages, her mouth slightly open, and a line of text running beneath the photo that read, "I deserve to be spanked, I'm a very naughty girl."

"So don't go pretending to be my mate and my mum's mate when all you're doing is making fun of her."

Oh my America . . . The words of the poem sprang into Matt's head again and he thought of the incredible thrill that had raced through him when he pulled Ellen's dress away from her breasts, the excitement of discovering the unknown. He picked up the magazine and looked at the image of Kelly, airbrushed and manipulated into impossible perfection; she looked about one step away from a blow-up doll.

Matt sat down at Hannah's shiny white table, clear of any sign of use except for an orange set of condiment containers.

"Men are simple things," Matt said. "Mainly we think about sex. And when we think about sex, mostly we think about breasts and bottoms, and somehow at some point it all started to be about girls who looked like this." He gestured toward Kelly. "In the olden days, it was big pale flabby birds who were where it was at."

"What?" Charlie asked skeptically.

"Yeah, I saw a program about it once, when the Tivo was broken in the flat and we could only get BBC2. This artist called Rubens used to paint, like, seriously big women and everyone thought that was the bee's knees. Naked paintings of fat birds were the olden-day *Bang It!*"

"Gross," Charlie said, wrinkling his nose.

"And then when I was growing up it was all about skinny. No breasts or hips or bottoms. All the fit girls were the skinny ones. At that moment, it was all about this." He tapped Kelly on the face, which seemed like the only appropriate place to touch her. "But this isn't real. Big round breasts aren't what make a girl beautiful or make you love her."

"What about the girl you had sex with and wrote about? You said she was blond and had big tits."

"Did I?" Matt said uncomfortably, thinking about Lucy and how she'd listened to him bleat on about Ellen, how funny and bright she had been once he'd stopped looking down her cleavage and started looking into her eyes.

"She had more than a handful, you wrote," Charlie said. "Enough in her bra to sprain your tongue, you said." Charlie wrestled briefly with some internal dilemma and then asked, "How do you sprain your tongue on a girl's . . . bosom?"

. . . *My newfound land.* Matt replayed the line again. He'd wanted to write a novel once, or poetry. How had he ever ended up writing about tongue sprain and Nevada cathouses?

"You can't, not really. I was trying to be funny. I was making it up. Most of that I made up, just like most of this photo is made up. Kelly's waist isn't that small, and her breasts aren't that big and her legs aren't that long. She's got a little bit of acne on her chin, and on the day of the shoot she had shadows under her eyes because she'd been up all night. And I'll tell you something else: she looked a million times prettier in real life than she did in this photo."

"Did she have her top off?" Charlie asked, wide-eyed.

"No," Matt lied. "She had all of her clothes on." Charlie looked disappointed. "And that girl I wrote about, I lied about her, too. In real life she's funny and smart and kind, but I didn't write about any of that—any of the stuff that makes her a great person. I just made up a load of stuff to make me look big and clever. I feel pretty shitty about it actually."

Matt sighed. He was starting to wonder exactly who he was. This identity that he'd been nurturing for so long was slipping like a mask and he wasn't exactly sure that there was anything behind it.

"One day you'll realize, wanting someone, falling in . . .

you know—like sort of love, isn't just about bits of bodies. It's about attraction, yeah, but not the obvious sort. Like your mum. When she thinks you're talking rubbish, she sucks in the left corner of her bottom lip, just a fraction. She doesn't even know that she does it and it makes you think . . ." *It makes you think about kissing her until she laughs,* Matt wanted to say, but he refrained. "It makes you think about how nice her mouth is, and how she expresses what she's thinking even when she thinks she's not."

"Like Emily's hair," Charlie said thoughtfully.

"Whose what?" Matt wondered if he was talking about another *Bang It!* model.

"This girl at school, Emily. She's got long hair that reaches all the way down her back; it's sort of a dark yellow color, but when the sun shines on it, it looks amber, like honey running down her back. And she plays the electric guitar in a band and when she's onstage she looks like . . ." Charlie trailed off. "Like the whole world can go and jump in a lake because she doesn't care about anything but the music. She's the coolest girl I've ever met."

"Sounds to me like you like this Emily bird," Matt said seriously, without a hint of mockery or condescension.

"I really, really do," Charlie confessed earnestly. "But every time I try to talk to her I go all stupid and say crap and she looks at me like she thinks I'm mental and pathetic."

"Maybe you should write her a poem," Matt suggested.

"What, so then she'd think I was gay too?" Charlie exclaimed in horror.

"No, trust me, poetry can be one of the best ways of pulling a girl ever. Look at Shakespeare, or this bloke John Donne, who wrote this poem I can't get out of my head recently. They knew exactly how to woo a lady with the power of words."

"To what a lady? Is wooing a lady how you sprain your tongue?"

Matt shook his head. "That stuff you said about Emily's

hair, about it looking like honey and shit. That's romantic. You should write that down and give it to her, and I bet you she wouldn't think you were gay. She'd think you were sensitive and romantic, and not because you're acting sensitive and romantic to get her to snog you, but because you are that way, Charlie."

"Am I?" Charlie looked skeptical.

"You are if you're anything like your mother."

"I don't know," Charlie said thoughtfully. "All I can think about is what it would be like to touch a girl's . . . bosom."

"Yeah." Matt nodded. "And that probably won't change until the day you die. Even after you've touched a girl's bosom, you'll be wondering what it would be like to touch another girl's bosom and another's. That's just being a bloke. It's just this thing we're lumbered with. But it doesn't mean you can't care about a girl or, you know, like love her and shit."

Charlie looked at him with his level blue eyes and Matt shifted uncomfortably on his chair.

"So are you saying that you could fall in love with my mother then, even though she's old and a bit fat?"

"She's neither of those things." Matt chuckled. "She's . . . she's lovely, and brave, and strong in ways she's doesn't know, and she's beautiful. And yeah, I could fall in love with your mum, I reckon. If things were different."

"If what things were different?" Charlie challenged.

"Well, you know, it wasn't long ago that your dad died, and then there's all this stuff with her sister and the going-out business and . . . other stuff."

"You helped her today," Charlie stated.

"I got her here, I don't know if that actually counts as helping. There's a small possibility that I've permanently traumatized her."

"She likes talking to you," Charlie said. "You make her smile. I hadn't seen her smile or laugh, not a real smile that she means, not until you came."

"That's not exactly surprising. You've both had a shit year."

"Yes, but I don't want next year to be shit, too. I miss Dad, and I love him, but I want to be happy again. I want Mum to be happy and you make her laugh. So if you promise not to write about her and not to be mean to her, then I don't mind if you ask her out on a date. But I don't think you should have sex right away."

Matt pushed the plunger through the coffee, watching the dark liquid swirl and surge through the filter. "I don't reckon she'd say yes," he said. "I don't reckon she'd think it would be a very good idea. I mean, like you say, I'm not exactly boyfriend material."

"You could write her a poem," Charlie suggested. "Show her you're sensitive and romantic."

Matt snorted a derisory laugh. "I don't know, I've been writing bollocks for so long now that I'm not sure I could."

"Tell you what," Charlie said. "You write her a poem and I'll write Emily a poem and we can read each other's and see if they are bad or not, and if they aren't too bad we'll give them to them on the same day and ask them out. Like a pact."

"A suicide pact?" Matt joked, but he saw that Charlie was deadly serious and he remembered what it was like to be Charlie's age for a moment, when anything was possible and the future was a place waiting to be filled with dreams come true. "You know what," Matt said, holding out his hand, "let's do it."

Charlie spat in his palm, took Matt's hand, and shook it.

"Deal," he said.

"Cool," Matt replied. "But the spitting was a bit over the top, mate."

"Hannah?" Ellen knelt beside the bed so that her face was level with her sister's. "Hannah? Wake up, sis. You need to eat."

Hannah stirred, mumbling something unintelligible, moaning as she rolled over, turning her back on Ellen, reminding her of the days when it had been her job to drag her teenage sister out of bed and cajole her into going to school.

"Hans, Hannah—wake up, come on now." Gingerly, Ellen shook Hannah's bruised shoulder, scared of hurting her again.

Slowly, stiffly, Hannah rolled onto her back and opened her eyes, although only one was able to open completely. She turned her head and looked at her sister. "Ellen?" she whispered through dry, cracked lips. "Are you here?"

"Yes," Ellen said awkwardly. She had no idea how to reconcile her feelings, the fury and anger that she still felt every time she looked at Hannah because of what she had done to her and the pity and horror at what her sister had been through. She felt like she needed to be two people, or have two sisters, to be able to slip through a hole in time and exist in two parallel universes simultaneously. She had no idea how to handle this. There was no choice but to take it second by second. "Charlie came round this morning, we had a bit of a disagreement and he came round here. I wasn't sure what you would say to him."

Ellen thought Hannah might have frowned, but her features were immobilized by swelling. "You thought I'd tell him about me and Nick?"

Ellen felt stung, just as if Hannah had slapped her in the face. She hadn't been making it up, then; Ellen hadn't imagined it. It really was true.

"You didn't really tell me before, exactly what happened between you and Nick," Ellen said steadily. "And I need to know before I drive myself mad. Was it a one-off thing? Were you drunk? Where did it happen?"

With some difficulty, Hannah turned to look at Ellen. "It wasn't a one-off thing . . . it was a relationship. We were together for about a year."

Ellen pressed the back of her hand to her mouth to stifle the wave of nausea that swept over her. She nodded, gesturing that Hannah should go on.

"You know that I never really liked Nick, not when I first met him. I thought he was pompous and overbearing and that he was changing you. I always thought you were so cool, so together, and then Nick came along and . . . you weren't my big sis anymore, you were his wife. Your whole life was about being his wife. You never seemed to understand how much I looked up to you, wanted to be like you. I was so jealous of you, but the more I tried to be like you, the less you liked me."

"You were jealous of me?" Ellen asked, disbelieving. "You hated me ever having anything that was mine, you always tried to take it, always—even . . . even my husband."

"Ellen, that's not true!" Hannah sobbed. "Look, I know I like the limelight, making everyone look at me, me, me—but only because I don't have what you have. I don't have your . . . presence. I'm all smoke and mirrors, hollow inside. You . . . you are everything I've always wanted to be, but that isn't why Nick and I . . . that just happened. I wasn't looking for it, he came to me."

Ellen didn't say anything; she couldn't.

"We were at a family thing, a Christmas thing, and I'd been feeling a bit down. You know, another New Year's coming up and still no Mr. Right. I was in Mum and Dad's kitchen, knocking back the Baileys, and he came in. He asked me what was up. I can't remember what I said, something rude probably, telling him where to go, and he just leaned over and kissed me. Not a massive snog or anything, just a kiss on the lips, and he said that no woman like me should be alone on New Year's Eve. That's when it started, when I started to see him, when I started to fall for him."

Hannah paused and reached for a glass of stale water by her bed; her voice was paper dry.

"I tried to stay away from him, I swear. I suddenly got it. I suddenly got how much you loved him, and why he saw me. He saw the good in me, and I knew that's why you loved him so much. And I never, never wanted to . . . but then one night he just turned up at the flat. It was dark and raining and he just arrived. He stood there on the doorstep in the rain, just looking at me, and then we . . . we kissed. He said he'd tried to stay away, too, he'd tried but he couldn't. He said he needed me. It started then and I . . . I loved him, Ellen, I loved him and he loved me, too. We were going to tell you. We were going to face up to it all and be together, until . . . The last year, it's been hell because I've had to grieve for him in secret, knowing how I've betrayed you. Torn between wanting to be near you, with you and Charlie, and running away so that you two would never find out what I've done."

"But if Nick hadn't died, if you two had run off together, Charlie would have found out then. You can't have cared about that."

Ellen watched for a second as Hannah struggled to sit up and then she hooked her arms under Hannah's and helped her rise, plumping pillows behind her to support her back.

"I did. I thought about it all the time and so did Nick. We worried and worried about it. Nick never wanted to hurt Charlie or you. If it had been up to him he would have left it as it was. Living at home with you, coming round to me two or three times a week. If I loved you, I should have been able to live with that. But I'm not like you, Ellen. I'm not the sort of person who can live on the sidelines. I wanted to be everything to him, so I forced his hand. I gave him an ultimatum. I told him he had to choose, either me or you. Just before he died he promised me that it was going to be me, that he just wanted to wait a few more weeks and then we'd be together. We decided we'd talk to you together and then he'd talk to Charlie. I made him promise that he'd look after you, financially. That you'd be able to keep the house and he'd make sure you were comfortable."

"How big of you," Ellen said coolly.

Hannah burst into painful-sounding coughs, clasping her ribs with each spasm. "I know what it sounds like," she said. "I know that I sound like a heartless bitch, but, Ellen, nobody ever loved me the way he did. No one ever looked at me the way he did. He made me feel so special, so beautiful."

"Yes, he was good at that," Ellen said bitterly. Hannah had recited almost word for word what she had told Allegra about her husband only a few days earlier.

"I know you loved him," Hannah went on. "And I know he loved you, too, once. But people change and grow apart."

"I know that he changed me," Ellen said. "I know that he stopped me in my tracks at a point in my life when I could have been anything or anyone and he made me into his wife. He would have changed you, too, Hannah, in the end."

"Well, perhaps I needed changing. I mean, look at my life without him. Look at what happens to me when I'm left alone."

Ellen straightened and stood up. "This, this is not your fault. This has nothing to do with Nick."

Hannah nodded, silent for a moment. "What do we do now? Is this the last time I see you and Charlie?"

Ellen looked at her sister. "Charlie can't ever know about this. Whatever Nick was, he was a good father and Charlie adored him. We can never let him have a reason to think differently about his father."

"And what about you?" Hannah asked.

"I loved Nick, I loved being his wife, and if I hadn't found out about you, then I suppose I always would have. You've taken that away from me, Hannah. I can never get that back."

Hannah turned her face away. "I know. I never meant to tell you, I wouldn't have if—"

"But I'm glad I know," Ellen interrupted. "I think I needed to see the life I had with Nick the way it actually was, not the way I thought it was. I don't think he was a bad man, I think he was just a man who wanted it all, and all his way, and I let him get away with that. Maybe you wouldn't have, but then again, maybe you would. There's no way of knowing now. Either way, at least now I can go forward again, knowing that the best part of my life isn't over. That it's yet to come . . . and one day, so can you."

Hannah turned back to look Ellen in the eye.

"Can you ever forgive me, Ellen? Will it ever be like it used to be between us again? When we were girls, you used to hold my hand 'til I went to sleep. Do you remember that time you wanted those shiny patent leather shoes in that shop in town? You were fifteen and I was about six? Mum said no, you couldn't have them, and you were gutted. Do you remember that I saved up my pocket money for a month and then asked Mum to buy them for you with my money? She thought I was so cute that she bought them for you and let me keep the pocket money. I've always wanted you to be happy, Ellie. And I know you won't believe me but I love you so much. And now you hate me."

Ellen shook her head, thinking of those shoes that she had treasured so much, and how she had let Hannah play in them, parading up and down the hall in them, making Ellen laugh until the tears streamed down her face. It was a happy memory, but one that Ellen found painful to recall.

"I love you, Hannah," she said quietly. "That's all I can tell you right now. And I won't let you deal with this on your own."

As Hannah began to sob, Ellen put her arms around her and pulled her into her embrace.

"I keep trying not to . . . not to think about it, but every time I close my eyes, it comes back in flashbacks, a little bit more each time, and . . . Ellen, what if I've caught something, what if I'm pregnant? I'm so scared."

Ellen held her sister for a long time, rocking her back and forth, letting her tears soak through her clothes. Then after a while she gently pushed Hannah away a little so that she could look her in the eye.

"Hannah, we have to face this. We have to get you the help you need, get you emergency contraception and tested and . . . Hannah, you were beaten and raped," she said with deliberate blunt force. "You can't think that it doesn't matter, or that you deserved what's happened to you, because of Nick—because it does matter and you didn't deserve it. You need to go to hospital and get properly checked out, get proper care, and you need to report it to the police. Because if they've done it once, they'll do it again. You are the only person who might be able to stop that happening. I know it will be horrible and hard but I think you need to do this for your own sake, and I promise you I will be there every step of the way. Because I love you and I can't stand that this has happened to you and you think that it's just something you'll get over, like a bad cold or . . ."

"Someone dying?" Hannah said, a tear rolling down her damaged cheek.

"Will you go to hospital?" Ellen asked. After a moment, Hannah nodded once.

"Right now, we're going to get some coffee into you and some food, and then we're going to casualty to get you checked over and we're going to report this to the police. We have to, Hannah, there is no other choice."

"But there's no evidence," Hannah said. "I got changed, I had a bath."

Ellen thought of the bundle of clothes that remained unwashed at her house.

"There is evidence."

"They'll think I deserved it, that I'm a drunk and a slut." Hannah sobbed with such feeling that Ellen almost reached out and touched her. Instead, she sat on the bed, softening her voice.

"Maybe, maybe that's the way you think, too. But whatever happened, Hannah, you don't deserve to feel that way. Maybe it is impossible to catch the people who did this to you, but if you don't do something, tell someone, get some help, then you will always feel that way. And I don't want that for you."

"Saint Ellen," Hannah whispered, a tiny smile pulling at the corner of her mouth.

"No," Ellen said. "Just Ellen, just me again. For the first time in a long time, I'm just being me."

CHAPTER Twenty

W ell, it certainly is different," Allegra said thoughtfully once Ellen had stopped reading the ending that she herself had written for *The Sword Erect*. "It's not at all the sort of ending that my readers will be expecting. . . ."

"I know," Ellen said. "And of course I only did it for fun, but after we got back from the hospital, it had been such a difficult day, my mind was racing and I couldn't make my heart slow down. I needed to take my mind off of everything that had happened, because I could feel the panic there in the corner, just waiting for me to fixate on something and fall apart."

Ellen thought of the journey that she and Hannah had made to St. Mary's Hospital in Paddington a couple of days before. Charlie and Matt had wanted to come, too, and Ellen had wanted them to come, but she also wanted to protect Charlie from finding out anything more, at least for now. She had persuaded Matt to take Charlie home, but only after he had installed Ellen and her sister in a black taxi.

"Remember, you are in the safest place in the world," he had whispered in Ellen's ear as he secured her seat belt. Ellen had clutched the bright yellow handlebar as the cab pulled away, struggling to control her breathing, but as she looked at her sister, who had faced real and not imagined monsters, she forced herself to be calm, reaching out and covering the clenched hand that Hannah rested on the seat with her own.

Calming Hannah's nerves calmed her own in turn, and as long as she didn't stop for one second to think about herself, she could just about cope.

Once they had arrived at the E.R. Hannah hung back while Ellen bypassed the queue at reception to stop a nurse and tell her exactly why she had brought her sister in. Within minutes she and Hannah found themselves in a private room with a female doctor, who gently asked Hannah several questions and then asked permission to examine her. Ellen held her hand as the examination took place, keeping her eyes on her sister's face as tears streamed silently down Hannah's battered cheeks. They had stayed there for hours, until two women police officers arrived and took Hannah's statement. Ellen told them about the clothes that she still had at home and they told her they'd check the CCTV footage of the places that Hannah could remember going to.

After the ordeal was finally over, Ellen and Hannah had stood at the hospital exit for a long time, clinging to each other, neither one wanting to set foot either back inside or outside. "Matt said he'd come to collect us," Ellen said, reassuring herself as much as her sister. "He'll be here in a minute."

"This is hard for you, isn't it? All these people, all this noise and the smell. Especially here, I know how much you hate hospitals."

"This is a living hell," Ellen told her candidly. "I don't want to be here a single second more, but I wouldn't leave you here, either."

"I never told you how sorry I was, after you lost the baby and everything else that happened. I never told you that I cried for you; I knew how much you wanted more children. I wish I'd told you that I cried for you . . . but it seemed that anything I said made it worse."

Ellen smiled wanly at Hannah. "I wish you'd told me that, too, it would have helped." She took a deep breath of hot, exhaust-heavy air. "I had to come here to identify Nick, you know. They took me that afternoon to look at him. All the way here I was praying, praying that they'd got it wrong because I just couldn't imagine him not being alive . . . it was impossible. I was so certain that they'd got it wrong, I don't think I took it seriously until I saw him . . . I remember there was someone outside laughing in the corridor. I remember wondering why they didn't shut up. And thinking, how is it possible that life can go on for anyone when it's stopped for me? Maybe that's when I decided that I didn't ever want to go out again. Maybe it was then."

"You went through all of that alone," Hannah said, linking her arm through Ellen's.

"I don't think there is really any other way to do it. You've just done the same."

"If it helps you, even though everything that just happened was so awful and so horrifying, I feel better. I feel like I've done something about it. I mean, I hurt like fuck and it's no fun having three broken ribs but . . . thank you. I must be the worst sister in the world."

Ellen did not look at Hannah. Instead, as she saw Matt's face in the window of a nearing cab, she simply said, "But I love you, I keep on loving you. How can I do anything else?"

"Will you drop me off at my place?" Hannah asked.

"Don't be an idiot," Ellen told her. "You are coming home with me. Where else would you go?"

When they got back, Sabine had helped Ellen get Hannah into her bed, while Allegra had prepared soup for both of them. Ellen had sat with her sister and spoon-fed her until the new pain medication she had been given had kicked in, and for the first time in a long time Hannah looked almost relaxed.

"You know," she had murmured sleepily, "I think I knew that Nick would never choose me. I knew that he would drag me down and hurt me, but it didn't matter, nothing mattered. I just wanted to be loved, and he loved me. Maybe it was all a game to him, and maybe he never meant it, but he made me believe that he loved me and I thought I needed that more than anything else. That's all I've been clinging to ever since."

"So did I, once," Ellen had said as her sister drifted off in a mercifully painless sleep. "Now I'm not so sure."

A succession of dark images and shadows parading through her mind, threatening to engulf her at any minute, and unable to sleep in the unfamiliar box room, Ellen had got up and gone downstairs to the kitchen, half hoping, half expecting Matt to be there, but it was empty. She had taken her writing pad and pen out of the drawer it had languished in for the last year, sat down, and begun writing. She'd written to keep the tigers at bay, and for the whole of Sunday had concentrated on making Hannah as comfortable as possible and readjusting her mind once again to change. But she'd been aware of the notepad sitting in that drawer, waiting to be written on. She conjured a whole new ending for Allegra's book—one where Eliza made good her escape on her own, killing her hunters and then rescuing Captain Parker from certain death. And finally she had written the most erotic love scene between Eliza and the captain that she could think of, passionate, graphic, and best of all, with Eliza on top, taking charge.

Now, Monday morning had come and Ellen felt a little embarrassed that she had ever thought her amateur offerings were fit even for Allegra's scrap-paper pile, but still, her new life was not about sitting on laurels, it was about grabbing thistles—even if Allegra could be a particularly prickly one.

"So anyway," Ellen explained carefully, "normally when I felt like that I'd read one of your books, but last night I was so desperate to know what happened to Eliza next that I thought I'd write my own version; I mean, why should Eliza have to get rescued, why should she always be the helpless victim? After everything she's been through she'd be a stronger, world-lier woman, wouldn't she? I think she would, anyway, and it worked—writing did make the panic go away. It all seems a bit foolish now. I only read it to you because I thought you'd think it was funny. So anyway, let's start work on the real ending. I know that Simon is waiting for the next Allegra Howard."

"Yes, he is, he always is," Allegra said. "And I think I might have found her."

"Huh?"

"Ellen, haven't you noticed that it's not really me who's written this book at all, it's you. You had a vision for how it should be, it was your thoughts and ideas that shaped the characters and the plot. In truth, this book really belongs to you."

"To me?" Ellen laughed. "Allegra, that's so silly. All I've done is a lot of typing and had a few thoughts. I've been here listening to you telling the tale, weaving the words together to make a story. I can't possibly do that!"

"But you've just proved that you can," Allegra said, nodding at the sheets of lined paper filled with Ellen's scrawl. "That ending was as well written as anything I could have done. It's not the right ending for my book, my readers would have mass heart attacks, but it could be the right ending for a book—for your book." Allegra tapped one long finger against her thigh.

"No, I'm not a writer, I'm just me, Ellen Woods. I read books, I don't write them. I can't do that, Allegra, it's too hard and too late now. You are very sweet to be so nice about my efforts, but I know my limitations."

"Do you want to know my real name?" Allegra asked.

"Um, I do, don't I?"

"Joan Fisher," Allegra stated. "My real name is Joan Fisher. I wasn't born Allegra Howard. I was born Joan Fisher, daughter of a dentist, who grew up in Hull. I am Joan Fisher, who just about scraped through secretarial college and got a job in a bank, who got married at the age of twenty-three in 1960 to Graham Howard, who gave up work and moved into a semi in Surbiton and spent the next ten years keeping house, cooking, wearing an apron, letting all the fun and frolics of the sixties pass me by while I read and daydreamed and waited for children. But children never came, and in 1972 Graham Howard told me he was in love with another man. Another man, Ellen. He said he couldn't hide his true feelings from me anymore, that he loved me but that he would never love me in that way. We agreed that we would stay married, and perhaps adopt a baby. That he would have his life and I would have mine and we wouldn't ask questions." Allegra smiled faintly. "Graham was a lovely, kind man. He never wanted to hurt me, and at first I thought I would be happy with that. I'd lived one way for so long that I thought I would be . . . content. And then one morning I woke up alone and I realized that I was never going to be happy stuck in my semi in Surbiton and married to a man who felt more passionate about my Biba knee-high boots than he did about me. So I changed my life; it's a long story, there were many ups and downs, mistakes and triumphs, but at the end of it all I had become Allegra Howard, romantic novelist. Simon's father gave me my first book deal at Cherished Desires and I divorced Graham in 1978. By 1980 I was published in nineteen different languages. I changed my life, Ellen, I changed who I was, from the inside out. But the most important thing is that I didn't change *from* the real me into someone false and made up. I changed *into* the real me, the person I was always supposed to be. It's a cliché, but I found myself, and rather wonderful I turned out to be, too."

"Wow," Ellen said. "I had no idea, I just thought that you were always you."

"No one arrives in this world like Aphrodite, born from the sea the image of perfection. It's a struggle to become yourself, to find the path in life that is going to afford you the greatest satisfaction and joy. Many people never try, they simply let their lives dwindle away down whichever path takes them, and for some that is enough. But it wasn't for me and it shouldn't be for you, Ellen. Perhaps you don't know it yet, but there is so much more to you than you realize. I see a lot of me in you, and you are like a butterfly who's been trapped in a jam jar.

Now is your time to be free, to spread your wings and find yourself. And besides, you'd be doing me a huge favor. I've been trying to retire for years, but each year Simon persuades me to write just a few more books while he's looking for 'the next Allegra Howard.' I keep telling him I'll be dead soon. I'm tired of writing about beautiful, half-naked nineteen-year-olds. I want the chance to write something for myself, something about a woman my age—something for my own vanity and pleasure."

"So you want me to take over as Allegra Howard?" Ellen asked, her head dizzy with thoughts and feelings that didn't quite connect yet. "To become you?"

"Good God, no, darling. Let's not try running before we can walk." Allegra shook her head. "First, you should get all the credit—or otherwise—for whatever you write in your own right. And I don't see you as writing carbon copies of my books; I think you have a lot more modern and forward-thinking ideas than I do. And second, I've earned this name, it belongs to me, I would never simply give it away. Even to someone I am as fond of as you. It took me a long time to become myself, Ellen, and I intend to hold on to that until I'm ashes in the ground."

"Yes, but—Ellen Woods, romantic novelist. Somehow it doesn't sound quite right, does it?"

"Of course not. Yours is a terrible name for grandeur. You'll need to make something up. Try the porn-star-name formula. Your first pet's name combined with the street name where you were born, that's a good one."

"Well, we had this long-eared rabbit and we lived on Waters Crescent, so that would make me . . . Velvet Waters," Ellen said uncertainly. "It does sort of sound more like a porn-star name than a writer's name."

"Which is perfect," Allegra assured her. "Velvet sounds exactly like the kind of woman who would write powerful, sexy women in charge—historical romantic fiction. Good.

Now all you need to do is have an idea, write a proposal, and we'll show it to Simon and get you started on your first book. You'll have to write it in between helping me put together my magnum opus, of course, but that shouldn't be a problem—you seem to have a fondness for staying up all night 'chatting.'"

"*That's* all I need to do? That's *all* I need to do!" Ellen exclaimed. "Allegra, life is not that simple. I can't just have an idea—"

"You can if you try, oh, I don't know, say, thinking of one."

"I have no idea how to write a proposal."

"I'll help you," Allegra said.

"And I wouldn't have the first idea where to start writing a book."

"Why not? You've read thousands of them, you've had plenty of ideas for *The Sword Erect*. Why couldn't you put all of that insight and imagination into your own project?"

Ellen hesitated. She couldn't think of a reason why not right then, except that it seemed so . . . otherworldly, as if Allegra were suggesting that she take up time travel or fly to the moon.

"Well, Simon will never take me seriously, not as a writer—why would he?"

"Because he knows you, he knows how good you are at your job and how much you bring to a book, how much creativity and vision you've brought to my book. And he is no fool, he wouldn't let a talent like yours pass him by."

"A talent like mine?" Ellen blinked.

"You heard me correctly. Now we have to think about getting Velvet into print and me off the hook."

Ellen sat perfectly still behind Allegra's desk, attempting to focus her thoughts. Could she really do this? Could she really have an idea and write a book? She felt a giddy sense of excitement at the idea, a half-baked childhood dream that she had assumed would always be impossible to make come true, but could she have been wrong? After all, if the great Allegra Howard believed she was capable, then . . . well, she might be, mightn't she?

"I suppose I have always been fascinated with the early settlers in America. You know, the pilgrims on the *Mayflower*," Ellen mused. "I wrote my dissertation on it."

"Perfect," Allegra said. "Then you'd have the American market in your sites, too."

"I suppose I could try to think of something, you know—a plot or something to weave around the history."

"I suppose you could. You could take a chance, do something a little different, take a risk, and see if it just might change your life forever." Allegra's smile was warm but brief. "Now, as for my book—I have my ending ready and I think you'll agree it is rather splendid. Let's get it typed into the computer and finally deliver *The Sword Erect* to Simon. The poor man will die of shock when he realizes that I've actually finished at last. Although hopefully not before he's paid me."

"You first," Matt said as he and Charlie sat on a bench in the park behind the house.

"Well, I thought you should go first, because you are an actual writer," Charlie said, fingering a grubby piece of folded paper that looked like it had been ripped out of the back of a notebook.

"Which is why you should go first," Matt told him, tapping the closed lid of his laptop. "I don't want you to feel intimidated by my skill."

"Hah." Charlie rolled his eyes. "Coward."

"Look, just read me what you've got and let's get on with this. Neither of us wants anyone to see us sitting in a park talking about poetry, right?"

"Right," Charlie said, glancing over at a group of his mates who were kicking a ball around a few yards away. Sighing, he unfolded his piece of paper and flattened it on his thigh.

In the sunshine your hair looks like honey,
Running down the handle of a spoon.
And your skin as smooth and soft as the petal of
*   a rose.*
I like the way you laugh, like you don't care what
*   anybody thinks.*
And I wish that I could be more like you.

Hastily Charlie folded up his scrap of paper and stuffed it in his pocket.

"It doesn't rhyme and I'm not sure about the last line, because maybe she might think that I want to be a girl and that makes me look a bit gay."

Matt said nothing for a moment and then he clapped his hand firmly over his laptop lid.

"That's it, I'm not reading you mine," he said. "Yours is a million times better than mine."

"Really?" Charlie seemed appalled by the prospect.

"Yeah, yours is simple and heartfelt with imagery and shit. Mine is bollocks. I'm not reading it to you."

"You have to, that's the deal!" Charlie protested, eyeing Matt's laptop as if he was considering snatching it.

Sighing, Matt flipped open his laptop, angling the screen away from Charlie so that he would not be able to read over his shoulder. He looked at it for a second, opened his mouth as if he was about to speak, and then slammed it shut.

"No. Sorry, Charlie, I know it was the deal. But the thing is, your mum, she makes me feel weird and a bit soppy. This poem sucks; I can't ever show it to anyone. Not you and especially not your mother. She'd laugh me out of London."

"But are you still going to ask her out?"

"Are you still going to ask Emily out?" Matt hedged.

"I am if you are," Charlie said. "But now you've chickened out of the poem thing, you have to do it first. You have to do it tonight."

"Tonight?" Matt shook his head. "You don't impose a deadline on a man about to make a romantic declaration, mate. It's an organic thing—you have to bide your time, wait for the right moment."

"Tonight," Charlie repeated. "When we get back. Like how hard is it to go up to my mum and say, 'Ellen, would you like to go out with me?' How hard is that?"

Matt shifted uncomfortably on the bench. Never before had he hesitated about asking a woman out; in fact, he'd asked out a good many women without giving it a second or, on some occasions, a first thought. But this time it was different, it was very different. It mattered if Ellen turned him down. If Ellen turned him down, then he'd . . . Matt didn't want to think about it.

"You do it tonight, I'll do it tomorrow. After music. Deal?" Charlie held out his hand and fixed Matt with his steady blue gaze.

"It's great being nearly twelve," Matt said as he shook on the deal. "Everything's black and white, right or wrong, deal or no deal. Life is so simple."

Charlie shook his head. "All I can say is that you must have a very bad memory."

Twenty-one

Ellen and Hannah stood in the kitchen doorway, each with a cup of coffee in her hand.

"So you don't even want to go down there?" Hannah asked, nodding at the cacophony of unruly color that was splattered all over the rear of the garden.

"I didn't . . . I didn't have the impulse to go anywhere, but now—I want to go. I just . . . can't."

"We could hold hands," Hannah offered. "Like you did with Matt when you came to rescue me. Or wouldn't that be quite the same thing?"

Ellen gave her sister a sideways warning glance, but it was accompanied by a small smile. It was good that Hannah was here, it was good that they were talking again, that Hannah was well enough to be teasing her ever so gently. Ellen only wished that she could remember why they had stopped talking like this in the first place.

"When I came over to your house I was pumped up full of adrenaline and still half drunk, most likely. Matt more or less dragged me there, talking all sorts of nonsense on the way over to keep my mind off things. Now I don't feel that way. I feel . . . okay."

"So feeling okay means you can't get to the bottom of the garden?" Hannah said. "Freaky."

"Yeah, thanks, sis, freaky—that sums up my condition perfectly," Ellen said mildly. "If I tried now, the world would turn inside out, I'd have a panic attack, and you'd have to scrape a gasping, gibbering wreck up off the patio. It's quite something that I'm standing here with the door open, and that I'm thinking what fun it would be to take a trimmer to that grass and sort my plants from the weeds. That's progress—after all, I haven't got my hands dirty in quite a while."

"That's not what I heard," Hannah muttered into her coffee.

"I beg your pardon?"

"Nothing." Hannah paused and then shrugged. "It's just Sabine happened to mention in a bid to cheer me up that she'd found a pair of panties in the plastic-bag drawer that didn't belong to her or Allegra."

"Oh, I forgot about those!" Ellen exclaimed before she could clap her hands over her mouth. "How embarrassing."

"So?" Hannah asked. "Come on, it's your duty to spill. Take *my* mind off things. What happened between you and Matt that meant your undies ended up . . . off?"

Ellen hesitated. The truth was that she was desperate to talk to somebody about what had happened so that she could make sense of it herself—but she wasn't sure it should be Hannah, not when most of the reason it had happened in the first place was because of Hannah. And yet . . . maybe Hannah was exactly the right person.

"I'd just found out about you and my husband," Ellen said. "I was angry and drunk and I just wanted to be seen again—the way that Nick used to see me, the way that Matt sometimes looked at me. So I waited for him to come in and I threw myself at him in the most unseemly way. And for about a minute or two it, we . . . well, it was pretty exciting, and then I realized what was about to happen and Matt sensed I wasn't sure and he developed the most annoying conscience about it all and was ever so gentlemanly and sweet. So my knickers came off but that was about it really."

"Wow," Hannah said. "Matt's gorgeous. I would."

"Well, we all know *you* would," Ellen said before she could stop herself.

There was an awkward silence between the two women. Since arriving back from the hospital, neither of them had mentioned what had happened with Nick, as if in some unspoken pact or truce. But Ellen supposed that they couldn't go on like this, not if they were ever to be really close again. There was no point in shying away from it. Hannah and Nick had had an affair, Nick might have even loved Hannah—there was no way of knowing now. And somehow Ellen had to live with that, she had to accept it just as Hannah had to accept that the man she had fallen for would never, ever belong to her.

"I've hurt you so badly," Hannah said, turning away from the garden and retreating inside to sit at the table, as if she were the one who was suddenly afraid. "I don't know how you can even stand to look at me, Ellie, let alone have me here."

Ellen followed Hannah inside and sat down, too. "The only reason I find it hard to look at you is because of the state of your face. When I think about what happened to you . . ." Ellen paused as Hannah turned her face away, aware that her sister was not ready to think about that yet, perhaps would not ever be. "The odd thing is, Hannah, now I'm over the shock and the anger, I don't hate you, in fact I'm sort of grateful to you."

"Grateful?" Hannah looked at her, perplexed.

"You've given me the key to moving on. I was stuck with this memory of my marriage, a perfect, happy, loving marriage—but it wasn't like that. It wasn't bad, it wasn't awful—as far as I knew. But it wasn't perfect, either. Whether he meant to or not, Nick diluted me, he watered me down. He made me dependent on him and he spent so much time caring for me that when he'd gone I could barely care for myself, let alone Charlie. I loved him, I loved him with all my heart, and he was the best dad that Charlie could ever have had and I miss him and I'll still grieve for Charlie, for the family life that he had and he lost. But I can move on now, I can be myself again, once I've worked out exactly who that is. And I think if it hadn't been for you telling me what you did, it would have taken a lot longer. So, yes, I am sort of grateful to you."

Hannah nodded, chewing the tip of her thumb, waiting for a wave of emotion to pass before she could speak.

"I miss Nick," she whispered, tears streaming over her bruises. "I've missed him so much for every second of the last year. I'd watch you getting all the flowers and the sympathy and I'd want to shout, 'What about me? He loved me, you know. I lost him, too!' But I couldn't, so I just tried to be near the nearest thing I had to him—you and Charlie. But the more time I spent with you, the more I realized that what I had with him . . . it was nothing compared to the life he had with you and his son. And the more I came around, the more annoyed you seemed to get with me for being there. I used to think that you knew, that you'd found out somehow but hadn't told anyone. Do you think you sensed it, sensed something was wrong?"

"I doubt it," Ellen said. "I don't think I could sense anything very much for most of the last year. I think I was just caught up in all the pain. I don't suppose I wanted to share it."

"I was jealous of your pain, jealous of you," Hannah said thoughtfully. "Just like we always have been since we were little girls."

"Jealous of me?" Ellen exclaimed. "Don't be so ridiculous."

"Why on earth wouldn't I be jealous of my beautiful, clever, kind big sister who everybody always admired, always said was so lovely, such a wonderful mother with such a wonderful family? And then there's me, going from one bad relationship to the next, always single, living alone, working all hours because I had no one to go home to. Of course I was jealous of you."

Ellen laughed, "Well, that's just crazy—because I was always jealous of you. Younger, thinner, prettier, with your life all sorted—direction, a career—your independence. I felt old and frumpy and useless next to you."

The two sisters regarded each other across the kitchen table, and after a moment Hannah extended her hand tentatively across the table, where Ellen regarded it for a second and then covered it with her own.

"Hey," Hannah said. "Do you remember that time when Charlie was about five and he lost his favorite bear down at the park . . . what was it called?"

"Midnight," Ellen recalled. "Black fluffy thing. He couldn't eat, sleep, or even go to the loo without it. I told Nick not to let him take it out of the house, but he was insistent. Said it would be fine. Typical Nick, he always thought everything would be fine."

"And they came back an hour later, with Charlie howling his head off because Midnight was lost and they couldn't find him anywhere. I was here . . . why was I here?"

"Because Mum and Dad were coming up for the weekend," Ellen reminded her.

"I just remember Charlie sitting at this table asking you if Midnight was dead and you said, don't be so silly, he's just gone on a little trip to visit Father Christmas. You said he'd be back on Christmas Day. And suddenly Charlie stopped crying and he was all smiles again, laughing about what fun Midnight would be having with the elves. You made everything all right."

"Until I found out that they didn't make Midnights anymore and he was obsolete," Ellen said.

"We searched high and low for another one of those blasted bears, didn't we?" Hannah laughed. "And Christmas was getting closer and Charlie was getting more and more excited, and we couldn't find one anywhere and then . . ."

"And then you paid about ten times what it was worth for one on eBay," Ellen remembered. "You were so pleased with yourself, and I was so relieved."

"So we spent ages writing a letter from Santa, explaining why Midnight looked so new and his bow was back again and that missing eye had been replaced with a new one . . ."

"And on Christmas Eve I crept into his room and lay Midnight on the pillow beside Charlie's head," Ellen recalled. "I don't think I'd ever been more excited about giving him a present."

"And the next day . . . Charlie didn't even notice he was back. He didn't even play with him once. Because that was the Christmas he went off bears and on to train sets."

The two sisters laughed.

"I can't keep up with how fast he's growing up," Ellen said. "It makes my head spin. It seems like five minutes since he was a tiny baby in my arms, or howling his head off over Midnight. And now here he is interested in girls, giving me advice, sorting *me* out."

"He's a brilliant kid," Hannah said.

"Yes he is," Ellen agreed.

"So you're going to do what he wants, get some help—some treatment so that you can go down to the bottom of the garden and weed again? Maybe even have alfresco sex with Matt?"

"Hannah! Poor Matt must be scared to death of me by now, I shouldn't think that would be in the cards again. And yes, yes—I am going to get help. I am going to get down to the bottom of the garden and out of the house again. I am."

"Good," Hannah said. "Because then I'll be able to take you out and buy you some decent clothes at last."

When the doorbell sounded, Ellen assumed that it was Matt and Charlie, even though both of them had a key, so she was a little surprised to find a stranger standing there, a fair, short-ish, stocky man in a pair of Bermuda shorts and flip-flops.

"Hello?" Ellen said, eyeing him up and down.

"Hello. Is Sabine here please?" the man asked, and Ellen guessed that his accent was German.

"She's not quite back from work yet. Can I take a message?"

The man looked very disappointed. "I'm Eric, Sabine's husband," he explained.

"Oh, you!" Ellen was surprised. "Aren't you supposed to be in Austria declaring your love to a married Catholic woman?"

"Oh, she told you about that then," Eric said, his neck flushing bright red.

"Yes, she did." Ellen nodded, crossing her arms. "And can I just say that I think you are very lucky to have a woman like Sabine in your life and if I were you, I'd pick up my socks, cut back on the lap dancers, forget this Austrian woman, and try your best to hang on to a really wonderful woman."

"She showed you the list?" Eric looked supremely uncomfortable.

"All three categories," Ellen confirmed.

"You're right," Eric said. "I know that you are. Sabine told me to go to the woman I loved. So I did. I came to Sabine." Just at that second, the garden gate swung open and Sabine stood at the top of the path, staring at her husband. "Sabine is the woman I love, and I don't deserve her but I hope she might reconsider leaving me."

"Ask her yourself," Ellen said, nodding over his shoulder.

"I came for you," Eric turned and told Sabine. "I came to tell you that you are the woman I love, and that I've been a fool. I want you back, Sabine."

"You treacherous, stinking, hideous pig," Sabine said as she marched down the garden path. And then she kissed him.

"Blimey," Matt said as he and Charlie arrived a few seconds later. "It's busy, busy, busy here."

"Love is in the air, that's why," Charlie said pointedly, winking at his mother as he walked past the embracing couple as if it were a sight he saw every day.

"Random bloke?" Matt asked Ellen.

"Returning husband," Ellen explained, before calling to the couple, "I'll just leave the door on the latch. Do come in if you fancy a cup of tea."

They did not break their embrace to reply.

When Ellen made her way back into the kitchen, she found Allegra making herself a pot of Earl Grey tea.

"I do believe I have finished my book," Allegra stated as Ellen joined her. "Normally I like to celebrate with a bottle of vintage champagne, but we are in Shepherd's Bush and needs must, so Earl Grey it is. I telephoned Simon to tell him all about our plans for you, my dear. He was very excited."

"What plans?" Charlie and Matt asked simultaneously.

"Oh, it's nothing," Ellen muttered.

"It's *everything*. I have discovered that your mother has a rare gift for writing that if nurtured correctly might one day almost rival mine. So I intend to turn Velvet Waters here into the next big publishing sensation!" Allegra declared. "I do so love a challenge."

"Cool!" Charlie exclaimed.

"Brilliant," Matt said, smiling steadily at Ellen. He wondered how it was possible that she could seem even more beautiful every time he looked at her. She was like a flower blossoming before his eyes, which was what he had tried and failed to write a poem about.

"So go on then." Charlie elbowed Matt in the ribs.

"What?" Matt looked at him.

"Ask Mum that thing you wanted to ask her," Charlie growled out of the corner of his mouth, as if he could not be any more conspicuous.

"What thing?" Ellen asked.

"Oh . . . um, it was about . . . um—the loo—I've run out of toilet cleaner." Matt winced.

"That's not it!" Charlie laughed. "You are *so* gay."

"Charlie, how many times!" Ellen exclaimed. "Don't use the word *gay* in that context please."

"Well, he is," Charlie muttered.

"There are about a million people here," Matt said. "I'm not doing it in front of an audience."

"Doing what?" Ellen asked, confused.

"Ohhh," Hannah said as she caught Charlie's eye. "Oh, I

see—I've got it. Allegra, would you like to join me for a turn around the garden? And you, too, Charles."

"Well, we might need a machete to get through some of the undergrowth, but I should be delighted." Allegra nodded, gesturing at Charlie to follow. "Come along, young man. I will teach you the Georgian art of flirting. It's all about the angle of the fan, you know."

"What? What's going on?" Ellen looked anxiously at Matt. "Have you got bad news or something?"

"Depends." Hannah winked at Allegra. "Come along, Charles."

"I always get to miss all the good bits," Charlie moaned, following the others reluctantly.

Matt suddenly found himself standing alone in the kitchen with the woman who had somehow come to embody every single one of his dreams. *Funny how love is so unpredictable,* Matt thought as he looked at her, evening sun dusting her skin with gold, lighting her green eyes from within. He had never thought that the woman who would capture his heart would be an older, widowed agoraphobic. But she was.

"What are you grinning at and what's going on?" Ellen asked. "Have you done something, have you burned a hole in my carpet because you iron your shirts on the floor? I know you do it, you know."

"No," Matt said. "I . . . look, there's this poem. I didn't write it, I tried to write one but it came out all wrong, but there's this other poem that another bloke wrote and . . ."

"And?" Ellen looked at him, the intensity in his gaze causing her to catch her breath.

Matt took a step toward her as he quoted:

> *"Come, madam, come, all rest my powers defy;*
> *Until I labour, I in labour lie.*
> *The foe ofttimes, having the foe in sight,*
> *Is tired with standing, though he never fight."*

For Freddie born August 22, 2009

Acknowledgments

It was during the writing of this book that I got to know lovely Kara Cesare, and I would like to thank her so much for all the support and inspiration she has given so generously. Also thank you to the team at Gallery Books, especially Katherine Dresser and Ayelet Gruenspecht, for doing such a wonderful job on my behalf and for continuing to believe in me.

I count myself very lucky to have two wonderful agents working so hard for me on both sides of the Atlantic. Thank you so much Lizzy Kremer and Jill Grinberg.

On a personal note, thank you to Adam, source of so much support and inspiration, and to my wonderful daughter, Lily, who truly is my best friend, and not forgetting my baby son, Fred, who always makes me smile, even at three in the morning. Love to you all.

Introduction

Ellen Woods hasn't left her home in nearly a year. Mourning the death of her husband, Nick, she stays sheltered inside, quietly doing her freelance work while her eleven-year-old son, Charlie, refuses to eat anything but fish sticks. Grief-stricken and unable to pay her mortgage on her measly salary, Ellen knows she has to do something. But when she takes her sister Hannah's suggestion to board lodgers, she doesn't expect to find anything more than a way to keep a roof over her son's head. She certainly doesn't expect to find herself.

Now, with the help of her newfound friends—Sabine, a bold German woman on the run from her cheating husband; Allegra, a cranky bestselling historical romance author; and Matt, a handsome young magazine writer and serial dater—Ellen's numbness begins to fade. But when she finds out a shocking secret about her late husband and is accused by her son of being not only agoraphobic but also unable to take care of him, Ellen has a choice to make. She can either fall apart or she can pick herself up and start to live again.

Discussion Questions

1. A well-known English proverb claims that the grass is always greener on the other side of the fence. Discuss how this saying is relevant to *The Home for Broken Hearts.*

2. Ellen mourns Nick's death for most of the book, as do Charlie and even Hannah. In what ways do their behaviors reflect their grief? How does the grieving process differ for each of them, and in what ways is it the same?

3. Ellen and Hannah have a complex relationship fraught with envy, hidden anger, and jealousy. Is their conflict simply a case of sibling rivalry? How is it more than that?

4. Throughout the story, both Matt and Charlie undergo major changes. In what way does the twenty-six-year-old Matt come of age? How does it compare and contrast to Charlie's growth from child to adolescent?

5. Discuss the phrase "it is better to have loved and lost than never to